In the Palm of His Hand

Loretta Y. Stewart

Copyright © 2016 by Loretta Y. Stewart. All Rights Reserved.

Cover design copyright © 2016 by Loretta Y. Stewart. All Rights Reserved.

Scripture quotations are taken from the King James Version of the Holy Bible.

In the Palm of His Hand is a work of fiction. Where real people, events, establishments, organizations or locales appear, they are used fictitiously. All other elements of the novel are drawn from the author's imagination.

ISBN-13:978-1532806940
ISBN-10:1532806949

Acknowledgments

To God for giving me this crazy dream that I could write. If anything good comes from this book, it is because of Him. May all glory and honor go to Him.

My husband Dale, we've been through a lot of highs and lows in our marriage. Sometimes I didn't know if we would make it. Thanks for putting up with all my idiosyncrasies. I can't imagine life without you. You are the love of my life.

My sister Brenda Pearson for always being there to encourage me and sometimes kicking me in the butt! We've been through a lot of trials and tribulations of trying to sell my art—and now this! You have always believed in me more than I have. Thanks for being my sister and my friend.

Ricki Guthrie, you have been such a good friend. You were the first to read anything I ever wrote. Thanks for all the enthusiasm and encouragement. I know that our friendship has grown because of this.

My wonderful family, I thank you for all the wonderful stories I heard while growing up. You taught me the art of weaving a great yarn. Thanks for always being there for me through the good times and the bad. I love all of you dearly and wish we had more time together.

My church family at Broadway thanks for the support, the prayers and encouragement you have given me through the years. You are my family.

Penny Woolley. God brought us together for a reason. I thank you for your friendship and helping me work through my fears and phobias. You have an incredible ministry and are truly the hands and feet of God.

May the road rise up to meet you.

May the wind be always at your back.

May the sun shine warm upon your face,

The rains fall soft upon your fields

And until we meet again,

May God hold you in the palm of His hand.

Traditional Gaelic Blessing

1

The Mining Town

The sky was steel gray and hung heavily over the village of Brynmawr that sat in the middle of nowhere in a place more commonly known as Wales. The dusty dirt grays that encapsulated the depressing little town were a far cry from the luscious green fields of Mary O'Shea's homeland of Ireland.

Her father had transplanted her and her sister to this godforsaken mining town in search of work. They had barely escaped the famine that was now plaguing her precious home. When the plague had reached their farm and they saw their own crops shrivel up and turn black, Michael O'Shea had the foresight to seek another venue to raise his family. Unfortunately, Mary's mother Iona died shortly after the voyage to Wales. She had been exposed to diphtheria on the ship and had quickly succumbed. On that dreadful day, Mary lost two parents, for her father had turned to the bottle to console his troubled spirit. Every day was a struggle for him, but at night he lost the fight, drinking himself into a state of oblivion, just so he could find sleep. Drinking had become his life.

Mary, being the oldest of his daughters, shouldered the burden. She worried about his drinking. It had cost him numerous jobs since they had come here and they could not afford for him to lose yet another one. She had taken in laundry as well as cooking meals for some of the miners, trying anyway to contribute to the family's finances. But the harder she worked the less money they seemed to have. Secretly, Mary believed her father was taking the money she had tucked away. He had recently developed a penchant for gambling to add to his drinking. Michael was no longer the dad she once knew.

She straightened up from the washboard and bent backwards trying to remove the kink in her back. Her soapy hand raked across her forehead to brush back her auburn hair that had tumbled into her eyes. It immediately fell back. Disgusted, she pulled off the scarf she had tied on her head. She gathered up the loose strands and retied the cloth, securing the locks from her face. She rubbed her hand under her itchy nose and then returned to the task. Every muscle in her body was aching for some relief from her hard labor. Her hands were dry and cracked from the abuse of the harsh lye soap.

Mary felt the sudden sting of tears. What was the use of all this effort? A voice deep inside her whispered that she should just lie down and die. The voice had been invading more of her thoughts lately. It asked her why she was trying so hard. Was this all there was to life? Why struggle? In her distant memory she could hear her priest back home, preaching about it being a mortal sin to kill one's self. Was it the same as giving up? Would this jeopardize her reward in heaven if she did? Would God forgive her? She shuddered to think of the consequences. The thought put enough fear in her to keep her from entertaining it any further.

She paused to arch her back again and then studied the bleak landscape. Everything seemed to be muted in shades of gray. The sky was thick and dark and the ground was coated with black dust that spilled from the mine. The men's clothing was permanently stained gray. Their faces were blacked and their eyes ringed like reverse raccoons. They trudged back and forth like soulless beings without hope, of which Mary's father was one.

As she scrubbed, her sister Aubrey hung the clothes to dry. She came to Mary toting a basket of clothes, fresh off the line. "I'm goin' into house to fold them, Mary." A breeze kicked up and flapped the newly washed items that had been exchanged for the dry ones. With a little luck, they would soon be dry.

"I may need ya to relieve me. Me body's about to give way," Mary said in her thick Irish brogue.

"I will directly," Aubrey replied and disappeared into their house. Mary couldn't wait for relief. She walked over and sat down in a rocker. Her eighteen year old body felt more like eighty; her youth was quickly being spent. She closed her heavy eyelids to dream of emerald fields. She longed to run through the tall grass and watch the breeze wave through it like a gentle ocean tide. She could almost smell the sweet scent of wildflowers. Would she ever see her beloved home again?

A shadow fell over her face. Even though her eyes were closed, she sensed that someone was standing over her. She refused to acknowledge them by opening her eyes. She continued to cling to her dream of Ireland with its rolling green pasture fields.

"Mary," she heard her name softly spoken. Recognizing her father's voice, more than ever she did not want to open her eyes. He should have been in the tunnels of the mines, but instead he was in their front yard. This was not going to be good. He called her once more and she peered up at him, seeing his face silhouetted against the haze of the sun.

"What have ya done, Dad?" she asked accusatorily. She raised herself from the rocker and stood before him. The alcohol smell on his breath had said the rest. "Oh Dad, not another job."

He hung his head and turned from her. He had seen the disappointment in her eyes and couldn't bear it. Defending his actions, he mumbled, "I just took a nip to stave off the cold in me bones." But Michael's nips never ceased until the bottle was completely empty.

"Get yarself in the house," she said. "I'll put a pot o' coffee on the stove." As they proceeded into the house, Aubrey, who was still folding clothes at the kitchen table, exchanged a worried look with her sister. Mary put it bluntly. "Dad lost his job again." Aubrey let out a long sigh and gave her father a pitiful look. Michael dropped on the wooden chair at their table, utterly defeated.

Mary didn't say anymore to him, but began to knead her problems over in her mind. She worked it like a master craftsman. Their debts were piling up and without the steady income from her father, how were they going to dig themselves out of the pit? She wasn't sure if she could take on anymore jobs or if there were any new jobs out there. Everybody in the community was pretty much in the same boat.

Questions swirled in her mind. Oh, Daddy, why did ya bring us out here to this bleak and dreary land? Why didn't ya leave us in Ireland? Surely the famine won't last much longer. We could have survived. At least back home, we had people that cared for us. Now what are we goin' to do?

She took the reheated coffee, poured it into a mug and set it before him. There wasn't a lot of coffee left in the cupboard or anything else for that matter. As it was, she had been reusing coffee grounds, only mixing in a little of the new to give it some strength. She wasn't sure how much more she could stretch it. She sat across from her father and rested her forehead in her hand. Her thoughts continued to run in circles. There were no ready solutions or quick fixes. The tears she had felt earlier could no longer be contained. Silently she prayed, *Lord Jesus help us.*

Michael took a timid sip of coffee and then said apologetically, "I'm sorry, Mary. I'm sorry I let Aubrey and ya down. I'm a miserable excuse for a father."

He got no arguments from either daughter. Ordinarily, Mary would kid him out of his depression, but she was finding very little humor as of late. She remained quiet, contemplating. She had received a marriage proposal a few weeks back. He was an older gentleman who had recently lost his wife to sickness, leaving two small children that needed to be raised. Mary had declined his offer politely holding out for something more. But she supposed that in light of these new developments, she should reconsider his offer. At least the family would be taken care of. It wouldn't be much, for he had so little, but at least there would be one man working.

She quietly resigned herself to her decision. She would have to accept this marriage of convenience, even though she had hoped for more. She had wanted a husband to love her more than life itself, but she needed to be practical. So she resolved that tomorrow morning, before the men headed for the tunnels, she would swallow her pride and offer her services as a wife. A heaviness settled in her heart. The voice tempted her again. Why do you bother? Why do you go on? She murmured aloud, "I have no choice."

That night, she thrashed around in her sleep. Her dreams, muddled and confused, seemed to merge into another. At one point, she dreamed she was going down into the tunnels. She determined that if her father couldn't work in the mines then she would take his place. She would be the one to support her family. She stepped into the cage and as she was about to be lowered into the pit, something happened. The ropes that held it suddenly snapped and it plummeted down into the abyss. She felt herself falling as darkness engulfed her. Just before she hit the bottom, she awoke with a start. She sat up trembling, trying to catch her breath. In her dream, she was certain that she was going to die, but waking to reality didn't help. Her heart was weighed down with impending doom.

She lay back down, trying to calm herself enough to return to sleep, but instead found herself wrestling with the sheets the remainder of the night. She just hoped that her restlessness did not disturb her sister who shared her bed. Morning finally arrived, but the sun brought no comfort with it. Mary reluctantly slipped out of bed and hurriedly dressed. She put a fresh pot of coffee on the stovetop, grabbed a basket and headed out to the chicken coup. She found six eggs, enough for two apiece. They would at least have nourishment for breakfast. She sliced off a piece of bread for each of them and warmed them up as she fried the eggs.

There would be no butter or jams to spread on the toast. She longingly thought about the cow that they had left behind. They had at one time, the luxury of having milk and butter every morning and on some occasions her mother had taken the curds and made cheese. She had taken that for granted while growing up, but now she wished that she had some sweet cream for butter. But this place was so desolate; she had only seen a couple of cows.

Aubrey joined her in the kitchen. She was fully dressed and ready for the day that lay ahead for both of them. She offered her sister a hand with breakfast, but Mary declined. Soon she set their food on the table and said, "That's all there is. We are fortunate to have that." They ate, not waiting for their father to join them. Since he took to drinking, he never kept a regular schedule for his meals.

Mary didn't take time to savor her food. She swallowed her portion almost whole for she had an important errand to run. If it worked out, it would change the course of her family. She took the last swig from her mug and then got up from the table. "Ya'll have to clean up," she said to Aubrey. "I have somethin' important to tend to this mornin'."

"This early?" Aubrey questioned.

"Best to get it over with," she said without explanation. "See if ya can get Dad up soon. He needs to eat to keep his strength up—and his spirits. Besides, we can't be wastin' food at a time like this." She threw her well-worn shawl around her shoulders and leaned over to kiss her young sister on the cheek. "Don't worry," she assured her. "Our troubles may be over soon."

She rushed out the door, determined to go through with it. She put her hopes and desires aside for the good of all and quickly walked the path to Miles McKinney's place. She could hear the grit of coal dust under her feet and it set her teeth on edge. As she walked, she pondered past regrets. If she hadn't been so full of pride, she would still be back home. She had had plenty of offers of marriage, for admittedly, she was a tease at times with the opposite sex. But she was looking for someone to love her for whom she really was, that would treasure her beyond what she could do for them. The only problem was Mary wasn't even sure who she was.

But it was her pride that always got in the way. Her mam had repeatedly reminded her of what the Good Book said about it—it always came before a fall. But Mary wasn't ready to settle down for she had an adventurous spirit. She wasn't looking forward just yet of the drudgery of being a wife and mother with a whole houseful of children. She wanted to see things and experience life to the fullest. Again her mam warned her. "Mary, be careful for what ya wish for. A prospective suitor doesn't wait long. He's libel to turn his sights on another if ya put him off too long."

Mary's mother turned out to be right. A few prospects did find other game more willing towards their attention. Then of course, this adventure didn't turn out to be what she had hoped for. Now she longed to be back to the way things were, but that could never happen. Their farm was gone, and along with it, her mother. Mary felt so alone.

As she approached McKinney's house, she was suddenly overtaken by a feeling of trepidation. Inwardly, she hoped that she was too late and that Miles was already headed for the colliery. She hesitated at the gate outside his home. The fence around his property was sorely in need of some fresh paint. It had once been white, but now was weathered gray by the elements. Mary took in a deep breath, unlocked the gate and swung it open. It made a loud protest as it squeaked to its resting place, just wide enough for Mary to squeeze past. It hung lopsided intending to someday escape the hinges that held it.

Just as she was struggling to close the gate, the front door opened and Miles stepped out into the dim sunlight. Mary felt herself shudder at the thought of marrying this tall, gangly scarecrow of a man. His long skeleton legs and arms made him look uncoordinated and his gaunt face accentuated his beaklike nose. At thirty years of age, Miles' emaciated body made him appear much older. He was not the least bit attractive to her.

When Miles saw her, he cordially smiled and said, "Mary O'Shea, what a pleasant surprise." Mary had been so fixated on her task, that she took no notice of the young woman behind him. It wasn't until he took the woman by hand and gently pulled her forward that it even registered. "Mary," he began. "This is me new wife."

Mary's heart stopped and so did her feet. Her mouth gaped open in surprise. All her hopes sank into an ocean of despair. There was not going to be any rescue of her family, at least by these means. She would have to find another way.

Miles blue-gray eyes sparkled as his grin broadened. He rested his hands on either side of the woman's frail shoulders and gently pushed her towards Mary. "This is Eloise. We were married a couple o' weeks ago." He turned to his wife and said, "Eloise, this is Mary. Her dad works in the mines."

"Did work," Mary corrected him.

Miles countenance fell. "I'm sorry, Mary. What happened?"

How could she explain that her father was a drunk and that he loved the bottle more than his own daughters? She tried to protect his reputation or what was left of it. "Difference o' opinion," she simply said. Miles just nodded as if he understood and maybe he did. After all, he probably saw him drinking plenty of times on the job.

Mary took Eloise's hand and shook it. Politely, she said, "Tis nice to meet ya. Congratulations on yar marriage." Eloise shyly nodded. Mary felt her heart go out for this young girl. She appeared to be nothing more than a child, possibly Aubrey's age, but more likely even younger. What kind of life was she going to have? What dire circumstance had Eloise's family been in to allow her to marry at such a tender young age, especially to a man she barely knew. In any case, it was none of her concern—now.

"What brings ya here, Mary?" Miles asked.

She couldn't very well tell him the real reason was to inquire about whether his marriage proposal was still valid. Her mind raced to come up with a new excuse. "I was wonderin' if ya knew of anyone who had some laundry that needed done for them." She hoped that the Lord would forgive her lie. The last thing she really wanted was more laundry to take in, but that might be her only alternative.

"No, I don't, but I'll keep me ears open. If I hear anythin', I'll sure let ya know. If it wasn't for Eloise, I'd hire ya meself."

Yeah, if it wasn't for Eloise, she wouldn't need another job; she would be marrying beak-man. She thanked him for his time and quickly made her exit. Even though her plans were foiled, she felt a great sense of relief. In some strange way she felt like God had exonerated her from a loveless marriage. She was grateful and took the time to let Him know. Then she prayed that God would give an answer to her about their situation, because she was running out of ideas.

2

The Deal

Somehow over the next few weeks, the O'Shea's managed to survive. There was enough food in the cupboard, not an overabundant supply, but enough to keep in their bellies. Mary pinched their pennies and kept track of every coin that left the house. They were somehow able to make their rent payment for which she thanked the good Lord for. It was as if the story of the five barley loaves and two fish were happening in their own lives. God was multiplying what little they had and the sisters were not wanting for anything.

Michael continuously looked for work, but was turned down. It was hard enough for the Irish to find work in this country, let alone one that was developing a reputation for the drink. Mary refused to give him any money for fear it would be spent on spirits. When his supply came to an end, he began to show signs of withdraw. He became highly agitated and shook terribly. The wild look in his eyes frightened both girls, but Mary stood her ground. His condition worsened until one night they were awakened to horrible screams.

"Get 'em off o' me! Get 'em off o' me!" Michael cried as he danced around his bedroom, trying to brush off invisible creatures that only his infected mind could see.

"There's nothin' on ya, Dad," Mary said, raising her voice over his.

"Can't ya see 'em? They're crawlin' everywhere," he said and to prove his point, he stamped on a few he thought were scampering across the floor.

"They're all in yar mind, ya old fool," she shouted, trying to sound brave. She was far from it as her heart nearly beat out of her chest from fright. Aubrey was behind her, eyes wide with her own fear. Mary turned to usher her back to bed. "There's nothin' ya can do for him." Aubrey looked warily at her, but obeyed. She went back and closed the door behind her, but refused to go to sleep. Instead, she sat on the bed, her legs drawn up and the covers pulled as far as they could go; her body was trembling.

Mary went back into Michael's room to try to console him. She found him clawing at his face, trying to remove whatever was attacking him. "Mary," he pleaded. "Be careful. They're all over the place." His pale blue eyes had turned dark with fear.

"There's nothin' in this room, Dad."

His eyes narrowed and he said angrily, "Don't be lyin' to me. I can see for meself. They're crawlin' on everythin'. There's one climbin' up yar gown, now!"

Mary instinctively swept her hand down her gown, in case maybe there was some validity to his claims. She felt foolish when she saw nothing. Solemnly she asked, "What *do* ya see?"

Michael made a horrible face. "They're awful lookin' creatures; some kind o' hairy spiders with glowing red eyes." He looked at her with pleading eyes and asked, "Don't ya see 'em?"

Mary sadly shook her head, "No, Dad. What ya're seein' is in yar mind; tis withdrawal."

He went to her and began to beg. "Mary, I need a drink. Just a little one to get me through this bad patch."

"No," she said firmly, but the pain in his eyes made her softened. "Even if I wanted to, there's none to be had. I don't have a speck o' it in the house." Michael slowly turned in defeat. There was no sense in trying to combat the spiders anymore. He would let them have him and then he'd be done. Mary took him by the hand and gently pulled him towards the kitchen. "Come on. Let me make ya some tea. Maybe it'll calm yar nerves."

Michael sadly shook his head, but like a little lost boy, he obediently followed her. She sat him down on one of the chairs, lit the kindling in the stove and then put the kettle on to heat. Her dad still in distress looked guardedly around the floor to see if anything followed them into the room. So far, so good. Mary sat across from him and tried to calm his fears. It set him to begging for a drink once again.

When the tea kettle sounded its alarm, she raised herself from the chair and poured some steaming water in two mugs and then added the tea. She let them steep as she sliced off a couple of pieces of bread and thinly spread some jam that she had been holding back. Her dad hungrily took the bread and devoured it. Mary had intended on having some, but after seeing his response, she felt sorry for him. After taking only one bite, she relinquished the rest to him. She stirred a small amount of sugar in his tea and then set the cup in front of him. This he savored a little longer.

She sat down and quietly sipped her tea, pondering what she was going to do with him. He still had a wild look about himself, but at least he was no longer ranting. She silently prayed for direction and would have appealed directly to the saints, but couldn't recall if there were any that specialized in getting someone off the drink.

Michael suddenly put his tea down and began to cry like a baby. Mary found this more frightening than his hallucinogenic state. She got up and sat beside him and took him in her arms trying to soothe him. Instead, he began calling out to Mary's mam. "Iona, I'm so sorry for everythin'. I tried to be a good husband. Didn't I bring ya here to give ya a good life?" He wept harder. "I killed ya with me own hands, I surely did. If we would have stayed, ya'd still be with me." His cries descended into apologies for bringing on her death.

Mary rocked him in her arms, her own eyes flooded with tears. She was too young to have to deal with such things. She should have been thinking about starting a new life, not supporting a drunkard father. Yet she would never desert him; she loved him so.

Eventually, Michael calmed down enough to lead him back to his room. The spiders had ceased their torturous ways and it didn't take long for him to drift off to sleep. Mary wished it were that easy for her. As she crawled back in bed, Aubrey asked if everything was alright. Mary answered in the affirmative, but she really didn't feel that way. If she had only known what was on the horizon, she would have separated themselves from him. The nightmare that had begun tonight would continue until it came to completion. Mary saw little sleep the rest of the night.

She awoke to the Sabbath, a day of rest. She hoped to take advantage of it later in the day. In the meantime, she got Aubrey up and ready for Mass. There was no sense in bothering her dad. He had only gone sporadically since the passing of their mother.

At church she heard the awful news about her homeland. It seemed that the British official in charge of relief efforts in Ireland, Charles Edward Trevelyan was offering little or no aid to those starving there. The British had been sending corn meal to the poor to sustain them, but now with it at short supply, they refused to replenish it. Trevelyan had even ordered the closing of the food warehouses that had been selling Indian corn to the people. One of the parishioners stated that Trevelyan said that the Irish were far too lazy and had become habitually dependant for help from the British. He thought that the Irish property owners needed to support those who were impoverished there.

Mary was incensed when she heard the talk. It was beyond her that men could let politics stand in the way of feeding desperate people. How they could make impassioned speeches about whether a man put in an honest day's work or not, while innocent young children starved to death.

It was unfathomable. Reluctantly though, she had to admit that her people did not have the best reputation. They worked hard, but they could also play just as hard. She said a prayer for her people, many of them her own kin and offered her thanksgiving for her own family. There, but by the grace of God, they could have been suffering the same fate.

She went to confessional and knelt before the partition that separated her from the priest. She confessed all the wrong doing she could recall during the past week, but it seemed they were always the same. High on her list was of course her pride, followed closely by her temper. She also had added a new one in recent weeks, the sin of disrespect for her father. It seemed that one was trying to squeeze past the others at the top of her list.

The priest had given her some *Our Father's* and a few *Hail Mary's* to recite along with absolution, but Mary wasn't feeling very forgiven. She wished that somehow she could pull her soul out of her body, soak it in hot water and lye soap and then scrub it until it was white as hyssop like the Good Book said. Maybe then she would feel better about herself and her predicament.

As the days progressed into weeks, Michael finally got away from the alcohol. Mary was pleased with him and made every effort to say how proud she was of him. Things stayed pretty much the same as far as their finances went. On occasion, Michael picked up an odd job or two, but they were always short lived. Mary continued to manage their money and to her surprise they had accumulated a small nest egg. It pleased her, but not wanting to take credit, she quickly gave praise to God for how well He had provided for them.

But it wasn't long until that surplus suddenly began to dwindle. She couldn't understand what was happening, but she had suspicions. She had hidden the money, but now she was afraid it had been found. She would have to be alert for any signs that Michael might be drinking again. So far, she detected no alcohol. However, three nights later, her worries were realized. Michael came home in the wee hours, high as a kite. He awakened everyone with his celebration. He delightfully waved a fistful of paper bills under Mary's nose, exclaiming, "I won! I won!"

Mary was appalled and asked despondently, "Where did ya get that?"

"I won it!" he announced again with a satisfactory grin, as he tottered on his feet. "I placed some money on a couple o' winnin' horses."

"Where did ya get the money to place yar bets?"

That wiped the smile off of his face. He stammered trying to come up with a good answer. Finally he spit out, "I earned it. Ya're not the only one that does work 'round here."

"Ya stole it from the family is what ya did!" Angrily she turned away from him. He grabbed her and spun her back around.

"I did it for the family," he shouted.

Little licks of fire were ignited in her eyes. "Give me the money," she said grabbing at it. She had no intentions on keeping all of it, just what he had taken from them.

Michael held it out of her reach. He shouted, "Tis me money, I earned it."

"Ya stole it! That money belonged to the family."

"If it belonged to the family, it belonged to me. I'm part o' this family."

"That was to pay for food and our expenses, not to be squandered on spirits and gamblin'."

Michael set his jaw. He had flames of fire burning in his own eyes. "Tis me money and I'll do what I please with it." With that he stormed into his bedroom and slammed the door shut.

Mary was distraught. She determined that she would have to find a better hiding place for their money. With her father returning to his drunken ways, he could drain them dry overnight. She turned to go back to bed and found Aubrey hugging the doorframe. Her eyes were full of the same anxiety that Mary felt. Mary smiled weakly trying to reassure her. "Don't worry baby sister; thin's will work out." Aubrey tried to return it, but both women felt the fear of an unknown future.

Weeks passed and the women continued to work hard to provide. Michael took the money he *earned* and quickly went through it. He had nothing to show for it, so Mary assumed that he squandered it on gambling and drinking. The two seemed synonymous with each other. She had hidden their funds where she was certain he would never look, but that didn't ease her mind any. In the time being, she kept up her exhausting pace of washing laundry and odd jobs. Somehow they managed, but she was wondering for how long.

A few more weeks went by when Mary made a dreadful discovery. The rent on their cottage was due in a couple of days which shouldn't have been a problem. They had been socking away every penny that was made. But as she went to her hiding place and pulled out the small tin container, she found it was completely empty! Fury and panic entwined themselves. She needed to find her dad quickly and stop him before it was too late. She wasn't sure how much of a head start he had on her, but she aimed to catch him before he spent their entire money. She dropped the tin box to the floor and rushed out of the cottage, brushing past a confused Aubrey. Her sister called to her, but Mary didn't stop; she was on a mission.

She marched resolutely into the center of town and unashamedly went in every pub she encountered. It created quite a stir, for the men were not used to seeing a woman enter their den, let alone one as attractive as Mary. Yet it didn't slow her down. She inquired if they knew Michael O'Shea and whether they had seen him or not. She got no information, just shaking heads. She then asked about any horse races in the immediate area and got some hang-dog looks from some, but they refused to tell her anything. Dejected, she returned to the cottage.

Aubrey waited for her return. She sat on the front stoop with her chin resting on her fist, not knowing what she should do. When she saw Mary dragging her feet down the dusty road, she stood, dreading to hear the news. As Mary came to her, Aubrey held out the empty tin. Mary took it and then let out a deep sigh. She looked sadly at Aubrey and simply said, "Tis gone. All our money is gone."

Aubrey stared at the ground in disbelief. Quietly she asked, "Dad?"

"Dad."

Aubrey's eyes welled up with tears. She looked pleadingly at Mary. "Why would he do that to us?"

Softly she answered, "I don't know why he does what he does. I cannot begin to understand him anymore."

The two walked silently into the cottage. The shock had numbed them. Mary sunk into a chair and worked everything over in her mind, trying to find a solution to their dilemma. Aubrey joined her and the two sat without saying anything for a long time. When dusk came, Aubrey rose to light the oil lamp that hung on a nail by the window. Mary began to prepare some supper, but neither had any appetite. Instead she made them some tea and they nibbled on a little bread.

When darkness came and still no Michael, Mary encouraged Aubrey to go to bed. She balked at first. Then Mary said, "Ya need yar rest. The both of us will have to put in more than our fair share to make up for what was lost." Aubrey nodded in agreement and reluctantly went to bed while Mary stayed up and waited for their father.

Michael finally staggered into the house near morning. This time there was no celebrating. He held a lone bottle of whiskey that was nearly drunk. It was all that was left of the family's money. He shuffled his feet as he entered the kitchen and found Mary asleep, her head resting on her folded arms. He tried sneaking by her, hoping not to wake her. He had hoped that his daughters would both be asleep in their beds when he got home.

As he tottered in the near dark, he bumped into one of the empty chairs. It let out a honk as it scooted across the floor. The alarm woke Mary immediately. It didn't take long for her to commence firing at her dad. "Where have ya been? What have ya done with our money, ya old fool? That was to pay our rent and put food on the table. Now we have nothin'!" Her despair punctuated her last statement.

Hanging his head in defeat, he began to cry. He put his hand up to cover his pinched face as he blubbered, "I was only doin' it for ya girls; ya work so hard. I wanted for ya to be proud o' me." Mary shook her head. She wanted to say more, to unleash all her anger that had simmered all day. But as she looked at the pitiful man, she no longer felt the need to inflict anymore pain.

Michael sensed that he had gotten a reprieve. He stopped crying and began explaining what had happened. "Oh, Mary, I had a winner. He was the grandest horse ya ever saw. I've never seen a horse with better breedin'. He was sleek and well-groomed. Ya could tell he was taken good care o'. He was spirited too; ready for the race. He was a prize horse; a real winner."

Mary narrowed her eyes in disbelief. "But he lost, didn't he?" Michael didn't answer, just bowed his head to look at the floor. "And he took all our money with him." With that, she was finished with the conversation. She picked up the dirty cups and saucers and placed them in the dish pan, intending to wash them later. She walked past him, headed for her bedroom.

Michael stopped her. "I'll get yar money, Mary. I promise, I will." She quickly dismissed his empty guarantee and closed the bedroom door behind her.

That morning when the sisters awakened, Michael was nowhere to be seen. Mary surmised that he had gone looking for a free handout of alcohol. She was greatly surprised when he showed up stone-faced sober that afternoon with all the money he had taken. Puzzled, she asked him how on earth he could have replaced it so quickly. He just replied, "Tis done; I won't be bettin' anymore. I've learnt me lesson." Nothing more was said about it, but Mary had an awful gnawing in her stomach. She suspected that he had done something dreadful in order to return it, but for the life of her, she couldn't figure it out.

Two months went by and she got her answer. Michael had been acting peculiar, as if hiding from someone or something. Then one dark night, two men came looking for him. They gave Mary the willies. She promptly told them that he wasn't there and didn't know when he would return. It wasn't a lie; Michael kept his own hours. She never knew when he would be around to help them.

The men left, but she had a feeling they were lurking around, keeping watch. When Michael finally showed up later that night, Mary warned him. He was about to flee when the two men let themselves into the house. Michael's face turned ashen at their sight. Mary felt her blood turn cold with fear.

"Michael," the thin, blond haired man said pleasantly. "We have business to discuss." His calm demeanor should have relieved Mary's anxiety, but it only heightened it.

"I know," he said quietly, trying to think of how he was going to get out of the mess he created. "I'll pay ya what I owe; I promise."

The Welshman's eyes darkened, his steel blue eyes were hard. He said firmly, "Yar interest is mountin' daily. I'm havin' doubts o' yar honesty, Michael. We need assurance that yar debt will be paid. Do ya have anythin' o' value that we can hold for collateral until ya pay us?" He gave Mary and Aubrey a once over and what she saw made her tremble in sheer terror.

Michael didn't like what the man was insinuating. With great resolve, he said, "I have nothin' here that the likes o' ya would want."

A sly grin spread across the man's face as he looked at his companion. They exchanged a knowing glance. The spokesman responded, "Oh, I think maybe ya do, Michael."

Michael was adamant, "Leave 'em be. They've got nothin' to do with what's between me and ya."

"I don't know 'bout that. I think it be a good solution for everyone concerned. Here's the deal: we take the collateral and keep 'em until ya pay off yar debt or they pay it off for ya. In return, Brian here, he don't use his gun on ya. Everyone's a winner. What do ya say? Ya want to live now, don't ya Michael?"

When he put it that way, Michael felt he had no recourse; he didn't want to die on this night. Sadly, he made the deal to save his own skin. But in return, he would spend the remainder of his short life wishing that they would have plugged him instead.

3

A Change of Ownership

Matthew Denham was the devil himself. He laughed after he had taken Mary's virtue. He slid out of bed and as he dressed, said to her, "Ya better get used to it, wench. Ya belong to me now. Ya'll be doin' whatever I say from now on, includin' servicin' other men."

"Ya got yar payment," she spouted. "Now let us be."

"Ya don't understand, love. Ya belong to me; I own ya." He laughed again and it further deepened the anger burning within her.

"Ya cannot own us; slavery's been abolished. Tis not legal anymore," she said defiantly.

Denham laughed even harder. "Prostitution is illegal too, but ya don't see anyone puttin' a stop to it, now do ya." He started to leave, but turned and said, "Now don't be gettin' any funny ideas, mind ya. Or I might have to lay a hand to ya again and I hate doin' that; it's such a pretty face." He reached out to caress her cheek and Mary pulled back in revulsion. Instead of being insulted, Denham laughed again; it was part of the game.

When he left, Mary rolled onto her side, curled up in a fetal position and hugged one of the pillows. She tried hard to hold back her tears, but they ran unabated down her cheeks. Her body ached from the abuse, but what was worse was the humiliation and shame she felt. How could she ever be clean again? She wanted to sit in a washtub of hot water and scrub herself with soap until her skin bled. In anger, she cried out to her heavenly Father. *Where are You? Don't Ya care? Is this punishment— my penance for my sin o' pride and selfishness?* She wanted to die this very moment and God forgive her, but she begged that He would be merciful and take her now. But as she pleaded, she got no response.

In the back of her mind, a new resolve formed. She had to be strong. Who would take care of her sister? Oh, Aubrey! Little Aubrey, not quite sixteen years of age. What was happening to her? She had seen the one that was called Brian, take her by the arm and drag her away. Mary's heart tore in two as she recalled her sister screams for help and not being able to do anything. She touched the bruise under her left eye that was darkening. She had to stay strong for both of them and somehow get them out of this damnable situation. She muttered, "Oh, Dad. Look what ya done to yar daughters."

That was nearly eight months ago. Since then Denham had made quite a bit of money off of them, entertaining lonely miners who were willing to give up a few shillings. But Denham was a smart businessman. There was plenty of money to be made in the city. So they packed up the women and headed for London. Once there, he made money hand over fist at the girls' expense. It seemed that the British men couldn't get enough of the peasant girls from Ireland.

But eventually, Denham grew bored. He was pleased he had made considerable more than what Michael O'Shea had owed him. But it was time for him and his brother to return to Wales to look after their other interests. He went looking for a buyer for his girls and soon found one. Charles Fortier was a *business man* that ran a lucrative brothel right off of Haymarket Street in the heart of London. It was just down from the entertainment district where all the theaters were. He offered an entirely different entertainment for the men of the city.

Denham got a fair price in exchange for the girls. Then he gave them both a going away gift of himself one last time. As he left the brothel to board the train, a satisfied grin stretched across his face. He was proud of what he had accomplished. It had been an exceptional investment. Up to this point, it had been by far the best business deal he had ever made.

Fortier was more sophisticated than their previous owner. To anyone on the street, he appeared to be a respectable business man. He was impeccably dressed with his tailored black frock coats and beautifully embroidered vests. He never left without first donning gray dress gloves and his walking cane, even though he didn't need it. His piercing gray-blue eyes and his immaculately trimmed beard held the fancy of many young ladies. If they only knew what evil lurked in his soul, it would have turned their blood cold.

As Mary and Aubrey were brought into the bordello, they were greeted in the usual way. It sickened Mary to be subjected to it, but she resigned herself until she could devise a plan of escape. She prayed often that God would help them, but there were times when she was no longer certain He heard her. It had been so long since her last confession. There were so few Catholic churches in the area and Fortier never allowed *his* girls to leave the house. Besides, how could she ever get up enough courage to go to a priest and confess all she had done? Had they gone too far for God to rescue them?

The other women of the brothel welcomed them into the fold. Each came from various backgrounds, most coming out of desperate situations. They had formed a sorority of sorts, a strange sisterhood, with their own unique role to play in the family. The darlings of the group were two fair haired girls named Maudie and Polly. They were about Aubrey's age. They both had been abandoned when they were children. Most thought they were real sisters, but each had grown up in separate orphanages. Still one had to wonder if they could have been related somehow. Arleth and Hazel were two other girls. They were more aloof than the others, keeping mostly to themselves and seemed to take great comfort from each other.

The matron of the house was Abigail. Her sullen dark eyes painted a sad story. She had lived the life that these girls could only dream of. At one time, she had been happily married and had two beautiful little girls with dark curly hair like their mother. But in one night everything was lost. A fire had swept through their tenement building. Both her husband and girls perished. She was alone in the city without a cent to her name. Fortier came along, promising to take care of her. He had a strange way of keeping his promise.

The one that made the biggest impression and stood out from the rest was Dolly. She was the big sister of the group. Everyone confided their problems and even their secrets to her. She had nearly snow white blonde hair and a twinkle in her blue eyes. Her impish smile, along with a wicked sense of humor, endeared men to her and had them lining up to be with her. She was younger than Abigail, but in some ways seemed older. By far she had the most experience of any of the girls, being in the business for more than a dozen years; she had started when she was only fourteen.

Unlike the other girls, she seemed to enjoy her work. Mary had asked her about it once and she answered with her thick cockney accent, "Deary, why would I wan' a real job. I did dat once. I worked as a servant girl; got me nowhere. Look 'round. I got the 'ole world at me 'ands. I got a lovely room to meself, fancy clothes, fine foods and dozens o' male admirers. What more would I wan'?" She howled and her brash laughter was a little unsettling. Mary quietly got up from Dolly's bed and went to her room, feeling rather foolish. But one morning, as their night's work was concluding, Mary thought she heard a woman crying as she passed Dolly's room. She may have had the world at her hands, but she wasn't any different than the rest of them. She was just as hurt and lonely as they were.

Fortier rarely made an appearance at the house, just long enough to collect the profits. He chose to turn the business over to his henchman Ryland. He was a tall, muscular brute that enjoyed making women cry out in pain. He continuously made threats against the girls. Mary wondered if he didn't enjoy that more than a good tussle in bed. In any case, he was always stalking the hallways, making sure that the ladies were going about their business and that no one got any ideas about leaving.

Late one night when some of the girls had had too much to drink, they relayed a heartbreaking story of a young girl named Harriet. She had fallen in love with a man and he had promised to marry her, but Fortier wouldn't release her. The man had even offered to buy her freedom, but he refused, so the two had run off together. Ryland tracked them down and brought Harriet back, badly beaten. No one ever saw the man again and Harriet never spoke of him. From that point on, she was never the same. Weeks went by and Harriet healed from her physical scars, but continued to carry emotional wounds that would never heal. When she got another chance to run, she took it. Ryland went after her, but after a few weeks, he came back empty handed. They all hoped that she found her freedom, but many were afraid that Ryland beat her so severely that she had died. They all feared him.

As the girls told the sad tale, Mary noticed that Dolly, who usually had a comment on everything, quietly left the room. Arleth explained in a hushed tone, "Dolly, doesn't like talkin' much about Harriet. They had been close as sisters. I think she feels responsible for what happened to her. She had hoped so much that Harriet would get out o' the business and have that fairy tale life. But now she's…" Mary felt her stomach twist wondering what horrible things Ryland committed against this poor girl? That was the reason no one ever tried to escape.

She tried not to dwell on the story, but it continued to haunt her. She had become deeply concerned for her sister for she was sinking lower into depression. Aubrey wasn't eating and rarely left her room. Ryland continuously harassed her, smacking her around to *persuade* her to put out more, but she refused. She'd just lay there and spread her legs for the customers and nothing more. Many complained that they weren't getting their money's worth. Ryland punished her by twisting her arm behind her back until he nearly broke it. She'd cry out in pain and he'd respond with a sinister laugh. At times he'd throw her down on the bed and threaten to rape her. It was only a hollow threat; Fortier didn't like him *touching* the girls. Mary sometimes tried to intervene, but Ryland then took it out on her. Afterwards, Aubrey would apologize and promise to do better, but she was creeping closer to the edge and it worried Mary.

Early one morning, Mary tried to speak to her. "Don't ya give up. We'll get out o' it somehow." Aubrey didn't even respond. She lay staring at the wall, not focused on anything. "Aubrey," she said sharply, trying to get some response. She grabbed Aubrey's shoulder and turned her sister towards her. Slowly, she focused her eyes on Mary. "Ya're scarin' me," Mary said. Aubrey apologized and then turned back to look at the wall again. Mary wasn't through. "Aubrey, ya can't give up—*we* can't give up. God will rescue us."

Aubrey turned back to her sister and with fire in her eyes said, "God? God? When are ya goin' to realize that He has forsaken us, Mary?"

"No, He hasn't," she said refusing to accept it. "He has His reason for the delay, but He will save us." Her voice raised and sounded even louder in the quiet house. There was a part of her that was struggling with her own doubts. "Ya have to keep prayin'. He'll come through for us, ya'll see."

Aubrey turned away again and said nothing more. Mary tried comforting the girl by stroking her strawberry-blonde hair, but it seemed to make things worse. Her sister began to cry softly without making a sound. Mary prayed for her, pleading that God would at least rescue Aubrey. She couldn't hold back her own tears now. Sorrow flooded her soul as she remembered two young lasses running together on emerald fields. Mary had played the protective parent to her and now regretted it. Aubrey had always been the weaker of the two. She realized that her coddling had ill-prepared her for the real world. What she had done in love had caused harm. Now Aubrey was suffering the consequences. The only way out of this was to continue to shield her until they could get far away from this wicked place.

Slowly she got up from Aubrey's bed and returned to her own. She dissolved to her knees, beseeching the Lord once again on behalf of her sister. She wept violently, praying He would forgive them of all they had been a party to and mercifully rescue them. Spent from her emotional outburst, she started to get up, but something under her bed caught her attention. She knelt lower and saw that it was a folded up newspaper. How it got there, she had no idea. Possibly, one of her clients had lost it and it was swept underneath. She reached out, caught it by her fingertips and pulled it towards her. As she got to her feet, she unfolded it and caressed the paper. She marveled at the symbols and shapes that spelled out meaningful words.

She sat down on the edge of her bed and perused the paper, hoping to recognize anything. Even though she couldn't read, there were a few words she knew. One of them was Ireland, which she quickly found. She wondered if it had anything to do with the famine. The last she had heard was that those who were physically able were deserting to England. Others were said to have left on ships marked for Canada. They were being referred to as coffin ships, because of the widespread disease and death. The luckier ones came to America, but even then many were quarantined. How Mary wished that she and Aubrey could be on one of those ships getting a fresh start.

She studied the article, but try as she might, she couldn't find any other words she recognized. It frustrated her. The newspaper might as well have been written in a foreign language. Disgusted she folded it closed. Just then, on the back page written in large print, was a long word she recognized. She couldn't remember the exact word, but she was quite certain it was used to identify men. The other word she was sure meant women. There was also an intriguing etching of a pretty woman beside the article. She didn't know if they were related.

Once again she poured over the text, but found nothing that made any sense to her. She started to crumple it up to throw away, but something stopped her. For some inexplicable reason she smoothed it out and then refolded it. She hid it under her mattress as if it were a highly valuable treasure she needed to keep concealed from the rest of the girls. Truth be told, she didn't want to try to explain why she was keeping a newspaper she couldn't even read.

She pulled back the covers and then slipped between the sheets. She punched at the nearly flat pillow, trying to bring some life back into it and then settled in for some much needed sleep. Only sleep wouldn't come. She couldn't get the newspaper off her mind. It was beckoning to her. She changed positions, but the thoughts inside her head wouldn't let go of her. She rolled over, but it didn't help. The harder she tried to block it out, the more it seemed to possess her mind. Eventually, she threw the covers aside and got out of bed. She lifted the mattress just enough to remove it and then climbed back in her bed.

Somehow she felt compelled that God had something to do with this. There was something He wanted her to see or something she was supposed to learn. Was it about her homeland? No, it didn't feel like it. She gravitated to the advertisement on the back, with the etching of the woman. Something about it was pulling at her. *God, why are Ya wantin' me to look at this paper? Ya know I can't read. What are Ya tryin' to tell me? How can I figure this out when none o' these words make any sense to me? Someone that knows how to read will have to tell me.* As she prayed, suddenly she remembered that there were two women in this building that knew how. One was Abigail and the other one Dolly. Which one could she confide in?

Abigail was more refined and better educated of the two, but she could be temperamental at times, even standoffish. She could be pretty intimidating when she was in one of her foul moods. Yet Dolly's brashness could be just as scary in its own right. Mary had once thought herself as being reasonably intelligent, but after spending time with her, she often came away feeling stupid and foolish. Dolly may not have been well educated as far as book learning went, but she had knowledge that was infinitely more valuable, tucked away in the recesses of her brain.

As Mary thought about the paper and the secret that was locked inside it, she felt an assurance that Dolly was the one she needed to confide in. She made up her mind that she would approach her about it when the time was right. She glanced at the article once more hoping that maybe by some miracle God would reveal to her this mystery. With great optimism, she studied the words, but nothing changed. Reluctantly, she refolded the newspaper and then tucked it once again under her mattress.

With her decision made, Mary found a peace come over her that she hadn't felt for a very long time. She slept and then dreamed about a place that seemed familiar to her, yet strange. It felt like home in some ways, but in another it felt foreign. Even after awakening, the dream stayed with her. If she had been more in tune with God, she would have been aware that He was preparing her for something in her future.

4

The Newspaper

It took a few days for Mary to get the courage to go to Dolly. She didn't want to admit to anyone she'd never learned to read and write. It wasn't that she was too stupid to learn. It was just that most girls in her village were never afforded that opportunity. Even most of the boys lacked this education for their parents never saw it as a necessity. Like the generations before them, they would more than likely become farmers. Book learning was viewed simply as a waste of time.

But for Mary there was something magical about making sense out of all the lines and symbols. She marveled at the wondrous thing of picking up a book and reading the thoughts of people, some who had been dead for hundreds of years. Or what would be even better, would be to read the Holy Scriptures and not have to rely on someone else's interpretation. That would be the greatest experience of her life.

Timidly she knocked on Dolly's door and waited for an answer. When she didn't immediately get a response, she felt her courage wane and started to leave. The rattle of the door knob stopped her and then the door was rather noisily pulled open. Dolly peered up under heavy eyelids; her robe hastily put on. "What ya wan', deary?" she mumbled, her tongue still heavy from sleep or possibly whiskey.

Mary let the woman intimidate her. All she could get out was, "I-I-I…" The confidence and brashness she had once possessed was gone. A few years ago, she could have given a good tongue lashing to anyone that crossed her and not think anything of it. But as she stood before this woman, she was tongue-tied. The atrocities of her recent past had done something inside her. She had been robbed of many things, but mostly it had taken away her own identity. She no longer recognized herself.

"Spi' it out, love," Dolly said, spraying her own spittle in the air. "I got 'nothuh for'y winks I'm missin' out on."

"I-I-I'm sorry," she stuttered. "I-I-I didn't mean to wake ya."

Dolly pulled the door open wider and said, "Don' stand in the 'allway all die; come inside." Mary quickly darted in. She hoped no *Nosey Nellie's* would see her and ask questions later. Dolly offered her a seat on her bed which she took. Then Dolly joined her and asked, "so what so urgent, love?"

It got on Mary's nerves the way Dolly seemed to use *love* or *deary* in every other sentence. It was just an idiosyncrasy that some people have. Some found it endearing, but Mary found it as an irritation. In any case, she tried not to let it side track her. She pulled out the paper she had tucked inside her robe. "I've got this newspaper…"

"A newspapuh!" Dolly interrupted. Her eyes sparkled like gems. "I 'aven't seen one o' dese in weeks." Mary placed it gently in her hands and she accepted it as though it was made of the finest china. She looked it over and exclaimed, "Oh, deary, what a treasure. Dis isn't just any ord'nary papuh. Dis came all the way from San Francisco. Where did ya get it?"

"I found it. It was under me bed. I have no idea how it got there."

Dolly examined it like a curator of a museum going over a work of art. She scanned the headlines and then carefully turned the page. "It's not too old; only a couple o' weeks." After perusing it, she gently folded it and then returned it to Mary. She pulled out a handkerchief from inside her corset and dabbed at her eyes. She explained, "It's the only tin' I miss from me dies as a servant girl. The fam'ly I worked for got the papuh reg'lar. I used to steal it from the rubbish. Readin' was me only joy back den."

Mary placed the paper in her lap and gathered her thoughts. Hanging her head, she shamefully said, "I don't know how to read."

Dolly blinked. She looked dumbly at her a few seconds and then said, "Deary, it's not uncommon in our line o' work. Now me bein' able to read, dat's rare. The only reason I know is dat the nuns in the orph'nage made me learn."

"Ya're Catholic!" Mary said excitedly.

Dolly shushed her. "Don't be sayin' such a tin'! I'm not Catholic, but me Mum sent me to a Catholic orph'nage for two 'ears when she couldn't take care o' me. Dey tried to convert me, but I wan'ed no part o' it." Mary blushed with disappointment and said nothing of her faith. Once again, she felt stupid and wished she'd never approached her. Dolly must have sensed it, because she gently asked, "so, what are ya wan'in', love?"

Mary swallowed hard, to get rid of the lump in her throat. Quietly she began, "The paper..." Then her courage evaporated and she changed her course. "I recognized the word *Ireland*. I was wantin' to know what the article said about me homeland."

Dolly took the paper back and looked over the article. She glanced at Mary and asked, "Ya wanna know what it says?" Mary nodded her head. Dolly looked back at the paper, cleared her throat, and began to read. She stumbled over a few of the words and had to sound out the harder ones before figuring them out. Her lack of skill made her a little self conscious, but Mary sat enthralled at her skill.

The news was not good. The article reported that rebellion was igniting throughout the land as people were becoming desperate. Those that were starving had dissolved into eating their dead. Mary blanched and stopped her from reading more. She sat silently, trying to comprehend what had happened to her people. Dolly slowly folded the paper and laid it in her lap. She put an arm around her to try to console her, but Mary was so stunned she couldn't even shed a tear. Her mind could not grasp the inhumanity of it. Neither said a thing.

After some time, Dolly returned the paper to her. Mary figured that it was her polite way of asking her to leave. She took the paper and tucked it back under her robe. As she stood to leave, an overwhelming sense of foreboding came over her heart. At first, she thought it was from that dreadful report, but something else was going on. She sensed an urgency that she needed to pursue the real reason she brought the paper to Dolly. If she didn't, she felt she would be missing out on something that could change her life.

She turned to her and said, "I need one more thin'."

Dolly furrowed her brow and asked, "What is it, love?"

She opened the paper to the back page and boldly said, "I need to know what this says."

Dolly took the paper back and looked at the advertisement. She couldn't contain a slight chuckle that escaped. "Dis? Dis is what ya wanna know 'bout?"

"That I am," she answered, a new source of courage sprung up from somewhere. She leaned over Dolly and pointed, "I know this word has somethin' to do with men and this one has to do with women."

Dolly smiled sweetly at Mary; she was taken with the fact that she had some knowledge of words. She said, "Dis word is actually *gen'lemen* and dis one here is *lay'ies*. 'ow did ya know dat?"

"I don't know," she said shrugging. "I guess I've seen them enough that I kinda just know what they mean." She looked down at the paper straining to recognize more. "What is this article about?" Dolly responded by telling her it was an advertisement for mail order brides. Mary didn't quite understand. "What might that be?"

Dolly read: *"Lonely men lookin' to cor'espond troo duh mail wit' single women in 'opes o' findin' a wife".* Dolly explained. "'ave ya 'eard about duh strike, deary? Duh gold strike in California?" Mary shook her head and Dolly did her best to fill her in, although her knowledge of the thing was a bit sketchy. "Now dey're out dere wit' no women to care for 'em, so dey're lookin' for female comp'ny troo dese advertisements."

Curious, Mary asked, "What does it say?"

Slowly she began to read more. "It says: *We will as a trial, forward five let'uhs to five personals, insert a free personal an' send one copy for three months for fifty cents. Or to any lay'y who will send us five personal advertisements for five lay'y friends, which we will print free o' charge, we will send one copy for three months, free post paid. Lay'ies accept dis good offuh.*" Dolly joshed. "I almost took 'em up on the offuh once, until I got to tinkin' 'bout what it's like in a mynin' camp."

Mary *was* thinking about it. She had been so critical of living in a mining town. Now she wished that they were back there. Surely living in a gold mining camp wouldn't be nearly as bad as that and at this point it sure beat being a *working* girl. "Fifty cents. How much is that?" she asked.

"I don' know," Dolly said shrugging. "A couple o' crowns, I suppose. But for ya, it might as well be a couple o' guineas." She paused and then added. "Ya not get'in' any ideas are ya, deary?"

"Why shouldn't I?" she asked, a little defensive. She raised her voice. "Do ya think me sister and me want this kind o' life?"

"Simmer down," she said quietly. "I suppose ya don', but even if ya got someone to send for ya, Fortier and Ryland won' be let'in' ya go dat easy."

"I'll worry about that later. For now I have to find a way to get some money. Will ya help me write me letters?"

Dolly shook her head. "I won' be a par'y to yar funeral."

Indignant, she said, "Then I'll go to Abigail and have her write them."

"She won' do it. She won' take duh chance on get'in' caught by Ryland."

Mary wasn't about to give up. She determined that this was her lifeline and she was not going to it let go easily. "If ya won't help me, then I'll find another way."

Dolly hung her head and said, "Just a minute, love. I might 'ave a solution for ya." She looked at Mary's expectant face. "I 'ave a reg'lar customuh. 'e's been dealin' women to lonely men for a few 'ears. 'e recently 'as been in contact with someone in America about dis very tin'. 'e's duh one dat offuhed to get me outa dis place. Dat was aftuh Harriet left." She paused, thinking about her dear friend.

Mary emboldened herself to ask, "Is that where Harriet went?"

Dolly nodded her head sadly and then said, "I 'ope she found a good life." She thought a moment and then added anxiously, "Don' evuh breath o' word o' it. Ya'll get me in a world o' 'urt if ya do."

"I won't tell anyone as long as I live," she promised.

Reluctantly, Dolly said, "If dis is what ya wan', I can get ya in contact with 'im."

"I think this is our only hope o' gettin' out o' here."

"Alrigh'. But once yar in 'is 'ands, I'm out o' it. I'm not takin' the chance on messin' up me good tin'."

"Fair enough," Mary said and then she added. "Thank ya for yar help."

"Don' be tankin' me yet. Tank me by not get'in' yarself hurt or killed."

Dolly made good on her promise. It was about a week and a half later that her customer showed up. At the conclusion of their business, she snuck Mary and into her room. Fortunately, Ryland was occupied elsewhere.

Mary had come alone. She saw no need to concern Aubrey with her scheme for the moment. When the time was right, she would fill her in with the details. She hoped that Aubrey would go along just for the simple fact that they would escape this pit of hell. If by chance she did balk at it, Mary would force her one way or another. She would not leave her sister behind.

"Mary," Dolly said, "Dis is Marcus Ellin'son, duh man I been talkin' 'bout." She turned to Marcus and said, "Dis is Mary, duh one dat be wan'in' ya services." She quickly excused herself and left the room, leaving Mary alone with him. She didn't know whether to be frightened, repulsed, or grateful to the man. Right now he held her future in his hand.

Ellingson began, "Dolly says ya be wan'in' to go to America. Dat ya would be willin' to be a mail orduh bride." Mary wondered if he was really an old friend from Dolly's childhood. He appeared to be about the same age and had the same cockney accent.

"That we are," she said breathlessly. She was surprised to feel her heart beating so rapidly. "It would be me and me sister, Aubrey. But let me say up front, we have no money."

"Don' worry 'bout dat; I'll get reimbursed from duh 'usbands-to-be," he assured her. She saw his eyes darken and it gave her great concern. His pale complexion and beady little eyes reminded her of a rodent and made her skin crawl. She feared that this was not on the up and up.

"Tell me how this works," she said.

"It's simple real'y. Dey pay all the expenses o' get'in' ya to America. I just add in me finduhs fee."

"Ya won't be overchargin' him; takin' all his money, would ya?"

"Don' worry; I won' be bleedin' 'im dry," he said with a laugh. He sounded like a hyena. "Dey'll be plen'y left ovuh for ya."

"Where do we start?" she asked. The sooner they got things going the sooner she and Aubrey would be on their way.

"Well, let's start wit' duh article in duh papuh. Do ya 'ave it wit ya?"

Mary pulled out the paper from inside her robe and handed it to Ellingson. He looked at the different personals, trying to gauge which ones may best suit her. He began to read a few out loud to get her response to them. "'ere's one: *A gen'leman o' twen'y 'ears old, five feet three inches...*" He paused and looked up at Mary. "'ow tall are ya?" he asked. Mary had no idea, so he stood her up and looked her square in the eye. "Ya're a tall one, for sure. I'm five-nine and ya're almost as tall. Ya must be 'bout five-seven. Ya wouldn' be wan'in' some one shortuh would ya?" Mary shook her head and he returned to the personals. "'ere's anothuh one," he said after a few moments. "*An intel'igent young man o' twen'y-two, says 'e's six foot, one 'undred an' seventy pounds...lookin' for a lay'y between eighteen an' twen'y-two...*" He paused and gave Mary the once over.

"I'm not quite twenty," she informed him.

"Good. Dat one 'as possibilities." He continued to pour over the ads, trying to settle on the promising ones for both Mary and Aubrey. Then he wrote up her very own personal ad and read it back to her. *"A young lay'y o' nineteen, tall, o' slenduh built wit auburn 'air an' green eyes. Considered very good lookin' an' 'as kind disposition. Lookin' for kind man o' means."* Mary objected, but Ellingson explained that he had to be fairly wealthy to be willing to pay for her passage to America. She then relented. *"Lookin' for marriage and chil'run. Photos exchanged."*

"Wait a minute," she protested. "I don't have any photos."

"When duh time comes, I'll take care o' it."

"How does this all work?" she asked.

"Ya get to put in a free ad, where men can respond by writin' to ya through duh papuh. In duh meantime, ya can write to any five personals ya wan' and duh papuh will forward 'em to duh men. Ya see dese numbuhs." He pointed to the numbers that were before every ad. She took his word for it. "Ya write to dese numbers. Duh papuh 'as duh names an' addresses dat match dese numbers. Dat's how dey know where to send yar let'uhs."

"But it said somethin' about fifty cents. Isn't that to pay for the ad?"

"No, love. Duh fifty cents is for duh papuh. Duh ad is free to ya lay'ies; the men, dey charge." It was starting to sink in. The world ran on currency and nothing was ever truly free. In the end, she wondered if she and her sister might not be paying the highest price of all. But considering the circumstances, it was a chance she was willing to take. Ellingson smiled at her and asked, "Well, Mary, do ya still wanna do dis? I promise I will find ya a home away from dis place. I 'ave to or I don' get paid." He laughed hardily at his own joke.

His laughter left Mary feeling a little disturbed. In any case, she said, "Ya've got yarself two mail order brides, Mr. Ellin'son." As they shook hands, Mary had an uneasy feeling. Ellingson's hand was cold and clammy, like something fished out of the ocean after it had been dead for a week. It sent a chill up her spine. All along she hoped that God was providing a way of escape for them. But now she was having doubts. As she stood in Dolly's boudoir holding this man's hand, she felt like she was shaking hands with Lucifer himself.

47

5

A Prospect for a New Life

Mary's salvation did not come as swiftly as she hoped. It took time for a letter to cross an ocean, circumnavigate a continent, and then journey through another ocean before it landed at its destination of the Pacific Northwest. The responses then had to travel back the same route. Communication was nearly at a standstill. At this rate, the sisters would be using canes to walk down their wedding aisles.

When the letters trickled to only a couple of responses, Mary began to feel as though Ellingson was reneging on the deal. When she approached him about it, he was evasive and said he was weeding out the bad ones. Once a week he'd show up at her door on the guise of reporting their progress on the matrimonial trail. But since he had to pay to see her, he demanded to get his money's worth. Mary had objected, but when he informed her that he was going to Ryland and tell him the whole story, she gave in. Now she wondered if all this was a ruse just to use her services. She was stuck with the rat and she was beginning to hate him all the more.

Everything came to a head one night, when he revealed his true intentions. He had acted nervous when he entered her bedroom. He tossed his overcoat and hat on the chair beside the bed and then he began to pace like a caged animal. Suddenly he grabbed her and announced, "Runaway wit me, Mary." She was stunned at the revelation and just stared at him. "I been tinkin' 'bout it. I got a few quid put away. We can be married; I'll take ya to America. Ya can even bring yar sister along; I don' mind. I love ya, Mary. I'll make ya 'appy."

Mary turned away from him and buried her face in her hands. She couldn't believe what she was hearing. How could he say that he loved her after treating her the way he did. The reality of what he was proposing began to sink in and disgusted her. A flame of anger ignited inside her and she turned on him with a vengeance. "How dare ya use me like that? Have ya been plannin' this all along? Was any o' the letters real or were they all written by ya?"

Ellingson took a step back, trying to steady himself. He had not seen such fury from a woman before. He tried to explain, "Duh first let'uhs were, but aftuh 'while I couldn't bear to see ya go to someone else. Mary, I did it 'cause I'm in love wit ya."

"Love? Ya don't know the meanin' o' the word *love*. Love doesn't deceive…love doesn't use another person for his own pleasure." She set her jaw and said firmly, "We made a deal and we shook hands on it. I be expectin' ya to keep yar end o' the bargain."

"I can't," he said dejectedly and with as much dignity as he could muster, grabbed his hat and coat. He turned and let his own anger spill over. Pointing a finger in her face he said, "Ya will marry me! If it's the last tin' I ever do. I'll marry ya and take ya from dis godforsaken 'ell'ole." He stormed out of her room and slammed the door behind him.

Heads popped out of adjacent rooms trying to find out what all the commotion was about. Dolly darted across the hallway and into Mary's room, quickly closing the door behind her. "What 'appened, love?" she asked.

Mary groaned and sunk onto her bed. The last thing Mary wanted to do was talk about it, but Dolly pressed her. "The fool wants to marry me," she blurted out.

"'e wants to marry ya?" she asked incredulously. She gave Mary the once over and added, "Ya mean to tell me, 'e rather 'ave ya instead o' me?" Mary blinked. She couldn't believe her response. If she wanted the little rodent she was certainly happy to let her have him. Dolly realized her insensitivity a little late. "Sorry, love." She hesitated and then asked, "Are ya takin' 'im up on it?"

"I am not. We had a deal, but now I guess that's over. I suppose he'll go to Fortier and tell him everythin' and then I'll be in a royal pickle."

"Don' be too sure o' dat," Dolly said mysteriously. "Me an' Marcus 'ave a lit'le 'istory toget'uh. Ya 'ang in dere, deary. Let me see what I can do 'bout it." Dolly smiled faintly and then patted her on the cheek. "We'll get ya a 'usband one way or 'nothuh."

"Just as long as it doesn't end up being Ellin'son," she said grimly. The thought of having to spend the rest of her life with him was in some ways worse than working as a prostitute. At least as a prostitute, she still held out some hope of escaping. But to Mary, marriage was an honorable estate that she took seriously. When she joined a man in matrimony, it was a lifelong commitment. She wanted it to be to an honorable man, not a dishonest rodent.

The next time Ellingson came to her room, he was much more somber. He apologized for his behavior and said that he would make good on his promise. Dolly had somehow come through. But before they sat down to deal with that issue, he demanded his time with her. He was much rougher with her than any of the previous times, taking out his hurt and rejection on her. When he was finished, he quickly dressed and then took out a packet of letters from his coat pocket.

"Dis are some o' the responses dat ya got," he said quietly. "Dere be one dat sounds promisin'." He pulled the letter from the others, opened it and began to read: *I am twen'y-eight 'ears o' age and av'rage in looks. I 'ave an established bizness and can provide well for a fam'ly. I am lookin' for a lay'y to make as me wife, as I am tie'ed o' bach'lor life. She must be unduh tirty an' willin' to 'ave chil'run. Must be a hard workuh.*" He looked up at her with such hurt in his eyes that Mary guiltily looked away.

She almost felt sorry for him. "Well, do ya wanna write to dis one?" he asked.

Softly she responded, "I reckon we should; he sounds the most promisin'." Ellingson nodded and got out his pen and paper, along with a bottle of ink. He sat in the chair by the bed, using the night table as a desk. He took down her dictation and thus began a correspondence with what Mary hoped would be her future husband. But there was one thing that Ellingson did not share. The writer had concluded his letter by saying: *She must be of Protestant faith. Nationality makes no difference, only I prefer not to have a lady of Irish birth.* In some insidious way, he hoped that she would end up with this one. He determined that if he could not have her as his own then he would see to it that she would regret ever turning him down.

As the weeks went by, the letters came a little more frequent. Through her correspondence, Mary learned that the gentleman writer was James Whitaker. He lived in the small town of Windsor. It was in the heart of Williamette Valley in Oregon. He had settled there almost seven years ago with his brother Jethro by way of the Oregon Trail. Each had come looking for a sense of adventure and of course seeking some fortune. He had assured her that they had accomplished both. During this time, they had acquired a nice spread of land and began farming it. It was fertile ground that provided more than enough food for the two of them and the surplus was sold to areas miners.

But their real wealth came from the timber they harvested. As the gold rush erupted in California, spurring a mad rush westward, the Whitaker brothers took advantage of it. There was lumber needed to build new homes and plenty of trees, straight and tall, on their land. So they built a small sawmill and began a lucrative business.

It sounded quite promising. Mary had even wondered about the brother and whether he too was a bachelor. He could be a possible match for Aubrey. It would be the perfect scenario; two sisters marrying two brothers. So in one correspondence, she took the initiative to inquire about his status. She withheld her reason momentarily, in case he was already married. It was too presumptuous at this stage to mention her sister's need for a husband. Besides, Mary had her own problems getting Aubrey warmed up to the idea of marrying a stranger in a foreign land. She was giving up on life.

The next letter she received nearly broke her heart. James informed her that his brother had tragically lost his life nearly a year ago in a timbering accident. His death was still too hard for him to talk about. As Ellingson read the letter, Mary empathized with his anguish. She felt a longing to comfort this man that she only knew through their correspondences. She wondered if she was actually falling in love with him.

As his letters continued, James described the beautiful rolling hills of this strange land called Oregon. She could envision it in her mind and longed to smell the sweet grass once again. After enduring the pollution of London's industrialization, she had a greater appreciation for the simple country life. She laughed sarcastically to herself as she recalled how she had wanted adventure and to see the world. Her mother's words continued to haunt her: *be careful for what ya wish for, Mary*.

One day Ellingson came by with a new letter. Mary waited in anticipation for the news. Of course, he wanted his payment first and she begrudgingly obliged. She would be so glad to be rid of him, but for the time being, she had to try to keep him happy. He was her only lifeline to this mysterious James Whitaker that she was becoming smitten with.

When Ellingson was satisfied, he opened up her letter and pulled out a small photograph inside. Mary's heart skipped a beat when she found out. Ellingson toyed with her, holding it at arm's length, refusing to give it to her. He enjoyed watching her beg; it gave him a sense of power over her. When he had gotten all the amusement out of it he could, he gave her the picture.

Gazing at the photograph, she felt a turning inside her. He was lovely. In the picture, he was sitting in a chair, looking a bit uncomfortable. She supposed it was from wearing a suit. Being an outdoor's man she didn't imagined him being the type that liked suits. He had dark curly hair that was rather bushy and a full beard, but fairly trimmed. But it was his eyes that drew her attention. She detected a sadness in them. Determined that given the opportunity, she would cure him of it.

She turned to Ellingson and asked, "When are me sister and me gettin' our photographs taken?"

"Who says dat ya are?" he replied with irritation in his voice.

"Ya said that ya would take care o' it," she retorted.

"Ya know 'ow bloody expensive it is?" he said turning his back to her. His resentment towards her was growing.

"I thought that ya were goin' to add it to the expenses."

"Dat's anothuh tin; when is 'e goin' to propose to ya. I've got me own expenses mountin'. When am I goin' to get me pie?"

"I thought ya were gettin' it every time ya came to see me," she snapped.

He came back with venom. "Well, I tink I'm get'in' short changed."

"Ya got paid in full every time." Her eyes shot daggers at him when she added, "It was fine a few weeks ago when ya wanted to marry me."

"Well…" he mumbled. "I was wrong 'bout dat. I tought ya'd be a good wife, but now I see I was wrong." With that he picked up his coat and left.

Mary was glad that he was gone. Good riddance! That was until she realized that he had left without reading her letter. At least he had left it on the bed. She'd have to have Dolly read it to her later. She didn't seem to mind when Mary asked her to reread them to her, although she did say reading cursive was much more difficult. She looked at the writing, and saw how everything seemed to run together into a jumbled mess and couldn't imagine ever being able to decipher it enough to read. It was such a pity; she would have loved to spend her free time relishing each of his letters. But at least for now she had a picture of him. She could lay awake, thinking about him and dreaming of his handsome face.

When Dolly got around to reading it, she said that James had requested her photograph. She was afraid of that. Dolly put her arm around the distressed girl and comforted her. "Don' worry, love; we'll get ya picture. Don' tell anyone, but I've got a lit'le tucked away. Duh three o' us will go on the morrow and get it done."

Mary furrowed her brow and asked, "What about Ryland? He won't let us go."

She smiled reassuringly and said, "Don' ya be worryin' 'bout 'im. 'e knows not to mess with me. I'm the bread an' but'uh for 'em and dey know it." She gave her another squeeze and then asked, "By duh way, 'ow's Aubrey's prospects comin'?"

"She actually has two. One is in California and the other in Oregon. O' course, I'm leanin' for the one from Oregon."

"I 'ope dat tin's work out for duh two o' ya," Dolly said, sounding genuinely sincere. But then she warned, "just make sure dat ya keep yar let'uhs hid; ya don' want Ryland get'in' 'is 'ands on dem."

"Can he read?" Mary asked alarmed.

"Don' real'y know, but I wouldn't take the chance; 'e's no one to fool wit'."

The following day, Dolly stepped boldly past Ryland on the way out the front door. She had both Mary and Aubrey in tow, keeping them slightly shielded from Ryland's grasp. When he saw where they were headed, he sprang forward catching Aubrey by the back of her collar and yanked her backwards. She let out a yelp and Mary immediately went after Ryland. He was not going to hurt her baby sister.

Dolly grabbed her and gently pulled her back. Let go o' 'er," she said confidently to Ryland. "We 'ave important bizness to attend to."

"Now do ya?" he said sarcastically. "Well, who died and left ya in charge?" His brutish looks didn't improve with his mean scowl.

"Don' be messin' wit' us, Ryland," she insisted. "We 'ave some tin's we need to get done. Ya wouldn't wanna make us late for our clients' tis aftuhnoon, now would ya, love."

"Ya not goin' anywhere, without Fortier's permission," he said shoving aside Aubrey. His hulking body overshadowed both Mary and Dolly as he tried intimidating them, but Dolly was not having any of it.

"Fortier let's me take walks an' run errands all the time," she retorted.

"Ya maybe, but not the two o' 'em; they stay."

"What do ya tink we might be doin'; runnin' away toget'uh?" Dolly fearlessly said. Then she bluffed, "We got women tin's to take care o'; ya wanna come and watch, deary." Mary felt all the blood run from her face in fear that he might take her up on it.

He glared at each of them and then pointing a fat sausage finger at Dolly, barked, "I'm holdin' ya responsible if these two don't return." He looked intently at Mary and added, "I'll hunt ya down and break every bone in yar body."

Fear seized Mary. She closed her eyes trying to block out the image of what a beating from him would be like. But Dolly didn't give in. "No, ya won'. Ya know dat if anytin' were to 'appen to me, Fortier would 'ave yar 'ead for it." That stopped Ryland in his tracks. He was the first to blink in this showdown. "Come on girls," she said motioning to them.

They quickly slipped out the door and Ryland couldn't do anything to stop them.

They exited the front door and entered freedom if only for a short time. It was the first time the sisters had stepped outside their building since Denham sold them to Fortier. Mary had nearly forgotten how crowded the city was. Being outside among people, gave her a strange claustrophobic feeling. In some bizarre way their building provided a twisted sense of security. She almost turned to duck back inside and probably would have if Dolly hadn't gotten behind both of them. She took each of them by the arm and then escorted them down the sidewalk.

"Don' be nervous, lay'ies," she said in a hushed tone. "It gets easier duh more ya get out." Mary wondered how she knew what they were feeling, but didn't ask. Dolly was the only one of them allowed to venture out on a regular basis. She wasn't sure if she was always allotted the privilege or if it had been earned over the years. Whatever the case, it really wasn't her place to ask. Dolly continued to usher them through the crowd and down a few blocks until they were at a photographer's studio.

They had to wait at the studio, but eventually they were worked in. Even Dolly had hers taken. For Mary, the experience was not what she had expected. She wasn't quite sure why, but they had to stand perfectly still for a long period of time. She had a new understanding why James had looked so uncomfortable in his picture—it *was* uncomfortable! Dolly paid the exorbitant amount and they left. She would make the trip back to pick them up when they were ready.

As they walked down the street towards their building, Mary apologized for costing her so much. "I don't know how to repay ya for yar kindness."

Dolly smiled sweetly and said, "Don' be worryin' 'bout it. If I didn't wanna do it, I wouldn't 'ave." They walked a little farther and they came across a chemist shop. "Oh, let's stop in 'ere for a bit." Before they could protest, Dolly darted inside. Mary looked at Aubrey and shrugged. They obediently followed.

The outside window of the shop displayed beautiful ornate bottles containing brightly colored liquids. The sunlight danced across each one illuminating it as if the light was radiating from within. They appeared like gemstones, as stunning as any stained glass in a cathedral. Inside the shop was another treasure trove of bottles and flasks that lined shelves on the back wall. On each side of the store were counters made of rich oak, scuffed and marred from age-long use. The floor of oak planking was burnished from decades of foot traffic; it creaked and moaned under the weight of the customers.

For the first time in a long while, a genuine smile spread across Mary's face. Even though she had never been here before, there was a familiarity that brought a wave of remembrances. Her parents had often taken her to a similar place as a little girl. She let the feelings wash over her, reliving the simpler time of innocence. But the nostalgia drifted into a sadness that things could never be the same. Life had become cruel, stripping away the love and security she had once possessed.

Dolly called to her, snapping her out of her trance. "Come ovuh 'ere, love," she said sitting down on one of a row of stools at the counter. Mary and Aubrey followed and sat beside her. "Me treat. What will ya 'ave?" Mary and Aubrey both looked at her in puzzlement. "'aven't ya ever been to a soda fountain before?" They both shook their heads. Dolly chuckled and said, "Well, ya in for sometin' special."

She ordered a drink for each of them and paid the man behind the counter. The young man gave the first to Dolly, who politely pushed it down to Mary. She hesitated, not knowing what to expect. It had an effervescent quality. Tiny bubbles rose to the top and escaped just above the surface. It made her quite curious. Before taking a sip, she sniffed it and found it had a pleasant lemony scent to it. She took a small sip and discovered it had a refreshingly sweet taste. She rather enjoyed it, especially the sensation of the bubbles trickling down her throat.

"Well, what do ya tink o' it, love?" she asked.

"Tis quite good; I like it."

Aubrey tried hers and smiled at Mary. The smile warmed her heart. She hadn't seen her beam like that for quite some time. As they sat quietly enjoying their drinks, Mary finally got the courage to ask Dolly the question that had nagged her all day. "Have ya always had the freedom to come and go as ya please?"

Dolly chuckled and said, "Oh, no. It 'asn't been until duh last couple o' 'ears, aftuh me marriage."

Mary almost dropped her glass. "Ya've been married before?"

She smiled slyly and then said quietly, "Don' be tellin' no one dis, but me and Fortier are 'usband and wife."

"What?" Mary shouted and then remembered herself. She said more quietly, "Ya're married to Fortier?"

"In name only," she answered with a slight irritation in her voice. "It just didn't work out. We never bah-duhed to get a divorce. But because o' dat, I 'ave me freedom. I reckon, 'e knows I'm not likely to go anywhere, although…I did 'ave a tought o' goin' to America like duh two o' ya. But den again I got it too good 'ere."

"How can ya like this life, Dolly?" Mary asked in frustration. "Ya're better than this."

A faint smile returned, curling up on Dolly's face. "Tank ya for sayin' dat. But I can't see me workin' me fingers to duh bone, cleanin' and scrubbin' for someone else. I got it soft right now; Fortier may not 'ave been a good 'usband to me, but 'e still takes good care o' me none duh less. And 'e keeps Ryland off o' me." She downed the rest of her drink and then asked, "Ya ready to go back?"

Mary sarcastically laughed. "Most assuredly not, but I guess we have to." She and Aubrey finished their sodas and got down from their stools.

"Well deary, 'opefully ya both won' 'ave to do dis much longer. I wish ya both much 'appiness in yar new life, wherever dat might lead ya." She put an arm around Mary and gave her a squeeze. "I must say, I will miss yar friendship."

"And I too." Mary said returning the hug.

It wasn't too many weeks after Mary sent her photograph away that she got her answer. In the very next letter James asked her to become his wife. She agreed, but there were a few details that needed to be worked out. One had to do with Aubrey. Mary would not leave for America without her. Ellingson put up a fuss saying, "Whet'uh ya leave or not I real'y don' care, but I'm get'in' me pie for it one way or 'nothuh."

But fortunately for both sisters, they each got the marriage proposals they wanted. It looked as if they were headed for America and a new start on life. It all hinged on sneaking aboard a ship without Ryland finding out until it was too late to stop them.

6

The Escape

James Whitaker was not a foolish man. He had heard too many stories of lonely men being swindled out of their money by so-called mail order brides. In some instances, they had actually been taken by men posing as women, writing promising letters of matrimony, only to take their money and run. It would have been easy for someone as far away as England to dupe him out of a fortune. So James wasn't taking any chances. He sent only a small sum of money to Mary, just enough to buy a first class ticket for passage to America, plus a little extra for any expenses she might incur. When she arrived in New York, she was to go to a specific post office and there would be another allotment waiting to pay for her passage to San Francisco. She would then find more money waiting for her at another post office. It was to take her the rest of the way to Windsor, Oregon.

Ellingson was infuriated when he discovered that James had short changed him. Full of fury, he stormed into Mary's room while she was with a customer, half-scaring the man to death. The man hurriedly pulled on his pants, gathered the rest of his clothes and flew out of the room, leaving a dismayed Mary behind. Ellingson was ranting so much that she couldn't make head or tails of what he was saying.

"Will ya take a deep breath and slow down," she said with a slight edge of impatience. She pulled on her robe, covering herself.

Ellingson waved the opened letter in her face as he frothed at the mouth. "Ya intended 'as reneged on 'is money. 'e only sent enough for yar fair to America—duh bloody cheapskate!"

"What?" she responded in confusion and then added another question; "Why?" When he told her what the letter said, Mary busted out laughing.

"It isn't funny. Ya owe me money." He took the dollar bills out of the envelope and shoved them into his inside pocket of his jacket. "I guess I'll have to set'le for dis."

Mary's mood changed dramatically. She grabbed at him and shouted. "Hey, that's me money. How am I supposed to get to America without it?"

"Dat's yar problem," he said pushing her back down on the bed. He would have done more, but Ryland came tearing into the room. He had heard the commotion from downstairs and was more than willing to bust a few heads.

"What's goin' on in here?" he asked.

"Nothin'," Ellingson said in disgust. He threw the letter at Mary and it fluttered slowly, landing on her as Ellingson hastily made his departure. Ryland zeroed in on the letter and deduced that it was behind the entire ruckus.

He asked, "What do ya have there?"

Mary's heart hammered in her chest. She feared that he would find out everything and her hopes of escape would be dashed. She stammered, "T-t-tis just a letter."

"A letter? From whom?" he asked accusatorily.

Mary's brain scrambled to come up with an explanation. All she could think to say in her panic was a lie. "Tis from me Dad." Ryland quickly ripped it out of her hands and began to peruse it. Mary's heart sank. Her body quaked as she closed her eyes and prayed, hoping that her punishment might not be too painful. He continued looking over the letter with great interest and then he handed it back to her.

"Looks like everythin' is in order," he said, handing it back to her. "But if ya get any more letters from yar dad, ya need to clear it with me or Fortier, ya got that?"

Mary couldn't believe her ears. Obviously, Ryland couldn't read anymore than she could. As he left the room, she felt a huge weight lift off of her and a new hope had been birthed. She might make it out of here yet. But how was she going to get the money for the passage?

A couple of weeks later, Aubrey's suitor came through with his money. He was either more trusting or more gullible, depending on how you looked at things. He sent nearly four hundred dollars to the girl to bring her to Oregon. Ellingson gleefully took two hundred of it and then left the sisters high and dry.

Mary was devastated. She wasn't sure how much two hundred dollars was compared to British currency, but one thing was for sure, it would not be enough for one of them, let alone both of them to make it to Oregon. She ran circles in her mind trying to come up with a solution, all the while time was slipping away. How long would their intendeds wait for them? Mary retreated to her bedroom, closed the door and got on her knees, beseeching God's intervention. But days slipped into weeks and she still had no answer. She wished she'd have had an opportunity to skim some of the money they took in nightly, but Ryland always made sure that he got his hands on it first. She was sure that he pocketed some of it from time to time.

Early one morning, after all the girls had finished their shift and had gone to bed, Mary remained awake. Her worries had eroded any the hope she once held. She resigned herself to the knowledge that this was her life. Nothing was going to change. She pulled a chair over to the window and sat down, drinking in the last remains of the cool night air. The soft murmurs of a sleeping city could be heard below and she took some small comfort in it. But soon the hopelessness she felt produced warm tears as she cried out to God. She began to sob, releasing the pain of the last two years. When her tears finally subsided, she retrieved her handkerchief and wiped her eyes. Silently she sat, staring down at the soft glow of the gaslights that lined the city streets.

A soft knock on her door, gave her a jolt. She thought she was the only one still awake. Wiping her eyes again, she tried to make herself look as though she hadn't been crying. Then she called, "Come in."

Dolly came into her bedroom and quietly closed the door behind her. She saw Mary sitting, silhouetted in front of the window. She whispered, "I tought I might find ya awake."

"Can't sleep," she simply said, wondering why Dolly was still up.

"I can't seem to either. I just toss an' turn." She sat down on the edge of Mary's bed. "I'm sorry for yar misfortune, love. I feel like a lit'le o' it's me fault." Mary shook her head and denied it. "I tought dat Ellin'son was legit. I've known 'im for some time an' knew 'e 'ad 'elped other women get to America. I never dreamed dat 'e would fall for ya. But I've come to realize dat 'e 'ad a good reason. Dere's sometin' special 'bout ya. I can't rightly figure it out, but ya're diff'rent from duh rest o' us."

"I don't know about that," Mary said, turning her attention back to the window to hide the fact that she was crying again.

"Well, I do," Dolly said softly. She took a deep breath and then said, "I've been doin' a lot'a tinkin' and I tink I can get ya out o' here. I've got a lot o' friends dat owe me favors and I'm callin' dem in."

"Oh no, Dolly. Ya need to stay out o' it. I don't want ya gettin' hurt."

"Now, don' ya be worryin' 'bout me. Ol' Dolly can take care o' 'erself. Besides, I got ya into dis mess; I'm gettin' ya out." She came over and cradled Mary's head in her bosom and said, "Ya got a chance o' real 'appiness an' I wanna see ya get it. Ya deserve dat an' I'm goin' to 'elp ya. Be patient an' keep yar chin up." She tilted Mary's head upward and smiled cheerfully, trying to reignite her hope. As she started to leave, she turned and gave Mary a wink and then closed the door softly.

Mary didn't put much stock in what she had proposed, but three nights later, Dolly came into her room brimming with good news. "Ya got yar passage, love. I've got everytin' worked out for yar sister and ya. 'ere's a bit o' money," she said handing an envelope with some coins in it. "Dis will pie for yar voyage across duh ocean. I got a man dat's comin' tomorrow night to 'elp ya sneak away. 'e's goin' to escort ya to Liverpool an' 'elp ya get on duh ship. From dere ya're on yar own."

"Tomorrow night?" Her heart began to race in expectation. "Dolly, how can I ever repay ya? Ya've done so much for us. I'm deeply indebted to ya."

"Just 'ave a good life, love."

They hugged each other and then Mary said, "I'll never forget ya, Dolly. I hope that ya don't get into any trouble over this."

"Don' worry," she assured Mary as she started to leave. "Fortier won' do anytin' to me; I'm much too valuable to 'im." She smiled sweetly at Mary as she left and headed back to her room. As she entered her bedroom, she looked around longingly at the luxuries she had accumulated over the years. Sighing, she quietly said, "Well, it was good while it lasted." There was a tinge of regret in her voice, but suddenly she announced, "If 'e makes it too rough on me, maybe I'll make duh trip across duh big pond meself."

The next night, everything was ready for big escape. Dolly enlisted the help of the other girls to keep Ryland occupied all night. Mary didn't think that was a good idea to let anyone else in on their plan. She feared someone would take offence and inform Ryland on them. But all the girls were willing to do their part. During the evening meal, the others quietly showed their support. As they returned to their rooms, many gave their tearful goodbyes and well wishes.

The sisters had very few possessions and easily stuffed them into their pillow cases. They nervously waited for the darkness of night to fall. The plan was simple: Dolly had her regulars come and request to be with Mary and Aubrey, knowing full well that neither girl would be in their rooms. They would wait around the appropriate length of time and then leave, allowing the next to do the same. As long as they paid, Ryland would be none the wiser. It would allow ample time for their getaway.

The first of Dolly's men friends showed up and requested the girls. It gave Ryland a pause for concern. He watched warily as one of the men approached Mary's room and the other Aubrey's. But when he saw the girls welcome the men into their boudoir, he went back downstairs to his comfortable chair by the door. He could afford to be a little lax tonight, for Fortier had gotten theater tickets and would not be back until the early hours of morning.

When the coast was clear, Dolly slipped into Mary's room as Aubrey and her escort quickly joined them. One of the men, a husky, athletic type, pulled out a man's shirt and pair of trousers he had tucked underneath his jacket. He tossed them to Mary and said, "Put these on and be quick about it." Aubrey's companion did the same. Mary looked questioningly at him and he explained, "No one will look at ya twice if they think ya're a man. Besides, ya can't bloody well run in that if ya have to," he said pointing at her long dress she had on.

They began to remove their clothes, as men stood back and watched. Aubrey indignant by their lustful leers said, "Do ya mind givin' us a little privacy?"

The men chuckled and the husky one said, "I didn't think that women of the evenin' had any modesty left in 'em."

"Well, I still do. So turn around." The men politely turned their backs. Mary found herself laughing inwardly at Aubrey's spunk. It was the first real sign that she still had some fight left in her.

They quickly changed into the clothes, rolled up their dresses and stuffed them into the pillow cases. Once dressed, Dolly quickly hugged and kissed the girls one final time. Tearfully she said, "I'll miss duh two o' ya. Ya 'ave been like sisters to me. Ya take care o' yarself."

"Oh Dolly, what can I say? Ya take care o' *yarself*. Don't let Ryland or Fortier get the best o' ya. And if ya get tired o' this life, ya can always look us up in America."

"I just might, love," Dolly said, trying to smile. Both women laughed softly between tears, knowing deep down that they would never see each other again. Finally Dolly said, "Go on. Ya need to get goin'."

The two men had set up a rope to lower them to the ground. The husky one took off his cap and put it on Mary's head. "Ya need to tuck yar hair underneath it," he instructed. As Mary obediently shoved her hair inside the cap and adjusted it on her head, Aubrey mirrored her with the other man's cap. Then the husky one tossed their belongings out the window and then tied the rope underneath Mary's arms. Slowly he lowered her to where their comrade was waiting below. Once she reached the bottom, the rope was sent back up and then Aubrey followed. When they were both secured on the ground, the man wasted no time. They quickly followed him down the street, but not too fast, for that would have drawn attention to the three of them.

When they got a couple of blocks from the building, he made his introduction. "Me name is Trevor. I'll be 'elpin' ya get to Liverpool. We need to step lively to duh rail yard. Dere's a train leavin' in about an 'our, so we need to make good time to get dere." He glanced over at the two of them. He could see their eyes wide with terror beneath the dim streetlamp. "Ya need to throw yar bags ovuh yar shoulduh an' carry dem dis way," he said pointing to his own shoulder. "Men don' carry deir loads like a sack o' groc'ries.

Mary promptly obeyed, but Aubrey struggled. They had only gone a short distance and Aubrey was already waning from the weight of her belongings. Trevor did the gentlemanly thing and took it from her. She thanked him, but he replied, "Don' be tankin' me. I don' need ya tie'rin' out an' 'ave to carry ya duh rest o' duh way."

They walked in silence, keeping a steady pace, but Mary felt her own energy begin to fade. Neither had had much physical exercise in almost two years. The simple task of walking across town was about to do them in. She wondered if they would have the strength to reach Liverpool, let alone onto America. An insidious fear grew in the pit of her stomach. She wasn't sure if it was the fear of not knowing what might lie ahead or of being caught by Ryland. She shuddered thinking about it. It gave her a new resolve. She quickened her pace determined to see this through or die trying. She was never going back to her old life.

7

Liverpool

It was well past ten o'clock when the trio reached the rail station, but it felt more like midnight. A thick fog had formed giving everything an eerie, fuzzy appearance. It hovered near the ground, providing concealment from any Bobbies that might have been patrolling for vagrants. The three squatted behind an abandoned car and then stealthily maneuvered in and around them until Trevor spotted the one he was looking for.

"'ere," he said in a hushed voice and motioned them in the direction they needed to go. They continued until he found a box car with its door slightly opened. He reached up and slid the door a little, until a scraping noise could be heard and then he stopped. He peered around to make sure that they weren't heard, then he hopped up inside. He motioned them to toss up their bundles and quickly threw them to one side. Then he reached down and pulled Aubrey up into the car. Mary followed. He took one more glance around the yard, before slowly shutting the door. This time it gave no protest.

Inside the box car, it was nearly pitch black. Only slivers of gray-light filtered through the cracks around the door. Soon their eyes grew accustomed to the near darkness. Mary staggered as she made her way to the far side of the car and sat down against the back wall. The unevenness of the floor and the blackness of their surroundings made it disorienting. Aubrey followed, stumbled and nearly fell, before she caught herself. She plopped down beside her sister. Mary instinctively pulled the young woman against her as if to give her protection.

Trevor picked up their bundles and gently tossed them to Mary. He said, "'ere, use 'em for pilluhs and try to get some rest. Ya 'ave a long night ahead o' ya." She took them and handed one to Aubrey, not really sure if it was hers or not. Not that it made any difference. Aubrey tucked it behind her head and laid on her side. Mary scrunched down and laid beside her on her back. She watched warily at their stranger. Trevor kept himself at a respectable distance, sitting down on the straw that was strewn on the floor. Eventually, he laid on his back, crossed his arms behind his head and settled in.

Before anyone could drift off, they were startled by loud voices along the track. Trevor sat up quickly in anticipation of being found out. Mary sat up too and said a silent prayer. They all held their breaths waiting expectantly. The voices were muffled and unintelligible. Mary strained to make out any recognizable words, hoping that their conversation had nothing to do with them. To everyone's relief the voices began to fade off in the distance. Trevor let out a deep sigh and Mary found herself slowly letting go of her own breath.

He said quietly, "I tought we 'ad it dere for a min'et."

"Me too," she echoed. She looked over at Aubrey and could see the whites of her eyes even in the dim light. If she could have seen better, she would have seen that Aubrey's face was pasty white with fear. Mary reached over and took Aubrey's icy hand in hers as she felt her own heart beating hard in her chest. "Are ya okay?" she asked her sister.

Aubrey nodded and then realizing she might not be able to see her, whispered, "I will be as soon as we put some distance between us and Ryland."

Mary concurred. Then as if their wish had been granted, the train lunged forward, slowly churning ahead and then gradually picking up speed. It swayed back and forth in a rocking motion and the rhythmic clickty-clack began to have a hypnotic affect on all of them. Aubrey closed her eyes and was quickly out. Mary felt her own eyelids begin to get heavy, but she forced herself to stay awake, keeping guard.

As she quietly laid against the base of the wall, she kept Trevor in her sights. It was becoming increasingly more difficult to see inside the car as the train pulled away from the city lights. A velvety blackness shrouded them. At this point, Mary couldn't even see her hand in front of her face. She wondered if their rescuer could be fully trusted. Apparently Dolly did or she wouldn't have placed them in his hands. But then again, she had trusted Ellingson and that hadn't worked out too well. Still, this man seemed different from the other two she had met tonight. He, at least, had been gallant enough to carry Aubrey's bundle for her. He seemed somewhat respectful towards the weaker sex, but also appeared like a loner; someone that would not ordinarily volunteer to help someone else.

Her curiosity got the best of her. "Thanks for helpin' us," she said quietly, but her voice seemed to be amplified against the walls of the empty boxcar. Trevor grunted in reply. She didn't let his unresponsiveness deter her. "I mean, ya didn't have to help us." Trevor continued to ignore her. "Ya sure seem to know yar way around the marshallin' yards. Ya must have a lot o' experience with them."

"I manage," he finally replied. Then he added, "Ya just 'ave to learn to get by in dis life."

Mary had learned that lesson as well. In the years of transitioning into adulthood, life had just pulled her along by its current. She discovered the trick was to keep your head above the water. She thought about what he had said and then poked a little. "Ya must have owed Dolly a big favor," she said more as a question than a statement. But as soon as she said it, she wished she could have pulled it back.

"Well, dat's between me an' Dolly," he said abruptly. "Ya need to be get'in' yar sleep. Tomorrow will come too fast for all o' us."

That was the end of the conversation. Mary turned on her side towards Aubrey and let herself relax enough to doze off. It was not a restful sleep. Her dreams were muddled with images of beastly animals that resembled a conglomeration of bulls and dragons. She and Aubrey were trying to capture one to ride. When they were finally able to get on top of it, they could barely get it to move. In the meantime, off in the distance, Ryland was riding one of his own and closing fast. As the monster approached, she could hear this strange monotone clicking sound. It was beginning to annoy her. She kept thinking that if it would only stop, she would be able to sleep and be safe. She wished she had a blanket too, because it was beginning to snow. It made the animal slick and difficult to ride. Aubrey ended up slipping off the beast. When Mary went back for her, she saw that Ryland had her. He reached down with a sword and cut off Aubrey's head. He held it up as a trophy. Mary awoke with a start.

She was still in the boxcar shivering, partly from the fear of the dream and partly from a chill. Her clothes were damp from the mist of the previous night. She reached in the pillow case and pulled out a dress and wrapped it around her shoulders for warmth. Inside the car it was beginning to lighten up. It must have been near daybreak.

"Don' get too com'table," she heard Trevor say. "We're almost to Liverpool. Ya need to get ready. We'll jump out o' duh train when it begins to slow down."

"Jump out?" she said startled. She could hear Aubrey rustling as she came awake.

"Yeah," he replied. "We don' wan' duh Bobbies findin' us when we pull into duh yard. We'll jump out just before dat."

"Won't we get hurt?" she asked as she got to her feet. She stumbled from the movement of the train and steadied herself against the wall. Aubrey sat up, just as alarmed as Mary at the news.

"Duh train won' be movin' fast as it comes into duh yard. Still, ya need to land on yar toes an' bend yar knees. When ya 'it duh ground, tuck yarself and roll away—just make sure it's away from duh train, not towards it," he chuckled, but neither of the women found it amusing. Trevor ignored their concerns; he'd shove them out of the train if he had to. He tottered as he walked towards the door and slid it partially open. The dim light of early morning invaded their car. The sky outside was still a deep azure with traces of purple streaked across it. The fog of London had long evaporated and left the sky clear and bright. Only a couple of stars were still visible as the sun waited anxiously just below the horizon.

Trevor rested one of his forearms on the side of the doorframe and the other on the door and peered out. It made Mary edgy just watching him stand there. She could envision him losing his balance and tumbling out. "Would ya please, do me a favor and step away from the door?"

Puzzled, Trevor turned around and saw the apprehension on her face. He laughed and asked, "Does dis make ya nervous?"

"It most certainly does," she responded.

Trevor's laughter died to a faint smile as he stepped back. He tottered as he made his way back to her. "Ya need to get yar tin's toget'uh," he said a little more lighthearted. He helped Aubrey to her feet and then walked her slowly to the side of the door. He laid her belongings off to the side and then turned to help Mary, but she had already staggered towards the door. As he instructed them once more, the women's eyes grew big as saucers.

The train began to decelerate; it was time for them to jump. To Mary's surprise, Aubrey went first. Mary hastily followed, but didn't land quite like Trevor had told her to. She felt something give in her right ankle as she rolled to her side. Trevor was right next to her with their bundles. He softly tossed them aside just prior to his landing. Out of the corner of her eye, she saw him gracefully land like a skilled gymnast and exercised a perfect roll. He came away unscathed.

Aubrey was to her feet, but limping slightly. She had ripped her pants and skinned up both knees. When she tucked and rolled, she must have hit her head on a rock. A nasty goose egg was forming on her forehead and blood was oozing from it. Still she fared better than Mary, who was still on the ground. She rolled over and sat up, cradling her foot as she grimaced in pain. She hoped it was only sprained and not broken.

Trevor came over and rubbed his face in frustration. "Now why did ya go and do dat? I told ya 'ow to land."

"I'm sorry, but this was me first jump from a train. I'm not experienced as ya are," she said angrily.

Trevor took his cap and slapped it in his hand. He let out an expletive and then apologized for his vulgarity. When his temper had subsided, he bent down to look at her ankle. Gently he pulled off her shoe and could see that it had already begun to swell and show some color. He asked, "Do ya tink ya can walk?"

She answered, "Not a chance."

"We 'ave a long ways to go yet," he announced to no one in particular and stood up. He surveyed the area and saw a few trees just beyond them and formulated a plan. "Stay 'ere," he said and trotted towards the trees.

"Where would we go?" Mary said sarcastically.

Trevor returned shortly carrying a long stick and a couple of smaller ones. He squatted down on his knees and asked, "Ya 'ave sometin' dat ya're not too terribly fond o' in yar bag? I need some strips o' cloths to wrap 'round yar ankle."

Mary rummaged through a few things and found a long gown. Trevor pulled out his penknife and began to cut strips off the bottom of it. He took them and gently wrapped them around her foot and ankle. As he did, he placed the two smaller sticks on either side as a splint. When he finished, he helped her to her feet. He instructed her to use the larger stick as a crutch as she put her arm around his shoulders and leaned on him. Gingerly, she tried it, but the pain was almost unbearable. She gritted her teeth and toughed it out, though her progress was much too slow.

Trevor lost his patience. "Ya'll 'ave to carry both bundles," he said handing them to Aubrey. Suddenly, he scooped Mary up in his arms and began to carry her. She started to protest, but he would have none of it.

"We need to find a room for us before nightfall. I don' know 'ow difficult dat's goin' to be." He circumnavigated the rail yard and then headed towards the wharf. The journey was long and Trevor had to stop every so often to rest. Mary again protested, but as soon as she started, he hoisted her over his shoulder and began walking again. She quickly learned to keep her mouth shut.

As they drew closer to the shipyards, they began looking for any houses that might be advertising a room for rent. Trevor saw a couple, but they looked pretty rough and run down. They would be his last resort. Finally, just down the street, there was one that looked promising. He set Mary down just outside the door and leaned her against the house. "Ya 'ave Dolly's money?" he asked with his palm up. She hesitated until Trevor explained. "I need to rent a room for us. Ya don' expect to buy a ticket on a ship an' immediately board her, now do ya? It may take as long as a week before ya can get on her."

Mary hadn't given it any thought and not wanting him to know just how naïve she really was, she said with a bit of an attitude, "I reckon not." Reluctantly, she reached inside her corset and pulled out the envelope with the money. Trevor rolled his eyes in response, but quickly took it from her.

He spilled out the coins and surveyed how much they had to work with. He dug out a few shillings and muttered, "It bet'uh not cost more dan dat." He replaced the rest in the envelope and handed it back. Mary quickly shoved it back in her corset. He looked sternly at her and then Aubrey. He warned, "Talk to no one; ya understand? I mean *no one*." He knocked briskly on the door. An elderly woman came to the door and spied the three of them warily. Trevor said to her, "Me brothers an' me need a room. I see ya got one for rent. 'ow much ya be needin' for a week?"

"Six shillin's," she replied.

"Dat's a lit'le 'igh; would ya make it four?" he asked.

"Six shillin's," she insisted.

Trevor hesitated and then offered, "Maybe five?"

"Six shillin's and no less."

Trevor relented and paid her the money. He could have gone back to the rat traps they had passed earlier, but he was in no mood to be totting Mary back the way they came. Besides, it would have been uphill. He had Mary put her arm around his shoulder and the three went inside, following the woman to their room.

"What 'appened to 'im?" she asked Trevor.

"'untin' accident," he quickly lied. "Fell out o' a tree."

The woman snorted and shook her head in response. Then she let them into the room. "Room doesn't include meals," she informed him. He nodded in agreement and then the woman left them. Trevor sat Mary down on the edge of the bed and then closed the door behind the old woman. Mary started to ask him something and Trevor cut her off.

"No talkin', remember?" Mary looked at him incredulously and started to voice her objections. He quickly muted her by putting his hand over her mouth. "Ya can't talk," he insisted. "Ya can't let anyone know dat ya're Irish." This brought a fire to Mary's eyes. "Ya don' understand, love. Wit' what's been 'appenin' in Ireland, yar people 'ave been abandonin' it like rats on a sinkin' ship. Dey've been comin' here in droves an' wit' it, bringin' all kinds o' diseases. People are scared o' 'em. For yar own protection, just keep quiet an' let me do duh talkin'. Alright?" Mary dutifully nodded her head and he removed his hand.

"Now let's get ya set'le in," he said softly. "Ya need to get yar weight off o' yar foot." He helped her lie back on the bed. Then he requested Dolly's money once again. "I need it to go an' buy yar tickets for yar trip."

Mary hesitated again, not totally trusting him. The last thing she wanted was for him to take their money and then desert them. Trevor must have suspected what she was thinking. "It's good dat ya're not trustin' anyone; ya'll not be takin' by anyone anymore. But right now ya need to trust me to take care o' ya. I'm not Ellin'son. I 'ave no idea what Dolly saw in 'im, but ya 'ave to trust me. I won' let ya down. If I did, I would be let'in' Dolly down. I couldn't bear dat."

Mary whispered, "Ya love her don't ya?"

Trevor smiled sweetly and said, "Yeah, wit' all me 'art. But it's not what ya tink. Ya see Dolly is me sister. She looked aftuh me growin' up, spesh'ly in duh orph'nage. She always took up for me. Well, I guess I owe 'er everytin'." Mary was surprised at this new revelation, but it explained why Dolly had put them in his hands. She took out the envelope and handed it to him. "I'll be back as soon as I can wit' duh tickets—I promise." He then slipped out the door and was gone.

Aubrey came over and sat softly next to her. "Do ya think he'll be back?" she quietly asked.

Mary looked forlornly at Aubrey. "I'm trustin' him with our lives." She laid back and began to pray.

Time passed and deep shadows formed as the sun lowered itself on the horizon. It was getting late and there was no sign of Trevor. Mary had Aubrey light a lamp in their room. She was surprised that the old woman didn't charge extra for the oil. And still they waited. Fear began to knot up in her stomach. It was dark outside when suddenly the door flew open and Trevor came busting in carrying a box of groceries. He shoved the door closed with his foot.

"I got yar tickets, love," he said breathlessly. "Ya leave in four dies. I 'ope yar ankle is bet'uh by den." He pulled out a loaf of bread and some cheese along with a bottle of milk and set them on a small table in the corner. Trevor would have preferred some ale, but thought these girls would rather have milk to drink. Other women in their profession might not have minded, but there was something different about them—he just wasn't sure what it was.

They ravenously devoured the food. It had been twenty four hours since any of them had had a morsel of food. Mary hadn't realized how hungry she was until they began to eat. Her anxiety must have kept her hunger at bay.

When it came time to go to sleep, Mary apprehensively waited to see what Trevor would do. Would he demand payment from *both* of them? But to her surprise, he asked to borrow one of their bundles. Aubrey handed hers to him and he laid down on the floor, using it for a pillow. Mary and Aubrey exchanged a look as they crawled into bed together. Their trust and respect was growing for Dolly's little brother.

As they counted down the days for their departure, Trevor continued to take care of them. He brought food for them every day. Mary wondered where he got the money for it; sure that he had spent all of Dolly's money on their fare. She suspected that he may have been stealing, but had no proof. She didn't insult him by asking, just prayed that he wouldn't get caught. During their wait, he would periodically bring a cool, damp cloth and place it on Mary's ankle. The swelling had gone down slightly, but the bruising had deepened to an ugly purple. She still couldn't bear wait on it.

The day before they were to leave, Trevor brought in a stick that he had found. He took out his penknife and did a little work on it, fashioning it into a walking stick for her. He hoped that she would be able to use it to get on the ship. That evening, she tested it out. It was painful but she was able to hobble on it. Trevor felt a little more comfortable about leaving them on the ship alone.

The last evening and they all felt a little morose. Both girls had grown an attachment to their chivalrous benefactor. They were going to miss him. In the small time together, they had developed a brotherly love towards him. Mary was a little amused as he timidly asked to see the money that Aubrey was carrying.

As she feathered out the dollar bills, Trevor let out a whistle and exclaimed, "Good golly! I've never seen so much money." He picked one up and examined it. "It don' look real," he commented and returned it. "Ya know ya real'y need to split duh money and each o' ya take 'alf." He didn't expand on his suggestion; they understood. Neither wanted to think about the possibility of something happening to the other. When morning came, they took his advice.

Trevor brought them a couple of apples a piece for their breakfast. They ate quietly; no one feeling much like talking. It was a bittersweet morning for the three of them. Mary was anxious to get started, yet she was sad to leave their new friend behind. But the moment had finally arrived. They gathered their belongings and Mary, leaning on her cane, limped out of the house. At Trevor's suggestion, they had remained disguised as they left. He didn't want to raise the suspicions of the owner of the house. He wasn't sure what would have happened if she saw two women instead of men. The old woman probably would have run to the nearest constable's office and reported suspicious activities. They didn't need that kind of trouble.

As they slowly trekked towards the shipyards, Trevor spotted a secluded place they could use to change into their dresses. As they dressed, Trevor continued his gentlemanly ways, by turning his back to them. It warmed Mary's heart to see that there were still good men in the world. After they had changed, he encouraged them to keep their disguises with them. "Ya never know if ya might need it again on yar trip. It's a long ways dere. Ya don' know what ya might encountuh 'long duh way."

Mary's eyes clouded with tears as they walked towards the ship. They would finally be free of Ryland and the bondage they had lived under the last two years. An excited expectation swelled in her as the ships came into sight. They were glorious wooden vessels with ecru sails, some rolled up and others hoisted in position, ready for use. It stood tall in the forefront of the bluest sky she had ever seen.

Trevor squinted his eyes against the glare and said, "I've never seen duh skies so clear before. Dere's usually so much smoke from the fact'ries dat ya could cut it wit' a knife. Someone must be smilin' down on ya today, Mary." She smiled faintly and nodded in agreement. Trevor directed them to the ship and as they stood on the gangplank, it was time for their goodbyes.

"I wish I were goin' wit' ya," Trevor said sadly.

"I wish ya were too," Mary echoed. "And I wish Dolly were with us." Trevor nodded. She noticed that his eyes were a bit watery, and that realization caused her own to tear up. She wanted so much to show Trevor how grateful she was for all his help. "Thank ya, Trevor. We will never forget yar kindness towards us. Ya're a good man. Ya take care o' Dolly."

Trevor choked back his emotions. He wouldn't have admitted it, but he had grown fond of the two. "Don' worry about Dolly. If Fortier makes trouble, 'e'll 'ave to deal wit' me. I know she loves all duh niceties dat 'e 'as afforded 'er, but it's time dat she takes a realistic look at tings. Fortier is not always goin' to be so gen'rus. I wan' 'er to leave. Maybe now dat she sees dat ya 'ave got'en away, she'll tink about 'er own future."

"I hope so," Mary said and without even thinking, she kissed him on the cheek. Trevor was so taken aback that he didn't know how to react. He gently touched where she had kissed him and bowed his head. His face flushed with embarrassment.

Quietly he said, "Ya need to be goin'. Take care o' yarself. Don' be trustin' no one." He shyly looked into her eyes and then on impulse, he quickly returned the kiss, only this time it was on the lips. "Goodbye, Mary," he said hastily, turned and then ran down the gangplank. She watched him disappear out of sight, as she felt a tug at her heart and wondered what had just happened. She wondered if she had mistakably given him the wrong impression. Distantly she heard her name being called.

"Mary?" Aubrey called once again. "I think he was beginnin' to like ya."

Mary shook it off and said. "No, he was just bein' kind. Besides we have some husbands waitin' on us in America. Best be gettin' along." She wiped a lone tear from one of her eyes and brushed past Aubrey, resolute on not looking back on what they were leaving behind. She was determined that a new and wondrous life was on their horizon. How she hoped that it was so.

8

The Journey to America

The accommodations in steerage were worse than Mary could have ever imagined. From friends, she had heard horror stories of emigrants traveling to America and hoped they were exaggerations of gifted yarn-tellers. She was wrong. A sick feeling of regret crawled in her stomach, but it was too late to turn back.

The sisters were ushered by a person of authority until they reached an open hatch below. Two ladders went straight down it that they, along with about fifty others, had to negotiate. With her bad ankle, Mary slipped and nearly fell from one of the rungs. Fortunately she caught herself, but her arm was wrenched in the process.

At the bottom of the ladder, they found themselves in a long, narrow room approximately thirty-five feet long. It was about twelve feet at its widest, but narrowed to five feet on one end. Running along the sides were wooden partitions that served as sleeping quarters. Mary looked around and saw that many of their fellow travelers had carried with them rolled up mattresses. She naïvely thought that they would be provided. She studied the wooden planks, not relishing the idea of spending the next month sleeping on hard wood. Reluctantly, she tottered along the sawdust strewn floor and took possession of one of the sleeping berths. After her spill, she was ready to get off her foot for awhile.

Aubrey shuffled after her and the two shared a bottom berth. It was a little better than being on the top, but not by much. Space between the two wasn't much more than a couple of feet. Claustrophobia had never been an issue until now, but lying in such close quarters gave Mary a feeling of suffocation. That, combined with the horrible stench of unsanitary conditions, made it difficult to breath. She tried breathing through her mouth so as not to inhale the putrid smells, but that just invited the disgusting odor into her taste buds. They were beginning to realize how long and arduous this trip was going to be.

The next few days at sea were difficult and even worse for the sisters. Mary struggled with the pain and swelling in her ankle, but her concern was more for Aubrey. When they had set sail, it had been a gorgeous day. The sun was warm and bright, but by mid-afternoon, clouds began to roll in. The wind picked up, causing the swells to rise. The ship was tossed up and down on the waves, adding to their discomfort. The first vestiges of seasickness began to show themselves. Aubrey had it worse; their chamber pot was being used for an entirely different purpose. Mary tried her best to keep from relieving herself, but with each heave from Aubrey, it was getting harder to deny it.

She decided it was time to get her out of the environment for awhile. They rolled out of the berth and made their way to the ladder for the next deck. Behind them, she heard one of the male passengers make a curt remark. "Yeah, get her outa here, before she makes us all sick."

His wife chastised him, "Leave 'em be. Can't ya see that they're in a bad way?"

"Oh, so that's what's wrong with 'em," he remarked. The two stopped and exchanged a look. They had both been fortunate up to this point, but some of the other girls had not. Fortier had ushered them to a doctor to take care of the situation.

Mary led her by the arm trying to get her away from the stench. With great difficulty, they climbed the ladder to the open hatch. What met them at the top was three barrels half full of kitchen refuse from the day before. Aubrey promptly threw up in one of them while Mary held her. Then they tottered on the drunken ship until making it to the railing. The deck was slick with rainwater but only a fine mist fell at the moment. The coolness of the breeze revived them as they took in some of the salty air. It smelled clean compared to what they had been breathing. But the rolling of the ship did not ease the roiling in their stomachs.

As they hung over the railing, Aubrey slowly turned towards Mary and asked, "What if I am? What will I do? No man will want me as a wife?"

"Don't be worryin' about it," Mary tried to assure her. "Tis just the rough seas makin' ya ill."

"But what if..." Aubrey trailed off. She returned her gaze to the swirling water below. After a moment of hesitation, she announced, "I'll kill meself if I am."

Mary grabbed her and spun her around. "Ya'll do no such thin'!" she said angrily. "Tis a mortal sin, Aubrey. Ya don't know if ya are or even if the man ya're goin' to marry might not be acceptin'. Don't do *anythin'* in haste." Aubrey lowered her head in shame and then Mary prodded, "Promise me."

"I promise," she murmured.

Mary swept her in her arms and held her. Aubrey returned the embrace, drawing strength from her sister. Suddenly a loud voice startled them. "What are ya doin' up on deck?" It was presumably an officer from the ship, in his pristine white uniform and fancy cap with gold piping around the band. When they didn't immediately answer, he gruffly asked again.

Mary spoke up, "We were just gettin' some fresh air. Me sister's sick."

On hearing this, the man instinctively took a step back. "Then ya need to get down with yar own kind," he said.

Mary's anger flared. "She doesn't have anythin' but a good case o' seasickness, like we all do." She stared him down, but the officer refused to give in. "What are ya goin' to do? Throw us overboard, if we disobey?" she fumed. One look in his eyes told her that it just might become their fate if they did not retreat to *their* place. They were worse than commoners—third class passengers with no sense of value. He'd just as soon squash them under his foot and wipe the debris off with a dirty rag than to give them the time of day.

Mary turned to Aubrey and said, "Come on. We need to get back downstairs." She put her arm around her shoulder and directed her towards the hatch. The man watched until they disappeared below, making sure they didn't return.

The waters eventually calmed and so did their sickness, although eating was a chore in itself. They had no dining room as the other classes did. Their food was dished out of a huge kettle into dinner pails; first come, first serve. The food was atrociously vile; the taste of cooking shoe leather would have had a more appealing flavor. To make matters worse, they soon discovered that all refuse was eventually stored in steerage, adding to the disgusting smells they already endured.

There was virtually no privacy for any of the women. The division of sexes was not well defined, with many of the young single women being quartered among married couples. Even so, Mary and Aubrey felt the wandering gaze of many of these husbands. They felt no safer than they were at the brothel. They took turns shielding the other as they changed their clothes and performed other acts of indiscretion. They continuously felt as if they were on exhibit. There had even been one incident when a man climbed into their berth with them. Mary made quick use of her cane and banished the man, but from that point on, neither slept soundly.

During one of the sleepless nights, as Aubrey cried softly, she confessed, "I'm not goin' to make it, Mary." She spoke softly as not to awaken anyone else.

Mary's heart sank. "Don't talk like that. We'll get through this."

"I'm not strong like ya are. I can barely keep any o' this disgustin' food down."

"Ya just take it one day at a time—one moment if need be. And ya pray. God will see us through."

"How can ya still believe in Him after all that's happened to us?"

"We're alive aren't we? Ya know how many o' our own people have died from famine? But God rescued us."

Aubrey scoffed. "Some rescue—into the hands o' Denham and then Fortier."

"His ways are not our ways. I don't rightly know why thin's happened the way they did, but I know that He is rescuin' us now. So don't give up. Life is goin' to get better." Aubrey didn't totally disagree with her sister. If they made it off the ship, it would be an improvement to say the least.

Along the journey, they did receive good news. Aubrey had her monthly visit and Mary followed close behind. It added to their physical despair, but both were relieved there would be no unwelcomed visitors. They could go on with their plans with no worries of having to explain to their future husbands that they were not as pure as they had portrayed themselves. But for Mary, this knowledge weighed heavy on her. She felt deceitful and sought a clear answer from God on this. She determined that when she arrived in America, one of the first things she would do was seek out a priest and make a full confession. She wanted to start this new life completely absolved of wrongdoing.

Thirty-five long days at sea and the ship finally sailed into the harbor of New York City. Everyone quickly gathered their belongings and waited. But before anyone could go ashore, they had to be examined by a health official. If any onboard were found to be with sickness, the entire ship would be quarantined on Staten Island for thirty days. Rumor had it that the housing there didn't fare much better than what they had already encountered. Everyone's heart sunk as they awaited the verdict. When Mary heard the news, she cried out in a silent prayer, *Dear Lord, please spare us o' this. We cannot take much more.*

After several hours, they allowed first class passengers to disembark. Some men in steerage let out a war whoop of delight, but Mary still held her breath. She wouldn't relax until they had stepped onto American soil. It took some time, but eventually those in the hold were allowed to climb to the next deck. Mary's ankle had surprisingly grown stronger, but still had a little tenderness to it. She and Aubrey mounted the ladder and climbed to the open hatch. Bright sunshine made them squint their eyes, yet it was a good harbinger, at least Mary thought.

They scampered down the gangplank and then onto the dock, where they were greeted with a crowd of people scurrying about. It surprised them to see so many people. Somehow in Mary's mind, she thought the new world would be less populated. Aubrey gasped and exclaimed, "Would ya look at that! Tis as busy as London ever was!"

"Tis a sight that's for sure," Mary replied. She dug out a crumpled piece of paper that she had tucked in with her packet of letters from James. In his letter, he had instructed her to go to the post office next door to a large hotel. Since she could not read, she had written down the address, in a language only she could understand. To help her remember, she had made a crude drawing of a person with an arrow pointing to their derrière. It was coupled with a drawing of an oar alongside a house. It all stood for Astor House. Then she had drawn a picture of a street that was very wide. This she had trouble remembering. Was it Broad Street? That didn't sound right. Neither did Broad Road. She squeezed her eyes tightly shut as she concentrated, trying to remember.

"Which *way* do we need to go, Mary?" Aubrey asked.

In an instant she knew. "Broadway," she nearly shouted. "We need to go to Broadway."

She had to ask a few people where it was before she found one that hadn't just got off a boat like they had. Finally an older man with a worn face, pointed to a high steeple and said, "You see that church? That's the Trinity Church; it's on Broadway. Follow it and then go another block or so and you'll find St. Paul's Chapel. The Hotel is across the street."

"Thank ya, sir," she said excitedly. Her heart was pounding in anticipation. As they quickly walked down the street, Mary slid her cane under her arm. She no longer needed it, but carried it just the same. It was a reminder of Trevor and all that he had done for them; it gave her a sense of hope for their future. Besides, it made an excellent weapon to ward off unwelcomed propositions.

They started down Broadway, keeping the church's steeple in view. It wasn't hard for it was the tallest structure in lower Manhattan. The massive stone building grew more impressive as they approached it. Under the shadow of its towering spire, Mary felt so small and insignificant. A terrifying thought entered her mind. Did God stand from His ivory tower and look down at her with the same impression? She shuddered and said to herself, perish the thought.

They continued until they came to the wrought iron fence that surrounded the courtyard of the St. Paul's Chapel. It was yet another impressive church building, although not nearly as tall as the former one. Where Trinity was a giant that towered over everything, St. Paul's was squattier, having more of a boxy appearance. It had a small portico in the front with four large pillars; its tall steeple was in the rear. Mary and Aubrey passed slowly, taking in the sight.

Across Vesey Street was the Astor House Hotel. It looked nothing like a house. It too was a massive stone building that stood six stories high with storefronts on the street level. As they approached, Mary pulled Aubrey back, in fear that they both might get mangled by the traffic on the streets. The great crowds of people both befuddled and intrigued her. She had never expected it to be as bustling as London.

Finally they chanced to cross Broadway to another immense building. The gothic structure turned out to be the post office she was looking for. They walked inside and the enormity of the building seemed to swallow them up. Not knowing where they needed to go, they sort of followed the crowd. A long line had formed and they joined in. They paid no attention to the fact that it was largely made up of men. A gentleman behind them tapped Mary on the shoulder. When she turned around he politely tipped his hat. "You may want to get in that line over there," he said pointing to the right. "It's for ladies only; you might get through faster."

Mary thanked him and then they made their way to the other line; it was noticeably shorter. When they finally got to the window, she wasn't entirely sure of what she should say or do. She said in a rush, "Me name is Mary O'Shea. There is supposed to be a letter waitin' for me from Oregon. Tis from James Whitaker o' Windsor, Oregon."

The teller quickly wrote down the information and passed it to a runner. He had her step aside briefly while he took care of other patrons. Soon the runner returned with the letter in hand. Mary eagerly tore it from the tellers hand, thanked him and then she and Aubrey went to a private corner of the room and opened it. There was some money inside; what appeared to be a little more than he had previously sent. Along with it was a letter. Mary's heart began to sink. How was she going to know what it said?

She thought for a minute and then was inspired. Going back to the teller, she asked, "Could ya be tellin' me if there be a Catholic church nearby?" It was probably a dumb question, for all she knew the church across the street could be one. It was strange to her how so many churches, whether Protestant or Catholic, looked so similar. She secretly wondered if there was really any difference in God's eyes. It was a thought she didn't dare voice to anyone of her faith.

The teller, a little put out with her, gruffly said, "Take a right down Broadway to Barclay, then make a left, go one block. On the corner of Barclay and Church Streets you'll find St. Peter's."

"Thank ya. Be holdin' to ya," she said as politely as she could. She didn't want to get off on the wrong foot in her new home.

"What are ya goin' to do, Mary?" Aubrey asked as they left the post office.

"I'm goin' to Mass," she said as if it was the most logical thing she could do.

"Why on earth would ya do that?"

"Because I need to seek God's face, that's why."

Aubrey grunted. "I suppose ya're goin' to confession as well."

"Most certainly," she replied. "And it wouldn't hurt ya too much either.

"Are ya goin' to confess everythin'?"

"As much as I can remember about the last two years, since me last confession."

"Ya'll make the priest blush," Aubrey said offhandedly. Mary didn't answer right away. "Ya think he'll absolve ya o' all yar sins?"

"I'm countin' on it," Mary said confidently. "God is faithful to forgive. It says somewhere in the Good Book somethin' to the affect that *if we confess our sins, He is faithful and will forgive us and will purifying us.* If not, then we are without hope." Aubrey held her tongue, not wanting to burst Mary's bubble, but she had felt for a long time that they were indeed without hope.

They had to ask someone where Barclay was, but eventually found their way to the church and stood marveling at the structure. St. Peter's looked like something out of Greek mythology, with its massive stone building and giant columns in the front. The temple had an air of dignity, but to the two young women from Ireland, it was very intimidating. Mary and Aubrey slowly climbed the steps to the portico. Three large doors stood open before them. Mary started in, but Aubrey balked, refusing to go in.

     Mary entered, stopping at the stoup. She took some holy water and crossed herself. Timidly she went into the sanctuary. Walking down the center aisle, she let the beauty of it overtake her. The dark wooden pews contrasted with the creamy white decor and the brilliant colors of the stained glass. The glass glistened, reminding her of that special day they had spent with Dolly. Throughout the sanctuary, numerous statues were displayed but the center piece was a painting of the crucifixion. Mary went to one of the pews, knelt and crossed herself once again. She bowed her head and prayed.

     When she finished, she waited for her turn to enter the confessional. During that time, she argued with herself not to be subjected to this humiliation. How could God possibly forgive her? She should just leave and accept this fact. But inwardly, something told her that this was a lie. Her God was a forgiving God. He knew everything that went on and that she was not a willing participant. Even so, she was ready to accept the part she played in this sin. She longingly sought after His forgiveness and a fresh start. In the end, the latter won out and she stayed.

     When it was time for her, she knelt in front of the curtain that separated her from the priest. She took in a deep breath, crossed herself and said, "Bless me, Father, for I have sinned. It has been over two years since me last confession." Then she began the long, difficult task of retelling all she could possibly remember that needed to be confessed. She couldn't name each one, but she trusted that God's memory was far better than hers. He would know and she put her hope in the fact that He would absolve her of even the sins she couldn't recall. She concluded her confession with admitting being disrespectful to her father. "I'm sorry for these and all the sins o' me past life."

The young priest, who was sitting in for the parish priest on this particular morning, was at a loss for words. He had never encountered such a confession before. He said a prayer for wisdom and then tried to council with her. He asked, "Have you given up this lifestyle, my daughter?"

"I have indeed," she answered. "That's one o' the reasons I have come to America—to escape it and to begin anew."

He contemplated her words and then said, "You said it is one of the reasons for coming here. What are the others?"

"Me sister and I are to be married. We are mail order brides on our way to Oregon to be wed."

This news gave pause to the priest. Finally he said, "You know that marriage is a sacred estate. It is a gift from God and should never be entered into lightly. It is to be a sacred union between like-minded believers. Is your husband-to-be a Catholic as well?"

She hesitated and then quietly confessed, "He is not, Father; he is a Protestant."

Quietly he answered, "Then I cannot give my blessing on this. For one to marry outside the faith, you are inviting misery on yourself and any children that may come from this union." She timorously agreed with him. For this very reason she had not wanted to go into this with the priest. He sensed this. "But you are going ahead with this just the same, aren't you?"

"I have promised him."

"Do you love him?"

"I believe that I do. I love the man that wrote the letters to me."

The priest slowly responded, "You know that the marriage will not be valid in the eyes of the Church? You will be living in sin as much as when you were living at the brothel. Your children will be considered illegitimate. Are you willing to accept the consequences?" Mary turned it over in her mind. She struggled with the thought that God would condemn her for such an act. What made the difference if she were Catholic or Protestant, as long as they were baptized believers? She never answered his question. The priest continued, "You need to make all this known to your betrothed before you marry. Hold nothing back, including your involvement in prostitution. If you deny this truth, you will be acting deceitfully. It is not a way to begin a marriage."

Mary's heart sank, but she agreed. The priest then instructed her to recite the prayer of contrition. Mary prayed softly, *"O me God, I am heartily sorry for havin' offended Thee, and I detest all me sins, not only because o' Thy just punishments, but most o' all because I have offended Thee, me God, who art all good and deservin' o' all me love. I firmly resolve, with the help of Thy grace, to sin no more and to avoid the near occasions o' sin. Amen."*

The priest offered her prayers of penance for her to recite and then once again pleaded that she would reconsider her actions. He then concluded by saying, "I absolve you of your sins in the name of the Father, the Son, and the Holy Spirit." They both gave the sign of the cross and then he concluded the confessional by saying, "Go in peace to love and serve the Lord."

Mary replied, "Thanks be to God." But before she got up to leave, she timidly asked. "Father, I have a letter I just received from me intended. I cannot read. Could I impose on ya to read it to me?"

The priest was reluctant at first but then agreed. Mary slipped the letter through the curtain. He opened it and began to read to her: *"My dearest Mary, if you are reading this..."* He paused. It did not slip by his reasoning that she had already lied to this man. *"...if you are reading this, then you have made it safely to America. I have enclosed money to pay your passage to San Francisco. When you arrive, go to the post office—anyone in the city can tell you how to get there. I will have another letter waiting for you with enough money for a stage to take you the rest of the way. Be careful on your trip, especially through the Isthmus of Panama. It is not a safe place and I dread sending you through there, but the alternatives are even more frightful. Be on your guard with strangers and let no one know that you have any money on you. I love you dearly and wish that I could be there to protect you. I longingly await your arrival. James."*

He refolded the letter and returned it to her. Quietly he said, "Think about what we have talked about, Mary. The journey you are about to embark on is not safe for any woman. Please reconsider."

"I cannot. I have made me promises."

The priest suddenly pulled out a chain with a medallion on it. He thrust it through the curtain towards Mary. "Take this. It's a Saint Christopher's medal. My mother gave it to me when I went to seminary."

Stunned Mary replied, "Oh Father, I could never take that from ya."

"If you're going through Panama, you need it far more than I do. Saint Christopher will protect you. Please take it," the priest pleaded. Reluctantly, Mary took it from him and placed it around her neck. The priest concluded, "May the Lord watch over and protect you, dear child."

"Thank ya, Father," she said with great gratitude and then exited the confessional. She returned to a pew and knelt once again. Clasping her hands together, she bowed her head and began to recite her prayers of penance. When she was through, she waited for Mass to begin. She joyfully accepted the Eucharist, feeling God's presence and being fully washed with His forgiveness. She had such a feeling of freedom that she had not felt in a long time.

But as she left the church building, she sensed a foreboding. What waited on the horizon troubled her spirit. What was she to do about James? She hadn't feared him rejecting her for her faith. She had Ellingson write to him about the importance of her Catholic beliefs and he seemed accepting, because he never commented on it. Even so, she could not see herself confessing she had not simply been a servant working in London, but was in actuality a prostitute. Yet the young priest's words continued to echo inside her heart: "*If you deny this truth, you will be acting deceitfully. It is not a way to begin a marriage.*" She would have a few weeks to ponder it and to seek God's guidance. Hopefully by the time she arrived in Oregon, she would have her decision.

9

The Journey Continues

The steamer ships bound for the coast of California left every two weeks, carrying mail to the gold country. The women booked their passage to San Francisco, but were disappointed that the next one would not leave for another five days. They needed to find a hotel that was fairly inexpensive. They were at a decidedly disadvantage, not knowing much about American currency and the actual cost of things. Mary was afraid they'd be swindled out of their money or even worse robbed. She instinctively reached for the St. Christopher's medal the priest had given her and said a prayer.

They walked along the streets in search of any hotels that looked inexpensive that might have vacancies. They inquired on several, but were repeatedly turned away. Perplexed, they continued on. As they stepped into the next one, they heard the manager yelling at another man, "Can't you read the sign? It says *No Irish Allowed*." The man took his hat and thumped it with his other hand. With his head bowed, he turned and left the hotel. Mary was indignant and wanted to give the manager a piece of her mind. But she remembered what Trevor had said about her people spreading diseases. They had a right to be scared. She contemplated their next move and was suddenly inspired.

"Don't say a word," she insisted.

Aubrey furrowed her brow and whispered, "But ya heard what the man said…"

"I know, but they don't have to know we're Irish."

"Huh?"

Mary started towards the desk while Aubrey remained close to the door in case there was trouble. She walked up to the man who was seated at the desk, smiled seductively and then doing her best Dolly impersonation said, "'ello, love. Ya gotta room for a coupla girls fresh off the boat from London."

The man immediately warmed up to her. He glanced past Mary to Aubrey then back to Mary and said with smile, "Well, I think I could probably manage to find something." He turned to the rack of room keys, looked them over and then removed a set. "I've got one right at the top of the stairs, so you don't have to walk very far."

"Now aren't ya so kind," she said continuing the flirtation. She hoped that it would get them a room and nothing more.

"How long will the two of you be staying with us?" he inquired.

"We'll be needin' the room for the next five dies, deary."

"And what about the nights?" he said grinning.

Mary let out a howl, sounding just like Dolly. "Oh, now aren't ya a flirt." She padded him on the arm as he leaned on the desk.

The man joined her laughter and then said as a matter of fact, "The room's a dollar twenty-five a night…that makes it six twenty-five. You know, it's cheaper by the month." His eyes glistened with lust.

"Now aren't ya the temptuh, but we'll only be needin' it a short time," she giggled, as she pulled out some bills, hoping she didn't give him too much. She coolly handed them to him.

"You need to sign the register," he said collecting her money. Mary froze. She didn't think about that. The man returned with a few coins of change for her. He repeated himself and pointed to the registry. Mary picked up the pen and dipped it into the ink well. Her hand was shaking as she put it to the paper. She scribbled something trying to make it look like a signature. The man frowned and said, "It's not very legible."

"Penmanship isn't me strongpoint, love," she said tossing her head to the side as if she were an empty-headed dame.

"I need something a little more readable," he responded. Mary got the impression that her charm was wearing thin. He took the pen from her hand and dipped it again. "What's your name?'

"Mary O…" she caught herself just before exposing her true identity. In a split second, she pretended to cough and then said, "Whitakuh. Mary Whitakuh."

He looked warily at her, but wrote it beside her scribble. Then he handed her the key. He said, "It's the first door on the left." He smirked at her and added, "Do you need any help?"

She wagged her finger at him teasingly. "No, no, no. I tink I will be safuh if ya stay here." She giggled flirtatiously and started up the stairs with Aubrey in the rear. When they were safely in their room, she breathed a sigh of relief.

Aubrey stared at her sister and said, "Ya amaze me!" Mary just looked at her. "Ya sounded exactly like Dolly."

"I don't know about that. But I think I did well enough that this American couldn't tell that I wasn't cockney. I just hope I didn't encourage him *too* much." Aubrey nodded in agreement.

During the next five days, the women explored the city. It felt good to have that freedom again. As they walked, the enormity of the city astonished them for it seemed to stretch into infinity. But what impressed them the most was the gathering of people from every ethnicity. It was hard to fathom that more people lived on this little island than the one they had grown up on. Of course, their population was rapidly declining.

While they took in the sights, they remained cautious about what they spent. They only ate at a restaurant a couple of times, and that was because they were curious about the cuisine. Mostly they sustained themselves on bread and cheese from the market. Their one indulgence was the purchase of a carpet bag for each of them. They were tired of carrying their belongings around in a pillow case. In the evenings as they returned to their hotel, they quietly snuck up the stairs, trying not to draw the attention of the man at the front desk. Fortunately, when it was time to check out, someone else was manning the counter.

On the day that they were to leave, they excitedly mounted the gangplank to the steamer appropriately named the *America*. This time the trip would be different. They had an actual cabin that was fully furnished with a mattress to sleep on. They both plopped down on it in pure delight.

The enormous ship left the New York harbor and headed southward, circumnavigating the peninsula of Florida, before making stops at Cuba and Jamaica to refuel on coal. There were some five hundred people on board, many loaded down with mining equipment for the gold fields. As second class passengers, Mary and Aubrey were allowed to roam the decks freely and take their meals in the dining room, although they felt a little under dressed with their well worn clothing. Still it was far better than being sandwiched in the bowels of the ship for the entire cruise. Unfortunately, their accommodations changed as the ship made its final stop.

The Isthmus of Panama is a narrow strip of land that separates the Caribbean Sea from the Pacific Ocean. Their ship anchored just off the coast of the village of Chagres, because of the reefs and sandbars. The passengers were then ferried inland to find passage up the Chagres River. The sisters, ill-prepared for the sixty mile journey across the tropical rain forest, disembarked with the others. When they reached Chagres, they were at a loss at what they should do next. Mary made inquiries of some of the other passengers, but many turned away refusing to help them. Finally, a young man in a rumpled linen suit approached them. He had an engaging smile and a line blonde mustache. The three days growth of stubble on his face added to his rugged good looks. He explained to the women their dilemma. "You're going to have to take a boat up the Chagres River to Las Cruces and then travel by pack mule until you get to Panama," he said removing his wide-brim hat and wiping the perspiration from his brow.

The gravity of James' words about this being a dangerous place was sinking in. A familiar twist of fear knotted in her stomach. If she had fully understood the situation, she would have purchased some sort of weapon—a knife or a sword or anything to protect themselves. As it was, she only had her walking stick to use as a club if need be. She reached up and touched the medal around her neck, making sure it was still there.

The man beckoned them to follow him as he sought out one of the natives for passage up the river. Many of the men had already rented out their canoes, but with some persistence and some extra money, the three finally secured one. Two others quickly joined them in the boat. The natives were no discriminators of the sexes, charging the women as much as the men for the ride. It cost each of the ladies a hefty three and a half dollars for a seat in the canoe, along with an additional dollar and a half for their bags. Mary and Aubrey gingerly climbed into the hollowed out log and sat near the rear where they were at least covered by a canopy made of palm leaves. It would shield them from the hot tropical sun for the next forty-five miles up the river.

A team of three half naked men used long, skinny poles to negotiate the murky waters of the Chagres. It would take them four days and nights to ride upstream. The sweltering heat of the days was a sharp contrast to the cool nights. On one evening, as the temperatures dipped, a torrential downpour set in. The women were drenched and chilled to the bone. They huddled close together for warmth and safety, not trusting any of their companions, except possibly their Samaritan. He had offered his jacket to drape over them, but they declined. It was a long night.

When they finally arrived at Las Cruces, they rested that evening on a cot they shared. The following morning, they munched on some stale bread cake and drank some coffee. It was at this time Mary thought it would be good for them to change into their shirts and trousers. It would make traveling by mule much easier.

Neither one had any experience riding a horse or mule growing up, but Mary remembered a time when she was very small, her dad had put her on top of their milk cow and she had ridden her. She supposed that it wouldn't be much different. She climbed up and sat astride her mule like the rest of the men, while Aubrey, intending to be more dignified, rode side-saddle. But before the trip was through, she too decided to straddle the animal. If the two had thought that the trip up the river was expensive, it didn't compare to the cost of the mules. Fourteen dollars a piece was quickly subtracted from their funds.

The road was not much more than a track of dirt. It was hilly and steep most of the way. The forest closed in on them, making them feel as if it was going to swallow them up. Neither girl slept much on the trail. They had heard rumors in Las Cruces that this was the most dangerous part for travelers, especially those returning from the gold fields. Many were robbed and left to die. Mary kept her walking stick handy, just in case and constantly caressed the Saint Christopher medal around her neck. But that didn't keep her from being on continual alert. With every little sound, she jerked her eyes in that direction, ready to attack anything that moved. The sheer terror of the last fifteen miles would revisit her in nightmares for years to come.

After two days, they reached the safety of Panama City. It appeared as a haven of refuge to them, as they rode through a city of adobe houses and monasteries built by the Spaniards over a hundred years ago. Mary was delighted to see an immense Catholic cathedral near the town square. She would visit it before they left, giving thanks to God for His protection. They found a room at a hotel and Mary said they should splurge and pay the extra quarter to take a bath. She said, "It would be good to wash away the stench o' ridin' a mule for two days." Aubrey quickly agreed.

Fortunately, they only had to stay one night in Panama City. The Pacific Mail Steamship vessel, the *SS California* was docked and waiting to sail back to San Francisco. The women boarded early in the morning, eager to begin the last leg of their journey to California. As they traveled up the coastline of Mexico, they marveled at the sight of dolphins playing in the ocean and an occasional glimpse of a whale breaking through the surface of the water and then plunging back into the deep. This was the adventurous life Mary had envisioned, enjoying the wonders of God's creation. It was an amazing reprieve from hellacious prison they had escaped. Mary paused briefly to remember all the girls they had left behind, especially Dolly. She said a silent prayer for each of them, hoping that someday they too would be set free from their bitter bondage.

But the time the sisters shared on the ship was bittersweet. Although they enjoyed the gentleness of this part of their voyage, both were vastly aware that these were in all likelihood the last days they would have together. Soon each would depart to start new lives with their husbands. The probability of them ever being reunited was slim. The knowledge of this hung over them like an ominous storm cloud.

Their newly acquired traveling partner, who had rescued them in Chagres, turned out to be a writer from Massachusetts, name Robert Timmons. He was a bit of an adventurer that had taken a shine to them. He persistently questioned them about their life stories, but Mary would only tell him the reason for coming to Oregon. The mystery intrigued him and nearly became an obsession, but Mary refused to disclose anymore. Still Timmons clung to them throughout the rest of the trip, holding out hope that eventually he'd get a story from one of them.

They arrived at the San Francisco harbor, approximately two weeks later. Upon entering the port, they found it polluted with sailing ships, many deserted by its sailors. These men had simply left their ships abandoned for promises of riches in the gold fields. The steamer adeptly navigated through the maze of clippers and docked at the pier. Mary and Aubrey gathered their meager belongings and quietly disembarked. Mr. Timmons was quickly on their heels, which was a good thing, because they were immediately accosted by a small group of wild-eyed men.

Mr. Timmons gently took them by the elbow and pulled them close to him. He firmly announced to the lusting men, "Sorry, boys. These ladies are with me." They continued onward at a brisk pace, in case any decided to follow them.

As they walked away, Mary heard one of them ask, "Do you have to take both of them?"

Timmons ignored him and when they got a safe distance away he said, "It's not safe for women to be traveling by themselves in this country. There are far too many lonely men looking for the companionship of a woman. Then once they get liquored up…well, it's never a good outcome." Mary shuddered. She thought they had left the danger behind them in Panama, but once again they were entering a wild, lawless country, only the most valuable commodity these men were seeking was them.

Reluctantly she asked him, "Would ya be so kind to escort the two o' us to the post office?"

"The post office?" He looked at them in puzzlement and inquired further. "Why do you need to go to the post office?"

Reluctantly Mary replied, "I have a letter waitin' for me; I need to pick it up."

This seemed to fuel his intrigue. He smiled mischievously and said, "I'd be delighted to."

They asked several people before eventually finding someone who could tell them where they needed to go. They discovered that it wasn't too far up the street. They trekked up a hill away from the cluster of fishing shacks and came to Justice Court. Just beyond it was the post office. They went inside and saw that things were fairly quiet compared to the bustle of

New York. Mary got in line and waited. When it was her turn, she inquired about her letter and soon had it in hand. She opened it and discovered a small amount of cash along with a letter from James. She immediately sucked up her pride and asked Timmons if he would read it to her.

"I'd be delighted to," he said, thinking how he would be privy to some private information. Timmons began, *"My dearest Mary, if you're reading this..."* He paused and looked questioning at her just as the priest had done. Mary lowered her eyes, refusing to meet his gaze. He continued, *"Then you have safely made it through Panama. I'm sorry to have subjected you to that route, my love, but to send you around Cape Horn would have been even more treacherous."* Timmons stopped to interject his own commentary. "He's right. The fierce winds and high seas make it one of the worse shipping routes in the world. Many ships have been lost through there. Besides, it takes over four months to sail. Conditions are ripe to come down with some dreaded disease like yellow fever or cholera. There's a high mortality rate."

"I don't understand," Aubrey began. "Why couldn't we have just taken a train across the country?"

Timmons couldn't keep from chuckling at her naivety. Gently he said, "My dear woman, that's because the railroad doesn't even reach the Mississippi River as of yet." Aubrey looked at him blankly, clearly not comprehending what he was saying. He tipped his hat back and then rubbed his forehead trying to think of how he could explain it the women from Ireland. "Look, it takes three days to travel to the end of the line in Indiana. That's not even quite a third of the way across the country. You'd have to get a wagon and go to Missouri and join a train…er a *wagon* train."

"What's that?" Aubrey interrupted.

"It's a group of wagons traveling together. It makes it safer to travel in a group."

"Why didn't we do that instead?" This time it was Mary asking the question.

"It's not an easy journey. You have to leave in the early part of the spring, hoping that you don't get caught in any heavy spring rains that might get your wagon stuck in the mud. Then once you got into the plains, you worry that you don't get there too soon, when there isn't much grass for the animals to eat."

"Then why not leave later?" Mary asked.

"Then you worry about getting into the mountains too late. There are deadly consequences if you encounter snow while in the mountains. A few years ago a wagon train traveling to California, got caught in the heavy snow of the Sierra Mountains. Nearly half of the eighty-seven that started out perished. In the end they had resorted to cannibalism to survive. Now which route would you have preferred to travel?"

Breathlessly, Mary answered, "I guess the one we took." Timmons nodded in agreement.

He finished reading the letter to Mary and then folding it, slipped it back into its envelope. He handed it back to her and then asked, "Now what?"

"I guess we need to find a stagecoach like James said," she answered.

"I hear that there's a new company called Wells Fargo that runs a line clear up to Portland. I guess we should check it out."

Mary raised her brow and asked, "We?"

He smiled mischievously and said, "You don't think I'm missing out on the end of this story, do you?

Mary just shook her head. She guessed that they would have their traveling companion a little longer.

10

Aubrey's Wedding

The city of San Francisco was the picture of decadence. It was unsophisticated and bawdy, engaged in every kind of wickedness known to man. Gambling houses and saloons populated every city block. And there was no shortage of brothels either. This once peaceful Spanish mission had deteriorated into a den of iniquity. Over the past year, four major fires had decimated large portions of the city. Many residents began to wonder if the hand of God had come against them and that Heaven itself was chastising them for all their evil works.

Mary, Aubrey and their traveling companion Robert Timmons walked up towards Montgomery Street looking for the two-story red brick building of Wells, Fargo and Company. Fortunately, Timmons was with them and could read the signage on all the buildings they walked by. It would have been embarrassing and possibly dangerous if the ladies had accidentally walked into the Union saloon next door by mistake.

Entrepreneurs Henry Wells and William Fargo, taking advantage of the opportunities presented from the gold rush had recently established themselves out west. They set out to meet the growing banking and transportation needs of the miners, plus make a small fortune for themselves. In the past year, they had just set up a stagecoach line that ran all the way up to Portland.

The trio went inside and inquired when the next stage was due to leave for Oregon. It was not expected to return for a couple of more days.

They went ahead and paid the fare, which cost them considerably. Aubrey's fare was slightly less because she would be settling in the southern part of Oregon. To Mary's dismay, Timmons bought a ticket to accompany her to Windsor.

"Don't ya have a story ya have to cover," she said, showing her agitation. His interest in the sisters seemed to be settling on one in particular.

He smiled impishly and said, "I am; you're my story." Mary started to say something, but changed her mind half afraid it might end up as part of whatever story he thought he might have.

After they purchased their stage tickets, they walked down the next block and found a hotel. Like many hotels in the city, there was gambling on the first floor. Timmons again rescued the ladies. He signed the register for them and then escorted them to their room. It was a good thing for it seemed every male followed them with their eyes as they walked through the lobby. They found it unnerving and decided to forego any sightseeing as they had done in New York. The only time they left their room was for meals, all the while in the company of Timmons.

In some ways it was good for the sisters to be holed up. It was a chance for them to spend their last days together without any interruptions. They reminisced about happier days of growing up in the country, when life was simple and innocent. They laughed at things their dad had done to entertain them, neither wanting to think about what might have become of him. They talked about how Mam had always been the voice of reason when Dad got carried away. She always had some thoughtful Scripture she'd share in times of distress.

"Ya're like her, Mary," Aubrey said quietly.

She chuckled softly. "How is that?"

"Ya got her faith. Ya always believe that God has yar best interest, no matter how bad things get."

Mary was thoughtful and then asked, "Don't ya still believe in Him, Aubrey?"

Aubrey had her own thinking to do before she answered. "I guess I still believe, but I think that He's too busy to bother Himself with us."

"He's not too busy. He loves us and He promised that He would never forsake us."

"That's easy for ya, Mary."

"Tis not; I struggle to understand too. I don't know why we have gone through what we have. I think that there are reasons that we may never understand, but God has not forsaken us. Thin's will get better."

"Me sister, the eternal optimist," Aubrey said chuckling and then Mary joined her.

The sun glistened off the rich burgundy paint of the Wells Fargo stagecoach. One could tell that the coach was fairly new, because the amber colored wheels were barely scuffed. The coach driver took the ladies' carpetbags along with Timmons' backpack and stowed them securely to the wrought iron rack on top. Aubrey carefully stepped into the metal stirrup and climbed into the coach. Timmons helped steady her as she did. Mary was next and then Timmons followed. He took the seat beside her, not giving her much space. She gave him a sharp look and said, "Could ya give us a little more room; I'd like to breath."

Timmons' blue eyes sparkled with delight and he broke out in his characteristic impish grin. Mary's banter did something deep in his soul. He felt a strange connection with her, but wasn't quite ready to say that he was falling in love with her. "Sorry," he said, sliding over slightly, but not too far. She gave him a disgusted look, trying to discourage him.

On the other side of the coach was an elderly looking gentleman with silvery-gray hair and a bushy mustache. Sitting beside him was a couple looking to be in their early thirties. They had a young toddler that sat on the young man's lap. It looked to be a young boy, but with long golden locks of hair, it made it hard to tell. Mary didn't want to embarrass herself by asking, so she avoided it.

    The conductor slammed the door closed and hopped up onto the box beside the driver and rode shotgun. With a snap of the reins, the coach suddenly jolted forward. They bounded down the dusty road that had been chewed up from all the other wagons that had previously passed through. This was the first time either Mary or Aubrey had ridden in a coach. Mary felt a bit like royalty, but Aubrey was concerned that the team of six horses was traveling much too fast. She peered out the window as the scenery swiftly raced by. Mary couldn't keep from chuckling at her ever cautious sister. But one thing was for sure, they both were glad they were sitting forward instead of riding backwards. With their propensity for motion sickness, they would have been sick as dogs before they left the city limits.

    They climbed up and down the myriad of steep hills before exiting the city and then onto the beautiful countryside of Napa Valley. The rolling hills of wine country were reminiscent of their beloved homeland. The sight triggered more stories about their childhood. Timmons sat back quietly observing, making mental notes for his story. Fortunate for him, he had a good memory for details; it would have killed the spontaneity of the moment by taking notes.

    The first way station was approximately fifteen miles up the road. The coach stopped only long enough to exchange the tired horses for new, fresh ones. No one had time to exit the stagecoach. The conductor hopped down and quickly unhooked the team, while the hostler brought the other team along side. By the time the conductor had returned from the barn, the hostler had the second team harnessed and ready to go. All the while the driver kept his hand ready on his shotgun as he surveyed their surroundings for anyone that might be up to no good. As soon as the conductor was back on board, away they went down the highway, bouncing along the ruts and potholes, making sure they didn't miss any.

Sometime when the sun was high in the sky, they stopped at another station. As they approached, the conductor sounded a bugle announcing their arrival. This time the passengers were allowed to get out and stretch their legs and attend to other needs. Since there were no privies, the women went one way into the woods, while the men headed in the opposite direction. They returned to a simple one-story log cabin. By the door was a tin wash basin with a pail of water. The remains of what had once been a piece of soap, yellowed with age, sat next to the basin. Mary cleaned up the best she could, trying not to take up too much time. The only towel was a dirty woolen shirt that hung on a rusty nail close by. She opted to let her hands air dry.

The smell of beans cooking in the fireplace, hit them as soon as they entered. The aroma set Mary's stomach rumbling. She hadn't given much thought about eating until that moment. They sat down at a makeshift table of rough cut pine boards, with crudely made benches that were equally rough. The passengers squeezed in together making sure that the driver and conductor got the chairs at the ends of the table.

The station keeper dipped the pot of pinto beans into tin bowls for each of the paying customers. Unfortunately, the beans smelled better than they tasted. What was worse was the stale bread that they were served. Mary examined her piece of bread and discovered it was infested with bugs. She promptly placed it on the table and motioned to Aubrey not to eat it. She couldn't believe that they were charged a whole dollar for this meal.

As they sat quietly trying to choke down their food, Mary found herself staring at Aubrey. She wanted to memorize every laugh line, every freckle, and every feature about her face. She thought about the way her strawberry blonde curls liked to fall around her face and how sometimes Aubrey would become disgusted with it and wrap it into a bun. Or how her sister liked to twist a single strand around her finger when she fretted over things. She wanted to keep these memories locked forever in her mind, because she was acutely aware that memories fade very quickly. After nearly four years since her mam had died, she could scarcely recall any details of her face. Time was running out for the two of them.

As soon as the meal was eaten, the passengers were ushered back on the stage and off they went. They trekked back down the trail until they just about reached the horses limits and once again traded them off for rested ones. They continued onward at breakneck speed, never dawdling at the way stations. Along towards evening, they came to the *home* station. It was a little larger than the previous ones and included lodging. The station keeper and his wife made it their home. The wife did all the cooking and so this meal was a little more palatable, but still nothing to brag on. They had a little bacon with their beans and to their delight, the bread was fresher and bug free. They also had pie for dessert, but it wasn't very good. The crust was hard and tough with only a thin veneer of dried apples and a smidgen of brown sugar. At least the coffee had good flavor.

Mary was looking forward to stretching out on a cot and getting some sleep, but to her disappointment, they were once again escorted back to the stage. A new driver and conductor took over and they were down the road again. Exhausted, the sisters leaned into each other and tried to get a little shuteye. Timmons offered his shoulder for Mary, but she promptly declined.

Their journey continued much the same until they reached Aubrey's destination. It was early afternoon on the fourth day when they rolled into Jacksonville, Oregon. The town had originally been known as Table Rock City because of its view of two mesas in the distance. A little over a year ago, gold had been discovered in Jackson Creek and miners quickly flooded into the valley. It soon swelled to a city of over two thousand complete with gambling halls, saloons, shops and businesses and one lone bank. It had only recently had its name changed to Jacksonville after the creek where the gold was found, but early settlers still referred to it by its original name.

The coach stopped and all the passengers got out to stretch their legs. Only the trio would stay behind when the stagecoach pulled out. The ladies scanned both sides of the street, trying to figure out their next move. Aubrey at a loss turned to her big sister and asked, "What now, Mary?"

Mary sighed heavily. She narrowed her eyes and with determination said, "We start lookin' for Pedersen's General Store."

They turned left and started down the street when Timmons grabbed Mary by the arm. "What are we supposed to be looking for?"

"The man Aubrey is to marry owns a general store. His name is Pedersen. Henrik Pedersen."

"As in Pedersen's General Store?" he asked pointing over her shoulder. Mary turned and saw a mercantile, but there were no distinguishing marks making it stand out from the other shops. The only difference being the name that was on it. Mary inwardly chastised herself for not being able to read it.

The three road weary travelers walked across the street and entered the store. The wooden planks creaked underneath their feet, amplifying the hollow sound of their steps. A fresh aroma of newly ground coffee mixed with the scent of leather tackle that hung on the walls. The place was abuzz with customers, mainly loud talking miners in search of bigger and better tools.

The proprietor was a young man in his late twenties with light blonde hair and spectacles over his ice blue eyes. He was built like a Ticonderoga pencil, tall and thin. As he was finishing with a customer, Mary and Aubrey browsed, not really looking at anything in particular, just biding their time. When he finished with one of his customers, Mary gently nudged Aubrey forward, before she could make a sudden dash out the front door.

Henrik Pedersen peered up from his ledger and started to ask if he could help her. His voice trailed off and his expression suddenly changed. He wasn't sure if he recognized the woman in front of him or not. He questioningly asked, "Aubrey?" When she nodded her head timidly, he nearly leaped over the counter. "Aubrey!" He came around and suddenly, forgetting himself, gave her a tremendous hug. The few remaining patrons stared at them in dismay. When Henrik realized what he had done, he backed away, flushed with embarrassment. Aubrey was displaying her own unique shade of red.

"I'm sorry…that vas a little forvard of me…I…uh…" He muttered something low and unintelligible from his Danish tongue which further deepened his blush. "I vas so vorried about you. I vas afraid something might have happened to you or that you might have changed your mind."

Aubrey in her shyness lowered her head and stared at the floor. She said barely above a whisper, "we ran into some difficulties." She sneaked a peek at him and then returned to gaze at the floor. No one would have guessed that she had ever been with any man, let alone hundreds. To Mary's relief, it appeared that the farther they distanced themselves from their past, the more Aubrey become her normal bashful self. Aubrey stammered and said, "I want ya to meet me sister." She turned towards Mary and introduced her and then Timmons. She added, "Mr. Timmons has been, I guess ya'd say, our guardian angel. He helped us through Panama and then the craziness of San Francisco."

Henrik gave Timmons a firm handshake and said, "Thank you for protecting them." He then addressed Aubrey once again. "I vanted to meet you there, to help you get through, but I could not leave the store or Mama all alone. It vould have been too much for her." Suddenly he remembered that he needed to introduce her to his mother. "I'll get Mama. I know that she'll be happy to see you." He disappeared behind a curtain, much to the dismay of the impatient customers. Mary would have jumped in and helped out, but she knew nothing of the mercantile business.

Henrik reemerged with a diminutive woman with graying hair. Freda Pedersen may have been small in stature but she was physically strong from years of hard work. She had gentle features and an engaging smile. She immediately welcomed Aubrey with the same affection that her son had. Her blue eyes glistened with tears of joy as she invited Aubrey into the parlor to get better acquainted. Henrik remained in the store taking care of business, while Mary found herself alone with Timmons. It was the first time since they had met; it wouldn't be the last.

Aubrey was quickly filled in on the family history. Henrik's father Johann Pedersen had married his bride and immediately set sail for the new world. They settled in the frontier of Ohio, just as it was opening up to be the passage to the West. The couple had built a thriving business, supplying settlers with their growing needs as the territory beyond them began to expand. The former Lutherans soon found themselves caught up in the Methodist movement that was spreading throughout the Americas. They quickly became staunch followers of the methodic ways of John and Charles Wesley. So much so that when an expedition of Methodist missionaries excitedly returned from the Oregon territory, after prayerful consideration, the Pedersens decided to sell out and embark on a new adventure. Johann and Freda, along with Henrik and his younger sister, Mathilde, set out on the Oregon Trail in the spring of 1847. Little did they know that a short time later, gold would be discovered in California setting off a great exodus to the Pacific Northwest.

But not all went well with the move westward. Along the trail, Mathilde contracted dysentery and was buried somewhere along the lonely miles of Nebraska. Heavy with grief, they continued on, until reaching Table Rock City before the first snows began to fall. That first winter, they built a makeshift shack and lived off what the land provided with good game. It was a long hard winter, but they made it through. When spring came, Johann drove a wagon a two days journey to Windsor to the closest sawmill in the area. He came back with a start of lumber for their new store. He and Henrik worked long days to get it under roof, but getting the provisions all the way up from San Francisco proved to be the most daunting. With no delivery service, Johann made the journey all alone and brought back what they needed. By the beginning of the next winter, the Pedersens had seen dividends to their hard work.

Then one night Johann went to sleep only to awaken on the other side of the Jordan River. When Freda found him the next morning, he had a peaceful smile of contentment on his face. Now the business belonged entirely to Henrik. He was more than capable to take over.

Henrik placed Aubrey and Mary up in a hotel for the following week. It would allow him and Aubrey to spend the next several days getting to know each other a little better before the circuit preacher returned the following Sabbath. They would then be married. During the week, Mary found her time with her sister limited. She seemed to be finding herself alone with Timmons more and more. It made her uncomfortable and exhilarated at the same time. He had a way of looking at her that made her heart race, and then as if on purpose he would say something to irritate her. What really infuriated her was that he seemed to like it when they argued back and forth. It was as if she was lighting a fuse of passion in him. It confused her and even more, it scared her. She would have to try to keep him at arm's length.

The morning of the wedding, Aubrey made a startling confession to Mary. "I don't know how ya goin' to feel about this. I've been talkin' with Henrik about God and church." She hesitated, not wanting to hurt her sister. "I think…I think I might be…becomin' a Methodist." She lowered her eyes, not making eye contact with her sister.

Mary was so surprised she didn't know how to reply at first. Finally she asked, "Why do ya think that?"

"Because for the first time in me life I talked directly to God and I think He heard me prayers. I asked for His forgiveness and I feel at peace. I know I didn't go to a priest and ask for absolution or even say prayers o' penance. But Henrik said to me *that if ya confess with yar mouth the Lord Jesus, and believe in yar heart that God has raised Him from the dead, ya'll be saved.* I did it Mary. I confessed that I believed in Him. And then I confessed everythin' that I had done and asked Him to forgive me. I put me trust in Him as me Lord…believin' everythin' about Him… Is this what it be like Mary…to be at peace with God? Is this what ya been tryin' to tell me all along?"

Mary's eyes misted and her throat constricted with emotion. She was barely able to say anything. "I've been tryin' to tell ya; God hasn't given up on either one o' us." They embraced each other and wept. It was a memory that Mary would hold onto forever.

They dressed in the new gowns Henrik had bought for them and Robert Timmons had the honor of walking Aubrey down the aisle. It was a strange relationship that had developed from a simple question of what are we supposed to do…to him being part of the wedding party and maybe insinuating more. After the wedding and as all the celebrating was winding down, Aubrey and her new husband escaped to their honeymoon abode, leaving Mary and Robert alone once again.

It was a clear night and Robert asked her to take a walk in the moonlight. Mary should have declined, but she didn't. They strolled in the dew soaked grass and listened to the crickets play their symphony. Neither said anything for awhile. Robert broke the ice. "It was a beautiful wedding."

"That it was. Aubrey made a beautiful bride. I think she will be happy. Henrik seems to be a good man. He'll be good to her."

"What about you, Mary? Do you think this James fellow will be good to you?"

"All I know is what his letters say. I believe that he will. If I didn't, I wouldn't be marryin' him."

"Don't you think it's kind of strange that you're going to marry a man you hardly know?"

She looked at him puzzled, wondering what he might be thinking. For some strange reason, her heart was beating a little faster. She stammered, "Aubrey barely knows Henrik, but they seem like a good match."

"And you think you and James will be a good match?"

"I'm countin' on it."

"Better than the two of us?"

Mary couldn't say anything; her head was spinning. Anxiously, she insisted, "I made a promise."

Robert wouldn't let it drop. "If it wasn't for that promise, I might very well marry you." It caught Mary by surprise, but before she could react, he pulled her towards him and kissed her long and hard. When he was finished, Mary could barely catch her breath. Something stirred inside her for she had never been kissed like that before. She couldn't say anything. It was Robert that spoke. "You think about that tonight while you're sleeping." Then he walked her back to the hotel. And Mary did think about it—all night long. She got very little sleep.

The next morning was time to say goodbye. Aubrey and Henrik came down to the station to see Mary and Robert off. Henrik went aside to talk to Robert, giving the sisters some privacy.

Mary whispered to Aubrey, "Everythin' okay between the two o' ya?"

Aubrey smiled softly and answered, "He doesn't suspect anythin' and I'll never tell him." Mary nodded in understanding. "What are ya goin' to do Mary?"

She sighed. "I don't know. Me conscience says I have to tell him, but me heart says not to."

Aubrey remained neutral. She had made her decision, now it was Mary's to make. Instead she asked, "What about Mr. Timmons?" Mary looked bewildered. Did she somehow find out about what happened last night? "Henrik and I have been talkin' and we think he might be sweet on ya. What do ya think?"

Mary didn't deny or confirm. "I have a promise to James."

"Mary…" she pleaded softly. She hesitated to say what was on her mind. "Mary, I think maybe ya might have yar own feelin's for him."

Mary swallowed hard and then answered, "Like I said, I have a promise to James."

Before Aubrey could implore further, the stagecoach pulled in. She felt a rush of things she wanted to tell her sister, but they had run out of time. She began to cry as she said, "Mary…how do I tell ya how much I love ya and how much ya mean to me? That if it wasn't for ya, I would probably not be alive?"

Mary kissed her sister and then thrust herself into Aubrey's arms and they held each other sobbing. "If it weren't for ya, I would not have been able to go on. Ya kept me alive."

Robert reluctantly interrupted. He put his hand on Mary's shoulder and said softly, "I'm sorry, Mary. But the stage is ready to leave."

They continued to cry and hold each other. Mary wanted desperately to say something profound, but words escaped her. Aubrey was the one that was inspired. She suddenly remembered a blessing their dad liked to quote. She quietly said, "May the road rise up to meet ya…"

Mary chuckled through the tears, remembering the blessing with her. She echoed her with the next line, "May the wind always be at yar back."

"May the sun shine warm upon yar face," Aubrey said.

"And rains fall soft upon yar fields," Mary answered.

Together they recited the next line, "And until we meet again…"

Mary couldn't finish it and Aubrey said it to her sister as a prayer. "May God hold ya in the palm o' His hand, Mary. May He always keep ya there."

Robert almost had to pry her from Aubrey. He gently led her to the stage and helped her in. He sat close to her, taking her hand in his to comfort her. As they rode away, Mary leaned out the window and waved goodbye. It was the last time that they would ever see each other.

11

The Meeting

Mary tried to stifle her tears, but failed miserably. Robert drew her into his arms and she didn't resist. This brought the ire of their fellow passengers, a middle-aged well-to-do couple. The matronly woman had such a sour disposition you had to wonder if her pinched face was caused by her hair being pulled back too tightly or was it her surly attitude. She made a snide remark to her henpecked husband as he sat beside her, silently agreeing. The other two passengers paid little attention. One was a well dressed, mild mannered man who had his face buried in a book and the other was a stubble faced cowboy, who simply slouched in his seat, pulling his hat down over his face so he could nap.

Robert let her cry herself out, not trying to discourage her from showing her emotions. During the deluge, he pulled out a handkerchief and offered it to her. She graciously accepted it and wiped the tears from her drenched cheeks. Over the last few weeks, he had become acutely aware of how much the sisters were dependent on the other. It was going to be hard the next several days, not only for her, but for him as well. He had grown to love this short tempered, stubborn woman, who had a deep passion for life.

"Thank ya, Robert," she said hoarse from her display of emotions. "Ya've been very kind to me—better than I deserve."

He chuckled at her remark. "What makes you say that?"

"I haven't been too kind to ya," she said, blowing her nose.

"Nonsense. If anything, I'm the one that's been a bit ornery. I have to admit that I enjoy teasing you. I like it when you get your dander up."

She narrowed her eyes and asked, "Now why would ya like that?"

He smiled and answered, "Because I think you're beautiful when you're angry." Mary immediately became miffed with his remark. Robert laughed out loud and said, "Just like now." Mary pretended to become even more annoyed, but soon broke out in a sly smile. Soon they were both laughing together. It served as a little emotional relief and lightened her heavy heart.

Unfortunately, Mr. and Mrs. Prude that sat across from them, found no humor in either one of them. Mrs. Prude thought their behavior was vulgar and offensive. She determined that once they reached Windsor, she was going to make a formal complaint about them. Letting her disapproval be heard, she said to her husband, "It's bad enough that we have to be subjected to riding this distance with a bunch of ill-mannered ruffians, but to have them be brazen enough to practically perform indecent acts in front of us, it's beyond me."

This comment brought the cowboy awake. He slid his hat back and said, "I guess I must have missed something."

Robert retorted, "No, but I'm about to get something started." He leaned forward to speak his mind to the woman, when Mary pulled him back.

"Let it be," she said softly. "'Tis not worth it."

"It is to me," he said looking at Mary. But her soft eyes said something else. He saw a flicker of pain in them that disarmed him and made him wonder what she was hiding.

"Just let it go, Robert," she pleaded gently. "Once we reach Windsor, we'll be done with this." For her sake he did.

After two days of traveling, the stagecoach rolled into Windsor. When the conductor informed the passengers, Mary immediately felt her stomach tie up in knots. "We're here," she said, almost sounding like a question.

Robert responded forlornly, "I guess so."

She sat still not fully ready to leave the coach. She wasn't sure what she needed to do next. Robert sat quietly beside her as Mr. and Mrs. Prude hastily made their exit. She made a beeline to the station manager, leaving her husband in her wake. Neither Mary nor Robert really cared. Mrs. Prude was the type of person that loved to criticize and stir the pot. No one really took her seriously. Most people just tolerated her insolence as best they could and hoped her wrath would either burn out or move to another location.

Robert hopped out of the coach. He put his hands around Mary's waist and helped her down. The conductor lowered their belongings from the rack and handed them to him. Robert suggested they might check into a hotel for the night. "It's getting late and seeing that you don't really know where to go, it might be best. We can get a fresh start in the morning." When Mary didn't immediately respond he asked, "Do you have enough for a room?"

Reluctantly she answered, "I'm not sure." She counted her change, trying to estimate how much she had. She was beginning to figure out the currency somewhat, but it was still a little confusing. "I think I might have a couple o' dollars in some change," she said spreading the coins out in her hand. Robert looked them over and agreed. To ease her mind though, he offered to pay the rest if she didn't have enough. This greatly alarmed her. "I could never do that. It wouldn't be proper for a lady to owe a gentleman any money."

"Don't worry about it. I'm sure your *husband-to-be* will take care of it," he said a little too curtly. When he saw that his remark had cut her, he quickly apologized. "I'm sorry. I don't know what made me say that."

Mary quietly replied, "Ya know why…and so do I." She didn't say anymore and the two of them crossed the street to a hotel. When they checked in, to her relief, she found she had enough for the room and if she was careful, enough for a light supper and possibly an apple or two for breakfast. They made their way to their separate rooms. Mary couldn't resist stretching out on the bed. It felt so good to lie down after the long journey. She could still feel the rocking of the coach as she closed her eyes. It didn't take much for her to sink into a deep sleep. A knock on the door startled her awake. She went to answer the door as she tried to get her heart rate back to normal.

Robert was at the door, inviting her to dinner. "My treat," he said. Mary quickly protested with the same excuse as before, but he would have none of it. "It's our last night together; let's not argue. Truce?"

She smiled shyly and agreed. "Truce."

They went to a restaurant just down the street. It was simply called the Lantern House, because of all the oil lanterns that lit the place. There wasn't anything fancy about it. It was a two story wood plank structure with a balcony on the second floor. Along the front was a hitching rail that was currently serving its purpose with five horses aligned side by side. Inside were large wooden beams that held up the Ponderosa pine ceiling. The outer walls were made of the same wooden planks, but the interior wall was constructed of handmade bricks crudely slapped together with mortar. Although the dining room was dimly lit, it did lend a certain charm to the place.

Robert escorted Mary to a small wooden table off to the side. He graciously pulled the chair out for her before sitting across from her. A waiter came by and handed them a menu and then left them to make their decisions. Mary feigned reading it so others in the restaurant wouldn't suspect her ignorance. She quietly asked him what was on it and he read it to her. By the time the waiter came back, Robert was ready to order for both of them.

They sat and talked, as they waited for their food. It was just small talk, nothing of real importance. Eventually, the conversation turned to Mary's reluctance for him to pay for her meal. "How can ya afford all this?" she asked him.

He looked at her sideways and said, "I make a decent living writing."

Puzzled she asked, "How does someone make a livin' by writin'?"

Robert couldn't keep from quietly laughing. He marveled at her innocence. "I have actually had a few books published. But what I'm most proud of is actually having some pieces published in Harper's. I'm not Charles Dickens by any means, but I've had some success." He stopped and noticed the blank look on her face. "You have no idea who Dickens is, do you? The Pickwick Papers…Oliver Twist…"

She slowly shook her head and then asked, "Is he famous?"

Robert couldn't contain his laughter this time. "Is he famous? He's probably the greatest novelist of our time," he exclaimed a little too loudly. He watched Mary's countenance begin to fall. Quietly he explained, "He's an Englishman and I thought that by coming from that part of the world, you might have heard about him."

"I have not," she said looking down at the table in shame. "Ya must think o' me as an imbecile."

"By no means, Mary. I think you're probably the most intelligent woman I've ever met; you fascinate me."

She peered up at him and with tears clouding her vision, she said, "Me? I have no formal education. I cannot even read. How can ya think that about me?"

"It takes more than book learning to be intelligent. I don't know what's in your past, but I can imagine that you've had to live by your wits all your life. You *are* smart and let no one tell you otherwise."

Embarrassed, she hung her head again and softly said, "Thank ya for yar kindness, Robert."

He smiled softly and reached across the table and touched her hand. Confused, Mary let him hold it for a few moments before she withdrew it. She looked around and wondered if any of James' friends could possibly be here and see her cohorting with another man. Robert was obviously disappointed by her reaction, but before he could say anything, their meal was brought to them.

They enjoyed their food, but Robert enjoyed her company more. After the meal, they went for a stroll along the boardwalk. Everything was closed down for the night save for a few saloons and gambling joints. Even in this small farming community, the houses of ill-repute were solicited whole heartedly. As they made their distance from the noise of the gambling establishments, a quietness fell around them. A cool breeze caused Mary to draw her shawl tightly around her. The sounds of night creatures began to serenade them. It had a soothing effect on her. Being with Robert had become comfortable for her. There was an ease in their relationship that she had never experienced with man. It felt wonderful and awful at the same time. She couldn't stop thinking about James and her commitment to him. He had sounded so wonderful in his letters. Could he make her feel like Robert made her feel?

As if he were reading her mind, Robert asked, "What are you going to do about him?"

"James? I reckon I'll marry him," she said quietly.

"Why?" He didn't stop for her to respond. "You know that there is something between us; you can't deny it, Mary."

She stopped and looked him squarely in the eye. She said, "Ya got me emotions so stirred up that I can't think straight right now."

Robert set his hands on either side of her shoulders. "Then you shouldn't marry him. We don't have to stay here, Mary. We can bypass Windsor and keep going. Run away with me."

She broke free from his grasp and turned away, trying desperately to sort things out. She thought that she could live with the man that wrote such beautiful letters, even possibly have feelings for him. She had felt great empathy when she had learned of his brother dying. And then there was the matter of all the money he had spent to bring her to this land. Could she turn away from her obligation to him to run away with a man she hardly knew? Then again, she barely knew anything about James and yet she was willing to spend the rest of her life with him? In her confusion, she reconciled that she needed to pray about this and hopefully find an answer by morning.

She turned to Robert and before she could give him an answer, he kissed her passionately again. She felt her knees go weak and her heart beat faster than a scared jackrabbit. When he was finished, she was again breathless. She couldn't find her voice for a moment, but then quietly said, "I need time to think about this." Then as they turned to head back to the hotel, she suddenly stopped. She asked him in all seriousness, "Do ya believe in God?"

Robert was taken aback by her question. He stammered, "I guess, I've never really thought about it. I suppose deep down I believe that there is someone or something out there in control of the universe, but I'm not sure he pays much attention to me. I guess, as long as he doesn't bother me, I won't bother him."

"Don't ya want to have a relationship with Him? Don't ya want to feel His love?"

He grinned mischievously and answered, "I'd rather feel your love."

Once again it stirred something in Mary's heart and clouded her thoughts. She tried to steer back to the question at hand. "Don't ya ever think about Him?"

"Nope," he answered simply and honestly.

"Didn't ya ever go to church when ya were a little boy?"

"Sure, but I outgrew it," he said jokingly.

His answer greatly disturbed her. How could she even consider being yoked with someone that had such little regard for God? If it were a sin against the Church for marrying outside her faith, what would the priest say about her marrying a man who had no faith? And come to think of it, he never really said anything about marriage. "When ya said to run away with ya, were ya proposin' marriage?"

Robert rubbed his mustache and slyly grinned. "Well, if that's the only way you'll come away with me, then I guess that's what we'll do."

Mary didn't like his flippant answer. She didn't respond to him, but slowly walked back to their hotel. There was so much to think about—pray about. She had to have an answer by morning, but was afraid she already had it.

After a long, sleepless night, Mary came somewhat to a conclusion. She determined that she had to at least meet James before she made up her mind. She got up early and dressed in the lovely gown that Henrik had bought for her for Aubrey's wedding. She fixed her hair as best she could, hoping to make a good impression on him when they met for the first time. She then packed her things and left the hotel without stopping to tell Robert. She had to do this all alone. She went by a general store that was just opening and bought a couple of apples for her breakfast and then inquired about the sawmill. She was told that it was on the edge of town along the Umpqua River.

She ate her apples as she started towards the northern end of town. She switched her carpetbag from one hand to the other, to give her arm some relief of the strain of carrying it. As she drew closer, she could see the outline of the wooden structure from the distance. Mary became apprehensive of their meeting. What was she to say to him when they met face to face? Dread was creeping its way into her soul. She was torn between what was right and what her heart was telling her. Resolutely she walked the last couple of hundred yards to the sawmill.

The mill looked so serene setting on the river surrounded by evergreens. But as Mary got closer, she discovered it was anything but peaceful. As the giant water wheel turned outside, it powered the saw blades inside, making a deafening high pitch buzz. The ear splitting noise pierced the early morning silence, causing Mary's ears to hurt. She tried putting her hands over them to protect them, but it did little. As she approached, fortunately the men shut the machine down.

She heard some of them talking loudly as if the saw was still going. Evidently, the years of working at the mill took its wear on the hearing of the workers. As they were yelling, she heard a few choice words come out of their mouths, words that should never be said in the presence of a lady. Unfortunately, she had never been considered a lady and had heard all those and then some. When they saw her, they quickly quieted down and signaled to the others as well. They stared at her, not only because it was uncommon to see many women in this territory, but it was even rarer seeing one so attractive. They watched her gracefully walk towards them as if she were floating on air.

Every man turned to look at her, except one lone soul who was bent over the saw blade, trying to fix it. He was so absorbed in solving the problem that he barely noticed that it had suddenly grown quiet. When it finally registered, he straightened himself up and turned towards them. He immediately saw Mary standing in front of him, framed by the doorway. His initial reaction was one of irritation. The mill was no place for a woman; they were too much a distraction to the workers. But as his eyes adjusted to her image, he realized that this wasn't just any woman.

He quickly ran to her, but when he became aware of his disheveled appearance he stopped. His flannel shirt and cotton twill pants were stained dark brown from work. He had black grease on his hands and face and his dark curly hair was bushed out, making him look like a wild man. As he came to her, he still had a large tool in his hand. The crazed look of his appearance made her take a step back. Realizing he had scared her, he threw the tool aside. A broad smile appeared on his face as he asked, "Mary…is that you?"

She smiled shyly and upon seeing so many men staring at her, she instinctively bowed her head in embarrassment. It seemed that no matter where she traveled in this world, men always seemed to be leering at her. She swallowed hard, and quietly answered him, "Tis me…Mary O'Shea."

He laughed heartily and said, "It won't be for much longer." He approached her, not knowing how he should act. "I'm sorry for how I look. I wasn't expecting you. We're having a little difficulty with one of the blades this morning." He stopped talking long enough to take her all in and suddenly exclaimed, "You're beautiful! You're even more beautiful than the picture you sent." Mary felt the color rush to her face. She had not expected this kind of reaction. James unexpectedly turned to the men that worked under him and announced, "This is my wife to be!" This sent a cheer from the men and slaps of congratulations on James' back.

James then led her to his office so that they could be alone. Again he apologized for his appearance. "Makes no difference. Ya had no way o' knowin' I was here. Besides, ya've been workin' hard this mornin'. Ya bound to get a little dirty."

As she talked, James narrowed his eyes in confusion. He blurted out with some disdain in his voice, "You're Irish."

"Tis so," she answered. His reaction confused her. "I told ya that in me letters."

James continued to look at her oddly. He didn't remember reading that. Something like that would have stood out to him. "I thought you were from London."

Mary felt alarmed by his response to her ethnicity. She tried to explain, "I worked in London. I was livin' there when we corresponded."

James rubbed the back of his neck trying to reconcile it all in his mind. His past experiences with the Irish had never been positive. As a young boy, he had had run-ins with hooligan Irish gangs and then later, as a teenager in New York City…he didn't even want to think about it. He didn't like the idea of having a wife of the same ethnicity. It disturbed him greatly. What was he to do now?

"Have I done somethin' wrong?" she asked.

"No, I just didn't understand that you weren't English."

"Does it make a difference?" she asked with concern.

He looked at her intently. Even with her brow furrowed with apprehension, she was the most beautiful thing he had ever seen. He smiled softly and said, "No, it makes no difference. I was just confused that's all." Mary relaxed a little, but she was still not sure why he didn't know that she was Irish or why it upset him so. She wondered if he was now having second thoughts about marrying her. Part of her secretly hoped that he was. It would give her a way out so she could go away with Robert. The storm of uncertainty began churning again in her mind. Before she wandered down the road too far, James gave her an answer. "I guess we need to start making some wedding plans."

The feeling of anxiety she had did not recede. Her fate was seemingly sealed. She was going to marry James. Now she had to break the news to Robert. She wondered how she was going to do that.

12

Another Wedding

As they topped the knoll to James' farm, Mary had the strange feeling of déjà vu. Looking down on the green pasture fields with the rolling hills off in the distance, it mirrored her ancestral home. She felt tears of joy well up in her eyes, but it was quickly tempered with the realization that this was not her beloved home. There would be no mam or dad to greet her and Aubrey was a two day journey away. The things that made her home so special were now gone. Tears slid down her cheeks for another reason.

James had decided to take her home after they met with the preacher. They made plans to be wed the day after tomorrow. Although it seemed sudden, Mary went along with it. If this was to be her lot in life then she might as well get it over with. As she briefly thought of Robert, another type of sadness closed in on her heart. She quickly dismissed it and thought about what was at hand.

James showed her around the place. It was good rich, fertile land. The fields had already been plowed and the first seedlings were beginning to spring up. Everything was coming into full color. A beautiful carpet of grass lay before her with wildflowers starting to bloom. James stopped to show her the barn where he kept a milking cow and a set of oxen to do his plowing. There was also plenty of room for the horses and the wagon when it was not in use. A hen house sat off to the right of the barn.

He finished with a tour of the farmhouse. It was small and made of rough hewed logs that had obviously been cut before the sawmill had been established. A porch with a crude railing was on the front. Inside was a sitting room with a fireplace to one side. Through a doorway in back of the house was the kitchen that amounted to a couple of cabinets, a cupboard and some shelves. They were stocked fairly well with all the essentials. A small cook stove was wedged between the cabinets and the wall. Adjacent to it was a small table with two wooden chairs. To Mary's satisfaction she spotted a hand pump with a wash pan underneath. At least she wouldn't have to carry water. A window was hung behind the hand pump providing a scenic view of the farm.

On the left hand side of the sitting room were two bedrooms. She peered inside as James was gathering his belongings. The bed was made of tangled sheets that probably had never been washed since they were first put on the bed. That would be one of her first chores of the day. The other would be straightening the disarray of the room. On the other side of this room was a second bedroom. It had a simple bed and nothing more. James explained that his brother Jethro had slept there.

Once James had gathered up a few things, he went to the barn to get cleaned up. He planned on going back into town to stay at the sawmill until they officially tied the knot. He didn't want people to talk. Once she was settled in, he left for town promising to return by supper time. It would be Mary's first test of her domestic skills before they married.

As soon as he was gone, she set about making the house right. It was in dire need of a woman's touch. Everything that was not used on a daily basis had a thin film of dust covering it. Before she started, she changed into a worn out dress and then dove into her work. She was so focused on her tasks that when she heard the sharp rap on the door, it nearly startled her out of her skin. She couldn't imagine who it might have been. Timidly, she drew close to the door. Just as she was about to open it, the person on the other side knocked again, making her jump. She caught her breath and opened the door. To her surprise she saw a very upset Robert on the other side.

He brushed past her and stormed into the house. "Where is he?" he asked angrily.

"He's not here," she answered trying to appear calm, but inside she was shaking. "How did ya know where I was?"

"I figured as much. I asked around where your *betrothed* lived." Robert made it sound like a dirty name. He turned to her and almost shouting said, "You went and did it, didn't you? You went and agreed to marry him—or are you already married?"

She didn't answer him right away. Instead she closed the door behind them and then sat quietly in a rocking chair. She tried to gather her thoughts before she spoke. "I'm sorry, Robert," she said softly, not looking at him. "I made a commitment and I have to follow through with it."

"And what about me…what about us? Can you deny that there isn't something between us?"

She peered up at him, with tears in her eyes. "Robert, this is so hard for me. I have never felt like this about any man. I don't know if it be love or just strong feelings. But know that I do care deeply for ya."

"Then why marry someone you don't even know?"

"I know ya cannot understand this, but I made a commitment to him. He invested money in me. I have to pay him back…" She laughed cynically at what she had just said. "I guess that sums up me life: givin' a man what he pays for." Robert looked at her incredulously as her words began to make sense to him. This was the secret she had been hiding. He couldn't find any words to say, so Mary said it instead. "Here's the kicker to yar story. Me and Aubrey were forced into bein' whores. *This…*" she said stretching out her arms. "This was our only escape. So ya see I have a debt that I have to pay. I have no choice." A lone tear dropped from her eye, trickled down her cheek and around the curve of her chin. Soon a twin followed on the other side.

Robert just stared at her not knowing what to say. He took a deep breath and gathered his thoughts. "You do have a choice; you don't have to do this. Come away with me, Mary. I'll find a way to pay whatever you owe him. But please come with me."

More tears began to flow and her lower lip quivered. "Robert, I cannot. I've made a promise." There was no way that she could make him understand that the promise was more than her betrothal to James. It was the promise to serve God. If she went with Robert, with his lack of commitment to God, she would more than likely end up turning from God. She had chosen James because he believed in God. Her shoulders heaved as she began to weep.

Robert walked over to the window and looked out. He spoke to no one in particular, "I just don't understand." He was quiet for the moment, trying to find a way to convince her. In the end, he concluded that there was no way of changing the situation. She was determined to see this through. He sarcastically laughed and said, "You know, you're the first woman that almost got me to go down the aisle. I would have married you, Mary. I actually fell in love with you."

"I believe that I fell in love with ya as well," she said with a trembling voice. Her face pinched in pain as more tears fell. "I will always remember ya and all the kind thin's ya did for me."

He turned and looked intently at her, wanting to memorize her face. He sadly smiled and said, "When I get the book written, I'll send one to you and to Aubrey."

She shook her head slowly and replied, "Ya know I won't be able read it."

His smile broadened. "You will, Mary. I have faith in you. One day you will learn." He went to her and lifted her from the chair. With his thumbs, he wiped away the tears on her cheeks and then softly kissed her one last time. "Take care of yourself. If you ever get tired of the lumberjack, look me up. I'm sure that I will still be single."

They shared a sorrowful laugh. Then Mary patted Robert's face softly. "Goodbye, Robert. I won't forget ya."

"Neither will I," he said and then turning, he walked out the door. Mary watched him from the window until he disappeared over the knoll, tears continuing to stream down her face. She wondered if she had made the right decision.

She turned from the window and quickly busied herself trying to get her mind off of her troubles. But she couldn't seem to control her thoughts as they continued to compare James and Robert. Could she ever grow to love James in the same way? Then she began to worry about the impending nuptials and what would happen on their wedding night. It was too soon to want to have relations with him, but if that was expected she would approach it just as she had previously. She would close her eyes and pretend to be someplace else until it was all over. She didn't think that part of marriage would ever be enjoyable to her.

She spent the remainder of the day scrubbing and scouring everything. The house took on a fresh clean scent. When she was finished she wasn't sure what time it was, but judging by the rumblings of her stomach, James would be home soon. She would have killed a chicken and cooked it for supper, but was afraid that he might not like that. With her luck, she would end up killing his favorite or something like that. She looked in the cupboard to see what he had on hand. She found some potatoes that weren't too shriveled up. She peeled them and set them aside in a pan of water to keep them from turning black. She would cream them after she milked the cow. She also found some turnips that she could cook. Along with the freshly baked bread she had made earlier and the pie she made from the dried apples she found, it would be filling.

She went to the barn and found a pail along with a small wooden stool. She gave the cow a small bribe of a handful of potato peelings, which she seemed to enjoy. Then she petted it to try to keep her from getting nervous as she milked her, but it was more to calm herself. It had been a long time since she had done this. She sat down and gently squeezed down on the cow's teat and soon it came back naturally. When she finished, she took the pail of milk back to the house. In the kitchen, she poured most of it into a stone jar that she found. She would later skim the cream off the top and set it aside to make butter. She noticed that there was neither butter nor a churn in the house. That would have to change. If anything, she would ask for a churn as a wedding present.

She used the rest of the milk for the potatoes. Once she got the food simmering on the stove, she quickly cleaned herself up and changed her clothes. She wanted to make a good impression with their first meal together. She readied herself and waited. As the sun lowered to the horizon and the shadows lengthened, Mary went around lighting the oil lamps in the house. And still she waited.

She went to the window and looked out. It was getting dark outside and she was growing worried. She didn't relish spending the night alone, but at least the knowledge that James would be here for supper helped. As she squinted against the darkness, she thought she heard the distant sound of wagon wheels. Soon she saw a faint outline of the buckboard as it came over the hill. He pulled the wagon to a halt in front of the door and jumped out. Mary waited in the doorway for him. The soft glow of light spilled out around her silhouetted form. James stopped in his tracks to take it in. He felt his heart begin to beat faster at her sight. The knowledge that she would soon be his wife thrilled him. As he approached her, she said to him, "I was gettin' worried."

"Sorry. The problem we had earlier this morning got us a little behind. We had a huge order of lumber that we had to get ready to ship out by morning. Trust me; I was trying my best to get home as early as I could." He looked at her not sure what he should do. He wanted to kiss her, but thought it best to wait until they were married. After all it was just a day and a half away now. As he entered the house he said, "Supper smells good."

"I hope ya like it. Tis just creamed potatoes and turnips. I wasn't sure what ya liked to eat."

"Anything has to be better than my cooking."

As she set the food on the table, James looked around his home. If he didn't know better he would have thought he was in the wrong house. "You sure cleaned up the place today," he said, pleased to find that she was a hard worker. He hoped that she would remain that way after they were wed.

"I wanted the house to look nice when ya came home tonight," she answered quietly, putting the last of the food on the table. She stood by the table waiting for her future husband. She wasn't sure if she should go ahead and sit or wait for him to pull out the chair for her. She had her answer when James ignored all proprieties and sat down. Living in the backwoods of civilization had obviously erased any memory of good manners he may have learned as a boy.

James looked at her quizzically and said, "Are you going to stand there through the meal or sit down?" She disappointedly sat down. Thinking about how gentlemanly Robert had treated her, she concluded that she needed to keep those things out of her mind and stop comparing the two.

Before they ate, James blessed their food. She was touched when he asked that God would bless their impending marriage and provide them with numerous children. When he finished praying, Mary gave the sign of the cross as was usual. James was so intent on the food that was at hand he took no notice. He helped himself to a heaping helping of potatoes and a good amount of turnips. He was well pleased when he tasted it. "You're a good cook, Mary," he complimented. "Everything tastes good."

"Thank ya," she said, letting a little color rise to her cheeks. She was delighted that he was pleased with her cooking. It was one hurdle that she had crossed. "Tis been some time since I've had some potatoes."

"Potatoes are a big staple of food for your people, isn't it?"

"Tis true. The climate and the soil are good for growin'—or at least it was."

"Did your family suffer during the famine?"

"Me dad, when the blight first hit, decided that he had had enough o' farmin'. So he decided to move us to Wales. But me mam got very sick on the journey and never made it. Dad blamed himself; he was never the same afterwards."

James seemed genuinely concerned when he asked, "And your father? Is he still alive?"

Mary picked at her potatoes with her fork. Suddenly they no longer seemed to have any flavor. "I'm not sure. We got separated and me sister and I ended up in London."

James continued to eat heartily. "You never really told me what you did for a living."

Mary continued to move her food around. There was a huge knot in her stomach. She tried to think of a good way to break the news to him and hoped that he would understand. The words of the young priest echoed in her head reminding her of her deceit. It was not the way to start a marriage, but neither was telling your intended that you were a prostitute in your former life. Mary couldn't bring herself to tell him and decided to be vague, hoping he wouldn't press it. She simply said, "I worked as a servant." She reasoned in her mind that she had served men.

"Really? I suppose they don't pay you much for a job like that."

"I was provided for," she said quietly. She wanted to change the subject. "I'm sorry about yar brother. How did he die?"

James countenance changed. He stopped shoveling food in his mouth and tried swallowing. It kind of stuck there and struggled to go down. He cleared his throat and softly said, "I'd rather not talk about it. What's done is done."

Mary felt her heart sink, feeling like she had committed a cardinal sin against him. "I'm sorry. I thought it might help to talk about it." James said nothing else. An uncomfortable silence fell between them. She tried to think of something to say…anything at all, but nothing came to her. She couldn't help but think that there had never been this awkwardness between her and Robert. Immediately she chastised herself for such thoughts. She needed to quit thinking about him.

After the meal concluded, it was time for James to leave. He apologized for not spending much time with her. "I'll make it a point to get home for supper early tomorrow, so we can get to know each other better."

"Do ya want me to bring some breakfast or lunch or anythin'?"

"No, don't bother. I'll pick up something in town. Just take care of the farm and the animals while I'm gone. It'll only be another day and we'll have the rest of our lives to get to know each other." He bashfully grinned at her and Mary was surprised that she felt a rush of color rise to cheeks. "Hey, don't worry about spending the night alone. It's fairly quiet around here and as far as I know nobody knows that you're here alone. You'll be fine."

Mary tried to be brave, but after James left she began to worry. There was one person that knew she was alone. Even though he would never hurt her, what if somebody else had accidentally discovered she was here by herself? She closed the door and noticed that there was no lock. To ease her mind, she slid a chair under the doorknob. But she was quite aware that if someone wanted to get in bad enough, they could always get through a window. She thought about the leers of the hungry miners and it sent a shudder through her. Then another worry invaded her thoughts: were there any Indians in the area?

Mary survived the two nights she spent alone. She didn't get much sleep either of those nights. Every strange noise awakened her and set her heart beating fast. So on her wedding day, she was not at her best. James picked her up that morning and promised to take her to a restaurant for breakfast just for the occasion. Sadly, he had not volunteered to buy her a special dress for the event. She reasoned that Henrik did because he could afford it more than James. She settled on wearing that dress for the wedding. In some way, it allowed Aubrey to be a part of her wedding.

There was nothing special about the ceremony. It was just her and James, the preacher and two perfect strangers acting as witnesses. The ceremony was pretty cut and dry, with James slipping a ring on her finger, proving that they were legally wed. When it came time to kiss the bride, James gave her a simple peck and that was it. It was a far cry from the passion she experienced with Robert. She dismissed the thought by reasoning that in time, things would change.

As they exited the church, she looked across the way and saw Robert as he was about to board the stagecoach. He looked at her sadly, but managed a weak smile. He tipped his hat to her, which brought a new wellspring of tears. While James' back was turned, she gave a small wave and mouthed, "Thank ya." He then climbed into the coach as Mary perched herself on the buckboard. As the stage pulled away, James and his bride headed in the opposite direction. She tried not to cry, but she felt her heart being torn in two.

James must have noticed her quiet countenance. He turned to her and took her hand. "Everything alright?" he asked.

She smiled faintly and said, "Just overwhelmed. I'm married now."

James busted out laughing and then gave her a squeeze. "You're a treasure, Mary." Perplexed that he found humor in it, she went along with him and laughed. They headed down the dirt road to their new life together. But she soon found that this was going to be a strange life. As they reached the house, James let her out and then informed her that he needed to get back to work. "I've missed too much time as it is. We can't fall too far behind; we have too many orders that need to be filled. I'll see you at suppertime." And with that he turned the wagon and left.

Mary stood staring at the dust cloud that followed after him and then wandered to the house. She looked down at the golden band on her finger and wondered if she had really gotten married or had it all been a crazy dream. Her special day wasn't anything like the celebration of Aubrey's wedding. The whole town had been invited to share in their nuptials. There had been food and music and dancing…and there had been Robert. Her heart sunk and she heard herself say out loud, "What have I done?"

13

The Wedding Night

This day had been far from what she had expected. Not that she had anticipated a large crowd at their wedding, but she thought that James would have wanted a few close friends there. She certainly didn't foresee being left alone all day while her new husband went back to work. It was certainly a strange day. And it would be a stranger evening.

She took care of all the things that needed to be done on the farm, feeding the animals, milking the cow, doing chores. Being a special occasion, she had gotten permission from James to kill a chicken for supper. She didn't relish the idea. She wasn't sure which task she hated more, killing or plucking it. It almost made her not want to eat it.

She grabbed the chicken and it fought gallantly, but in the end the ax fell and it was dead. It continued to flop around for while, disgusting her further. She had a large pot of water heating on the stove. It was not quite boiling when she pulled it off of the stove. Grabbing the chicken by its feet, she dunked it into the hot water. She swished it around a bit and then took it out to see if the feathers came out easily. She had to dunk the bird four times before they would. After she finally got all the feathers pulled out, she cut it up, rolled it in flour and fried it to a golden brown color. She placed it in a shallow pan, covered it with a towel, and put it on the back of the stove to keep it warm. Then she took the drippings and made some gravy to go with the mashed potatoes.

When she thought that it was about time for James to return, she stuck a pan of cornbread in the oven. Then she went and changed back into the dress she had worn that morning. She checked her hair in the dim mirror that was hanging on the wall. She wanted to look nice on this special night. She paused and stared at the bed, wondering what it was going to be like. She had been with so many men, none showing any tenderness or affection towards her. On occasion one of them would be gentle. Those were the ones she believed were married, cheating on their wives for the first time. She wondered what approach James would take with her tonight. The familiar knot of anxiety grew in her stomach. As she left the bedroom, she closed her mind to the thought and sat down in the rocking chair, waiting for him.

James was more prompt tonight. He pulled the wagon up to the house and greeted her with a kiss; it was the best so far. He looked at her with a boyish grin and said, "I'll unhitch the horses and take them to the barn. I won't be long." He drove the wagon to the front of the barn, unfastened the harness and then stabled the horses. True to his word, he quickly came back to the house. The marvelous aroma of chicken and cornbread hit him as he came inside. It set his stomach to rumbling. He walked into the kitchen and saw Mary standing by the table waiting. She had spread out all the products of her labor. "What a beautiful sight," he said smiling.

"What? The food or me?" she asked.

James' smile broadened and he nervously rubbed his beard. "Both I think." He went to her and took her into his arms. Gazing into her placid green eyes he said, "I'm sorry about today. Things just seemed to pile up and it couldn't be helped. The timing couldn't have been worse. But I promise, in the future, we'll have more time together."

He kissed her softly at first and then with more passion. It was what she had hoped for all along. It stirred something in her, but nothing like what Robert's kisses had done. Again she admonished herself for comparing the two. It was going to take awhile for her to move on. She prayed that someday she would have the right feelings for her husband.

"We need to be gettin' at this food before it gets cold," she said breaking from his grasp and sitting down at the table. James shrugged and then joined her. They prayed together and then James took a hearty helping of everything.

"I'm starving!" he exclaimed, digging into it. "Mary, you're an excellent cook—better than any ol' restaurant that I've ever eaten at. Looks like I got me a prized wife." Mary peered up from her food and thanked him. She then asked about his day. "You wouldn't want to hear about it. It'd bore you."

"Tis not true. I'm interested in what ya do. I want to know what ya do all day."

"Well, a lot less since you came," he said jokingly. "I certainly appreciate you helping out with the farm. I have to say that since Jethro passed away, things have been mighty difficult."

"Thank ya for the kind words. Now tell me all about the sawmill."

James smiled shyly and said, "Okay, you asked for it." He began to tell her about how they had come up with the idea of building the mill and how it all came together. As he talked his enthusiasm grew. "You know a lot of people appreciated us coming and clearing off part of their land for farming. It helped them out and helped us too. There weren't too many mills in the area, so people came from two or three days journey just to buy from us. Of course, in the last year, there's sprung up a few more mills, but by now we have a good reputation; people trust us."

Suddenly he grew quiet and didn't say anything for a moment. He swallowed a forkful of potatoes that seemed to stick to the back of his throat. When he spoke again it was filled with emotion. "Everything was going well until the accident." Mary reached across the table and placed her hand over his. He looked up at her and smiled weakly, but it quickly faded. "Me and some of the other fellows…Luke Myers, Art Jackson and a couple of others, were timbering not far from here when the tree we were cutting suddenly broke free. It fell the wrong way. Jethro was on that side. He tried to run…but he had no chance."

He looked down at the remains of his meal and decided that he had had enough. He pushed it aside. The pain she saw on his face tugged at her heart. She wanted to comfort him, but wasn't sure how. She took a deep breath and slowly let it out. "I'm sorry. I know how difficult this must be for ya. Losin' a love one is never easy."

James apologized. "I shouldn't have brought it up—especially not on this day. I'm sorry."

"Don't be. We share our burdens now. Whatever hurts ya, hurts me."

"You're amazing," he said shaking his head. "I am a very blessed man."

After dinner, Mary cleared the table and cleaned up the kitchen, as James went into the sitting room. It struck him that it might be nice to have a fire tonight. He went outside and brought in a bundle of wood, placing it on the hearth. Then meticulously he set up small pieces of dried kindling in a tepee fashion along with some dry straw. He took down the tinderbox from the mantel and struck it several times with the flint until the charred rag inside caught a spark. He quickly set a long straw to it and then used it to catch the kindling on fire. Soon it was ablaze and James added larger pieces of wood. He stood back, enjoying the fruits of his labor. Then he took out his pipe and a small pouch of tobacco. He lit a long straw from the fire and set it to the tobacco, then tossed it into the fire.

When Mary finished her work, she stood in the doorway watching him. He felt her eyes on him and he turned to look at her. "What are you grinning about?" he asked.

"Memories," she replied. "The smoke from yar pipe made me think o' me granddad. He used to smoke a pipe. I don't have a lot o' memories of him, because he died when I was so young. But the ones that I do were good ones. He was a funny man and always made me laugh."

"Memories can be good sometimes," he said quietly. He stared into the fire, deep thought.

Mary came in and sat on one of the rockers and James joined her. They watched as the intensity of the fire grew, little licks of flames danced upward creating an almost hypnotic affect. Neither said much at the moment. Then James finally spoke. He leaned forward and nervously cleared his throat. "You are probably wondering about tonight," he began. He couldn't look at her, but instead continued to stare at the fire. "I figured that since we don't know each other very well that you might not be ready for relations." He cleared his throat again; it had suddenly gone dry. "I thought maybe it would be best that we wait until we're more comfortable with each other. I can sleep in Jethro's old room until then."

Mary didn't know what to say. It had taken her by surprise. She didn't know if she should be relieved or insulted. She thought for moment and then said, "Maybe that would be wise."

James nodded in agreement. He turned to look at her and added, "I just hope it doesn't take too long." His mischievous smile had returned. "Hey, listen. I've made arrangements for us to spend all day together. I'm turning everything over to Luke tomorrow. I told him not to bother me unless the mill was burning down. I thought maybe we could go to town fairly early and pick up anything you might need. Did you happen to have any money left from the trip?"

Mary turned her attention to the fire again as she answered him. "Only a few coins" she said softly.

"Well, I'm glad you had enough," he said almost gleefully. Mary didn't dare tell him how hard it was to make the money stretch. She had grown resentful during the trip that he hadn't trusted her with his money. If she had opened her mouth about it, her anger would have gotten the best of her. The last thing she wanted was to have a row on their wedding night. She simply nodded her head. James went on. "Of course, the day after tomorrow is Sunday and I'll get to show you off at church."

That seemed to infuriate her even more and she nearly said something. If she was good enough to show off, why wasn't she good enough for him to invite them to the wedding? But she bit her tongue again. She wasn't entirely sure why she held back, because she never did with Robert.

After a few yawns, they decided to turn in. He walked with her to the bedroom door as if walking her home from a date. He kissed her softly and then went into the adjacent room. Mary went into the other room and closed the door behind her. She wasn't sure what to make of the turn of events. She thought it odd that in some ways, she was a little disappointed. She slowly took off her wedding dress and hung it in the closet; she would wear it again on Sunday. Then she crawled in bed wearing only her dainties. She didn't have a nightgown, leaving it behind at the brothel. She never wanted a reminder of those days, yet somehow the memories shrouded her, leaving a darkened place in her heart.

She lay in the near dark with only the dim light of the moon shining through the gauze curtains. Even though she was tired, she couldn't sleep. Too many thoughts raced through her mind. And she couldn't get her mind off of Robert, wondering what he was doing on this night. She rolled over on her side, trying to close off her thoughts and go to sleep. But soon she found herself thrashing about in her bed, finding no relief in sleep. Suddenly she heard the door to the other room open. Her heart leapt to her throat. Had he changed his mind? Would he come barging into her bedroom demanding satisfaction? What would she do if he tried?

She lay quietly, trying to hear every little sound. His footsteps went past her room and continued on; apparently he was unable to sleep either. She then heard him go into the kitchen. Maybe he had gone in to find something to nibble on. She remembered how he had pushed aside his supper after talking about Jethro's death. She waited, lying on her back wondering if she should get up and check on him. She argued that it was her duty as a wife to care for her new husband, so she threw back the covers and got out of bed. Putting aside all modesty, she didn't think about wrapping herself up in a blanket or anything, just went as she was.

She opened the door slowly and crept into the sitting room. The flames from the fireplace had burned down considerably and gave little light. Seeing a dim light from the kitchen, she stealthily moved through the house towards the room. She found James sitting at the table with a whiskey bottle and a shot glass in his hand. He was still wearing his clothes for he hadn't bothered changing. He jumped when he saw her. "What are you doing in here?"

"I heard ya walkin' around. I came to see if ya needed anythin'."

"I'm fine." He took a swig out of the shot glass and sat it down on the table. He felt her eyes on him, along with condemnation. "I thought a couple of drinks might make me sleepy." He placed the cork back in the whiskey bottle, got up from the table and returned it on the shelf, behind some canned food. For some reason he was compelled to hide it. He turned back and for the first time saw her in her camisole and pantalets. His heart leaped in his chest and he was overcome with desire. He swallowed hard and asked breathlessly, "Don't you have a nightgown or something?"

Finally conscience of her appearance, she instinctively folded her arms over her breasts. Nervously she tried to come up with an answer. "No…I…I don't own one."

James couldn't take his eyes off of her. His breathing had accelerated. "We'll have to rectify that tomorrow. We'll buy you a real pretty one."

She nodded, but didn't say anything. The look in his eyes scared her. Her own heart was beating rapidly, but not from desire. "Well, if ya not be needin' anythin', I'll go back to bed." But before she could turn to go, James was on her in two steps. He drew her into his arms and kissed her with such fury that Mary was sure that he would have his way with her. She tasted the liquor on his lips and was revolted.

He stopped and then just held her close to his body. Mary put her arms around him, but was only being polite. Her eyes were wide with fear and she wanted to run to her room, close the door and lock it from the inside. The problem was there was no lock. He whispered in her ear, "Mary you're so beautiful. You're more beautiful than the picture you sent." He pulled away from her, stuck his hand in his pocket and took out the photograph that she had sent him. It was slightly tattered and creased. He looked at it sadly and said, "I know I should have put it in a frame and placed it on the mantel. But I wanted it with me all the time, so I could take it out and look at you from time to time. It was like having you with me. I guess I thought that this day would never come."

Mary didn't know how much whiskey he had drunk, but he was clearly feeling the effects; his words were slurring. Her fear was heightened by the knowledge that men did things they wouldn't normally do when they became inebriated. She was on high alert, not knowing what he was capable of doing. "James, I think it be time to go back to bed," she said calmly, but she was anything but calm inside.

He looked intensely at her. Once again he said, "You're so beautiful." He took his hand and played with her hair. "You're hair is beautiful. I couldn't tell it was auburn in the photo. I've never seen hair this color before. It shimmers in the light." He began to caress her face and then cradled it in both hands. "You're skin is so soft, like a rose petal. I want you, Mary."

It sent a chill through her. She wasn't ready for this. He would be like all the other men that used her and she was deathly afraid that this would be how her marriage would be. She quietly reiterated. "Tis late James; time to go to sleep."

He let go of her and looked forlornly at the wooden floor. "You're right. Besides, I made a promise to you that I would wait. A gentleman *always* keeps his word," he said with a note of sarcasm. Mary took the oil lamp from the kitchen and then helped him back to his bedroom. He plopped down on the bed and then collapsed the rest of the way. He murmured something she couldn't understand. Setting the lamp down on the nightstand, she lifted his feet and placed them on the bed. Thankfully he was already drifting off to sleep. She picked up the lamp and returned to her room. She set it on her nightstand and crawled under the covers. Shivering, not from the cold, but from the duress, she decided to leave the lamp on. Even though it was dangerous to do so, the danger of being surprised by a night visitor was more frightening.

    She curled up on her side and tried to calm herself. The whole incident seemed bizarre and out of character from the man in her letters or even the one she had spent the evening with. She closed her eyes, but immediately saw the leering look James had in his eyes. It set her to shaking again. As she was contemplating the turn of events, three revelations came to her. One was that she had somehow married her father; her new husband was in love with the drink as much as her dad. Second, what James felt for her at this moment was not love, but lust. And lastly, the only man that had ever truly loved her had ridden away that morning. Mary felt so alone at that moment. She spent her wedding night crying herself to sleep.

14

A Fearful Beginning

The young bride was perplexed. She couldn't figure out this strange man she had just married. Their wedding night had been so bizarre yet the next day was pleasant and sweet. They started out doing a little shopping at the mercantile, which included getting a butter churn and a nightgown. Then they returned to the farm where Mary packed a picnic lunch of leftover chicken and James led them to a beautiful meadow. A small stream fed by the Umpqua River, meandered through the pasture, then along the edge of the woods. It trickled over the small, smooth rocks that projected from the water, creating a soothing gurgling sound in the background. Its beauty reminded her of her family's farm.

Mary spread out a patchwork quilt on the ground and then emptied the contents of her basket. She watched with growing delight as James hungrily ate. He seemed to be enjoying her cooking—and her. When he saw that she was looking at him, he smiled back with a twinkle in his eye. Her heart began to melt towards him as she pushed back the haunting memory of their wedding night. She reasoned that it had been an isolated incident and nothing more. She determined to give the matter no more consideration.

After the meal, they walked along the stream and talked. At one point, they took off their shoes and stockings and went wading in the water. It was cold, still having a bite from the thawing snows from the mountains. James rolled up his pants legs to try to keep them dry, but they got wet anyway. Mary kept her dress hiked up enough to keep dry. That was until James suddenly pulled her into his arms and kissed her rather passionately. In the midst of his fervor, she forgot herself, letting her dress tails fall from her hands and into the water. She wrapped her arms around his neck and returned his kiss. For a moment she truly felt like a married couple.

But once evening approached, James again balked at sharing a bed with her. She still had mixed feelings about it and found herself fretting whether he was dissatisfied with her or if there was something physically wrong with him. She lay awake for several hours, wrestling with it until sometime in the wee hours of morning she slipped into a state of sleep.

When morning arrived, James appeared quite chipper. He even teased her about getting out of bed a little late, saying that he had done nearly a day's work by the time she had lifted her head off of her pillow. She thought at first he was upset with her, but when he caressed her cheek and called her his *Sleeping Beauty,* she realized he was being facetious.

They went to church and James seemed to take great joy in introducing his new wife. During worship, they shared a hymnal and sang together. As they sat down, he gave her a quick wink, which caused her to break out into a shy smile. When it came time for the preacher to deliver his sermon, James opened up his Bible and held it so they could read together. She didn't have the heart to tell him that on either occasion she hadn't read a single word. She just continued to smile softly and pretend to be absorbed in the Scriptures. Everything seemed to be going well until the end of the service.

After the closing prayer, James suddenly became upset with her. He grabbed her by the arm and quickly ushered her out of the church without speaking to anyone. People stood in the wake staring in dismay. As they rode back on the buckboard, he said nothing, but Mary could see that his jaw was set firm in anger. She held her peace for the moment, waiting for the opportune time to approach him. She decided that this was *not* a good time as they careened down the dusty road that led to the farm.

He pulled the wagon to an abrupt halt in front of the house and jumped off. He went directly inside, slamming the door behind him. Not knowing what he might be capable of doing, Mary didn't know what to do next. The thought crossed her mind to grab the reigns and take off with the team. But where would she go? She knew no one. Could she leave and head towards the safety of her sister? How could she face her? And would she even make it that far before James caught up with her?

She slowly climbed down from the wagon and tried to steady her shaking legs. Fearfully, she walked towards the house, hoping that God would help her face whatever lay before her. She put her hand on the doorknob and slowly turned it and then opened the door. James was inside pacing like a caged animal. She cautiously entered, closing the door quietly behind her. She slipped by him and went directly into the kitchen to prepare their meal.

James continued to pace, working himself up into an agitated state. Soon he could no longer contain it and called brusquely for Mary to come into the room. She warily poked her head inside and then obediently came in. There was a wild look in his eyes that frightened her even more than her wedding night. She tried to keep her distance from him, but when he saw her standing by the doorway, he charged at her. He spewed, "You lied to me!"

Bewilderment, she tried to find her voice and managed to say, "What are ya talkin' about? I've never lied to ya about anythin'."

"What do you call this?" he asked, making the sign of the cross. Mary continued to be puzzled. Her mouth moved trying to form words, but nothing came to her defense. She remained silent. "Are you going to deny being Catholic?" he asked furiously.

"I have never denied it," she answered quietly.

His fury increased. "How dare you stand there and deny it. You lied to me about being Irish and you lied about being Catholic."

"I never denied any o' that. I was forthright in all me letters," she spoke softly, not wanting to agitate him further.

"There was *nothing* in the letters and you know it," he shouted. "And another thing, you knew from the beginning that I clearly stated that I did not want anyone who was Irish or Catholic, but you completely ignored it. Did you not think I would find out?"

Turning away, Mary wrinkled her forehead, trying to make sense of everything. Suddenly the revelation came to her. "Ellin'son!" she said under her breath. He had set her up on purpose. His words came hauntingly back to her, *"Dere be one dat sounds promisin'... Well, do ya wanna write to dis one?"* Her thoughts raced as she tried to recall what was in the very first letter. She was sure there was no mentioning of James' request. Ellingson had intentionally left out those details. If Ellingson couldn't have her, he was going to make sure that she'd pay for her rejection.

She turned back to James and tried to explain. "I did not intentionally try to deceive ya. For whatever reason, I was not aware o' yar prerequisite for marriage. I was sure that in return I had mentioned me faith and that I was Ireland. If I have left out those details, it was inadvertent and not a deliberate act o' deception."

James spun away from her, still enraged. He picked up one of the rockers and threw it against the wall, splintering one of its arms. Mary jumped. Her heart was now racing in her chest. When he turned back to her, she froze with fear. She closed her eyes, anticipating violence and began to pray for God's protection. She heard a voice from a distance and suddenly realized it was her own. She asked in a calm voice, "James, why do ya hate me so? Why are ya persecutin' me?"

James stared at her in disbelief. It was as if the Lord Himself had spoken to him. His fury changed to grief and he fell to his knees. Confused, Mary opened her eyes and saw her husband crumbled on the floor sobbing. It didn't lessen her fear. Cautiously she went and knelt beside him. She put her hand on his shoulder and he began to cry harder.

She let his sobbing subside, before asking, "James, why do ya hate the Irish Catholics so much?"

James' jaw muscles tightened and pain etched itself across his face. His answer came in spurts as the agony of one dreadful night came to light. "Because…they were responsible…for the death…of my parents." He got to his feet and walked over to the window, trying to catch his breath. It was a few minutes before he gained control of his emotions. He absently raked his hand through his hair and he began to explain. "We used to live in New York City. After years of toiling on a farm, my father decided to move us to the city, for all the *advantages* it offered. He set up a market and sold fresh produce. My parents had put a lot of hard work into it and were beginning to make a go of it. But one evening it all came to an end. My brother and I had left the store early to go home…" James began to sob again.

Mary waited for him to regain his composure. Soon he spoke again. "They were walking home that night when a gang of men tried to rob them. They said that my father had refused to give them what they wanted. The men attacked him. When my mother tried to intervene, they beat her too." He buried his face in his hands and sobbed. "My mother never made it to the hospital. My father lasted two days; he never regained consciousness. They said it was a local gang of Irish immigrants that had done it." He looked at Mary with eyes filled with so much pain and anger; she felt a dagger go through her heart.

She came and took him into her arms. Carefully choosing her words, she said softly, "James, I'm so sorry for what happened to yar parents. So much tragedy has come into yar life. Believe me when I say I wish I could take away yar pain." She stroked his hair as she talked and it seemed to soothe him.

But he didn't easily let go of his pain. He shook his head and said curtly, "the Irish are lazy, shiftless people. They wouldn't do an honest day's work if anyone offered them a job."

Mary was indignant, but held her temper. Quietly but firmly she asked, "Do ya think o' me that way? In the short time that I have been here, have I not done me share o' work?"

James blinked. He pulled back and looked at her. "I-I-I have to admit that you have done that and more." He paused briefly and then added, "But what's to say that after a time you won't become lazy?"

"What's to say that any woman won't become lazy? And what's to say that I might remain a hard workin' woman? Only time will tell. Don't judge me by what someone else has done, James. Judge me by me own actions."

The realization of her words brought a slight smile and a nervous chuckle. "You're right. I have unfairly judged you. I'm sorry."

Mary nodded slightly and started to walk away. James pulled her back into his arms. She whispered in his ear, "I understand now, but let us keep this in the past and move forward. I will prove to ya in time to be worth me mettle."

He cradled her face in his hands and apologized again on his part. Then he said, "But would you please not make the sign of the cross when we are in church. I don't want to make others uncomfortable with it."

Mary wanted to protest, but she obediently complied. "Okay, James whatever ya say. I'll be the good wife."

He smiled broadly and said, "That's a good girl." He kissed her hard, but Mary was still reeling from his display of anger. She cautiously accepted his kiss, but there was no passion in it on her part. Then innocently he asked, "What's for dinner? I'm starving." It was as if nothing had ever happened, but it left Mary feeling betrayed by her emotions. Something was wrong with this relationship, but she couldn't focus her thoughts long enough to figure it out. She quietly went back to the kitchen, while James righted the rocker he had thrown. She heard him say offhandedly, "I guess I'll have to fix that tomorrow." And then nothing more was said about the fight.

That night, James had taken a couple shots of whiskey just before bedtime. He said he needed it because there was a slight nip in the air, but it was only an excuse. When Mary got up to go to bed, he followed her and grabbed her by the arm. He said, "Don't you think we should make this marriage binding in God's eyes now?"

Mary wasn't sure what to say. After all that had taken place earlier, the last thing she wanted was to have intercourse with him. A new fear rose in her. She couldn't dare refuse him. What if he had another outburst of anger? The beating of her heart intensified, not from sweet anticipation of being with her husband, but out of concern that he might harm her. She couldn't think fast enough on how to escape this. Ultimately she submitted to his wishes.

So James had his way with her and the event had been less than tender or loving. Afterwards, as he fell asleep fully satisfied she rolled over onto her side and curled up into a fetal position. She thought of all the other men she had serviced in her old life. She felt hollow and empty inside and began to cry softly, not wanting to awaken him. The love she desperately sought was like a fleeting rainbow—beautiful and brilliant, but just out of reach, always unable to grasp. She laid in the dark, wondering what kind of life she had chosen for herself. She wished now that she hadn't been so hasty in fulfilling her responsibilities. If she had only known what had awaited her, she would have listened to Robert and ran far from this place.

"Oh Robert," she said just above a whisper. "I was wrong about everythin'. Where are ya?" She paused and then closing her eyes, prayed, *"Oh God, what have I done?"* Little did she know, but this prayer would be repeated throughout the ensuing years.

15

The Revelation

The weeks flew into months. Summer came and there were fields to be worked and a bounty of crops to be brought in. Mary worked from sunup to beyond sundown. She would drag her weary body to bed eager for sleep. So often it wouldn't come until after James first had his comfort. She tried her best not to fall asleep during it. The only day she really looked forward to was Sunday. The spiritual nourishment she got from church, enabled her to carry on throughout the week.

It was difficult at first to remember not to make the sign of the cross. She caught herself several times touching her forehead only to pretend to scratch a phantom itch. She saw James look at her crossways and continued to rub her forehead and it seemed to appease his ire towards her. She walked on eggshells for fear that she might embarrass him and he'd take away her only joy in life. It was hard to be a closet Catholic.

One night as they went to bed, James asked her about the Saint Christopher's medal she wore around her neck. He knew nothing about what it stood for or the importance it had to many of Mary's faith. She unwittingly told him that it was to protect her in her travels and proudly proclaimed that a kind hearted priest had given it to her just before leaving New York. In a sudden rage, he ripped it from her neck leaving a deep abrasion on both her neck and her heart. Then he violently threw it across the room. The medal ricocheted off the wall and disappeared from sight.

"No woman of mine is going to have an idol hanging around her neck," he said in disgust. Then he turned with his back to her and went to sleep. Sadly, Mary was grateful for the respite from his husbandly *affections*. She too turned her back to him and began to cry softly to herself. It was becoming her nightly routine.

The next morning, she waited until James had left the bedroom before getting out of bed. She knelt down close to the floor and found the medallion underneath the dresser against the wall. She reached as far as she could and retrieved it. Examining it in her hand, she saw that the medal itself was undamaged, but the chain was broken in two. It could never be repaired. Huge teardrops fell and splashed on the necklace, which she wiped away on the bodice of her nightgown. She thought once more about the priest that had given it to her. But with her memory, came his warning. *"You need to make all this known to your betrothed before you marry. Hold nothing back, including your involvement in prostitution. If you deny this truth, you will be acting deceitfully. It is not a way to begin a marriage."* There was a sense of foreboding to it.

"Oh Father, how can I tell him now?" she murmured a quiet prayer. *"Tis hard to tell what he might do to me if he ever found out."* She wept bitterly at the realization that she had indeed deceived him. She felt imprisoned again with no reprieve in sight. *"Father, what am I goin' to do? Is this punishment for all me past sins. Oh please forgive me for all me wrongdoings and rescue me from me predicament."* She crossed herself and kissed the Saint Christopher medal for she had no rosary beads. Then she wrapped it carefully and respectfully in a handkerchief, burying it underneath her clothes in the bottom drawer.

As she turned to leave the bedroom, she felt the room sway to the right. She threw her hand out and caught herself against the wall, steadying herself. Soon the feeling passed. She reckoned she either turned too quickly or the stress from the night before had caused it. She hadn't been getting much rest lately and her stomach was a little unsettled. It was probably just a combination of everything.

She slowly walked from the bedroom to the kitchen and set about her morning routine. She lit the kindling in the stove and as it heated, she took a small basket with her and headed for the henhouse. Gathering up the eggs, she returned with them. By this time the stove was getting warm and she set the iron skillet on it and began to peel some potatoes. She chopped them up and added them to the skillet, frying them up in lard. She preferred to cook them in butter, but she used it so sparingly at home, choosing instead to sell as much as she could to the mercantile. It provided a small income for her.

After the potatoes were fried, she cracked open a couple of eggs. The smell of the frying eggs began to cause her stomach to churn. She tried holding it back, but by the time she flipped the eggs over, she was making a mad dash through the back door. She promptly deposited the empty contents of her stomach onto the ground. Her dry heaves caused her head to throb and she feared she might pass out. Somehow she made her way back inside the house and wetted a dishtowel. She wiped her forehead and face and the feeling subsided.

James came into the kitchen just as she was placing his eggs alongside the potatoes on his plate. She quickly made her escape, saying she didn't feel well and went to lie down on their bed. The sight of James eating his eggs would have caused her to vomit all over again. She lay staring at the ceiling trying not to move, wondering what was wrong with her. She couldn't recall doing anything out of the ordinary, but all her energy seemed to be drained. Forcing herself from her bed, she went back to the kitchen. Even though the eggs had been eaten, the smell remained. She promptly gagged, but it didn't go any further.

"Aren't you going to eat something, Mary?" he asked.

"I think I'll just eat an apple this mornin'." She reached into the cupboard to a small basket and retrieved one. Biting into it, she concluded that she had overdone it yesterday. She had picked several large baskets of the fruit. That was what was making her feel so tired and rundown today. She decided that after morning chores and a trip to the mercantile, she would take it easier this afternoon. It might be exactly what her body needed.

The sun was nearing its apex in the sky when she finally started walking towards the store. Her tiredness overwhelmed her and she wondered if she needed some kind of tonic. She would ask the mercantile owner if he might have something to give her that would give her a little pep until she got over whatever was ailing her. She shifted her basket of wares on the crook of her arm and continued on her walk to town.

It was a glorious day, with not a cloud in the sky. The sun cheered her heart after the drama of the night before. She felt so good she began to sing, mostly old Irish tunes that her dad had taught her, but they were intermixed with hymns she had recently learned at church. She had never sung these songs back in Ireland, but they were beginning to grow on her. There was one song in particular that seemed to be a favorite among the congregants and with Mary as well. She topped a hill just as she came to the chorus, and let her voice ring out: *"Amazing love! How can it be, That Thou, me God, shouldst die for me? Amazing love! How can it be, That Thou, me God, shouldst die for me?"*

She let the words of the hymn speak to her heart. *"Father, do Ya really love me that much? Do Ya really love me enough to die for me and me sins? How can it be?"* Overcome with emotions, her eyes misted up and quickly breeched their floodgates. They streamed down her face as she began to sob. She had noticed how emotional she had become; crying at the drop of a hat. *"Oh God, do Ya really love me? Does anybody really love me?"* The heaviness in her heart had returned and she asked, *"Does me own husband love me?"*

Carefully she climbed the wooden steps to the large wraparound porch of the mercantile. A few wooden rockers sat outside and were fully occupied by a trio of ladies exchanging gossip. A couple of men sat whittling doing virtually the same thing. Mary wondered if she was ever food for their fodder. As she reached for the door handle, a young cowboy was making his exit. He politely held the door open for her, tipping his hat as she walked by. She went inside and waited to be served. At the counter was Mrs. Snider, an elderly woman that was easily distracted and rattled by the smallest things. It was going to be awhile before she would be waited on.

Mary browsed the aisles of shelves. There were a few things that they could use, but she would choose her purchases wisely today. She had always been frugal since she had grown up with so little. She ventured over to look at the material goods. Longingly, she caressed the more expensive fabrics and wondered what it might be like to be wealthy enough to afford such luxuries. Then again, she wondered what it would be like to be able to buy a store bought dress. Aubrey's husband could afford it. She couldn't understand why James couldn't. He was successful enough to buy her an occasional dress, but he was just too tight with his money.

As she continued to dream about a life of abundance, she was awakened from her slumber by the familiar voice of her new found friend. "Mary, how are you today?" the woman asked.

Mary turned and greeted the woman warmly. "I'm fine," she politely lied. "Thank ya for askin'. How are ya doin', Ida Rose?"

Ida Rose Beecham had the strangest look on her face as she studied Mary. A twinkle appeared in her blue eyes as her smile broadened. It was as though she was sharing a wonderful secret with her best friend. The truth was, Ida Rose was about to, only Mary didn't know the secret was hers. "I am doing just fine, but obviously not as well as you are." She paused to enjoy the moment and then leaning forward, whispered, "How far along are you?"

Mary raised an eyebrow and asked, "Excuse me?"

Ida Rose threw her head back and laughed softly. "Do you not know that you're expecting?"

Mary was confused. How could this woman possibly think she was with child? Wouldn't Mary be the first to know if she was pregnant or not. But as she began to review her symptoms, the slow realization took hold in her mind. "How did ya know? I didn't even know."

She giggled and answered, "I have this strange gift. I look at a woman and immediately recognize the glow of motherhood and—well, I just know." If anyone would know the glow of motherhood it would be her. Ida Rose already had five children and she hadn't quite reached her thirtieth birthday. "When it comes time for the birthing, let me know. I'm the best midwife around. I certainly have my own experience to help me." She heartily laughed at herself and Mary politely joined her. But she was beginning to feel nauseous, not from the pregnancy, but from the news of it.

Before they could talk further, the owner of the store called to her. "Mrs. Whitaker, how can I help you today?"

"I have some eggs and some butter to sell ya?" she said to him.

"Very good," he replied. "You know, I sell out of your butter as soon as it comes into the store. People come in asking for it. I don't know what you do differently, but people seem to know the distinction."

Mary smiled sweetly. She wasn't sure if he was telling the truth or just ingratiating himself to her. Curtis Thompson had an easy way of talking that could set a person at ease, but at the same time made them wonder if they were the butt of a private joke he had running inside his head. He was slightly balding, but had a thin mustache that curled up on the ends. He had a nervous habit of tweaking it every now and then.

He examined the contents of her basket and tallied what he owed her. "Is there anything I can get for you, Mrs. Whitaker?" She listed a few items and then asked about something for an upset stomach. With great concern Thompson asked, "Are you suffering from dyspepsia?"

"I don't even know what that is," she said perplexed.

Ida Rose stepped in. "No, just nausea and vomiting, I'm I right?" she asked Mary. She nodded in agreement. "Then I suggest that bottle of tonic bitters over there," she said pointing to a bottle on the top shelf.

Thompson reached up and took the bottle down. He gently placed it in her basket with her other items and then looked knowingly at her. "Congratulations, Mrs. Whitaker. Does James know yet?"

Mary was a little indignant that her condition was becoming common knowledge. "He does not. So if ya would please keep this under yar hat until then, it would be greatly appreciated."

"Your secret's safe with me," he said smiling. Then changing the subject he added, "Oh, there's a letter for your husband. I'll get it for you as soon as I get done with Mrs. Beecham."

"I just need this spool of thread," she said, handing him the money. Thompson deposited it in the cash register and then went to the back to retrieve the letter.

"Where are yar children?" Mary asked Ida Rose.

"Luella is watching them. That's the advantage of having several children. Eventually the oldest is able to watch the little ones so you can get a small break. Of course, I don't dare leave them for too long; I'm likely to find that the boys have tied Luella to a tree and are causing havoc."

Mary chuckled. Then she leaned towards Ida Rose and asked, "What's dyspepsia?"

She smiled softly and answered, "It's a digestive disorder. Trust me; you don't have it."

Just then Thompson returned with the letter. "Here you are, Mrs. Whitaker. Hope it's good news."

Mary accepted it with apprehension. She wondered who might be writing her husband. A disturbing thought occurred: Did he have another prospective bride on the side? She looked at the writing, but there was nothing detectable. It just looked like scribbles to her, but at closer examination, it did have a certain familiarity about it. Ida Rose made a comment, but Mary was too deep in her thoughts to hear her.

"Mary," she said, finally getting her attention. "It's not bad news is it? You look upset."

"I'm sure tis not," she said, trying to convince herself that it wasn't. "Ya know what it be like to get a letter. Tis so rare out here that ya always expect the worst. I'm sure tis probably from a distant relative just keepin' in touch."

"Well, I hope so. After all, I'd hate to see your good news diminished in any way."

Mary smiled reassuringly. "I'm sure it won't."

They exited the store and walked together until parting at the Beecham farm. Mary tried not to fret about the letter. She finally surmised that it probably had something to do with James' work. If she would have thought about it earlier, she could have dropped it off at the mill. As she let the thought go, she felt a little lighter walking the rest of the way home. When she got there, she placed the letter on the mantel and then finished a couple of chores that remained. Then she laid down and rested for awhile. She felt a little guilty doing so, but now she had a good excuse.

By the time James returned home, Mary had supper on the table. She hoped that he would be in a good mood for she wasn't sure how he would accept the news that she was pregnant. They had both written about wanting to have children, but that was before she had become a disappointment to him. Now she wasn't sure if he wanted her to be the mother of his children. Her hope was that in some way it would bring them closer. She would wait for the opportune moment to tell him.

James was in good spirits as he pulled the wagon up to the barn. Mary greeted him with a kiss that surprised him. "What do I owe the honor of this reception tonight?"

"I just wanted to let ya know that I missed ya today." She kissed him quickly again, but before she could pull away, he grabbed her and pressed his body against hers, kissing her more passionately. It felt hopeful that they could put their past mistakes behind them and move forward.

When Mary pulled back, James looked at her with desire in his eyes. He said, "Maybe we can help you get over your loneliness tonight."

She smiled shyly, hoping that would be the case. On rare occasions, James *could* be tender to her, taking his time making love. She treasured those moments, but unfortunately, they came sparingly. She returned to the house as James put the team away. When he came into the kitchen, she had the food on the table waiting for him. He sat down at the table, folded his hands and blessed the meal. Mary noticed that he was more talkative than usual this evening. She didn't think she had enjoyed a meal so much since they had first married. It had been a promising evening and she hoped that this was a prelude to a wonderful night between them.

As the meal concluded, James went and sat in the rocker to relax as Mary cleared the table. As she was washing the dishes, she heard him ask from the sitting room, "What is this?"

Turning, she saw him standing with the letter in his hand. She immediately felt apprehensive. "I forgot. Mr. Thompson at the mercantile gave that to me today. I hope tis not bad news."

James looked at the letter puzzled. It had been sent from London. He recognized the unmistakable handwriting. It was Mary's! He looked up at her dismayed. Could this have been a letter lost in transit? If so, why didn't she recognize her own handwriting? He looked back down at the letter and opened the envelope feverishly. He pulled it out, unfolded it and began to read. What he read made his heart sink at first, and then a slow and steady anger began to grow in his gut.

Dear Mr. Whitaker,

You don't know me, but I know your wife quite well. I'm quite sure she has not disclosed anything about her past and I thought you might like to know the woman that you married. You see, I know her better than you do. I was her former lover, but then again, she has had numerous lovers. You should know that before she accepted your proposal of marriage, she was a prostitute. She was paid for services rendered to any man willing to pay her price. She was quite good at. I enjoyed my time with her. I hope that you have as well.

Sincerely,

Marcus Ellingson

James reread the letter, not quite comprehending it. Slowly the fire in his gut spilled over like an erupting volcano. He began to shake violently. Mary entered the room and was standing by the doorway watching his reaction. She was unaware of what the letter contained and was becoming frightened with what she saw. Suddenly his eyes were filled with rage and he turned on her. She instinctively stepped back, but ran into the wall; there was no place to go. James was so furious, he couldn't form any words. He charged at her and pinned her to the wall. "How could you? How could you?"

"How could I what?" she asked, trembling with fear.

"This whole marriage has been a sham. You pretend to be some holy and righteous Christian and the whole time you're nothing but a lying whore. Is that what they teach you in the Catholic faith? That you can sleep with every man in creation and just receive absolution from a priest. How do you earn that…by sleeping with *him*?!"

Mary blinked. She tried to catch her breath, but James had pressed her so hard she was having difficulty inhaling. She tried to remain calm. "What was in the letter, James?"

He looked at the crumbled letter in his hand. Suddenly he shook it in her face and said, "It's from your former lover. It's from Marcus Ellingson."

The air escaped from her lungs and she could barely stand on her shaking legs. She could never have guessed that Ellingson would have sunk so low as to write James about her. If she had known, she would have destroyed it. But then Ellingson would have known that. He was probably at this moment relishing the thought of her handing the letter to her husband. She lowered her eyes unable to look at him. With resignation she asked, "What does he say in the letter?"

"That you were a whore," he said bitterly. He had tears in his eyes, but they were from anger and shame, not from sadness. He spoke with venom. "He said that men paid to be with you. That he was even one of them. Do you dare deny any of it?" Tears slowly descended her cheeks. They confirmed his accusations. "I want you out of here," he said resolutely. It was all he could do to not physically beat her. If he had had some liquor in him he probably would have. "I don't want to ever see your face again, do you understand me!"

Mary stood frozen, not knowing what to do. Where was she to go? The Beechams? She didn't know them well enough to lay her burdens on their doorstep. Aubrey was too far away. What was she to do? She reached down to her belly and instinctively caressed it. There was a life growing inside her. How would she care for her child? Their child. She closed her eyes and prayed. When she opened them, she looked intently at James. Somehow she summoned up the courage and said, "Would ya turn away yar unborn child?"

James stared in disbelief. "What?"

"I'm carryin' yar child. Would ya turn away yar child?"

James shook his head and angrily spouted, "How do I know that it's *mine*?"

"Because, I have not been with anyone else since I have left London. Tis yar baby."

He hung his head and for the moment, relented. But he resolved that once the baby came, she would be gone from his life…and their child's. He would not stand for a whore being in his house, sharing his bed. Angrily, he turned and went into Jethro's old room and slammed the door behind him. The promising evening had dissolved into a nightmare. If Mary thought her life had been difficult before, from now on it would be a living hell.

16

Exiled

Everything was out in the open. All the darkness of Mary's past was brought to light with a simple stroke of a pen. Now she was left with the consequences of not being forthright from the beginning. She was filled with remorse and regret. Had she been truthful, the engagement would have been declared null and void by James. She would have been free to marry Robert. She wondered if marrying an unbeliever would have been any harder than all this. James said that he was a Christian, acted all pious to those in the community, but there was a dark side of him that scared her as much as Ryland.

The battle escalated the next few days. When Sunday rolled around, Mary was given strict orders not to attend church. She was exiled to their house and forbidden to even go into town even to sell her eggs and butter. "How do I know you won't want to sell other things?" His words were laced with malicious sardonicism.

"How dare ya insinuate such a thin'? I've been faithful to ya."

"Really?" he said mockingly. "What about the man you were seen snuggling up with on the stagecoach. You don't think that it's not all over town. I'm already a laughingstock. What will people do with this when they find out that I married a whore?"

Mary was so indignant that she shook. Her eyes narrowed to tiny slits from her contempt towards him. "That was the man that saved me sister and me from the dangers of the Isthmus and San Francisco. He was tryin' to comfort me after I had to say goodbye to Aubrey, not knowin' if I would ever see her again. He was just bein' a friend."

"Well, that's not what I heard from Mrs. Cavanaugh."

"The old biddy that was on the stagecoach?"

"Mrs. Cavanaugh is a highly respected church goer."

Mary wanted to say, "Like ya," but bit her tongue instead. They stood toe-to-toe, neither one blinking. Finally, Mary announced, "I'm goin' to church, whether ya like it or not. I'll walk if I have to."

"I wouldn't if I were you," he threatened. "Not unless you want the whole congregation to know about your past."

"Ya wouldn't dare. Ya have too much pride for that."

"Don't be too sure about that. I think I will gain a whole lot of sympathy from them once they learn how I was duped by this sinful woman."

Mary stood staring at him in disbelief. "Won't people become suspicious when I don't show meself?"

James disdainfully laughed. "I have the perfect alibi; I'll just tell everyone that you're not feeling well. After all, you are with child; it's quite common."

"So what happens later on, after the period o' mornin' sickness passes? What will ya tell them then?"

James pulled on his hat and grinned contemptuously. He said firmly, "I'll just tell them that you're having some trouble with the pregnancy and are bedridden. Then after the baby is born, I'll send you away. I'll tell them that you couldn't take care of the baby and so you left me."

With the news that he would be so cold-hearted to send her away without her child, it left Mary stunned. She was without words for the first time. James laughed derisively once again and went out the door. A few moments later, she heard the wagon pull away from the house.

Her mind darted from thought to thought trying to reason a way out of her predicament. She should pack her bag and leave. Going straight way to the bedroom, she pulled out her carpetbag and threw her clothes in it. But by the time she had finished, the reality that she had nowhere to go hit her hard. She crumbled to the bed as she held her Saint Christopher medal to her breast and began to pray. A new thought emerged: there was no reason to panic. She still had plenty of time before the baby would weigh her down and make her journey difficult. She had found a way to escape the brothel—she would find a way to escape this prison as well. She'd just have to bide her time.

At church, James was the picture of an honorable Christian man. He sang out loudly during the worship time and when he was asked to pray, he didn't hesitate, praying a long reverent prayer that even made the preacher look insufficient in comparison. Whenever anyone questioned where Mary was, he proudly proclaimed that they were expecting a little one and that she was feeling under the weather this morning. Everyone seemed to accept his answer—all but one.

"She seemed fine the other day, when I saw her," Ida Rose said.

"Well, you know how quickly these things can come on a woman," he reasoned.

"Maybe I should come and check on her to make sure that there's nothing else wrong," she offered.

"No, don't bother; she'll be fine."

"I hear tell, that there's a doctor over at Middlebury; we could send word to have him check on her."

"That won't be necessary," he said curtly. Then realizing how stern his words were, he softened. "I mean, I'm sure this is all temporary; she'll be up and around in a few days."

Ida Rose let it drop for the moment, but something just didn't set right with her. She couldn't put her finger on it, but she felt that James had been putting on a performance today and was anything, but truthful. She would pray about it and seek the Holy Spirit's guidance. She wasn't the type that liked to butt in, but when she felt God's leading, she rarely resisted.

The next day, Ida Rose couldn't get Mary off her mind. She prayed earnestly for an answer and the feeling that something wasn't right seemed to intensify. She called to Luella to watch the children and then took the wagon and headed for the Whitaker farm. When she topped the hill that overlooked their farm, a dreadful fear overtook her. What if James had done something to her? It was preposterous to think of such a thing. In all the time she had known James, she never perceived him to be a violent man. But there had been a distinct change in him since the death of his brother that was not good. The thought raised her fear to the next level.

As Ida Rose drove the wagon down the incline, to her great relief, she spotted Mary coming from the barn. Mary stopped, shielded her squinting eyes from the sun. When she recognized the woman, she waved enthusiastically. Ida Rose pulled the wagon to a halt by the barn. She hopped off the wagon and threw her arms around her, hugging her warmly. Mary had never received a more friendly welcome from her before.

Ida Rose exclaimed, "You look the picture of health. Are still feeling poorly?"

Mary looked dumbly at her. Then slowly the realization of what James must have told everyone about her began to sink in. "I feel fine today."

"But you were sick yesterday?" Ida Rose pried.

"A little," she answered. It wasn't a complete lie. After her confrontation with James, she had felt sick to her stomach.

"The way James had talked; you were so sick that you couldn't even get out of bed."

Mary's eyes fell to the ground and she hemmed around for a good response to her inquiry. "I-I-I just wasn't able to go to church, that's all." When she made eye contact with Ida Rose, she felt as if the woman could see into her soul.

"Did you and James have a fight?" Mary nodded her head and looked down at the ground again. "Is it about the baby?"

"The baby isn't the problem—directly."

"Then what's wrong?" she asked with great concern.

"Somethin' about me past that I cannot take back," she said regrettably.

"You want to tell me about it?" Ida Rose asked.

"I don't think I can."

"Does it have anything to do with the letter?" Surprised, Mary looked intently at Ida Rose. How did she know? Did James tell her? No, he couldn't have. But somehow she knew. Ida Rose cradled Mary's face in her hands and asked, "What was in the letter, Mary?"

Mary couldn't answer her. She turned and slowly led her into the kitchen. Putting a pot of coffee on the stove, she sat down across the table from Ida Rose. She wanted to tell the woman everything, but the courage wasn't there. She simply replied, "I've done some thin's in me past that I'm ashamed o'. The letter came from someone who knew about it. He told James everythin'. Now he doesn't want anythin' to do with me."

"What could you have possibly done?" she questioned. It was unfathomable that she could have done anything that horrendous. She took Mary's hand and gave it a squeeze. Lightheartedly she said, "What? Did you kill someone?"

"If it were only that, it might be more forgivable."

Her new friend looked at her with great distress. Her eyes prompted Mary for more information, but none was forthcoming. "I wish you would confide in me."

"I cannot; tis too dreadful." Overcome with emotion, her tears betrayed her again. "I've tried to explain to him why I did it, but he's refused to listen. He cannot accept the fact o' what I have done. Since then, I have prayed continuously for God to help him see the truth. If it hadn't been James, I would still be locked in a livin' hell. I wish that he could see that he was an instrument o' God's deliverance."

"Do you think that if I talked with him that he would listen to me? Maybe I could make him see that if God can forgive you then it is our responsibility to do likewise."

"Oh, Ida Rose, ya cannot get yarself involved in this mess. If he found out that someone else had an inklin' o' what went on, I'm afraid o' what he might do. Right now, with the baby on the way, he won't kick me out. I just don't know what will happen afterwards."

"Well, you have a place to stay if he ever does. Roy and I will not turn you away." She paused and then putting her hand under Mary's chin, turned her head upward so that their eyes met. "Remember that!" Mary nodded, but felt so full of shame. How could she have found such a good friend as this? She then realized that God had sent her there to be an encouragement.

Ida Rose left that day, with a new respect for her friend. Whatever was in Mary's past had produced an incredible resolve in her over the years. It was a shame that her husband could not see that and have some compassion for her. She determined that she would keep watch over her, making it a point to visit regularly, but only when she knew that James would not be there.

During their times together, she began bringing her Bible and read it to Mary. It seemed to bring comfort to her, especially reading from the Psalms. It also spawned some interesting discussions about the Scriptures. One passage spoke specifically to Mary. It was about Elijah the Tishbite and how he was fed by the ravens morning and night during a drought in the land. Mary saw the spiritual connection. She too was going through her own drought, yet God had sent Ida Rose to nourish her through His word. It brought comfort to her soul and helped to carry her through the days ahead.

As the months went by and Mary became heavy with child, James was true to his word. He told everyone that she was having some difficulty and had to be bedridden. When some protested that he should let them look in on her, he made the excuse that the doctor from Middlebury had come and seen her. He was the one that recommended complete bed rest and no visitors. She was not to be disturbed until the baby came.

Of course, Ida Rose insisted that she check in on her since more than likely she would have to deliver the baby. Reluctantly, James allowed it, but only when he said that she could, so as to make sure that Mary was in bed. Both Mary and Ida Rose went along with the charade, not letting on that she knew the truth about the situation.

Christmas came without much fanfare. Mary honored the Irish tradition by placing a candle in the window welcoming Joseph and Mary. She put her hand over her bump and had a great empathy for her namesake, wondering what she must have felt that night. When morning came there were no gifts other than the crib James had made for the baby. It was a very bleak holiday. The only present Mary received was a knitted rust-colored shawl from Ida Rose and crocheted blanket for the baby. She also sent a few well worn baby clothes that she hoped she'd never need again. Mary was grateful for everything she had done for her. She was the lone connection to the outside world.

December crept into January at a snail's pace. Mary was more than ready for the baby to come. It was getting harder for her to do her chores. James had little compassion for her fatigue. He did pitch in by feeding the animals and milking the cow. She still churned the butter which James took to town to sell, although Mary no longer saw a dime of it.

Late January, the weather had been fairly mild. Previously, there had been a lot of cloud cover and some brief showers of rain off and on. But on the evening that Mary went into labor, the weather had taken a turn southward. As darkness descended, a strong breeze dropped the temperatures to well below freezing. The light drizzle had begun to turn to snow. As Mary's birth pangs intensified, so did the snowstorm. James hitched up the team and quickly rode off to the Beecham farm. Upon hearing the news that Mary was in labor, Roy hitched up his own team as Ida Rose gathered her things. She gave finally instructions to her children to mind Luella and then they set out right behind James.

The snow was so thick in the air that the lanterns were nearly ineffective. The tracks that James had just laid down as he journeyed to the Beecham's were quickly being covered. He slowed the horses to a crawl and the Beecham's did likewise. The blizzard-like conditions were creating a white out and James was having trouble recognizing any landmarks. He guessed where the road was by gauging the tree line along the way. It was a slow and arduous ride back to the farm. James worried that they wouldn't make it back in time.

Mary was propped up on pillows in her bed. Her water had broken just before James left to get Ida Rose. Fear and apprehension enveloped her. Although she had witnessed the miracle with farm animals, she had never had the opportunity to help out with a woman's birthing before. It was an experience she did not want to have alone.

A new contraction hit her and she gripped the brass railing behind her head. She grunted and tried not to push, but the pain was nearly unbearable. She wondered how close she was to delivering. Wasn't the first one supposed to be the most difficult and longest? For her sake and the baby's, she hoped it would be lengthy, because James was taking much too long. Where was he? She prayed.

The wagon nearly slipped off the road and into a ditch. Somehow James kept the wagon upright. Roy saw James nearly go over and pulled his team to the left. The snow was not letting up. James fought to keep the horses on what he thought was the road. He was becoming disoriented; nothing looked familiar. A new fear crept in; had he missed the turn off to his farm? If he had, how far back did he need to go? He brought the team to a halt, stood and surveyed his surroundings. Roy stopped right behind him. He told Ida Rose to stay put while he trudged through the snow. The wind buffeted against him, trying to push him back. He finally made it to James.

"What's wrong?" Roy shouted over the wind.

"I'm not sure where we are. Have we passed the turn off?"

"I don't think so, but with this wind blowing the snow the way it is, it's making it hard to see."

James got down and they took their lanterns as they ventured ahead of the team. The snow was more than halfway up their calves and continuing to pile up.

"I wish I had left earlier to get you," James shouted. "But who would have thought we'd get a storm like this?"

"It is a freak storm," Roy agreed. He wiped away the snow that was accumulating on his beard. They continued struggling ahead in silence.

Ida Rose was getting nervous. She had lost sight of the men as the dim light of their lanterns disappeared behind a wall of swirling snow. She sat in darkness wrapped in a blanket, trying to keep warm. She worried what she would do if they got lost and didn't come back for her. And she was anxious for Mary. What was going on there? She had to be terrified.

Mary was frantic. The pains were coming closer and intensifying. She tried not to let her emotions control her. When a pain struck her, she tried to stay calm and not push, but it was just instinctive to do so. She wanted this over with. She prayed out loud, *"Oh God, help me and help me baby. Please I need Ya to send someone to help me get through this, because I don't know what I'm doin' here."* Before she could finish her prayer another contraction came.

As Ida Rose finished her prayer, she could make out the faint light from her husband's lantern. The light grew as he came closer. He hopped up beside her and announced that they had spotted the fence post that marked out the turnoff to James' farm. They were almost there. Ida Rose exclaimed, "Thank, God."

Roy had less faith. He said under his breath, "We're not there yet." But his words were drowned out by a vicious gust of wind.

James slowly led the horses forward, squinted his eyes against the snow and tried to see beyond them. With a gloved hand, he wiped away the snow that had collected on his eyelashes, hoping to improve his vision, but it didn't. The snow had stuck to his beard and had begun to freeze. If he didn't find shelter soon, he would be in danger of frostbite. He scanned the darkness in front of him and swore. He couldn't see the fence post. He had estimated that he should have reached it by now. A knot was forming in his stomach. He was just about to stop the wagon, when he finally saw it. He made a left turn; soon they would be at the house.

Sweat was pouring from Mary's face. She half grunted, half cried. Where was her help? She was immediately reminded of a Scripture that Ida Rose had read just last week. She quoted it as a prayer, *"I will lift up me eyes unto the hills from whence cometh me help. Me help cometh from the LORD, which made heaven and earth."* She drew in a breath and let out a scream.

James heard her scream as he hopped off the wagon. He bolted through the door and into the bedroom. He found Mary, her eyes wild with fear and for the first time since the letter, he actually felt a pang of compassion for her. He knelt in front of her and could see the baby's head beginning to crown. He wasn't sure what to do. He had birthed animals on the farm, but this was his child. He didn't want to mess this up. He found himself crying out for God's help. Just then Roy and Ida Rose burst into the room. Ida Rose pushed him aside and took over. Within moments the baby made its entrance into the world.

Ida Rose shouted instructions for James and Roy, as she held the newborn. Roy handed her a scissor-shaped devise which she took and clamped the umbilical cord. Then she took some cotton thread and tied it off about four inches from the baby's belly. Roy then handed her a pair scissors and she cut through the tough membrane of the cord. Once it was cut, she lifted the baby up. The jostling was enough that the baby took its first breath. James had returned with a clean towel. Ida Rose wrapped the tiny bundle in it and then handed the child to Mary.

"You have a son, Mary," Ida Rose said tenderly. Her anxiety was beginning to diminish. "What will you name him?"

Without hesitation, she said, "Joshua. His name will be Joshua—the Lord saves." She lovingly cradled him in her arms. It was hard to believe that this little bundle had caused all that pain and stress. Miraculously, the memory of it was already beginning to fade as joy filled her heart. She held him close and kissed him on the forehead. "Ya're me beautiful son," she cooed.

The wonderment of the moment of the child's birth had temporarily erased the hard feelings between the couple. They each reveled in the amazement of the miracle of life. Mary prayed silently, thanking God for His grace and mercy through the ordeal and most of all for His boundless love. Tears of joy flowed from her eyes and James found his own had welled up. He blinked and tried to wipe them away unnoticeably.

Mary only relented her son long enough to allow James to hold him. The proud papa carefully took him in his arms. He couldn't believe that something so small could scare him so much. He felt his heart swell with love and it caught him by surprise. This time he allowed the tears to fall from his eyes. He took his index finger and caressed the tiny fingers on baby's small hand. Then he gently stroked the baby's cheek.

As he held the baby close to his face, he said to his child, "You will be named after my brother Jethro."

A knife went through Mary's heart. The reprieve from the battlefront was short lived and the war was about to commence again. She had hoped and prayed that the baby would bring them together and they could become a family, but she soon discovered that James would have no part in that. Instead of uniting his parents, Joshua Jethro would be a wedge driving them farther apart.

Six Years Later

17

The New Arrivals

A cool springtime breeze ruffled Mary's hair. Although the air still had a bit of a winter chill to it, the warmth of the sun all but made up for it. She closed her eyes, and turned her face towards it, drinking in the radiance. Smiling softly, she recalled a distant memory of a little auburn haired girl running barefoot through the pasture fields of home. She had never felt more free and alive than on that day. She wished she could go back and relive it all again, somehow changing the course of her life. But if she did, she would miss out on the greatest joy of her life. A faint cry brought her out of her revelry.

"Mama, Mama," she heard the child call with excitement. "Look what I found, Mama." The little boy totted a small box turtle in both his hands. He hurriedly ran to show his mother who was resting on a large rock just beyond the small stream. He approached her and proudly handed it to her, exclaiming, "I found it by the creek."

"Oh, what I fine discovery, Joshua. Do ya know what it is?"

The boy squinted up at her, not certain of his answer. "Is it a turtle?"

She threw her head back and laughed with delight. "That it is," she replied, handing him back his treasure.

The boy examined the turtle carefully, turning it over in his hand. Mary could see how intently he was thinking and waited for the questions to follow. She marveled at the inquisitive mind he had at just six years of age. It didn't take long for him to ask. "Why does he hide his head and legs?"

She smiled softly and answered, "He's tryin' to protect himself."

"From what?"

"From ya."

"I wouldn't hurt him."

"I know lad," she said, pulling him up and enveloping him in her arms. "But he doesn't know that."

"How can I tell him that I won't hurt him?"

Mary kissed him on the cheek and said, "Honey, he doesn't understand."

Joshua furrowed his brow as he contemplated her answer. Soon a new question was posed. "Do turtles talk to each other, Mama?"

"I don't think they have any vocal chords, so they cannot speak. I've heard that sometimes they will hiss or make a gruntin' sound, although I've never heard it. But then again, I haven't been around a lot o' turtles."

The boy continued to inspect it. When he was satisfied, he broke from his mother's grasp, ran back to the water's edge and let it go. Then he returned to her.

Puzzled, Mary said, "I thought that ya would want to keep it as a pet. Why did ya let it go?"

The boy shrugged and said, "I don't know. I guess it just didn't seem right to take away his freedom."

She was shocked by his mature answer. *Freedom* was a big word and difficult concept for such a small boy. She said to him, "Ya're wise beyond yar years, me son."

Joshua seemed embarrassed. He shrugged and tilted his head down towards the ground. He decided to join her and climbed up the rock and sat down beside her. He was quiet for a moment, thinking of something else. He had a curiosity about something, but had always been afraid to ask. He thought by asking this simple question it might deepen the rift between his mother and father. They seemed to always be angry with each other.

Joshua sighed, trying to will some courage, but it wasn't happening. Mary felt that something was troubling him. "What is it, lad? Tell me what's on yar mind."

He hesitated for a moment, but then suddenly blurted out, "Why do you sometimes call me Joshua when everyone else calls me Jethro?"

It was Mary's turn to sigh. She hung her head in shame, knowing it was wrong, but it seemed so right when it was just the two of them. Quietly she tried to come up with a satisfactory answer. "I wanted to call ya Joshua, but yar dad wanted to name ya after his brother that he dearly loved. I guess I never truly let go o' that." She hesitated and then asked, "Do ya mind being called Joshua?"

He looked up at her and smiled broadly. "No, I kind of like it; like we have a secret. It sort of makes me feel…I don't know…special."

Mary again smiled at his maturity. She put her arm around him and squeezed. She didn't know what she would do without him. But it was because of him, she would forever be tied to James. She could have walked away from this nightmare long ago, but now it was impossible. James' threats to send her away from the child kept her in line with whatever he wanted. He fully intended to send her away after the child was born. But he soon came to realize that he could not care for a baby on his own. So they each were stuck with the other for the time being. But Mary feared that someday, he would make good on his threat. She prayed continually that God would intervene on her behalf.

They sat quietly, listening to the babble of the nearby stream. A chorus of singing birds accompanied it. The beautiful melody of nature was soothing to her soul. This was her respite, her reprieve from life. Joshua interrupted the solitude with another question. "Do I look like him?"

"Like who?"

"Like Dad's brother?"

"I don't know; I never knew him. He died just before I came to America." She looked the boy over and tried to see if perhaps she had misread any of his features. He had the same tousled, dark brown hair of his father and eyes as blue as the ocean, but he also favored her. She felt in her heart that there was no resemblance to his uncle, but she found herself compromising. "I'm sure that ya probably do remind yar dad o' him in some ways."

She hoped that it would appease his curiosity, but Joshua was feeling emboldened now. He asked her a question that had troubled him for some time. "Why don't you come to church with me and Dad?"

Mary took a deep breath and momentarily held it. How could she explain such a complicated matter to a child? She wished he would have stuck with the turtle questions. She slowly exhaled and asked him, "Do ya know what a Catholic is?" The boy shook his head. Mary again sighed, trying to find the right words. "A Catholic is someone that worships God in a very liturgical way."

"What does litter…"

"Liturgical. It means that our worship is very structured and…could even be called ritualistic to some." She could tell that she wasn't doing a very good job of explaining. "There are things that we do at every service and tis done in a specific order. We have Mass, which is similar to when ya have communion, only we have it every Sunday. We have certain prayers we like to recite and we have confession."

"What's that?"

"That's when we go to the priest and confess our sins to him. He gives absolution to us…forgiveness. He also offers prayers o' penance for us to recite and advice to help us from ever doin' it again."

"And Daddy doesn't like that?"

Softly she said, "Daddy just doesn't understand."

The boy tried to process this new information, but it was more than he could comprehend. Again he asked, "But I still don't know why you can't come to church with us?"

Mary was blunt. "Because yar dad thinks it be less embarrassin' for people to think that yar mother is a heathen than to know the truth that she is a Catholic." Before Joshua could ask anything more, Mary closed the subject. "We need to get back home; there's work to be done before yar dad gets home."

She rose from the rock and arched her back to get the kink out of it. She felt older than her age. She reached back and helped the boy get to his feet. They started back, but before they got very far, Joshua had another question. "Why do we come here?"

"Tis me sanctuary," she said, knowing that the boy could never fully understand. "I feel God's presence here and it also reminds me o' me homeland. I wish I could take ya back there someday."

"I'll take you back there when I grow up and get rich, Mama," he promised.

Mary laughed softly. She wished that life could be as easy as it was for a small boy.

They got back to the farm and Mary set about doing her chores. She had left some laundry undone. She admonished herself for taking too much leisure time. If she had just started on it this morning instead of lollygagging, it would be hanging on the line to dry by now. But the beautiful weather had drawn her to this special place of refuge and once there it was so hard to leave it. It was her little piece of heaven on earth.

She heated up some water and then hauled it to a large wash tub just outside the kitchen door. When she had enough in the tub, she put in a few pieces of clothing with a bar of lye soap and stirred it with a long stick. When it had soaked long enough, she began to scrub them on a wooden washboard. Once clean, they were wrung out, the soap rinsed away and wrung again. Then she hung them up to dry on the clothes lines. She repeated the process until all the clothes were washed.

Joshua kept her company, much too young to help with her labor. It was just a comfort to watch him play in the yard. Her heart ached knowing that she would probably never have any more children. She and James still shared a bed, but not much more. On a rare occasion James would have too much to drink and want her to give him his due. Things weren't much better than they were in London, only that she just had one man to service now. Still, there was no love exchanged between them.

Mary's arms and back ached, but her work was far from being done. She dipped a bucket down into the washtub and took the leftover soapy water to the kitchen. She poured it out on the floor, took a large brush with short stiff bristles and began scrubbing the floor. Then she took a large rag and soaked up the excess water and then rung it back out into the bucket, changing the water often. She continued the process until all the floors of the house were spotless.

Soaked and sweating, Mary finally took a break and sat down on a rocking chair on the porch. Joshua followed her around like a puppy dog. He had collected small rocks and pebbles and was building an imaginary town out of them. She laughed at herself, watching how meticulously he lined and stacked each rock. She wondered if he would have a future designing and building houses or even cities. More than likely he would just remain here and be a farmer or go into business with his father.

Before she could give it much more thought, she heard an approaching wagon. She looked to see a family that she did not immediately recognize. Rising to her feet, she walked over and leaned on a support beam for the porch roof. She squinted her eyes, trying to focus them. Joshua joined her at her side.

"Who is it Mama?" he asked.

"I don't know, son. I can't make out who it is."

The wagon drew closer and Mary could now see a man driving it. A woman with a yellow bonnet sat beside him. She had a small bundle in her arms and in the back was a strawberry-blonde little girl. She reminded her of…"Aubrey!" she suddenly shouted. She ran to the wagon as it pulled into the yard and stopped. "Aubrey!" she shouted, only to be disappointed when she looked into the woman's face. Confused, she looked at the man and instantly recognized him. It was Henrik Pedersen, but the woman was his mother. He greeted her with a wave and then slowly climbed down from the wagon. He reached up and took the little girl from the back and set her on the ground. Then he took the bundle from his mother and helped her down.

Fear pierced her heart as Mary waited for an explanation. An uneasiness started to build in her stomach. Henrik gave the baby back to his mother and then put an arm around her. "Mary, it's good to see you. How have you been?"

"Aubrey? Where is she, Henrik?" she asked, fearing his answer.

The baby began to cry and Freda Pederson walked away. She rocked him gently in her arms, trying to quiet him. Henrik turned his attention back to her. There were deep lines across his forehead, lines of pain. "Did you not get my letter?"

"What letter? I never received a letter. Where's Aubrey?" She was in a near panic.

Henrik's face pinched and tears flooded his eyes. His lip trembled as he said, "She's gone, Mary. My sweet Aubrey is gone." He broke down and wept.

Mary began to moan, "No, no, no, no." Her denial turned to screams of anguish. "Aubrey! Aubrey! No…God, please, no." She collapsed to her knees and Henrik tried to console her. Joshua stood behind at a distance terrified at what was unfolding. He locked eyes with the little girl and saw only sorrow there. A lone tear escaped her right eye and trickled down her cheek. She clung tightly to a homemade ragdoll.

"I vrote to you telling you vot happened," he tried to explain. "I thought you vould have received it by now." Mary shook her head. She tried to speak, but no words came out, just sobs. Henrik pulled her to her feet and then held her, letting her cry. Softly he began to explain. "Aubrey had a hard time with this pregnancy. She had had a miscarriage before. Ven ve found she vas vith child, ve took precautions. I vouldn't let her do any vork."

Mary's sobs subsided and she pulled back from him. She asked, "She died in childbirth?"

Henrik nodded. The memory was too much for him. He drew in a breath and convulsed as he wept. They embraced again, but neither took any comfort. Mary now understood why his mother had walked away with the baby. It had to be hard to see your son this way. Eventually, Henrik was able to come to the point. "I sent you two letters. I assume that you did not receive the second either."

Mary puzzled over it. She didn't want to think what she was thinking. "What was in the second letter, Henrik?"

Henrik dropped his eyes to the ground. What he was about to ask was the most difficult thing for him, outside of burying his beloved wife. "I need you to take care of my children…Aubrey's children. Mama's health is deteriorating. I'm vorried about her making this trip, but I could never do it by myself. She's not able to take care of them. I can't do it. I have no one." He motioned for the little girl to come to him. Timidly she stood beside her father and Henrik knelt and picked her up. His emotions overtook him again. "Doesn't she look like a miniature Aubrey?" A proud smile spread across his face, but the tears continued. "She vanted her named after you; her name is Mary Katherine. Ve call her Mary Kate."

Mary's lips quivered with emotion. She reached out to take the child from Henrik. At first, the child clung to her father, but he encouraged her to go to Mary. "Hello, Mary Kate. I'm yar Aunt Mary."

The child smiled and then shyly said, "You sound like Mama." That brought new tears to both Mary and Henrik.

Mary invited them into the house and then excused herself to change into a clean dress. When she emerged she apologized for her appearance. "I'm afraid ya caught me cleanin' me house. I was just restin' from scrubbin' the floor."

"I understand," Henrik responded. "They could never say that the O'Shea women vere ever lazy."

Mary smiled softly at the compliment and then offered some refreshments. "I can make some tea or some coffee…"

"Coffee vould be fine," as he checked to make sure it was alright with his mother. The woman nodded in agreement. Mary could see the tiredness in her eyes.

"Would ya like to lie down for awhile?" Mary asked her.

"Oh no. I vouldn't vant to impose."

"Tis no imposition. Let me go and get the cradle so ya can put the baby down." She retrieved the cradle from Joshua's bedroom and then took the child from the woman. She gently placed him in it and then helped the woman into her bedroom. When she returned, she went into the kitchen and put on a pot of coffee and then rejoined Henrik in the sitting room. "So what's the baby's name?"

"Michael, after your father."

She smiled softly. It was just like Aubrey to keep her family close to her.

When James came home, he found a house full of strangers. He was none too happy about it. He grabbed Mary roughly by the arm and abruptly pulled her into the kitchen. "What are all these people doing here?" he asked. There was fire in his eyes.

"They're family," she said quietly, not wanting Henrik to hear their conversation. She tried explaining the situation to him, but in response, he just grunted. Mary couldn't keep her feelings to herself. "But ya already knew that didn't ya," she said harshly. Her voice was firm, but remained just above a whisper. James was taken off guard and just looked at her. She continued her tirade. "What did ya do with me letters?"

"What letters?" he played innocent.

"The ones that Henrik sent to me about me sister."

"I don't know what you're talking about?" He turned from her and went out the back door. He went to the barn to sulk and didn't even come in for supper.

Mary set the food out and they gathered around the small table. She had Henrik bless the meal and then they quietly ate. There was an uncomfortable silence between them. It was broken by Freda Pedersen. "Your husband is not so hospitable."

Quietly Mary made excuses for James. "Tis been a long day for him; he works hard."

"Still, he's too tired to be cordial?"

Henrik reached out his hand and grasped hers. "Mama, please," he said to her.

The woman shook her head in obvious disgust. In a hushed tone she replied to her son, "You vant to bring your children into this situation?" No one said anything. The only sound was the clinking of silverware.

After the meal, Mary readied a place for all of them to sleep. It was a long trip back to Jacksonville and she wanted them to get a good night's sleep and be well rested for the trip in the morning. Of course, the matter of the children had not yet been settled, but in Mary's mind, she had determined they would stay. She didn't care what James did, but they were not being turned away.

She settled Freda Pedersen in her bedroom, putting the cradle in with her. It was not her place to interject herself as his caregiver, at least until the final decision was made. Mary Kate would sleep in Joshua's bed, while Mary made a makeshift bed in the sitting room for Henrik. James, much to his objections, would have to sleep in the barn, along with Mary and their son.

After the three were settled in the hay loft and Joshua had fallen asleep, Mary broached the subject with her husband. The discussion soon became a heated debate between them. Mary pleaded, "They're me family; they're part o' me."

"I am not raising a whore's bastards!" he said a little too loudly; his words were laced with bitterness. Joshua stirred, but didn't open his eyes. He pretended to be asleep while listening to them argue. It wasn't the first time he had feigned sleep to find out what his parents were fighting about. Both stopped momentarily, until they thought he was still asleep.

Mary, against her better judgment, refused to hold her tongue. "They are not bastards; they have a good father. Henrik is a good man, just overwhelmed. He cannot care for them by himself." She should have stopped there, but she didn't. "Besides, nothin' has stopped ya from raisin' this whore's child!"

James' fury was ignited. He grabbed her by the hair, pulling her towards him. His other hand was around her neck so fast that she didn't have a chance to take in a breath. "Don't talk about our son like that." His eyes were coal black in the darkness and Mary felt her blood run cold. Her words had only added fuel to his anger. His grip tightened, sealing off any hope that she could breathe. Mary struggled, beating on his arms, before he finally released his hold. She gasped for breath and rubbed her neck. James then snatched his blanket and moved several feet away from her, lying in the hay with his back to her.

Mary trembled with fear. It had been the closest he had ever come to killing her. He had done other acts of abuse, but he had never gone this far. She rolled over onto her side and curled up beside Joshua. She wasn't sure if she was shielding him or protecting herself. In any case, she took some comfort in it. She didn't realize that her own son was trembling on the inside. He continued to pretend to be asleep, but was much too afraid to doze off.

And sleep would not come easy for Mary either. She wrestled with the events of the day and the decisions that had to be made. She could not let Aubrey's children walk out of her life, but did she dare stand up to James and bring these tiny souls into the midst of their war? Eventually she dozed off, continuing to plead her case to God. She needed an answer by morning. She hoped she'd make the correct decision.

18

Getting Settled In

James refused her any help. He looked hard at her and made it clear that if they stayed, she would have to care for them on her own. To punctuate his point, he declared that he would not be a father to them. After Henrik and his mother left, Mary set about making arrangements for the new additions. Her first priority was getting a bed for Mary Kate and also some things for the baby.

She took some feed sacks, stitched them together and then stuffed them with straw to make a tick for the child to sleep on. At least she would have something soft to lie on until a bed could be constructed. Mary went out to the barn to see if there were any loose boards lying around that she might use. She had studied how Joshua's bed had been constructed and determined that she could replicate the simple design. She found what she needed.

The next day, she cut the boards to size. Then using her husband's tools she was able to dovetail them to form a box. But before she assembled them, she took a hand-drill and carefully drilled out the holes along all four boards. Once the pieces were put together, she nailed the legs to the side rails. Now all she needed was some rope. But as she searched throughout the barn, she could find none that was suitable for the bed. She would have to make a trip to town.

She gathered the children for the trip. She placed the baby inside a sling-like device she had sown together the day before. It allowed her to carry Michael much like a papoose. It freed her arms to carry back the supplies that she needed. She took the small amount of money she had secreted away in the bottom drawer with her Saint Christopher Medal and then they were on their way. Joshua was given strict orders to hold Mary Kate's hand and that she would not listen to any backtalk on his part. Reluctantly he obeyed his mother.

This would be her first trip to town in several weeks. James had lifted her ban simply because life was more difficult for him when he had to do the shopping. She was allowed to come to town, but with strict orders not to speak to anyone. He had ostracized her so much that the only friend she had was Ida Rose. James still didn't know how close they had gotten, although the last few years Ida Rose wasn't able to visit as much. Two additional children had prevented it.

The walk to the mercantile was a little more laborious than she anticipated. Even though Michael was only a few months old, after walking two or three miles with him strapped against her, it winded her a little. She stopped and rested on a tree stump along the way. The children were glad for the short respite as well.

Finally they reached town. As they made their way to the mercantile, Mary noticed a few turned heads in their direction. She wasn't sure if it was from the fact that she rarely came to town or because of the new additions. They climbed the steps up to the porch and then entered through the door. The jingle of the bell that was mounted high on the door brought an outburst of tears from Mary Kate. Mary knelt beside her to see what was wrong. Through sobs, the little girl said, "I miss my Daddy. I want to go home."

Mary had great empathy for her. She drew her into her arms, making sure that she didn't smash the baby. "I know sweetheart. But ya're goin' to stay with us for a little while. Someday, when thin's get a little easier, yar dad will come back for ya. Until then, we'll have a nice long visit. I'll tell ya stories o' when yar mam was a little girl like yarself."

The girl's tears subsided and she calmed down for the moment. Mary straightened herself and took Mary Kate's small hand in hers. She smiled reassuringly at her. The girl briefly returned it, but it quickly disappeared. The transition was going to be a little more difficult than Mary had thought.

They walked to the counter just as the previous customer was about to leave. As she turned, Mary saw that it was old sourpuss herself, Mrs. Cavanaugh. She gave Mary the once over and then looked at the children with a disapproving stare. She turned with her nose elevated to the ceiling and walked out of the store as if she had a bee up her backside.

Curtis Thompson, the owner, couldn't contain himself. He laughed uproariously at the sight. "She's a wonder, isn't she? She thinks she's mightier than the Lord Himself." He turned his attention towards Mary. "It's good to see you, Mrs. Whitaker. It's been awhile. Who do we have here?" he asked looking at the brood that accompanied her.

"Ya know Josh—Jethro here already; this is me sister's children. This is Mary Kate and the baby is Michael."

"They visiting with you?"

"Me sister passed away," she answered softly. "Her husband was havin' a hard time takin' care o' 'em. They will be stayin' with us for a time."

"Oh, I'm sorry about that. I didn't know you had a sister. Were you close?"

Mary nodded. "Like two peas in a pod, we were."

"Did she kind of die all of a sudden?"

"Childbirth." She hadn't intended to share this much information. She hoped James wouldn't find out. He didn't like having their dirty laundry aired. The last thing she wanted was to start another row; it didn't take much to set him off nowadays.

Thompson seemed genuinely sympathetic. "Shame. It happens a lot in these parts. Now what can I get for you today?"

"I need a yard o' linen or muslin, anythin' that would be good to make into nappies."

Thompson looked at her with great curiosity. "Excuse me, but I don't rightly know what a nappy is."

Mary was puzzled at this revelation. Surely he and his wife were familiar with such things. "Ya know what a nappy is, don't ya? Ya fasten it around the baby to…ah…ya know…"

"Oh, you must mean diapers. That's what we call them here. Yeah, I've got some good material for that." He went around the counter and walked over to the bolts of fabric on a shelf. "How's this?" he asked spraying out the material for her to inspect.

She examined it carefully and determined that it would do for what she needed. "That will be fine," she said and Thompson began measuring and cutting the material. "I used to have plenty o' nappies…er diapers from when Jethro was a baby. But over the years, they became cleanin' rags."

"Yeah, that often happens," he answered off-handed, folding the material into a small bundle. "Anything else I can get you?"

"I need some rope, approximately a hundred feet. How much would that be?" When Thompson told her, she had to reconsider; she didn't have enough money. She weighed her options and then said, "I'll hold off on this for a little while. I'll just take the linen."

"Hey, if it's a matter of money, your credit's good here."

"Thank ya for yar kindness, but I cannot allow meself to be indebted to anyone. She paid for the material and then ushered the children outside. They stood on the porch as she gathered some courage to face James. She hoped that he would give her what she needed and not make a scene in front of his employees. More than likely, she would have to deal with the ramifications later.

She trotted down the steps with Joshua and Mary Kate in tow. She went straight way to the sawmill, but as she approached, Mary noticed that James' buckboard was nowhere to be seen. She surmised that it must have been needed to haul lumber somewhere. The loud whine of the saw blade could be heard. It shrieked as a piece of lumber was forced into the turning blade. Just outside the door, Mary stopped the children, giving them strict orders not to leave their spot until she returned. "There are far too many dangers in this place to have two children rummagin' around. So stay put!"

Mary went inside and found the place in a flurry of activity. At first, no one seemed to notice her. One man nearly bumped into her with a long board. He started to tell her in no uncertain terms that she needed to leave, but at the last second, he recognized the boss's wife. He apologized profusely for his clumsiness. This caught the attention of James' foreman, Luke Myers. He immediately approached her and then led her into James' office, where it was a little quieter.

The first thing out of his mouth was, "James isn't here." There was alarm written all over him, like a school boy caught playing hooky. "He's…he's over at Willard's Crossing—on business." The man's face was flushed, but not from work; he wasn't a particularly good liar.

"Oh, I see," Mary replied. She was caught unaware. All kinds of thoughts began to circulate in her mind. She was surprised that she actually had a momentary pang of jealousy and a sense of betrayal. It wasn't out of love loss, but merely out of humiliation. She wondered how many of his employees knew about this *business* he was engaged in. They were probably all laughing at her ignorance and stupidity. She shook her head and laughed bitterly to herself at the irony of the whole mess. He condemns me for me past, yet he'll go and spend time with some trollip.

Trying to downplay it, she said, "Makes no never mind. I just came down to see if ya might have some rope that ya could spare. I'm makin' a rope bed for me niece."

Myers seemed perplexed. "Shouldn't James be making that for you?"

Mary diverted her eyes. "He's far too busy to do that."

Myers didn't say anything right away. A feeling of indignation came over him. He didn't like how James had been behaving and he certainly didn't like the harsh things he said about his wife. He wasn't even sure if he believed any of it. He toyed with a notion that would probably get him in the doghouse with James.

"We've got some in the backroom that's never been used. How much do you need?"

"I reckon a hundred feet will do nicely," she replied.

Myers went back into the room and came carrying out a heavy roll of it. "You can't be totting that back to the farm by yourself. It's much too heavy. Let me take you home and then maybe I can help you string it."

"Oh, I couldn't take ya from yar work. What would James say?"

"Hang him," he said in disgust. "He should be doing this for you."

It was a pleasant surprise that someone was actually taking her side for a change, but knowing James, she would be the one that was hung.

Myers took Mary and the children back home. She hoped no tongues wagged over this. She didn't need local gossip stirring the pot anymore than it already was. During the trip, Myers didn't say a whole lot, but continued to seem a bit agitated. Mary eventually broke the silence. "Ya know, ya didn't have to do this," Mary said trying to let him off the hook. "As a matter o' fact, ya could just let us walk the rest o' the way. I wouldn't want ya gettin' into trouble with James."

"I *won't* get into trouble," he said emphatically. He worked the muscles in his jaw as he contemplated whether he should say more. He set a steady gaze on the road and held his peace. When they got to the farm, Myers took the rope and commenced working on the bed. "This is a fine frame, Mrs. Whitaker. You do good work. Ever think of getting into furniture making?"

"Not really. I have enough work around here as it is."

The two worked together weaving the rope through the holes she had previously drilled into the side rails. Then they laced the rope the other way alternating it up and down, creating a checkerboard design. The children seemed fascinated at first, but soon the novelty wore off. They ended up going outside and playing for awhile. Mary and Myers were alone to finish their work.

Once the ropes were secure, Mary went into her bedroom and retrieved the straining wrench that they used from time to time on their bed. It was a funny sort of thing, looking like a giant clothes pin only it had a handle sticking through it near the top. Myers took it and put it through the rope and used the handle to twist the wrench. While holding the rope taut, he jammed an awl into the hole to hold the tension while he continued to tighten the next length of rope. He repeated this until he reached the end. It was a long, tedious process, but it was finally done. Mary then took the tick she had made and put it on the frame. She was satisfied with the results.

"Thank ya for all yar help," she said with great gratitude. "I don't think I could have finished this by meself."

"You're welcome. I was glad that I could help." He diverted his eyes and nervously pawed at the wooden floor, struggling with what was on his mind. Eventually he decided to speak his peace. "It's not right how James treats you. You deserve better."

Mary's mouth dropped open. She didn't know what to say. It was the last thing she had expected to hear. "What do ya know about this?"

Myers lowered his voice. "I know that he's not on *business*." As soon as the words left his mouth he wished he could pull them back. He furrowed his brow and set his jaw once again. "I shouldn't have said anything."

"Ya did right. Thin's haven't been right between us since the very beginnin'."

"Why, if you don't mind me asking? I would think James would be honored to be married to someone like you."

Mary hung her head in shame and said, "Let's just say that I've done some thin's that James has never forgiven me o' and probably never will."

Myers shook his head. "That's not very Christian of him in my book," he said with disdain.

"Christian or not, God *will* judge his actions," she said sadly.

Myers drew in a breath and slowly let it out. He momentarily took off his hat to scratch his slightly balding head and then replaced it. With empathy he said, "I just hope that one day, for his sake he comes to terms with whatever demons he's been fighting. He ain't been right since his brother died. I thought marrying you would help."

"Well, if anythin' it just exasperated the situation. I was not the wife that he had hoped for." She looked him straight way in the face and Myers studied her, searching for clues to what she meant, but none came. He shook his head, not knowing what more to say. "Ya know it would be best if ya left. I wouldn't want people findin' out that ya were here all alone with me. And I certainly wouldn't want yar lovely wife to be findin' out, especially if me past came out."

Myers looked at her dumbfounded. What could she have possibly done that would bring such condemnation? He ran his hand over his mouth and mustache trying to think of something encouraging to say, but nothing came. Reluctantly he said, "I guess you're right; I best be on my way."

Mary nodded and then thanked him once again. She walked him to his wagon and watched him drive away until he disappeared behind the hill.

That night, James came home acting as innocent as a dove. Mary waited for the fallout from Myers helping her. But James never said a word about it. She hoped that it would quietly be swept under the rug and he would be none the wiser.

She put the evening's meal on the table and called the children to supper. James sat down abruptly at the head of the table; his mood had suddenly soured. It nearly broke Mary's heart when she turned and saw him staring daggers at the little girl. A fury ignited inside her, but she pushed it down, not wanting to start a melee in front of the children. She tried to keep Mary Kate from seeing the hatred he directed towards her.

"Here love," she said to her as she spooned out some creamed potatoes for her. "This will put some meat on yar bones." She smiled sweetly at the girl who shyly returned it. She dished out some for Joshua and then sat down, waiting until James had his fair share before getting some for herself.

James looked crossways at her; his animosity was growing. "I noticed that you fed the girl first before you did our own son."

"Ladies first," she said simply.

James grunted in reply. He ate, but continued to glare at the girl with contempt. Mary's indignation had just about reached the boiling point. She was about to say something when little Michael began to cry. She rushed from the table and went to him. She returned with the baby cradled in one arm. Then with her free hand, she poured some cow's milk into a bottle and fitted it with a glass nipple. The baby immediately sucked on it to get some nourishment. Mary was thankful that Henrik had left these strange looking containers. They served well as a substitute, but it still wasn't the same as receiving mother's milk.

She gently rocked him in her arms and began to sing a lullaby. *"Sleep me child and peace attend thee, all through the night. Guardian angels God will send thee, all through the night. Soft the drowsy hours are creepin'. Hill and vale in slumber sleepin'. I me lovin' vigil keepin'. All through the night."*

Mary's gentle voice seemed to soothe the child. He made little cooing sounds as he sucked on the bottle. It brought a tender smile to her face. After a short time, she put the bottle down and placed the baby against herself, gently patting him on the back until he produced a burp. "Oh that was a good one," she said softly. "Do ya have another one for yar Aunt Mary?"

James couldn't take the cutesy scene anymore. "Do you have to talk that way?"

"I'm tryin' to calm the baby," she said firmly.

James erupted, "You know, I'm sick of your insolence and I'm sick of that stupid sing-song accent of yours." Both Joshua and Mary Kate suddenly became fearful; the little girl began to whimper.

Mary tried to keep her temper. She answered quietly, but resolutely, "I'm sorry, but that's the only way I know how to talk. I cannot help that I am Irish."

"Well, you're the one that lied about that didn't you?"

Mary tried to calm Mary Kate and keep the situation from getting worse. She thought about how it had all been Ellingson's fault, but said nothing in her defense. The baby started crying once again. James couldn't take the noise any longer. He got up from the table and stormed out of the house. Mary was sure that he went to the barn to cool off. It suited her just fine. She hoped that he would stay there all night and give her some peace.

She got the children quieted down, but at this point Joshua and Mary Kate were no longer interested in their food. After she got Michael fed and put to bed, she got the other two tucked in as well. When she was finally ready to turn in herself, she glanced out the window towards the barn. The faint light of a lantern was glowing inside. She was contented to know that James would more than likely sleep in the barn. She changed into her gown and turned out the oil lamp and drifted off to sleep.

Sometime in the middle of the night, she was suddenly awakened. James had returned and was exceedingly intoxicated. He was on top of her before she knew it. "You're not a bad looking woman for a whore," he said spewing the noxious smell of alcohol with every syllable. Mary trembled violently. She had experienced this far too many times. Once inebriated, he expected her to fulfill her wifely duties even if taken by force. James eyes were wild with anger and lust. "With your looks you must have made a lot of money selling yourself. So why did you have to steal my money to come to this country?" He grabbed her by the jaw and squeezed hard, hurting her. He let go, kissed her hard on the mouth and then said, "I think I'll take some of my money back."

At times, Mary was sure that her life would end with him killing her. She braced herself for what came next. Like on so many other nights, she let him have his way. Afterwards she felt ashamed and dirty. In her prayers, she cried out before the Lord, *"How long Father? How long must I endure this? If this is all that You have in store for me, then take me now. I don't know how much more I can bear. Please, be merciful and just end it now. Let me fall asleep and awake in Yar lovin' arms, Lord."*

But when Mary awoke, she found that she was still living a nightmare.

19

A Day of Surprises

As spring rolled into summer, things improved slightly. Mary figured that James couldn't continue his detestation for Aubrey's children; it took too much energy. In time his hatred turned to tolerance, but she could never see him as being a real father to them. She assumed that his dalliances with whoever had caught his fancy, was still continuing. There were days when he came home in a little better mood than others and didn't seem to mind the children. But those were often the days he was the shortest with her. It seemed that he could do whatever he wanted, but as for her, he would never forgive her.

Recently, James found a new cross to bear. The talk in town was that Mary had an affair with the same man she rode into town with. The two children she was now caring for belonged to him. That's why she kept to the farm so much and why James was so out of sorts of late. The father must have taken the children, but recently, for some reason returned them to her. Mary sarcastically wondered who could have started that rumor. Only one person was vile enough—Mrs. Cavanaugh. Ida Rose tried to set the story straight, but in the end, people believed what they wanted to believe.

At first, the rumor had infuriated James. Even though none of it was true, he still felt humiliated. But then a strange thing happened. People began to sympathize with his dilemma and he took on the persona of a martyr. He figured that someday he might use that to his advantage. So, James put on his mask of piety and rode off to church with Joshua. Mary stayed at home and worshiped as best she could. After he left, she lit some candles she had placed on the kitchen table and knelt before them, crossing herself as she did. Little Mary Kate was beside her, learning the Catholic way. She too knelt and crossed herself and they bowed their heads as Mary began her confession.

"Bless me, Father, for I have sinned. It has been a whole week since me last confession. I have had bad thoughts about me husband and have even said some disparagin' thin's under me breath a couple o' times." She paused to think if there might be more and then she added, "And I've lost me temper more than I can count. Please grant Yar forgiveness for I am sorry for what I have done and truly repent."

Mary Kate began her confession afterwards. Mary had recently taken to calling her by her middle name, much like Joshua. It was like a game to the children and it made them feel special. The truth was, Mary felt a little embarrassed to have a *daughter* named after her. She smiled softly at the girl as Katherine made her confession. "*I took away a toy that Joshua was playing with. It didn't belong to me. I'm sorry.*" She looked up at Mary and smiled sweetly. Suddenly, she frowned and bowed her head once more. "*Forgive me, Father, for I sometimes think badly about Uncle James.*"

This revelation tore at Mary's heart. She pulled her into her arms and held her. "I'm sure that our Father will forgive ya o' that, child. Yar Uncle is not an easy man to live with."

The child drew back from her and asked, "Why can't we go to church with Uncle James and Joshua? Mommy and Daddy and Grandma always went together."

Mary took in a breath and tried to find a way to tell her, remembering the previous conversation with Joshua about it. She simply said, "Uncle James prefers it this way." Katherine didn't understand, but asked no further questions of her. Mary confessed that there were many times she didn't understand either. Before they concluded their service, Mary recited a few Scriptures that she had put to memory and then said a concluding prayer. She got to her feet and with the little girl's assistance, blew out the candles; it was Katherine's favorite part. She giggled and then ran off to play with her ragdoll that Aubrey had made for her. Mary put the candles away to be used next Sunday. She looked out the kitchen window and wondered if God really heard her prayers and forgave her. All she had was hope.

August came and it was unbearably hot. Temperatures were generally tolerable year round whether it was summer or winter. But a scorching wind had come up unexpectantly from the south. It was hot and dry, withering all the crops in the valley. Everyone hoped for rain soon. Mary and the children made their weekly trip into town. Joshua, thinking he was bigger than he was, offered to carry the basket of eggs, while Mary carried the blocks of butter in a satchel slung over her shoulder. Michael, who was growing like a weed, was still carried in his sling. She had to admit that since carrying the child on these weekly trips, her stamina was being built up.

When they arrived at the mercantile, they found the place abuzz with excitement. A group of ladies of various ages, but mostly young, had surrounded a young man that Mary had never seen before. She found this to be a little disturbing and wished she had chosen another day to come to town. While all the clamor was going on, Mr. Thompson tried to wait on her.

"Noisy, aren't they?" he shouted above the din.

"What's all the fuss?" she asked, trying to be heard. "Is he someone famous?"

"Nah. Just the new school teacher; he's single you know," he said, tilting his head towards the rabble of young women that were already enamored by him.

"Not for long it appears," Mary said and then got down to business. Thompson gave her cash money for the items she brought in. He had tried years ago to just have her credit the money to an account, but she wouldn't hear of it. She liked the tangibility of having it in the palm of her hand. Besides, she had a fear that somehow James would get control of it once again and she would never see any of it. She hid it away in case of an emergency or more likely when James sent her packing.

She collected her money and then returned a portion of it, buying essentials. As an afterthought she splurged and bought the children each a piece of penny candy. It was worth the added expense when she saw their eyes light up. By this time, some of the clamor had died down. Most of the mothers had rescued the teacher by escorting their daughters away. The teacher was most grateful for the reprieve. With the shortage of women in this part of the world, he never dreamed that he would end up being the center of so much attention. As the crowd petered away, his attention was drawn to Mary.

"Oh, just the person I wanted to talk to," he said to her.

Mary, looked around thinking he must have meant someone else, but there was no one behind her. Bewildered she asked, "Are ya talkin' to me?"

The man's smiled broadly and announced, "What a wonderful accent! Irish, isn't it?"

Mary was taken aback and stumbled to find her words. "Tha-that it would be."

"Marvelous. I have relatives from there. Allow me to introduce myself. I'm Evan Sullivan, the new school teacher."

"That I heard," she said and then got to the point. "I am Mary Whitaker. Now why would ya be wantin' to speak to me?"

He raised his eyebrows in astonishment. "Well, for your children of course. They are of school age, I assume."

"Josh—Jethro would be, but Katherine is still too young."

He nodded and said, "Then I can count on you sending him to school?"

"We will see; it will be up to his dad if he will be allowed," she answered, just wanting to get out the door. Something about his forwardness made her nervous.

Before Mary could make her exit, Mr. Thompson called to her. "Hey, Mrs. Whitaker, I almost forgot; I've got something for you. It came on the evening stage. It's addressed to you." He handed a small package wrapped in brown paper and tied with string.

She hesitantly took it from him and stared at it. "Wonder whatever it could be?"

"There's only one way to find out and that's to open it," Mr. Sullivan said jokingly.

She shot him a look of disdain for his brashness. She was in no hurry to open it. The last time she got unexpected mail it had met with disastrous consequences. She tucked the package under her arm along with the things she had purchased and thanked Mr. Thompson. Then she said to both of them, "Good day gentlemen."

But as she started out the door, Mr. Sullivan stopped her. "Here, let me carry those things to your wagon." He took her parcels, before she could make a formal objection and then was outside holding the door open for her. He looked around and saw no sign of a buggy or wagon other than his own carriage. "Where's your wagon, Mrs. Whitaker."

"I'm afraid me husband has it; we walked here," she said a little perturbed at him.

He looked crestfallen as he thought for a resolution to their dilemma. Snapping his fingers at his new inspiration, he said, "I can take all of you home."

"That is not necessary; just give me back me packages," she said, reaching for them.

"No, no. This will give me an opportunity to get to know some of the townspeople," he said with a twinkle in his greenish-blue eyes.

"Ya had plenty o' people in the store that ya could have gotten to know better. Please give me, me packages."

"No," he said playfully keeping them from her. "Those aren't the type of people that I want to meet—at least for now. I'm talking about getting to know parents, like yourself. I believe that when I get to know them better, they'll be more accepting of sending their children to school. So please, assist me as I assist you."

Reluctantly, she gave in. Mr. Sullivan helped Katherine and then Joshua into the carriage. He started to help Mary, but she balked. "I can do it meself," she proclaimed and then struggled to get in. The extra weight of Michael strapped to the front did not help. Mr. Sullivan gently grabbed her by the waist and gave her that extra bit that she needed. "I told ya, I can do it meself," she said more out of embarrassment than disgust.

"I can see," he simply said, shaking his head in amusement. He then went to the other side and climbed in. He asked her which direction and she pointed straight ahead. With a snap of the reins, they took down the road. A gaggle of onlookers stared as they drove by.

Mary sulked and then said, "Ya know, ya probably shouldn't be seen with me. I don't have the best reputation around her."

"Oh really? That intrigues me," he said playfully. "What dastardly deed did you do to earn such a reputation?"

She looked at him crossways and replied, "Never ya mind."

He threw his head back and laughed enthusiastically as they continued down the road with a cloud of dust trailing behind them. After a pause in the conversation he asked, "So what's in the package?"

"It be none o' yar business," she answered resoundingly.

"Ah, come on; what's in the package?"

She picked it and turned it over in her hands. A million thoughts ran through her mind. Could it be something from Ellingson? What could he be sending her now? But it was addressed to her, not James this time. She felt the package again. It wasn't large, but it had some weight to it. A sudden realization came to her and she began to rip the paper and string off its contents. Inside, she discovered what she had hoped—it was a book. But this wasn't just any book to Mary. She was sure that it was from her beloved Robert after all these years. She wished that she could read so she would at least know the title of it.

Mr. Sullivan's curiosity continued. He leaned over just enough to read, "The Two Sisters by Robert Timmons. Is this a book you sent away for?"

"A dear friend wrote it," she replied, smiling faintly. She rubbed her hand across the cover, gently caressing it. It was the first book she had ever owned. Absently she said, "I wish I could read it."

Her confession stunned him. It never ceased to amaze Sullivan how few people knew how to read. He realized how fortunate he was to have parents that believed in the importance of it. "Can I see it?" Mary fearfully looked at him as if he was asking to hold her precious bag of gold. Reluctantly she allowed him to have it. "Here, take the reins," he said taking the book from her.

Sullivan paged through the book stopping at the dedication page. He read it aloud. *"To the lovely O'Shea sisters that made this book possible. Thank you for the delightful trip across the Isthmus and beyond. I'll never forget you for I carry you around in my heart."* Sullivan looked up at her and said, "Nice dedication; is this you?"

"He was a good friend," she said sadly. "He helped me get here."

Sullivan nodded. He perused the book again and this time an envelope fell out. "What's this?" he said picking it up. "It says, *To Mary*. Do you want me to read it to you?"

Mary hesitated. Did she want a stranger to read such a personal letter? She certainly didn't want James to read it to her. Maybe Ida Rose would be better. Then again, she was her only ally. Would she remain her friend after reading the letter? She concluded that he was probably her best option. Giving her consent, Sullivan ripped open the envelope and carefully unfolded the letter. He looked it over and then began to read.

"*My dearest Mary,*

How I've missed you. Forgive me for taking so long to write this book. Every time I sat down and took pen to paper, the memories of you overwhelmed my soul and I could no longer continue." Sullivan glanced over at Mary and saw tears in her eyes. He felt great compassion for the woman and wondered if this had anything to do with the comment about her reputation. He continued. "*I spent the last few years immersing myself in other projects, waiting for the pain of our separation to subside. It has to some degree, but I have to admit that in my travels, I have never come across anyone quite like you. You are a precious jewel that should be treated as such. I hope that your husband realizes what he has…*"

Mary stopped the horses for fear that her clouded vision would cause her to wreck. A quiet sob escaped from her and she reached inside the left sleeve of her dress to retrieve her handkerchief. Sullivan's jaw dropped as he witnessed her reaction. He wanted to comfort her, but knew it was inappropriate. She looked intensely at the stranger and said, "Tis not entirely what ya thinkin' but I would appreciate if ya kept this to yarself."

Sullivan obediently nodded. He continued reading. "*By now, I am sure that you have a whole brood of children and are perfectly happy. I wish you the best. Enjoy the book. It is not exactly yours and Aubrey's story, but still I think it captures the spirit of your lives. Unfortunately the world is not ready to hear your story. I'm afraid that it might not be too sympathetic to the truth. I sent a copy to Aubrey. I'm sure that her husband* will read it to her. There's nothing that might be unsettling for those two. I'm also sure that by now you are able to read..."

Sullivan paused, not sure if he should continue reading such a private letter. But through unabated tears, Mary urged him on. "*You have a tremendous amount of determination that will never let anything stand in your way of accomplishing what you set out to do. By the way, you may not want your husband to read the book. It might stir up some hard feelings, since I embellished the story between us a bit. Don't worry; I changed the names to protect you. Take care my love. You will always be in my thoughts.*

Your loving servant, Robert."

Sullivan carefully folded the letter, reinserted it in its envelope and then handed it to her. Softly he said, "It's quite a letter. He must have meant a lot to you."

"That he did," she said barely able to talk. She tucked the letter inside the book and cradled it against her.

"He's right. You shouldn't let your husband see the book and most definitely not the letter."

"Please, don't mention this to *anyone.*"

"Your secret is safe with me," he said giving her a reassuring smile.

"Is this what ya had in mind when ya said ya wanted to get to know the parents in the community?" she quipped.

He chuckled and replied, "Not exactly." Then he took the reins from her and continued down the road to the farm, neither saying much more. At the farm he helped her down, against her protests of course. He saw firsthand that determination or more like stubbornness that seemed to endear her lover. Then he helped the children down. But before he left, he gave one final plea, "Think about sending the boy to school. You know the importance of knowing how to read and write."

"That would be up to me husband; he makes the decisions." Sullivan nodded and then rode back up the hill and out of sight.

Mary spent the afternoon mourning over the book. She had a hole in her heart that seemed unbearable. She leafed through it hoping to see something recognizable, but all she saw was the repetition of letters that made no sense to her. Still she treasured it. Her beloved Robert had written it; had held it in his hand. She lifted it to her nose and drank in the scent hoping that she could smell him. But instead all she smelled was paper and ink.

Reluctantly, she hid it away in the bottom drawer of their dresser with a few of her other keepsakes, like her Saint Christopher's medal. She took it out, remembering the priest that gave it to her. It gave way to memories of the trip around the Isthmus and of San Francisco. Fresh tears fell that dissolved into sobs of sorrow. How she wished she could go back and change the outcome. She put the medal back in its place and tried to regain her composure. She needed to check on the children and start supper. James would be home soon and she didn't want to try to explain her demeanor to him. She only hoped she'd be able to explain her carriage ride with the new teacher before the rest of the town did.

She had a hot supper waiting on him. She had fed Michael and put him to bed already. It seemed the best solution to keep the child from upsetting James. She didn't know what to do when he got a little older. She would just have to figure it out then. She had once tried feeding Katherine, before he got home, so that she would not offend him by sitting at the table. But that didn't work out so well. He accused her once again of favoritism; feeding the child before her own son. As the meal concluded, she dismissed the children to have a private talk with James. She told him about the new teacher and how he insisted on taking her and the children home as a neighborly gesture.

James was sarcastically amused. "Did you tell him about your past and offer him your services."

Her eyes narrowed. "I only offer those services to ya," she said regretting it as soon as she said it. It was greeted with a backhand across the mouth. Mary felt the irony taste of blood in her mouth and took her handkerchief to wipe it away. "I did tell him that associatin' with me might tarnish his reputation." With that, James chuckled in agreement. She got up from the table and walked over to the hand pump. Wetting her handkerchief, she put it against her upper lip that was beginning to swell. "The teacher wants us to send Jethro to school."

James grunted and then said, "He doesn't need to go to school. That's your responsibility. You teach him to read and write."

Mary looked him squarely in the eye. "I cannot."

"What do you mean? Are you too stupid to do it or just lazy?"

"I cannot teach what I do not know," she said firmly.

James blinked. He wasn't sure that he understood her right. "What do you mean? What about all those letters?"

"They were all written by Marcus Ellin'son. He was to write what I told him to write, but obviously he did not. He read all o' yar letters to me. For his services, I had to do things—for him. He was paid in full. Then he was supposed to help me get to America, but in the end, he took yar money and left me high and dry."

James stared at her. He fumbled for words to say and finally said, "Wh-why didn't you tell me this?"

Mary looked at him with contempt. "Because ya would not listen to me. Besides, would it have made any difference?"

He hung his head and said, "Probably not."

There was an uncomfortable silence between them. Mary weighed whether to tell him more about what she went through to get to the Pacific Northwest to be his wife, but then thought what use was it? Too much time had passed and the bottom line had not changed. She was still a whore in his eyes. She asked, "So what's yar decision about the boy? Can he go to school or not?" James was giving it some consideration when she added, "It would mean that he would be away from me most o' the day. I would think ya would like that idea."

James nodded and said, "You're right. He can go to school."

20

The First Day

The morning awoke to beautiful sunshine and a clear blue sky. Ordinarily a day like this would lift the lowest of spirits, but for a six year old boy facing his first day of school, nothing would come close to that. Joshua Jethro Whitaker was feeling an intense despair. He'd rather spend the whole day cleaning out the barn from rafters to dusty ground than to endure the scrutiny of a school teacher, no matter how nice he initially seemed. He spent the morning dawdling instead of getting ready. To make matters worse, his mother was making him wear his Sunday best clothes and shine his shoes. It was almost more than he could bear.

"Aw Mama, why do I have to get dressed up? None of the other guys will be," he protested loudly.

"I want ya to get off on the right foot today with yar teacher," Mary said.

Joshua looked down at his feet in bewilderment. "On the *right* foot?" he questioned.

Mary ran a brush through his hair, trying to flatten his unruly hair. It seemed to stick out everywhere. "I *mean* that I want ya to make a good impression and not be known as a troublemaker."

Joshua was relieved. "I thought you wanted me to hop all day. I don't think I could make a very good impression doing that."

Mary chuckled as she put the brush down and then cradled his head in her hands. "I'm proud o' ya, lad. Ya're the light o' me life and I love ya more than I could ever say." She kissed him on the forehead and hugged him fiercely, not wanting to let go of him. Unexpected tears came and she tried to keep them from falling and betraying her. The day was going to be harder for her than for him. She let go of Joshua and said, "Now get ya thin's together; we need to get goin' or ya'll be late."

The long walk into town took longer than normal. Joshua acted as if he was on a death march. Each step took him closer to the inevitable. Mary shifted Michael in his sling. He had already outgrown the first one and she stitched together a larger one. She held onto Katherine's hand as she craned around to see her son scooting his feet across the dusty road. So much for the polished shoes.

They finally reached town and were greeted with a great deal of excitement. A crowd of mothers with their children had gathered at the church; it was serving as the new schoolhouse. As they reached the bottom step, Mary started up with Katherine. She glanced back at Joshua. He stood on the first step looking painfully up at the building. A couple of mothers walked briskly past him and up the steps, dragging their children behind them.

"Come on lad," Mary coaxed him. "Ya don't want to be late for yar first day." Joshua screwed his face and reluctantly climbed the steps. When he reached the top step, Mary knelt before him. Her heart went out to him. He looked so small and frail compared to the other boys. She tried to smile reassuringly. "Ya know it be only natural to be feelin' a little afraid."

"I'm not afraid," he protested vehemently.

"Joshua Jethro, don't ya be lyin' to me," she retorted. The boy dropped his head and apologized. Mary put her hand under his chin and lifted his head. "Courage is being afraid, but choosin' to face yar fears instead o' runnin' from them. Ya need to remember that fear does not come from God, but from the enemy. When ya give into the fear, ya're puttin' more faith in the enemy than ya're trustin' in God. Bear in mind what the Good Book tells us: *God has not given us a spirit o' fear, but o' power and o' love and o' a sound mind.* And don't forget what God told yar namesake…"

"Be strong and very courageous," Joshua finished her thought. He had heard her tell the story often enough.

"And ya know what God did for *that* Joshua?"

"He brought down the walls of Jericho."

"And He handed the city over to the Israelites. If He'll do that for him, think about what He'll do for ya when ya're in need o' Him."

"Yes ma'am," he said politely. He could feel his confidence beginning to swell under his mother's encouragement. A faint smiled curled up on his lips.

Mary slowly got to her feet. "Now lad, be brave and march right in there like a soldier in God's army." She kissed him on the forehead, which embarrassed him. He quickly looked around to see if anyone took notice of it. Fortunately everyone else was caught up in their own dramas and Joshua wasn't alone in his experience. Some of the older boys were putting up a big pretense of bravery, but deep down they were just as apprehensive as everyone else. Joshua turned from his mother and started into the school. He briefly hesitated, staring up at the building again. He had been inside this place hundreds of times, but somehow this was different. He said a silent prayer, took a deep breath and bravely went inside, trusting that God would knock down any walls he might encounter on this day.

Mary shifted Michael slightly in his sling and then took Katherine by the hand. They started down the steps, as she silently said her own prayer. *"Thank Ya Lord, for Yar words o' encouragement to Joshua. I could never have thought them up meself."*

Inside, Joshua scanned the room looking for a place to sit. His eyes were as wide as saucers. He tried to swallow, but it felt like a large rock had lodged itself in his throat. His mouth had gone dry, chasing any hopes that he would have enough saliva to remove the lump. He continued walking forward until he found an empty seat near the front and sat down. He nervously fiddled with the old biscuit tin he held in his lap. It contained a small lunch his mother had placed inside.

Mr. Sullivan, who had been making the rounds outside, meeting some of the parents, finally came inside the classroom. He addressed the students and immediately went about collecting names for the attendance. When he came to Joshua, he said, "Ah, the Whitaker boy; what's your first name again?"

Without even thinking he answered boldly, "Joshua." But then he thought better of it; he didn't dare cross his father. "I mean Jethro." His face suddenly burst into a deep red.

Some of the other children snickered. Mr. Sullivan was a little annoyed at their behavior. He quickly established order by rapping a ruler on the top of the desk. "Here, here," he said. "Quiet down." He turned to the small boy with the turned down face. "So which is it, Joshua or Jethro?"

"Jethro," he mumbled.

A red haired boy with freckles, sitting across the aisle, piped in, "It's Joshua to *his* mother." He said it in a mocking tone. Other kids began to snicker and Mr. Sullivan had to once again call the class to order. Joshua sunk lower in his seat wishing that he had never left home this morning.

"Mmmm," Mr. Sullivan began. "If I remember my Bible correctly, these are two fine names. Let me see, Joshua, I believe means *the Lord saves*, while Jethro means *His excellence*. Now which do you prefer?"

Quietly he murmured, "Joshua, but you better call me Jethro. My dad likes me to be called that."

The corners of Mr. Sullivan's mouth faintly curled upwards. "Well *Joshua*, I'll be sure to refer to you as *Jethro* whenever I speak to your father." Joshua blinked and then looked at his teacher with great astonishment. It was as if Mr. Sullivan understood the situation he was in. The teacher's smile broadened and he gave the boy a wink of encouragement. Joshua sat up straighter in the pew with a renewed sense of trust. Then Mr. Sullivan addressed the boy sitting behind him.

Mary and Katherine walked over to the mercantile. She hadn't brought any goods to sell, but she did have a small amount of money to make a few purchases. On the way there, she ran into Ida Rose who was carrying her youngest in her arms and had another close to her side.

She spotted little Michael's sling and exclaimed, "What a clever idea! I need to make one of those. Where did you get the idea for it?"

"I saw some Umpquas go across our property awhile back. A couple o' women had somethin' similar that they carried their babies in. It seemed a good idea, so I put this together. It makes carryin' things home easier."

"I'll say. Hey, I saw you bring Jethro to school this morning. Have any trouble getting him to go?"

"A small amount, but he came through at the end. I'm sure he'll do fine."

Ida Rose shook her head slowly. "I've got my whole gaggle of kids there; only have these two still at home. The home place is going to seem awful quiet today."

"I reckon so," she answered, not really wanting to think about returning home just yet. Even though she still had Katherine and Michael to keep her company, Joshua was the one that she had come to depend on. He was always good for running and toting things for her.

They started up the steps of the mercantile and Mary was about to reach for the doorknob, when someone swung the door inward. With the additional weight of Michael, it threw her off balance and she had to steady herself on the doorframe. The young man standing in the doorway instinctively reached out and caught her by her left arm.

"I'm so sorry," he apologized, his forehead wrinkled with concern. "I didn't see you coming. Are you alright?"

Mary felt more than a little foolish. Her face glowed with embarrassment. "I am fine," she said not wanting to make eye contact. "I just lost me balance."

"Again, I apologize," he said earnestly.

"There is no need to apologize; no damage was done," she insisted. Mary finally looked up at him and felt a familiarity about him like they had met before. She noted that he was a nice looking man about her age. He had dark blonde hair and shoe-button eyes with the longest eyelashes she had ever seen on a man. When he smiled, it created a dimple on his left cheek. But it was his dark eyes that seemed to draw her in as if there was some strange connection between them.

"Good morning, Reverend," Ida Rose said, snapping Mary out of her déjà vu trance.

The young man tipped his hat and said, "Oh, hello Mrs. Beecham. How are you this morning?"

"Just fine," she answered. "Have you met Mrs. Whitaker yet?"

The reverend turned his attention back to Mary. "I don't believe that I have had the pleasure before this day."

Ida Rose made the formal introductions. "Mary, this is Reverend Seth Matthews. He's our new minister."

"New minister? What brin's ya out here to the wilderness o' Oregon?"

"My bishop, mainly," he quipped. "But seriously, I believe God has sent me here for a reason." Mary nodded politely. The reverend suddenly cocked his head and asked, "Mrs. Whitaker? Are you related to James by any chance?"

"He's me husband," she answered quietly. There was no presence of pride involved in her answer.

"Oh, I see." He narrowed his eyes and said, "But I don't remember seeing you Sunday. I hope you were not feeling under the weather?"

Mary quickly lowered her eyes. She didn't really want to get into this with the young man. "I don't attend with me husband," she said softly. She felt scrutinizing eyes on her and a flame of anger ignited in her. For some strange reason she blurted out, "Ya see, I'm Catholic." When she raised her head to meet his eyes with an equal intensity, she only found compassion and not condemnation. It immediately disarmed her fury.

He smiled sweetly and said, "I know a lot of good Catholics that went on to be good Methodists." Mary looked at him with bewilderment. "My mother for one; she was Catholic before my father convinced her to marry him." His smile broadened making his dimple deepen. Something about his demeanor made her nervous; it was as if he were looking into her soul. He offered his hand to her even though it wasn't proper etiquette for a man to initiate a handshake with a woman. She shook it politely. Then he turned his attention to the baby. "And who do we have here?" he asked, shaking the tiny hand of Michael, who squealed in response.

"This is me nephew, Michael and his sister Katherine." Reverend Matthews knelt to say hello to the little girl. She shyly turned away from him and buried her face in Mary's dress as if to hide. Mary reached down and patted her softly to console her.

"Well, it was good meeting all of you. Hope to see you in church real soon," he said, addressing Mary. She nodded out of politeness, not agreement. He touched the brim of his hat and said, "Ida Rose, it was good seeing you. You have a blessed day."

"You too, Reverend," she replied as he trotted down the steps of the store and then climbed into his carriage. He turned the buggy around and then went on his way.

Mary stated, "He's a little young to be a minister, isn't he?"

"Yeah...well, they have to start sometime. Anyway, he may seem young, but he's pretty knowledgeable about the Bible. You ought to come and hear him preach."

Mary narrowed her eyes towards Ida Rose. "Now ya know I can't do that. James won't allow it."

"Why? Just because you're Catholic? We're worshiping the same God, you know. Besides, what can James do to you if you come? You know he wouldn't do anything in front of the congregation; it would make him look too bad."

"He can take away me son," Mary said somberly. She turned her eyes away from her friend to hide her tears.

Ida Rose tugged at her arm and asked, "What are you hiding, Mary? What could be so awful that James could threaten to take your child away? What is he holding over you?"

When Mary turned back to Ida Rose, tears spilled over onto her cheeks. "Somethin' dreadful; somethin' unforgiveable."

Ida Rose furrowed her brow and said, "What did you do? I can't believe that you could do anything that dreadful."

"It be in me husband's eyes." She reached down and took Katherine by the hand. The little girl looked at Mary with apprehension. The conflict that ensued between her aunt and uncle had withdrawn her even deeper into her shell. It pained Mary to see that. She wished she could offer her a loving home like her sister had. Mary said to the child, "Let's go dear." Then to Ida Rose, "I'll see ya later." They descended the steps of the mercantile and started down the road. The purchases she was going to make today would have to wait.

"Mary, I'm sorry if I upset you," Ida Rose called out to her. "I wish you'd confide in me."

"It wouldn't be good," she replied over her shoulder. Then she and Katherine headed for home.

That afternoon Mary deliberately went out and swept the dust off the front porch. It was about the time that Joshua should be coming home from school. She watched for his return with great anticipation. She prayed throughout the day that everything had gone well for him. She hoped that this first day would be a positive experience for him. It would set the tone for the rest of the year and possibly for all his schooling.

It wasn't long until she was rewarded with a glimpse of a happy child scampering down the road. She felt a soft smile curl up on her face and sighed in relief. When Joshua saw his mother standing on the porch, he broke out into a run. "Mama, Mama," he shouted with excitement. He hurriedly came to his mother and embraced her. Breathlessly he said, "Wait until you hear what I've learned today."

Mary tried to restrain her own excitement. "Sit over here and tell me *all* about it," she said sitting on one of the rockers.

Joshua was too excited to sit. He stood beside her, dropped his biscuit tin at his feet and showed her a tattered tiny book. "Mr. Sullivan gave this to me…er let me borrow it." He opened it up to one of the pages and handed it to her. Katherine, who had been playing out front in the dirt, stacking up pebbles as she had seen Joshua often do, joined them. The three gathered around to look at the small treasure.

"He called it a primer; it's to teach us how to read." He pointed to the page and said, "This is the alphabet." He briefly took it from his mother, turned a couple of pages and handed it back to her. On the page were small illustrations that Mary easily recognized; she had often done the same thing to convey something she needed to remember later. Joshua pointed to the top picture that was clearly Adam and Eve. He then recited the rhyme for them: "*In Adam's fall; we sinned all.* That's to help us remember that the first letter of the alphabet is the letter A." He pointed to the next one. "The letter B: *Heaven to find; the Bible Mind.*" He continued down the page to the letter F and said, "That's as far as we got today."

Mary's heart was overflowing; her son was going to learn to read. "Tell me about the pictures again." Joshua recited them all again, not knowing that his mother was trying to memorize them as well. He had expected her praise for his hard work. When she didn't immediately reply, the boy's countenance began to fall. He took the book from her hands and then she realized what she had neglected to do. Making amends she said, "That's a fine job, lad. It makes me mind spin tryin' to take it all in. I think that deserves a reward."

She got up and the two followed her into the kitchen. She poured some milk into three small cups for each of them. Then she opened a special tin and gave them each a cookie that had been baked earlier in the afternoon. When they were through, she had him recite all over again what he had learned, stating that it would help him remember it better. But in fact, it was for her benefit. She would privately rehearse those rhymes over in her head throughout the evening and then fall asleep repeating them. She had a new hope in her heart. Maybe someday she would be able to read Robert's book after all.

21

Unexpected Guests

The next several months went by quickly. Joshua had fallen in love with learning. Each day he awakened to new discoveries and excitedly shared his new knowledge with his mother. Mary shared his excitement and drank in everything he said. At night, when all was still, she would slip out of bed and by lamplight study his primer. She tried to recall all that he had said earlier in the evening. She retained some of the information like each letter of the alphabet and a few common words, but her progress was much slower than Joshua's. If she could only spend time inside the classroom, she would learn so much quicker. But that was impossible.

There were times when she was working outside she'd doodle in the dirt, practicing each letter. Since paper was so scarce, the only resource she could afford was a stick in the dirt. It was awkward holding the stick between her fingers, forming the lines and curves of each letter. It was painfully slow, but in time she improved. Eventually, through Joshua, she was able to string a few simple words together and formed a sentence. Still it was a far cry from reading Robert's book or more importantly the Bible.

Springtime came and flowers blossomed; the grass deepened to a rich green. One Sunday morning, when the bright sunshine chased away winter's chill, Mary stole away to her favorite spot. She took Katherine and Michael with her since Joshua had already gone to church with James. The little blonde headed girl scampered through the fields gathering up wildflowers along the way. Michael crawled along the grass carpet with Mary keeping a watchful eye that he didn't wander towards the stream.

Mary climbed up on her rock and reveled in the beauty before her. She leaned back, closed her eyes, and drank in the warmth of the sun. Suddenly, she felt a shadow come across her face, and it wasn't the sun ducking behind a cloud. She opened her eyes and saw that they were not alone. She jumped in response.

Mr. Sullivan chuckled. "I'm sorry. I didn't mean to scare you."

"Ya didn't scare me—just startled me," she replied a little embarrassed. "Mr. Sullivan, what on earth are ya doin' way out here?"

"Wandering. It was such a beautiful day I thought I'd do some exploring. I haven't had much of an opportunity to do so since I first arrived. I didn't mean to trespass. I didn't know if anyone owned this property or not."

"James never fenced it in. I reckon he's been too busy or just doesn't feel it necessary. Every once in awhile I see a few o' the Umpquas pass through. It used to scare me, but they seem friendly enough." She paused, glancing over at the children to make sure they weren't doing anything they shouldn't be. Michael was doing his own exploring on his hands and knees. He suddenly stopped, plopped down his rump and pulled up a wildflower. Mary anticipated his next move. She called to Katherine, who was fascinated by Mr. Sullivan's horse. "Katherine, make sure Michael does not put that flower in his mouth."

"Okay Aunt Mary," she said. She went over and sat down in front of him. Taking his hands in hers, she swung them back and forth in time with a cute little Irish ditty she was singing. Michael quickly forgot about the flowers. He laughed and made gurgling sounds as if he was trying to sing with her.

Mary turned her attention back to her surprise guest. She asked in her straight forward way, "So Mr. Sullivan, ya're not in church? Don't ya believe in it?"

Mr. Sullivan cleared his throat. "To be honest…" He started to sit down on the rock beside her when he suddenly remembered his manners. "May I?" Mary nodded and he scooted up beside her. "To be honest, I haven't been to church for some time now."

"Why not, if I may ask?"

He shrugged and said, "Don't really see much need for it."

"Everybody needs God. How can ya not see that? He created us; gave us our very lives. He gives us every breath we take in. We should be grateful for that."

Mr. Sullivan just nodded politely. He cocked his head to one side and said, "I can say the same thing about you. Why aren't you in church this morning?"

Mary lowered her head and said softly, "Me husband doesn't like me goin'." The school teacher curiously raised an eyebrow and waited for her to elaborate. "Ya see I'm Catholic. He doesn't think that I believe in the same things he does."

"And do you believe differently?"

"Not entirely. We each have our differences in how we choose to worship God, but *I believe* that we are both worshipin' the same God."

"There are a lot of prejudices out there for the taking. Some people can be so hypocritical with their beliefs. I guess that's part of the reason why I've been put off by religion. People talk about love and compassion, but whenever there's a real need for it, they are the first to judge and criticize."

"Not every Christian behaves that way. Some do show compassion. They're usually the ones that have been through a lot themselves and know what it feels like to be in need." She paused and then looked him straight in his eyes. "Ya know ya should not judge God by the actions o' a few people who *claim* to be His children. We are all sinners in need o' a Savior and God has been gracious enough to provide one. We should be grateful for that."

"Do you believe all that?"

"With all me heart."

"Then *you* should be in church this morning and not out here in the middle of a field."

"Makes no difference. God is here; He's omnipresent. I can worship Him here as well as in the church."

"But it sounds as if the church could use a few more people like you to keep them on the narrow path," he chuckled nervously. Clearly this was not a subject he was readily comfortable with.

"Well, I wouldn't want to start a war with me husband over this. I'll stay and worship God in me house in the manner I was raised to worship Him. Hopefully, God will understand." With that, the subject was closed. There was a brief lull in their conversation as they watched the interaction of the children.

Mr. Sullivan smiled softly, amused at the simple joys little ones had at that age. He turned to Mary and said questioningly, "The little girl…she called you aunt. I thought she was your daughter."

Quietly she answered, "She's me sister's…so is the boy." She didn't look at him; her eyes were fixed on the children. "She died givin' birth."

"The other sister from the book?" he asked, referring to the book she had received the day they had met.

She was amazed that he remembered. "We came to America together. Robert—Mr. Timmons became our travelin' companion the last part o' our trip. He watched out for us. He was a good friend indeed." Her voice wavered at the end, betraying her.

"He seemed to be more than a friend. In his letter, he seemed quite smitten with you."

Embarrassed, Mary lowered her head. She grappled with just the right words to say. "We might have been more than that if given the time together, but as it was, I came to this country to marry James." She met his eyes. They seemed puzzled by her remarks. "Ya see I was what people call, a mail order bride. James paid for me trip to America to be his wife."

"Ah, so you felt obligated to marry him instead of Robert?" Mary didn't answer. Once again she lowered her head. A cool, spring breeze buffeted them, blowing a stray strand of her hair in her face. A shiver went through her as she absently tucked it behind her ear. "Are you cold?" he asked. "I can give you my jacket."

"I'm quite alright. There's just a wee bit o' winter chill still left in the wind. I probably should get the children back to the house, before they catch their death." She gingerly slid off the rock, but before she took more than a couple of steps from him, she turned and said, "Ya've done a wonderful job teachin' Josh…I mean, Jethro how to read. I've been tryin' to study alongside him, but I'm afraid that I am not quite the student he is." She hesitated briefly, swallowing some of her pride. "I was wonderin', could ya be teachin' someone like me?"

"You mean you'd like *me* to teach you how to read?"

"Most assuredly," she answered. Her cheek flushed as she lowered her eyes. She then regretted saying anything to him.

"I'd love to teach you. How can we go about this?"

She stammered, trying to come up with a good solution for both of them. "How about we start next Sunday mornin'?"

"Won't I cut into your alone time with God?" he joked.

Mary found no amusement in it. "I have me quiet time with the Lord every day. I can still find time to worship Him on Sunday, ya can be rest assured."

He heard the ire in her voice and knew he had struck a nerve. "I didn't mean any offense. I just didn't want to impose," he said respectfully.

"Tis no imposition rather it will be a true blessin'. If ya can teach me, I will finally be able to read His Word for meself."

A faint smile spread across Mr. Sullivan's face. "I have full confidence that you *will* be able to read.

The following Sunday Mr. Sullivan arrived at her house as planned. As he rounded the bend and descended the hill of their farm, he caught sight of Mary coming out of the house. She greeted him as he climbed down out of his carriage. She was dressed in a simple cotton print dress. It was pale yellow with tiny blue flowers on it. He smiled broadly and said, "Don't you look pretty today. Is that a new dress?"

"I made it meself; just got it finished last night. Do ya like it?" She pirouetted around, showing off her new creation.

He whistled and teased, "It sure looks good…and so does the dress."

She stopped and looked at him incredulously. "Mr. Sullivan, that's a little forward don't ya think?"

His grin only deepened. "Now you know you were looking for a compliment. Why else would you be wearing a new dress for me?"

"Who says it be for ya? I just felt like wearin' me new dress today, nothin' more."

"Is it?" His teasing was turning into a flirtation. Suddenly an alarm went off somewhere inside her. She unconsciously took a couple of steps backwards. But the teacher went on. "Now I wish you'd call me by my given name. Won't you call me Evan?"

Mary ignored him. "Mr. Sullivan, this is just business between us. Ya teach me to read and in exchange I bake a few treats for ya. That is all."

His smile turned sideways and he shook his head. "I'll right, Mr. Sullivan it is. You're one stubborn lady."

"I am not stubborn, just determined. And thank ya for callin' me a lady."

He laughed out loud and said, "You're quite welcome."

They went in and sat at the kitchen table. Katherine sat with them for a little while, but soon grew bored. She hopped down from her chair and sat on the floor next to Michael, who was playing with some wooden blocks that once belonged to Joshua. For the next hour they studied the primer that he had loaned Joshua. Frustrated, Mary stumbled over the words, but the school teacher was impressed that she had learned that much on her own. He encouraged her with some words of praise. But soon it was time for him to leave. They didn't dare chance meeting James as he drove down their driveway. Not that they were doing anything wrong, but it might have been construed that way.

A few days later, Mary received another unexpected guest. It was afternoon. A hot breeze from the south and the increase of clouds brought the promise of rain showers later in the day. Mary stepped out onto the porch to sweep the accumulating dust off of it, but the wind just blew more. She quickly gave up. She wandered over to one of the graying rockers on the porch and took a brief respite.

She heard the carriage approaching before it started down the road towards her house. She squinted her eyes to see if she could make out who it was. It was obviously not James; he never came home early anymore. It couldn't have been Mr. Sullivan, because school was still in session, but none the less it was a man. As he drew closer, she could see that it was the new preacher that had come to town. She wondered why on earth he would come here.

"Good day to you," he said with a warm, friendly smile. A strong gust of wind nearly took his hat off. If he hadn't put his hand on top of it, it would have. "How are you on this windy afternoon?" he chuckled.

Mary couldn't keep herself from chuckling as well. It was a funny sight, seeing the poor man sitting there with his hand on his head. "Why don't ya come in and sit a spell, Parson. It will at least get ya out o' the wind and dust."

"Thank you kindly," he said stepping down from his carriage. He naturally had his Bible in his hand.

"Can I put on a pot o' coffee for ya and offer ya some apple pie?" She asked as they headed for the kitchen.

"I wouldn't want to put you to any trouble."

"No trouble, it'll just take a little while for the coffee to get done. I could use a cup meself. Hope ya're not in a real hurry to be on yar way." Before he could object, she had the pot on the stove. Then she offered him a seat at the table and joined him. She got straight to the point. "What brings ya here today, Parson? I hope not to bring bad news."

"Oh no, I was out visiting with some of the congregants and thought I would stop to see how you're doing. I haven't seen you all winter. I trust you are well."

Mary felt a slight irritation rise up in her. Here was the reason for the visit. She expected a sermon from him about not attending church. It was expected any time a preacher came calling on a *sinner*. He would quickly admonish her for not being in church. If he only knew the real reason she couldn't come, he would leave her be.

"I've fared as well as the rest o' town I suppose."

Katherine interrupted their conversation. She shyly approached the young preacher, staring intently at him. Mary admonished her, "Tis not polite to stare honey." But the young girl continued.

Reverend Matthews smiled tenderly at her. He inquired, "Is there something I can do for you, sweetheart?"

Katherine mustered up as much courage as her frail five year old body could. Then she asked, "Are you a good man or a bad man?"

Perplexed, the pastor responded, "Well, I like to think that I am a good man. Why do you ask?"

"I was just wondering," she said in a tiny voice. "My uncle is a bad man."

"Katherine!" Mary cried out.

"It's alright, honey," he said, trying to keep the situation calm. He offered to pick her up and to Mary's surprise she accepted, climbing up on his lap. "What makes you think that your uncle is bad?"

Shyly she replied, "He yells and hits my Aunt Mary; he makes her cry."

Mary tried to protest, but Reverend Matthews gently held up his hand and she held her peace. "Does he ever do that to you?" he asked softly.

"Sometimes he yells at me," she said just above a whisper.

"How does that make you feel?"

"Like I don't want to be here."

"Does he make you cry?"

"Uh-huh," she said nodding her head up and down. "But I try not to 'cause he gets madder if I do."

Mary dropped her head in shame. Getting up from the table, she checked on the coffee. Then she got two cups from the cupboard and set them on the counter, discreetly wiping tears from her eyes. She put the cups on the table and with shaking hands tried to pour the coffee. All the while Matthews tried comforting the little girl.

"Sometimes people do or say things that hurt other people," he said trying to put it in terms a child could understand. "They don't always know what they are doing. You need to know that whatever they do has nothing to do with you. It's not your fault. They are the ones that are wrong. And don't ever forget that God loves you and He hates what is happening to you…and to your Aunt Mary. Do you understand?"

Katherine nodded her head slightly, but did not make any eye contact with him. Tears streaked down her cheeks and she threw her arms around the pastor's neck, hugging him fiercely. Quietly she whispered in his ear, "I wish we could come live with you."

He wasn't sure how to respond. He hugged her and felt his heart break for her and this family. A great indignation rose in him. It was probably a good thing that James was not around at the moment or he might not have been able to hold his peace. He needed a godly wisdom in how he should approach this new revelation. "Just remember little one, God sees all and hears all. You are never alone for He will always be with you."

They were good words, words that Mary had often used to comfort herself. But there were times when they were simply just words. She took a freshly baked pie from the cupboard, sliced a couple of pieces and put them on small plates. Then she drew out a cookie from its jar. She turned and offered the cookie to her. "Here Katherine," she said tenderly. The little girl wiped her tears with the back of her hand and then took the cookie. "Now, why don't ya run off and mind little Michael whiles the reverend and me have a little visit."

"Okay Aunt Mary," she said, jumping off the pastor's lap. She turned and ran through the doorway and into the next room.

Mary gently placed the piece of pie in front of him, which he politely thanked her for. "This is very good pie, Mrs. Whitaker," he said quietly. She thanked him and then an awkward silence fell between them. Eventually, he approached the subject of the elephant that was in the room. "I was going to ask why James never brought the other children with him. I guess I kind of know now."

Mary shook her head gently and replied, "Ya have no idea. Ya think ya do, but ya don't."

He looked intently at her, trying to comprehend. There were so many questions he wanted to ask. "How bad is it? Do you ever fear for your life…or for the children?"

"James would never hurt his son." She hesitated and then added, "I don't think he would ever get angry enough to…" She couldn't bring herself to finish her thought.

"If there is anything I can do…if you ever get to the place you think you're in danger…"

"Thank ya, but there's nothin' anyone can do. I'm afraid it would just make thin's worse."

"I'm sorry for what you are going through." Looking for a way to minister to her he offered, "You know if you're unable to come to the church services, I could come here sometime during the week. I know a little about Catholicism from my mother, remember? I know it may be a little unorthodox to have a Protestant preacher doing a Catholic service, but the way I feel about it, I've been called to minister to the community. And this includes you, Mrs. Whitaker." He smiled sweetly and Mary felt that he genuinely meant what he said.

"Well, I'll think about that, Parson and I thank ya kindly for the offer."

He finished off his pie and took the last swig of coffee. Then getting up from the table, he excused himself. "I best be getting on my way. I don't want to overstay my welcome."

"Ya haven't. I'm a bit sorry and ashamed for what ya had to hear today."

"Don't be. If there's anything I can do to help the situation…"

"There's nothin' except maybe prayin' for us."

"That I can do. Let me do that right now." He put his hand on her shoulder and began to pray for Mary and the entire family. He especially addressed James' temper and how it was affecting everyone. He felt a tug once again at his heart, wishing he could do more for them. "I'll keep praying for you."

They started out the door and headed for his carriage. Suddenly he stopped and turned towards her. "Do you have a Bible, Mrs. Whitaker?"

"James has one," she simply said.

"But do you?"

"I've never had one for meself."

He looked intently at her and then he said, "Then I think I'm supposed to give this to you." He offered his Bible to her.

"Oh, I cannot accept that, Parson; that's yars."

"When I was getting ready to leave this morning, I had the strangest sensation that I was to give this to someone today. I now believe I'm supposed to give this to you."

"I cannot take yar Bible," she insisted.

"Even if it's from God?" Mary blinked. She didn't want to do anything that might go against God. "I have another one at home, so you'll not leave me without one," he assured her.

She hesitated again, but then slowly took it from him. "Tis the Lord's will, then I'll take it. Thank ya." She hugged it against her chest.

"You're very welcome. I believe that it's going to a good place," he said and gave her a smile of encouragement. "I'll be back around to visit and we can talk more about...things."

"Thank ya again, Parson." He mounted his carriage and then waved goodbye. Mary watched him disappear behind the hill as he rode away. She still hugged the Bible he had given her, treasuring it. She had never dreamed of having her very own Bible and now she had it in her hands. She went and sat down on the old rocker and opened it. The pages fell open to the book of Psalms and she stumbled through reading a very familiar passage.

"The LORD is me shepherd; I shall not want. He maketh me to lie down in green pastures: He leadeth me beside the still waters. He restoreth me soul: He leadeth me in the paths o' righteousness for His name's sake. Yea, though I walk through the valley o' the shadow o' death, I will fear no evil: for Thou art with me; Thy rod and thy staff they comfort me. Thou preparest a table before me in the presence o' me enemies: Thou anointest me head with oil; me cup runneth over. Surely goodness and mercy shall follow me all the days o' me life: and I will dwell in the house o' the LORD forever."

She took comfort with each verse. They would be words she would need to get her through the next several months.

22

Reading, 'Riting, 'Rithmatic, & Repentance

Over the next several Sundays, Evan Sullivan kept his appointment with Mary. Along the way, he would pass James and Joshua as they were going to church. Each time, Evan would politely tip his hat. It intrigued him that he had an odd feeling as though he was sneaking around behind her husband's back. He chuckled to himself as he realized that in a way he was. Only it wasn't an affair that they were hiding.

On one particular occasion, as he was about to pass, James threw up his hand and brought him to a halt. "Mr. Sullivan," James cordially greeted him. "You seem quite a ways from home," he said trying to fish for information.

Sullivan nodded, returning the greeting to both James and his son, making sure that he called the boy Jethro. Joshua and his teacher exchanged a knowing glance. He responded, "Yes I am,"

"I've noticed that you've been making quite a few trips out this road."

"I have."

James rubbed his chin in mild frustration. He was getting nowhere. "So you have business out here?"

"You might say that," Sullivan answered. He couldn't keep from smirking; this was becoming amusing for him. The two men sat on their perspective vehicles and stared at each other. Finally Evan relented and volunteered a little more information. "I'm tutoring a student."

James cocked his head and asked, "On Sunday? Wouldn't it be better for you to be in church?"

Sullivan shrugged. "You make sacrifices for your students."

"Shouldn't *she* be in church?"

"Who said it was a *she?*" he parried.

"I guess, I just assumed," James replied, feeling a bit chagrined. "So your student is a boy?"

"I didn't say that either." There was a twinkle in Sullivan's eye and his smirk deepened to a grin. "*She* doesn't attend church. You might say that she has trouble getting out of the house."

"An elderly woman?" James once again assumed too much. "Why are you tutoring an old woman?"

"She wants to learn to read."

"What use does an old woman have for reading at this late date?"

"You're never too old to learn anything; that's what keeps us young at heart."

James snorted and said, "I guess so. Well, I won't keep you any longer. Good day." With his curiosity finally appeased, he tipped his hat and then snapped the reigns signaling the horses to continue on their journey.

Evan breathed a sigh of relief. He shook his head and found himself laughing softly over the incident. He was glad that he'd maneuver the conversation in such a way that he didn't divulge Mary's identity. He rather enjoyed making sport of her husband. It somehow made him feel a bit superior to him. Satisfied, he continued down the road towards the

Whitaker farm. But a strange thought occurred to him: what if Mr. Whitaker turned back to follow him? What if he caught him with his wife? An unexpected chill ran up his spine. He couldn't keep himself from looking over his shoulder the rest of the way.

As he neared the farm, his mind wandered to thoughts of Mary and a smile curled up on his lips. Each week he found himself longing for Sunday to come so that they would be together, even though it was only for an hour or so. She had been one of the few bright spots in his life since coming to this territory. It had been a long and lonely winter for him, but now that spring was here, it gave rise to a ray of hope. He came down the hill of her driveway and then stopped in front of the house.

Mary came out on the porch to greet him. "Good mornin', Mr. Sullivan."

He smiled broadly as he jumped from his carriage. "After all these weeks and I still can't get you to call me by my first name."

She said firmly, "A pupil does not call her teacher by his first name. Tis not proper."

Evan shook his head as he chuckled. "Maybe so, but I thought we were becoming more than that."

"Whatever do ya mean, Mr. Sullivan?" she asked with some apprehension in her voice.

"I mean, I thought we were becoming friends."

"That we are…I guess." Evan turned his head sideways, raising an eyebrow. Mary quickly clarified. "I just never gave it much thought." Again Evan had a good chuckle.

Katherine came running out of the house. "Mr. Sullivan! Mr. Sullivan!" she cried as she practically leapt into his arms. Evan enveloped her, astonished that she was getting over her shyness around him. Mary admonished her for being disrespectful, but she was overruled. He was thrilled by the outpouring of emotions from her. Secretly he hoped that one day he would get that kind of greeting from her aunt.

He put Katherine down and then turned back to his carriage to retrieve something. When he came back, he had a strange looking object in his hand. It was about two feet long, diamond shape and made of newspaper. It had a knotted piece of cloth tied to the bottom. Wooden rods formed a cross in the middle with twine attached to it. "I made this for you," he said to Katherine. She wrinkled her nose, not quite sure what to make of it. "It's a kite. If there's enough wind we can fly it." Katherine took it from him, still unclear about its purpose. Evan turned his attention to Mary. "Oh, I brought something for you too." He had a book in his hand that she had not seen before. "I thought maybe we would work on some mathematics while we are at it."

"What in heaven's name for? What would I ever use it for?"

"Oh, you never know, Mary. You never know."

On nice warm days they would go back to the open field, spread out a blanket and have school right there on the grass. On this day, it was a little warmer than previous times. Evan took off his jacket, leaving him in a white shirt and black vest. He unraveled some of the twine on the kite and catching a breeze, trotted along until the kite was able to take flight. It warbled and wobbled, but came back to the earth with a crash. It took a couple of tries until it was steady enough to turn it over to Katherine. Then he settled in on the quilt Mary had laid out on the ground.

Mary had proved to be a quick study and had graduated from Joshua's primer to her newly acquired Bible. It was mixed in with a little of Robert's book, which she found to be an incredible piece of imagination. It was nothing like the broken lives the two sisters had endured, but was filled with a lot of misadventures that she found quite amusing. Even so, Robert had captured their personalities and characteristics. All in all it was very entertaining and pleased her quite well. Her only wish was that her own life had mirrored the book.

As they got settled, Mary placed her Bible and Robert's book on her lap while Evan set the mathematics book to his side. He drew in a deep breath of fresh air. "I love how it smells out here; it smells so clean. And it's so beautiful and peaceful."

"Tis so. I sort o' have a love-hate relationship with it," she said with a touch of melancholy.

"How's that?" he asked.

"I love it because it reminds me o' me homeland of Ireland."

"And why do you hate it?"

"It reminds me o' me homeland of Ireland."

Confused, he chuckled and said, "I don't understand. How can you love and hate for the same reason?"

Mary became a little indignant; she thought he was making sport of her. "Tis not funny. I love it, because it reminds me o' happier days when I was innocent. I hate it, because it makes me miss it fiercely. It makes me miss me family."

"Have you ever had a chance to go back and visit?"

"There's no need. The thin's that I miss the most are me mam and dad and o' course me sister, Aubrey. They're all gone now; I'm the only one left." Her words seemed to hang in the air like Katherine's kite. A brisk wind swirled around them, carrying them away.

"I'm sorry. I didn't mean to laugh at you. I just didn't understand."

Mary quickly changed the subject. "We should get busy. We don't have much time ya know." She tepeed her legs and rested her Bible against her inclined thighs. She opened up to the book of Psalms, because they seemed to be the easiest to read and she also took a lot of comfort from them. But it didn't take long for Evan to lose interest and encouraged her to take out Robert's book. He teased her, "I want to see what's going to happen next to you and your sister."

"Like I've said before, this is neither me sister or me. Although it was fairly accurate about our trip across the Isthmus; it *was* pretty harrowin' trekkin' across it. But o' course, we never did the other thin's he said that we did. Thin's were more uneventful than he portrayed them to be."

"I think you protest too much." There was a glint of glee in his eyes as he continued to tease.

"Ya keep it up and I won't let ya know how the book ends."

"Really? I don't know…I think you still need some help with some of the longer words."

His banter had gone too far. "Are ya sayin' I'm too stupid to figure it out on me own?"

"Not at all," he said backpedaling. "I think you're quite intelligent. You've really taught yourself how to read. I didn't give you that much help."

"But I'm still not a very good reader. I stumble over too many words."

Evan sighed. He saw what his teasing had done. He reached over, took her hand and gave it a gentle squeeze. "Be patient; it'll come in time. Now let's get back to the book."

Mary opened it up to the next chapter. According to the story, the trio had spent more time in San Francisco than in real life. In the book, the sisters had actually found jobs and shared an apartment in the city. The two had attracted many a roving eye among the lonely miners that visited the city of sin. Robert's character, which he renamed Richard Thompkins, looked out for the two, keeping them from any harm.

As the next chapter began, Richard had taken Maggie, the auburn haired beauty that was supposed to be Mary, to dinner at a restaurant. Mary sometimes felt a little embarrassed to read these passages, even though the character wasn't really her. But if she was totally honest, she felt a little exhilarated, knowing that Robert saw her that way. That *was* until this chapter.

Slowly she began to read the text, sounding out each syllable. "After din-ner, they went for a st-stroll a-round the ci-ty. The moon shone brill-brill…"

"Brilliantly."

"The moon shone brilliantly. The e-e-echo o' their foot-steps could be heard on the wood-en bo-bo…"

"Boardwalk."

"Boardwalk. There was a com-for-table…comfortable si-lence be-be-tween them." Mary continued reading in a halting, staccato manner. It was painfully slow, but Evan was patient with her. But as she struggled with the words, an uneasiness stirred in her stomach. She had a feeling she wasn't going to like where the story was headed. Because of this, she stopped reading aloud and sounded out the words in her head. Suddenly she shouted, "That is not what happened!" Evan, who had leaned closer trying to get a glimpse of what could possibly make her so indignant, was left in the dark when she quickly snapped the book shut and hugged it against her bosom.

"What?" he asked.

Mary got swiftly to her feet and moved away from him. In a fit of fury she began to pace. "O' all the nerve. I have a good mind to write Mr. Timmons and give him a piece o' me mind. There's only one thin' that's holdin' me back."

"What's that?" he asked getting to his feet.

She turned down one corner of her mouth and answered, "I don't know where he lives."

Evan couldn't keep from howling and she became even more incensed. She turned her back to him. When he finally contained his laughter, he came up from behind and put his hands on her shoulders. "So tell me, what's the terrible thing that he wrote about you?"

"Oh no. I cannot say it out loud. Tis too awful."

"It can't be that bad. They do have certain standards on what can and cannot be published." He reached for the book and she stretched it beyond his reach. This initiated a chase and Katherine quickly abandoned her kite and joined in. She circled both of them enjoying the game, even though she had no understanding of what was going on. Michael dropped to his rump and clapped his hands in delight over the whole thing.

"Give me the book, Mary. Come on…give me the book." She continued to keep it out of his reach. "Oh come on. What could be so bad?" He changed tactics and feigned disinterest. As soon as her guard went down, he stripped her of the book. "Ha-ha!" he shouted with great pleasure. He quickly paged through the book and found where she had been reading. All the while, Katherine was leaping up and down in excitement.

Evan found it and began to chuckle. "This is what made you so upset? A kiss?"

"Tis not the kiss," she said with her jaw set. "Tis what he said about me." Again, Evan perused the page. He looked up in dismay. She answered, "He has *me* kissin' *him*." Evan still was not getting her point. "I would never initiate a kiss. What kind o' woman does he think I am?"

Evan closed the book and laughed heartily, which further infuriated her. "Come on. What's wrong with that?"

"I've done a lot o' thin's that I'm ashamed o', but I would never be that forward. How could he write such a thin'?"

"Maybe that's what he hoped would have happened," he said softly. He moved closer and put his hand on her shoulder again and looked intently in her eyes. Mary felt a stirring inside her. She wasn't sure she wanted him to look at her that way, but couldn't seem to break free from his gaze. Evan reached up and gently pushed a loose strand of hair away from her face. He moved even closer and time seemed to stand still. Mary was frozen in the moment as his face drew closer to hers. There was part of her that wanted what was about to happen, but suddenly a voice within her cried out, *this is wrong!* It snapped her out of her stupor and she pulled away from him.

Quietly she said, "I think it be best that we call it a day on the lessons, Mr. Sullivan."

Evan pulled out his pocket watch, popped open the cover to look at it. "We still have time." But one look at her made him realize that indeed his time was up.

"Ya need to be takin' the kite with ya," she said quietly. She felt so much shame that she couldn't even look at him.

"She can keep it. It was a gift."

Mary shook her head. "If James sees it, he'll ask questions. Ya have to take it with ya."

Katherine confused by the sudden turn of events, looked at her aunt pleadingly. Evan knelt down in front of her and took one of her hands. "Your aunt's right. We have to continue to keep this a secret, right? I'll bring it back next week when I come to visit. It'll be something to look forward to, okay?" She nodded her head, trying not to cry. Evan put his hand on her head and petted her. Then he stood up and turned to face Mary. He realized that he had overstayed his welcome.

"I'm sorry, *Mrs. Whitaker.*" It was all he could say. He picked up the kite, gave a faint smile to Katherine and then gathered his coat and book. Then he walked back towards the house to his carriage. Mary turned away, trying to sort out her emotions. She had come so close to letting him kiss her. She found herself wanting it, but she wondered if it was because she was falling in love with him or just wanting to be loved by someone. She felt the sting of tears burn her eyes and she quickly restrained them. Then she scooped up Michael and headed for the house with Katherine in tow.

A few days later, Reverend Matthews stopped by. He had kept his word by paying regular weekly visits to her. She found some comfort in the fact that he not only kept his promise to her, but he didn't seem to be put off by her Catholic faith. Maybe he did care more about people than about differences in religious practices. She found it refreshing. But even so, there was a part of her that was overcome with shame. The incident with Mr. Sullivan had haunted her from that day on. Her mind reasoned that she had done nothing wrong, but her heart feared that she was in danger of committing adultery. If the preacher knew her heart, he might not be so accepting of her.

She invited him into the kitchen and poured a cup of coffee for him. His visits were so timely that she always tried to have a pot ready. She wondered how the town's folk would feel about her if they knew that she had two attractive, eligible bachelors visiting her regularly. Suddenly she realized just how grave the situation could become. Both men's reputations would be soiled.

"How are things this week?" he asked sipping his coffee.

"Ya mean with James and me?" He nodded. "Nothin' has changed; they are likely not to."

"I wish you would let me talk to him on your behalf."

"It would do no good, Parson. James has his reasons for what he does. If ya talked to him, it would only make it worse."

"There is *no* good reason for his behavior," he insisted.

Mary snorted as she shook her head. "If ya only knew the truth about me," she said solemnly and in an instance she knew what she needed to do. "Reverend, ya said ya would be willin' to help me with me beliefs." He nodded once more. "Would ya be willin' to hear me confession?"

The pastor thought for a moment and then agreed. "If it would make you feel better."

Mary returned the nod. She drew in a deep breath for courage, crossed herself and then dived in. *"Bless me, Father, for I have sinned. It has been well over eight years since me last confession…to a priest."* Her eyes darted back and forth as she tried to determine where to begin. For the sake of the reverend, she began confessing her life of sin as a prostitute. She continued on until she came to her last transgression: the feelings for Mr. Sullivan that she was struggling with. When she finished, she was totally exhausted.

Reverend Matthews sat quietly gathering his thoughts. He had never heard such a complete confession before. Usually, when someone wanted to confess something to him, it was about something they were struggling with or they simply wanted prayer. This woman was in need of true counseling.

"Mrs. Whitaker," he said softly. "Have you at some point made a confession of faith?" Her puzzled look prompted him for clarification. "You have at some point in your life realized that you were a sinner, who without forgiveness was be lost and headed for hell and that you have recognized that Jesus is the only one that can make restitution for your sins. That confessing those sins, you have accepted His death on the cross as that payment, knowing that you *will* be forgiven and saved. That one day, when you come to the end of your life, you will be with Him in heaven for all eternity. You've taken that step of faith?"

"I surely have; when I was but only twelve years old. But I have done a lot o' disgraceful things since then. Sellin' meself to men for one," she said lowering her head in humiliation. "I know it doesn't change much, but I didn't want that life; it was forced on me."

"I understand, but have you asked for forgiveness and repented of it?"

"Repented? What does that mean?"

"It's having remorse or deep sorrow for what you have done. It's knowing that you've hurt God by your actions and feel bad about it. Because of this, you make the decision to turn away from your sin and turn towards God. You have a change of mind that you want to do things pleasing to Him. Do you feel that way, Mrs. Whitaker?"

"That I do," she said. For some inexplicable reason she had begun to cry softly. She wiped away the tears momentarily with her fingertips.

"Mrs. Whitaker, if you have confessed your sins to God, He will forgive you of all your transgressions—all of them. In First John it says: *If we confess our sins, he is faithful and just to forgive us our sins, and to cleanse us from all unrighteousness.* Your sincere confession makes you righteous before God. And you don't have to seek out a priest to confess your sins to him; you just need to confess to Jesus. Jesus is our high priest"

The preacher opened up his Bible to the book of Hebrews and together they studied the Scriptures concerning Jesus responsibility to intercede on our behalf before God. "In Hebrews chapter seven it says: *Thou art a priest forever after the order of Melchizedek.* Then it says, *but this man, because he continueth ever, hath an unchangeable priesthood. Wherefore he is able also to save them to the uttermost that come unto God by him, seeing he ever liveth to make intercession for them.*"

He went on to explain. "Earthly priests die, but because Jesus lives forever, He has a permanent priesthood. He not only is able to save us, but He also is able to make continual intersession for us." He quickly turned to

First Timothy chapter two and read: *For there is one God, and one mediator between God and men, the man Christ Jesus.* Mrs. Whitaker, Jesus is the only one you need to confess to."

Mary was stunned, "Ya mean, all those years I have prayed that God would hear me prayers…He really did?"

Reverend Matthews smiled a satisfied grin. She understood. "God has listened and He knows how much you have suffered. He shares in that suffering with you."

Her tears fell unabated. The pastor put his hand on top of hers to comfort her. Mary looked up for the first time since her confession and met his eyes. She saw the compassion of Christ there. "Are ya not goin' to preach condemnation towards me for what I've done?"

"Why should I? If God has forgiven you, you're a new creation, *old things have passed away and all things are become new."* Then he quoted from Romans. *"There is therefore now no condemnation to them which are in Christ Jesus, who walk not after the flesh, but after the Spirit."*

"But James…"

"Your husband is wrong. His responsibility is to love you like Christ loved the church, willing to give Himself up for her. I've been praying that God will open his eyes to this truth. The Lord knows that I have been preaching enough about it on Sunday mornings."

She looked at him with great admiration. She almost felt like she had just had a conversation with the Lord Himself. "Thank ya, Parson. Ya've given me a lot to think about."

"Anytime. I'm here to shepherd the people; I'm here to help you in any way I can." He squeezed her hand and then after praying with her, he left. She stood for a long time staring at the road after he rode away. Today, she indeed felt like a new creation, like her soul had been scrubbed clean. She took a moment to thank God for the reverend's visit and for the words of encouragement he had given her. She also thanked Him for loving her so much that He had never turned His back on her. For the first time in her life, she felt hope.

23

A Storm on the Horizon

The next few weeks, Mary's heart was torn between two worlds. She tried to stay focused on being a faithful wife to James, but it was difficult. The years of abuse and humiliation were taking its toll on her spiritually. The pain cut deep into her chest. As she continuously cried out to God to change the situation, things only seemed to grow worse.

Evan Sullivan was not helping one bit. She wasn't just attracted to his handsome features, but to his irresistible passion for fun. His jocularity became contagious. It felt good to be able to laugh and enjoy life again. But she had to fight hard to not give in to her feelings for him. And praying about it didn't seem to help much either. She supposed that if she searched her heart she'd find that she really didn't want to avoid his attention. It was nice to have a man appreciate her for more than her cooking and housekeeping skills.

Yet the battle raged on; her flesh fighting against her spirit. Even in the midst of the laughter, she felt an anguish of despair that all this was wrong. It wasn't so much condemnation, but more of sorrow. Her actions were grieving God's Spirit. Somewhere a voice kept telling her that there was something better for her, urging her to be faithful to God. But could she hope? And if there was hope, how long would she have to wait? So the tug of war continued.

During the spring hiatus, Evan had more time to reflect on his relationship with Mary. He realized that he had put his own desires ahead of hers. He tried keeping it all business like, strictly a teacher/pupil relationship, especially after he had nearly kissed her. He sensed that protective wall she had built around herself. After all, she had a commitment to another man and he should honor that. But what bothered him the most was how her husband treated her and that she still defended him. She deserved better and it ate away at him that there wasn't much he could do. So each Sunday morning, he came with his books in hand and taught her as much as he could in the small amount of time they had. But Evan couldn't keep himself from wanting more. If only James were out of the way.

Summer was coming and school would begin again for the children. Schooling in the community had to be worked around the planting and harvesting seasons. There was no rest for the students. They were either in school or helping on their farms. Workers were so few in the area, with most looking for that get rich quick gold strike. Many didn't want to work for the piddling amount the farmers could pay *if* they could pay anything. So farm children were expected to do their part.

This Sunday would be the last before a new session would begin. In some ways, Evan looked forward to it. It would keep his mind preoccupied and off his growing infatuation for Mary. But a sadness enveloped his heart. The time they were sharing would at some point have to end. Mary had learned so much in the short period of time they were together that soon she would no longer need his guidance. Futilely he tried to find some excuse to be with her. Beyond having an out and out affair, he had no answer.

As he pulled up to the house, Katherine was the first to greet him. She had grown to love his visits as much as Mary. He gave her the attention she desperately needed from a father figure. Unlike Uncle James, Mr. Sullivan and Reverend Matthews doted over her, filling a void in her life. She continued to have bad thoughts about her uncle. She told her aunt about it and Mary admonished her for it. But Katherine couldn't comprehend why it was wrong for her to think bad thoughts of him, yet he could say bad things to her and no one did anything about it. It was the one thing she prayed for each Sunday morning; that God would punish him for what he did to her and Aunt Mary.

Evan held out his closed hand to her, palm down. "Guess what I have in my hand?" he asked her.

"A frog," she squealed.

"No, not a frog. Guess again."

The little girl strained to come up with the correct answer. She guessed again. "A baby chick."

"No, you want to try again." Katherine shook her head no. He turned his hand over and slowly opened it. Inside his palm were ten odd looking metal objects and a small wooden ball.

Katherine's eyes grew wide and she exclaimed, "What is it?"

"It's a game; it's called Jacks," he said grinning. "Let me show you how to play." They went over and sat down on the wooden porch. Evan scattered the jacks and began to explain it to her. "You have to throw the ball in the air, pick up a jack and then catch the ball before it bounces a second time. The object of the game is to see who can pick up the most jacks. First we'll start with onesies." He demonstrated, picking up one jack at a time until all ten were picked up. "After that you go to twosies, picking up two jacks at a time, and then threesies and so one. Do you want to give it a try?"

Katherine was a willing participant, but quickly realized that her skill did not match the school teacher's. It wasn't so much picking up the jack, but catching the ball. Evan chuckled at her failed attempts. He patted her on the head softly and told her to keep practicing. "You'll get it eventually," he said, getting to his feet. Just then Mary came and poked her head through the door; she was wiping her hands with a towel.

"Sorry," she said. "I was busy in the kitchen. I'll be ready in a few minutes." She popped back in the house just as quickly.

"It's all right. Can I help you with anything?" he called to her.

She came back through and tossed a quilt to him. "Here, ya can carry this."

Evan went back to his carriage and retrieved a couple of books and a slate. He wrapped them inside the blanket. By this time Mary had come back, carrying Michael. She took notice of the jacks that he had brought. "Oh Mr. Sullivan, ya shouldn't have."

He shrugged. "I saw them at the mercantile and couldn't resist. I thought she'd like them. She needs to be made to feel special."

Mary lowered her eyes and quietly said, "I know. But if James finds out about the gifts…"

"Then she'll hide them from him."

"Tis not right to do so. It be deceptive."

"This whole thing is deceptive," he replied. Mary snapped her head up and looked at him. She wondered if he was insinuating more. "Come on. Let's get to the lessons.

They went to their usual meeting place and let the children run free to play. Michael was getting around well, running as fast as his chubby little legs could take him. Mary was concerned that he was getting around a little too well. It seemed that every time her back was turned he was into something. His curiosity for things was always getting him into trouble.

Evan spread the quilt out and the two of them sat down underneath a large maple tree. Its broad branches supplied ample shade, although they really didn't need it today. Mary peered up at the sky and said, "Looks like a storm may be brewin'."

"Yeah, it might cut our time short," he said somberly. "I guess we should get busy."

Mary had brought Robert's book and opened it. There weren't many chapters left to read. She hated the thought of finishing it. It would be like losing Robert all over again. There were times that her heart ached so much for him that she wondered if he truly existed or if he was a figment of her imagination. And then she would read his book and know that he was real and miss him all the more. Evan's mischievousness reminded her of Robert. That was probably why she was attracted to him.

They read a short chapter together and then put it aside. Evan had brought a book of poetry for her to read. It was full of emotion and romance; some even made her blush to read them aloud. Her temper flared a little knowing that Evan was taking delight in all of this. He lay on his side drinking it in. The intensity of his eyes made her nervous.

Suddenly he roused up and sat next to her. "Have I ever told you what beautiful eyes you have?"

Mary scooted away slightly, but it didn't discourage him. He scooted over to meet her. "Mr. Sullivan…"

"Yes?" he said playfully. He reached up and caressed her cheek. Then he reached around her head and pulled the pins out of her hair. It tumbled to her shoulders and as he combed his fingers through it, a wonderful sensation flowed through her body. She closed her eyes and allowed it to blossom within her. It had been a long time since she had felt such pleasure. She entertained it momentarily, but just as she opened her eyes to protest against it, Evan's mouth was on hers. His lips pressed firmly against hers. She could feel his hot breath. She should have fought it, but instead returned it with the same passion. When they parted, the reality of what she had done mortified her. She immediately withdrew from him.

"This is wrong," she said getting to her feet.

"Why is this wrong?" he protested as he got to his feet as well.

"Because I'm married, in case ya have forgotten." Her anger was directed more at herself than at him. How could she have allowed this to happen?

"No, I haven't forgotten; you remind me of it constantly. But are you really married? Just because a piece of paper says it, doesn't make it so."

She didn't want to hear it. She had heard these arguments before from herself. She turned her back to him as if to drown out his words. When she did, her eyes scanned the horizon. She saw Katherine playing in the field, but Michael was nowhere to be seen.

"Michael! Michael!" she called urgently. She felt fear compress her heart, as she ran towards the last place she had seen him. Evan's anger turned to great concern as he realized what was going on. He chased after her, looking frantically back and forth. The two scoured their surroundings with their eyes, Mary turning a full three-sixty degrees, but seeing no sign of him. Panic was about to set in. She looked towards the creek and her fear became unbearable. In her mind she could see his small body floating in the water. She tried to shake the image as she cried, *"Dear God, make it not so!"*

Evan had the same thought. They raced to the water's edge and searched up and down the creek. To their relief, they did not find him there. But where could he have gone? Mary again turned around anxiously looking for some sign. Her heart was pounding so loud she could hear it in her ears. She tried to will it to calm down for it was interfering with her ability to hear if the child was calling out.

Evan wandered upstream. He crossed over and knelt by the bank. He turned and called back to her. "Hey, I think I found something."

Mary ran through the water as fast as she could. She didn't care that her dress was getting drenched. She came along side him and her eyes focused on what he was looking at. It was footprints from a small child going up the bank. They must have been his. Without saying a word she leaped onto the bank and searched the woods. "Michael! Michael!" She stopped to listen. Evan climbed up beside her and started to say something. She held up her hand to silence him. "Do ya hear anythin'?" He shook his head.

Just then a few fat drops of rain began patting the leaves on the trees. They were momentarily protected under the leafy coverage, but soon the heavens opened up and pelted them. They were quickly soaked to the skin. Mary was not deterred. She said a silent prayer and then headed in the direction she hoped that he had gone. She continued to call his name, but heard no response. She went a little farther, stopped and called again. In the distance she heard a child's giggle. She stood perfectly still trying to hone in on the sound. Evan was making it difficult, as he traipsed through the woods making too much noise. When he reached her, she shushed him. Once again she called out. They listened. A faint giggle sounded over the rain.

"Over there," Evan said pointing. They both ran swiftly, weaving through the trees as they went. Finally she spotted the boy, just as he spotted them. Instead of running towards them, he turned and ran away, giggling the whole time. It was a game to him. Mary quickly overtook him and scooped him up in her arms. She didn't know if she should spank or hug him; she opted for the latter.

"Ya naughty boy. Ya scared me half to death." She panted for breath, more from fright than from the sprint. She looked in his eyes and said, "Ya mustn't ever do that again." The child giggled not understanding the gravity of the situation. "We need to get ya back to the house and get some dry clothes on ya."

Evan by this time caught up with her. "Boy, you sure can run fast for a woman."

"Woman, indeed; I out ran ya."

"You did," he said and couldn't keep from laughing. Mary joined him, laughing out of relief.

She said, "Ya never know how fast ya can run, until ya have to." She paused and then said, "How in the world did he get this far?"

"I have no idea," he replied. "It's amazing how fast their little legs can carry them in such a short time."

When the two returned to the other side of the creek, they found Katherine standing on the bank crying. She was sobbing so hard, Mary could barely understand her. "I didn't…know where…you went. I…thought…you…left me."

Evan took Michael from Mary. She knelt down, picked the child up and hugged her. "I'm sorry, honey. I was so scared that Michael might have gotten badly hurt, I forgot about ya. I didn't mean to scare ya." The child's sobs settled down to a soft cry and they went to gather up their belongings. Mary picked up Robert's book, which was now saturated by the rain. "Oh, look at that, tis ruined," she said mournfully.

"Maybe not, it just needs to dry out," he said trying to reassure her.

They walked back to the house in no hurry. The rains continued to pour and since their clothes were already sticking to themselves, it didn't really matter. When they got to the house, Mary had the children take off their shoes as not to track in any more mud than they had to. She took Michael back in the bedroom, stripped him and toweled him off. She changed his diaper and put on some dry clothes. She turned him loose with orders for Evan not to let him get into anything.

It was Katherine's turn. She pulled off the girl's dress and undergarments and then towel dried her hair. She dressed her in a light blue print dress. Now it was her turn. She left the children's room and started for her bedroom, but Evan stopped her.

He grabbed her by the arm and teased, "You're so beautiful when you're all wet."

Mary sighed. She couldn't believe how insatiable he was. She was very flattered by the attention, but at the same time it was like offering a starving man bread crumbs. He'd follow the trail wherever it led—only she was afraid where this was leading her. She started to protest again when she heard wagon wheels. Both of them stopped and listened.

"What time is it?" she asked, her eyes were wide with fear.

Evan took his watch out and his heart sank. "We must have taken longer than we thought finding Michael." He too had fear in his eyes.

"Quick out the back door," she said pulling at his arm. But Evan didn't move. "Come on, ya fool, before he gets in the house."

"It's too late, Mary," he said defeated. She looked at him in disbelief. "My carriage is out front; he's already seen it." Mary now understood. What was she going to do? More importantly, what was James going to do?

The door swung open and she saw a soaking wet husband and child. What she also saw made her cringe. She had seen that look in his eyes on numerous occasions and it was never good. It usually led to violence. She instinctively stepped back as he entered the room. Joshua, who had been standing partially behind his dad, raced past him. James reached out to grab him, but the boy was too quick. He ran and embraced his mother. He too was full of fear. Mary pulled him behind her so that she was between him and James. She would protect her son no matter the cost. Evan had stepped in front of both of them ready to take action if need be.

James closed the door behind him. He threw his wet hat aside. "Mr. Sullivan," he said a little too calmly. "I thought you spent your Sunday mornings tutoring little old ladies." He shot a look at Mary; he had only contempt for her.

"I never said that; you just assumed," he said trying not to add fuel to the fire.

James nodded his head in agreement, but his jaw was firmly set. "So have you been tutoring her—or has she been tutoring you?"

Evan furrowed his brow, not understanding. He looked at James and then back at Mary. The terror in her eyes spoke volumes. Mary pulled Joshua forward and said quietly, "Go to yar room with yar cousins." He started to protest, but then relented. He gave his father a wary look as he went inside.

James turned his attention back to Mary and Evan. A sinister grin spread across his face as he removed his wet coat and dropped it to the floor. "Oh, has she never told you about her many talents?"

"James, don't," Mary said quietly. Her voice was shaky.

"What? Did you not tell him about your past?" He didn't wait for an answer. He addressed Evan instead. "She didn't tell you about all the men she used to be with?"

Evan looked at him with disdain. He had more contempt for James than ever before. He wasn't quite sure what he was insinuating, but he wasn't going to be swayed from Mary's side. "It doesn't matter," he said, a little louder than he intended.

"Oh really? It doesn't mean anything that she used to be a prostitute?"

His words slowly sank in. He looked at her hoping that she'd deny it, but she didn't. He couldn't fathom this sweet woman ever doing such a thing. He turned back to James and repeated, "It doesn't matter what she may have done years ago. What she has done now is what's important. She has been nothing, but faithful to you—only God knows why. You certainly don't deserve someone like her."

Mary saw something ignite in James' eyes; it wasn't good. Her heart had accelerated to the point she thought it would explode. Maybe that would be a good thing and it would all be over.

James took a step forward and said with derision, "So are you willing to protect her *honor*?"

"If need be," he said, standing his ground.

Mary came up from behind him. "Mr. Sullivan, this is not yar fight. Please leave before anyone gets hurt."

He turned and said, "I am not leaving you alone with him, especially in the state of mind that he is in."

"It doesn't matter anymore," she said, resigned to take whatever James was going to do to her. "Please leave."

He grabbed her by the shoulders. "Mary! I love you! I won't let him hurt you anymore."

"Tis over Evan," she said, saying his given name for the first time. He blinked, not knowing what to say. "Me place is with me husband. Please leave." There was a finality in her voice.

He stared at her, trying to think of what he needed to do. It was obvious that neither wanted him to stay. He felt helpless, but he relented. He picked up his possessions and walked past James, but before he did, he said, "If you so much as touch her…"

"What? You'll come back and hit me over the head with one of your books?" he said sarcastically.

Evan restrained himself from decking James right then. He turned and went out the door. He lit off the porch and headed to his carriage. The rain continued to come down in sheets.

James turned his attention on Mary. There was fury in his eyes. She had humiliated him for the last time. "Come on," he said. "We're heading for the barn."

Mary trembled. "Whatever for?"

"I'll not be a laughing stock in my own house."

He started to drag her out when Joshua came storming out of his bedroom. "You leave my mother alone!"

"Boy, get back to your room!"

"Don't you touch her," he said, balling up his fists. His eyes had narrowed to little slits and were filled with hatred.

"Don't talk back to your father," he warned him.

Mary spoke up. "Do as yar dad says." He started to protest, but Mary insisted that he return to his room. She looked at James and somehow summoned up the courage to do what he asked. It was the only thing to do to save the children. She slowly marched herself to the barn. Her breathing was labored from fear. In her heart she cried out for Jesus to save her. She prayed for a miracle, but the miracle would not come at this hour.

She swung the barn door open and James followed her in. He closed the door behind them and said, "It's time for your punishment."

24

The Unthinkable

Evan raced his carriage recklessly back to town. He had one thought on his mind. He needed to find the one person that might be able to reason with James. He just hoped that he was not too late. His mind whirled in a thousand directions, thinking about what was happening at the Whitaker farm. He had a sick feeling in his stomach. He should have turned around and went back there, but now it was too late. He had reached Windsor.

As he made the sharp turn coming into town, the carriage tilted and rode on two wheels. Evan shifted his weight to the other side just before the carriage flipped over. It seemed impossible for his heart to pound any harder, but it did. He raced along the muddy street, nearly crashing into a farmer and his wagon. The farmer said some disparaging words, but Evan ignored it. Time was getting away from him; he needed to hurry. Pulling up to the front of the church, he stopped quickly, nearly sending him out of the carriage face first. He jumped from his vehicle, ran up the steps and tore open the door. When he went inside he was disappointed.

He cursed himself. How stupid could he be to think that anyone would still be at the church? He paced the aisle trying to think about his options. A strange feeling came over him like he wasn't alone. It was odd that he had spent long hours by himself grading papers, going over assignments for the next morning and never encountered this sensation before. Yet today—a Sunday, it was somehow different. He half expected to see something supernatural out of the corner of his eye.

He looked up at the cross that hung behind him. He paid little attention to it before, scarcely knowing it was even there. So why did it bother him now? *"I don't know if you exist,"* he spoke out loud. His voice sounded so loud in the empty building and seemed to reverberate. He hung his head and said to himself, "This is ridiculous." He paused and then tried again. *"I don't hold much to whether or not You're real, but Mary sure thinks you are. If you are, then prove it to me. You need to save her from her husband. If you don't, then I'm afraid he'll kill her. Maybe not today...but someday. I need to find the reverend. I don't know where to begin to look, so please help me. Not for my sake, but for Mary's."*

He stood in the silent church waiting for a sign from heaven. He didn't know what to expect—maybe some lightning and thunder. It would be apt, since it was still raining buckets. Or maybe a booming audible voice would have been nice. Whatever he expected, instead he only got silence. Disheartened, he went back out into the driving rain. He surveyed the town trying to figure out his next move. Then unexpectedly a thought came to him. He got the impression that he needed to go to the mercantile. If anyone might know where the reverend was it just might be Mr. Thompson.

He trotted down the steps and sprinted across the street to the store. The mercantile was always closed on Sundays because of the Sabbath. Thompson only made exceptions for emergencies like a sick child or such. Evan ran to the back of the building where Thompson lived. He bounded the steps and began pounding on his front door.

He could hear Curtis Thompson calling before he answered the door, "I'm coming, I'm coming. Hold your horses." He opened the door and could tell by the expression on the school teacher's face that something was wrong. "Mr. Sullivan, is there something I can help you with?"

"I'm looking for Reverend Matthews. I don't suppose you would know where he is?"

"Well, as a matter of fact, I believe I heard Luke Myers invite him to Sunday dinner."

"Where is it?" Evan asked. He had been to the Myers farm before, but he was so rattled he couldn't remember. Thompson pointed and explained that it was just past the sawmill a little ways. It jarred his memory and he took off like a flash back to his carriage.

Thompson called, "What's going on?"

"Don't have time to explain," he yelled back. He leapt onto the carriage and took off. He drove past the mill and continued on. Myers farm was about a quarter of a mile out of town, but seemed a lifetime away. As he climbed a long hill, he saw up in the distance the large barn that belonged to Myers. He rounded the bend to his driveway, almost upsetting the carriage again. He pulled up to the front door, jumped out, slid on the mud, and righted himself before he fell. He charged up the porch steps and beat on the door.

Luke Myers opened the door and found the nearly panic stricken school teacher. "Mr. Sullivan," he said startled. "Are you alright?"

"Is the reverend here?" he said urgently. "I need to see Reverend Matthews."

"Okay, just hold on a minute," he answered. "Why don't you step inside and get out of the weather."

"No, I'm too wet. I just need to see Reverend Matthews."

Luke turned his head and yelled back. "Reverend, there's someone to see you at the door."

"Yeah? Who is it?" he asked as he approached the doorway.

"Mr. Sullivan."

"Mr. Sullivan?" Luke moved back out of the way, so the preacher could get by him. One look at Sullivan, told him that something was wrong. "What can I do for you, Mr. Sullivan?"

"It's James Whitaker," he said breathlessly. "I think he might do something to his wife."

The pastor didn't have to ask how he knew. With what Mary had shared with him, he surmised that the man had been a witness. "How can I help?"

"I thought he might listen to reason if it came from you—being a man of God and all."

"Let me get my hat. I'll be right there."

He turned around and found Luke beside him. Luke said, "I'm coming with you. But let me get my gun first." The preacher didn't argue.

When he heard his parents leave the house, Joshua peered out his bedroom window that faced the barn door. He saw them go into the barn. Katherine came up beside him wanting to see what was happening. Joshua pushed her back, afraid of what she might see. She began to cry and he put his hand over her mouth to silence her. The little girl fought against it. Joshua lost his patience.

"Listen to me," he shouted. "I need you to be quiet." The fear in his eyes silenced her whining and he removed his hand from her mouth. "Katherine, something bad is happening. I have to go for help. Do you understand?" She slowly nodded her head. "Okay, you have to do as I say."

Joshua ran out of the room and retrieved a chair from the kitchen. He closed the door to the bedroom and then stuck the chair under the door knob. "Did you see what I just did?" She nodded even though she didn't understand why he would show her such a thing. "Listen, when I leave, I want you to stick this chair under the doorknob like I showed you, okay?"

"Yes, but…"

"It'll keep my dad from getting in here. Do *you* understand?" The girl's eyes went wide as she nodded her head. "I have to leave, but I'll be back as soon as I can."

"But I want to go with you," she said crying again.

Joshua shook her and said, "Listen to me! You have to stay and take care of Michael. Now be brave for me."

He didn't console her anymore. He left the room and closed the door. He made sure that she put the chair in its place, securing the door in the process. Then he ran out of the house and down the road as fast as he could. Fear gripped his heart as he ran. What was his dad doing to his mother? He had seen him get violent with her before, leaving marks and bruises. But he had never removed her from the house before. Tears ran down his cheeks as he thought about what she must be going through. He had to get help as soon as he could.

As he ran, Joshua prayed for God's help. At one point he stumbled, lost his balance and belly flopped in the mud. It knocked the wind out of him. For a moment he thought he was going to die. He sat on his knees and sucked in air. Slowly he got back to his feet, making sure that everything still worked and then he ran on. He felt fear chasing after him like a dark supernatural being hovering over him. Its greasy tentacles were about to wrap themselves around him. He stumbled again, slipped on the mud and somehow regained his balance. He cried out again to God. Suddenly he remembered what his mother said to him whenever he was afraid. He began to repeat it like a mantra: "Be strong and be courageous. Be strong and be courageous."

He climbed the hill and spotted the Beecham farm. With the last ounce of energy, he climbed up the bank and ran across the field. He sprinted to their front porch and slid his way to the door, grabbing the doorframe to right himself. He began yelling as he beat on the door. Roy Beecham opened the door but had no time to ask questions.

"Come quick, it's Ma," he said panting. "I think Dad's going to kill her."

"What?" Roy was having trouble comprehending. Ida Rose heard the commotion and was quickly by his side.

"What's happened, Jethro?" she asked, her voice was tense.

He rambled, running his words together. "I-I-I don't really know. We came home from church and Mr. Sullivan was there. For some reason Dad got mad about it. I've never seen him that mad. Mr. Sullivan left and Dad took her to the barn. That's when I ran here. I'm afraid he's going to kill her."

Roy turned to Ida Rose and quietly said, "I'm getting my gun."

"I'm going with you," she responded.

"No, it's too dangerous."

"If Mary's hurt someone needs to tend to her."

Roy gave in. He threw on his hat and coat and then grabbed his rifle. He went and brought the team around to the side of the house. Ida Rose gave instructions to her oldest, Luella as she wrapped a shawl around herself, covering her head. She and Joshua joined Roy in the wagon and they took off. Roy hadn't driven his wagon this reckless since the night Jethro had been born. The irony struck him; it was bad weather that night as well. When they returned to the farm, it seemed deserted. Roy jumped down and started towards the open barn door. Ida Rose gingerly lowered herself to the ground, trying not to slip in the mud. By the time she reached him, he gently pushed her back.

"Let me go in first. I don't know what I'll find." She agreed and he went inside. As Ida Rose stayed outside, Joshua came beside her. He looked in her eyes, trying to find any hope in them. He only saw the same fear that he was feeling. Moments passed and then Roy called for her to come in. She broke free of the boy, instructing him to stay put. When she went inside and saw Mary lying on the ground, she gasped.

Evan led the way in his carriage while the reverend and Luke were in the pastor's. Reverend Matthews hated that Luke had to bring along his rifle, mainly because he was afraid someone might have to use it. Luke didn't like the thoughts of it either. James was not only his boss, but he had been a longtime friend. Something had been eating away at James for a long time and Luke felt powerless to help him. He worked his jaw as he debated on whether to speak his mind. He finally gained some courage. "I wish you could have known him several years ago, Pastor. James was a good man then."

"What changed him?" he asked, trying to talk over the noise of the carriage wheels and the steady downpour.

"The death of his brother Jethro," Luke replied. He paused briefly, wondering how much he should say. "James was a godly man; he treated everyone with respect. It was Jethro who had been hard to deal with. He rode James and ridiculed him. Even though they went to church together and professed to be a Christian, it was James that seemed more dedicated."

"So what happened?"

"Just before the accident, James and Jethro had had some words. No one seems to know what it was all about. Maybe James had had enough of Jethro's bullying. If the truth were told, any success they had in business was because of James. He had good instincts when it came to business. I think Jethro knew that and was jealous of the fact. Anyway, on the day of the accident, we could hear them in the office arguing. James came out and slammed the door. He gathered up a crew of men and headed out to do some timbering. Sometime later, Jethro came looking for him. James didn't know it. He and I were too busy cutting down a tree. We thought everyone had cleared the area. We had already notched it…have you ever cut down a tree, Pastor?"

"No, I'm afraid I haven't."

"Well, you have to cut out a wedge on the side you want the tree to fall. Usually it'll fall that way. But on this day, inexplicably, the tree didn't; it kind of veered to the right. As we looked to where it was going to fall, we saw Jethro walking across the field towards us. He saw it coming just as we realized what was about to happen. We yelled, but it was too late. He was killed instantly."

Luke continued, "James took it hard; he blamed himself. It was clearly an accident, but he refused to be consoled. He quit attending church, neglected his responsibilities at work and at home. He withdrew from life. But just when everyone was afraid he would do something to himself, he came around. He suddenly came back to church and said that he had rededicated his commitment to God. Everyone was relieved, but I still sensed that things were wrong. He become hot tempered and impatient…and began to drink. I tried to talk to him, but he told me to mind my own business. It was like he was sinking down into a deep mine shaft and there was no one to rescue him. I had hoped that getting married might be good for him, but it's made things worse. I'm not surprised that it's come to this."

Reverend Matthews wasn't sure what to say. He tried to find words of hope. "Well, it's never too late for God to save someone, as long as there's breath in him."

The Beechams had wrapped Mary in a couple of blankets and carried her into the house, laying her on her bed. Ida Rose had Joshua check on his cousins while she attended Mary. She grabbed some towels and began stripping off her wet clothes. She needed her husband's help because Mary was out cold. Roy hesitated, not wanting to see another man's wife, but he had no choice. Ida Rose could not do it herself.

The only way they knew she was still alive was because she had moaned when Roy had rolled her over. She had a split lip that was swelling and a busted nose. Blood had seeped out and dried; her eyes had already darkened with bruises like a raccoon, a clear indication that her nose was broken. As they rolled her over, they saw the full extent of his fury. She had welts and bruises all over her arms and back. Apparently the strap he had used had some kind of buckle on it; it had repeatedly left the imprint on her. There was also some bruising around the middle. They suspected he may have busted her ribs by kicking her.

Roy felt his stomach pitch. How could a person do such a thing to another human being? He couldn't imagine doing that to a wild animal unless it was about to take his life. But to do that to someone you said you loved…that you had a child with…it was unfathomable. He shuddered at the thought. They managed to get some dry clothes on her and tucked her in bed. Ida Rose threw extra blankets on her to keep her warm. She put a cool damp cloth on her forehead and hoped that she would awaken soon. She too was nauseated by what she had seen and feared that Mary might not make it.

Evan Sullivan was the first to get back. He had driven like a crazed lunatic. He pulled up to the house and saw a strange wagon by the barn beside James' team. It momentarily slowed him as he tried to figure out what was going on. He went to the door, hesitated as if to knock, but decided to just go in. He stepped inside and found Roy Beecham crouched by the fireplace, starting a fire. Roy stood and greeted him, but before he could say anything more, Evan asked, "How's Mary?"

Roy raised an eyebrow thinking it was a little forward to call her by her first name. After all these years he still referred to her as Mrs. Whitaker. He cleared his throat and then simply said, "Not good."

Evan's heart fell. He looked at the door to her bedroom and started to go in, but Roy stopped him. "Leave her alone; she's resting."

"Is James here?"

"No," he answered with disgust.

"Tell me what he did to her?" he asked, regretting the decision he had made.

Roy turned back to the fireplace and added a couple of small chunks of wood to the fire. "He...he beat her pretty good." He stood back up, looked him squarely in the eye and said, "No thanks to you." He wasn't sure who he was angrier with, James or the school teacher. Evan hung his head and Roy didn't hold his tongue. "You couldn't even be man enough to stand up for her."

Evan started to defend his actions when the reverend and Luke came through the door, interrupting the two men. Reverend Matthews asked the same questions that Evan had. They defended his actions by explaining how he had come to get them. Roy put aside his anger for the time being. Then the four discussed what further action should be taken. They decided that it was best if Evan went back to Mr. Thompson and organize a search party. Evan wasn't too happy about that, but they all agreed that it would not be wise for him to be the one to find James or be here if he returned. Roy and Luke would begin searching the property in hopes that he just wandered off. He didn't take any of the horses so they felt that he couldn't have gone very far, but it was just a matter of which direction he went. Reverend Matthews would stay and keep vigil with Ida Rose.

Before Evan left he quietly went inside the bedroom. He took one look at her battered face and collapsed to his knees. He leaned against her bed and began to weep uncontrollably. He kept saying, "It's all my fault, it's all my fault. I shouldn't have left you. I'm so sorry."

Reverend Matthews came along side to console him. He put his hand on the man's shoulder and softly said, "You had no way of knowing it was going to be this bad."

"Yes, I did. I saw the look in his eyes. I should have came back to protect her."

"All you would have probably done was get both of you killed. You did the right thing getting us. We'll find him and he'll have to answer for this."

"And what about her? What's going to happen to her?"

"She's in God's hands. Now if you want to help, you need to get that search party together. The sooner we find James the better."

Evan raised himself up and wiped away his tears. "I'm sorry, Mary…for everything. I didn't mean for you to get hurt." Without saying a word to anyone he left the house, got into his carriage and rode off.

Reverend Matthews knelt beside Mary's bed. Taking her hand, he spoke to her. "Mrs. Whitaker—Mary, if you can hear me, its Pastor Matthews. We need you to come back to us. A lot of people are depending on you…Joshua…Katherine and Michael…your friends. We all need you. If you can, please open your eyes."

He and Ida Rose waited, but there was no response. Ida Rose asked, "What do we do now?"

"We pray." He took Ida Rose's hand and they both bowed their heads and began to pray that God would intervene. Outside, Roy and Luke stood on the porch. They watched the rain continue to beat down. Pulling the collar of their jackets up around their necks, they ran across the barnyard and pulled James' team inside. They unhitched the horses and then saddled them up. As they did, they discussed which would be the best place to start looking for him. Once the decision was made, they mounted their horses and lit out to the open field in the rear of the property. It was going to be a long afternoon; they just hoped they could find him before night fell.

25

Resolution

It was as if the heavens had opened up and shown its disapproval. The torrential downpour continued. James, in his confused state of mind had run blindly across the open fields of his property and then zigzagged through the woods. When he came to his senses, he realized where he had come—the place where it all began. He stopped to catch his breath, bending over and gulping in as much air as he could. As his breathing became steadier, the weight of his actions hit him. He was appalled at what he had done, believing he was incapable of such violence. From the deepest recesses of his soul, an anguished cry bellowed from him. *"Oh God in heaven, what have I done? I didn't mean to kill her. What's happening to me?"*

The memory of his brutality crashed over him like powerful ocean waves. He interlaced his hands behind the base of his head, cradling it with his elbows. He tried desperately to shut the memory out, but it was no use.

Mary had obediently gone into the barn, but once inside he shoved her backwards. She stumbled, but caught herself before falling. He ranted, "You think you can make a fool out of me? I won't continue to be an object of scorn any longer."

"Scorn? If anyone has been an object o' scorn, tis me," she argued and then regretted saying anything.

"How dare you sleep with him," he shouted. His eyes were filled with contempt.

"It wasn't that way," Mary shook her head, denying it. She backed away from him until she came against one of the stalls and could go no farther.

"The two of you were laughing behind my back the whole time." He shook his head and said, "I can't believe that you slept with my brother."

Mary's eyes grew wide with disbelief. "I didn't even know yar brother." James drew back his fist and struck her in the face. The force instantly broke her nose and split open her lip. Mary hit the back of her head on one of the post. She went down like a sack of potatoes, dazed but not completely out.

"He couldn't let me have one thing for myself," he continued to shout. "He had to take you from me. I'll show him. Someone's going to pay for this."

He reached up and took down a leather strap that had once been part of a harness; it still had the metal loop attached. He swung the strap back and began to thrash her. Mary threw up her arms to protect herself, but it did no good. The strap caught her across the forehead, putting her on her back. She was open and vulnerable and he seized the opportunity. He began kicking her in the ribs. The bones snapped in two like small pieces of kindling. She rolled on her stomach for protection and James swung the strap again, pummeling her back; the buckle digging deep into her flesh. Mercifully, Mary lost consciousness, but he continued beating her.

Finally exhausted, James stopped and dropped the leather strapping to the ground. He stood over her panting like a mad dog. In his twisted mind, he only saw a phantom from his past that needed to be exorcised. But as the cloud from his mind receded, he began to come back to his senses, realizing what he had done.

Kneeling down beside her, he shook her lifeless form trying to awaken her. He said in bewilderment, "Mary? Mary, are you alright?" She didn't respond. James stood up and began to pull at his hair. He began to cry, "What have I done…what have I done? Oh Mary—I'm so sorry." He took a step back and said quietly, "I've killed her." He turned and bolted out of the barn and began to run. He ended up here…the place where he had killed his brother.

Evan had gone back to Windsor and told Curtis Thompson that he needed help. Thompson told him to go over to the church and ring the bell. "The men will come running when they hear it," he said. "They'll know that something's wrong."

Evan did as instructed while Thompson went and unlocked his store. He gathered up firearms, along with ammunition. He met Evan at the church as the first responders came on the scene. As they gathered, Evan began to explain that Mary was found in the barn by the Beechams nearly beaten to death and there was no sign of James anywhere. He tried to keep it as vague as possible so the men didn't get stirred up and go gunning for James. Evan personally didn't care, but there were too many unanswered questions about why he did it. They needed him alive.

"What about the children?" someone asked.

"They're safe; the preacher and Ida Rose are there taking care of them, as well as Mary."

Someone asked point blank if Evan knew if James had done it. He sidestepped the question by saying, "We don't have time for discussion. We don't have much daylight and we need to find James before nightfall."

The men took their horses and headed over to the Whitaker farm. As they got there, Roy and Luke were just returning. They had circled the perimeter and found nothing. After a short discussion, the men decided to fan out and continue walking straight ahead until they found something. It was still unknown which direction he had gone.

James was weeping, but the rain water washed his tears away. Large drops of water fell from the saturated curls on his head. He leaned against a tree trying to steady himself. The memory of that fateful morning was as real and as painful as Mary's beating.

He had been in the office early like every morning. Jethro strolled in a couple of hours later, which wasn't unusual. Even though they shared the same house, they each kept different hours. Jethro often went carousing into the early morning. He came in that morning with a hangover. The first thing he did was pick up the pot of coffee James kept warm on the potbelly stove in the office.

Jethro jerked his hand away from the pot and exclaimed, "Dang, that's hot!"

"Helps to keep the coffee warm," James said absently, continuing to peruse the books.

Jethro got out his handkerchief and wrapped it around the hot handle. He poured the steaming beverage into a mug. He brought it to his lips and blew on it, trying to cool it. It still burnt his mouth and he let out an oath.

"I wish you wouldn't do that," James said.

"What? Drink your coffee?" he asked.

"Swear like that." Jethro rolled his eyes and otherwise ignored the comment. "I'm taking a team up to the Breckenridge place shortly. You think you can have your wits enough to take care of the place while I'm gone or is your brain like scrambled eggs this morning."

"I'll manage," he said petulantly. Secretly he was glad that James had not asked him to come along this morning; his head was killing him.

James got up from the desk and picked up his jacket. Putting it on he said, "I've been meaning to talk to you about something." He hesitated and then said, "I'd like for you to find other accommodations."

Jethro was livid. "Why? That house is as much mine as it is yours. I've put in just as much blood, sweat and tears into it as you have."

James knew that was not the fact. He was the one that had done most of the work, but he didn't force the issue. "We can start building a new cabin down by that open field by the creek. That would make a nice place."

"Why do I have to leave? Why not you?"

"Because…" James started. Again he hesitated, not sure how his brother would take the news. "I'm getting married in a couple of weeks."

"Married? You? Who's the unlucky girl?" he asked snidely.

"I doubt if you know her. She's a sweet Irish girl over at Willard's Crossing."

"An Irish girl? I'm surprised at you James after our parents were killed by a bunch of Irish thugs."

"She wasn't part of that," he said defending his choice.

Jethro took a sip of his coffee and then said, "Why so soon lover boy?" he said baiting him. "Can't control the urges?"

James fumed inside; he wanted to strike his brother, but he resisted. He wasn't generally prone to violence, but sometimes Jethro pushed him too far. "We just decided why should we wait? Besides, we won't be kicking you out immediately. But at some point, I would like some privacy with my wife."

Jethro had an insidious grin on his face. He chuckled and said, "Wanting some *privacy*, huh?" James didn't like his tone of voice, but he held his tongue. "Hey, by the way, what's the girl's name?"

"Her name is Finola, but most people just call her Nola." Jethro responded with an uproarious laugh. James grew indignant and asked, "What's so funny?"

He took a sip of his coffee and asked, "Does she have hair the color of sunshine and sparkling blue eyes?"

"Yes," James answered. A knot was growing in his stomach.

Jethro howled again. He came over and rested his hand on James' shoulder and said, "Buddy boy, did you just get off the boat? How stupid can you be? She must have seen you coming from a mile away."

James knocked Jethro's hand off of him. His eyes narrowed as his fury grew. "What do you mean?"

"Have you ever wondered how she takes care of herself?"

"She cooks and does laundry for people."

"By day maybe, but by night…"

"What are you insinuating?" James asked

He answered slowly letting every syllable sink into his brother's brain. "She's…a…pros-ti-tute…dear old brother of mine." James was stunned. He stood with his eyes darting back and forth, trying to make some sense of it. "You mean she hasn't performed for you?"

A spark ignited a firestorm of anger. James shook all over. What infuriated him the most was that there was some truth in what Jethro had proposed. James had not controlled his urges. They had given in one night and then just a few days ago, Nola had told him she was with child. James wanted to get married as soon as possible to cover up his sin. He couldn't stand being further scrutinized by his brother .If Jethro ever found out that his saintly brother had fallen, he'd never let him live it down. Slowly, James came to the realization that his brother could be right. If that was the case then James might not be the father after all. Maybe she had duped him.

Jethro saw his reaction and ran with it. He laughed again and declared, "You have slept with her haven't you!" He laughed again and James' face flushed with embarrassment and anger. Jethro continued to add fuel to the fire. "You're probably the only man that she's slept with that she's never demanded payment afterwards." He paused just long enough to add a real zinger to get to him. "You know, it's going to be pretty awkward to live with a sister-in-law that you've slept with."

James couldn't contain his anger any longer; he snapped. He threw a punch and struck Jethro squarely on the jaw, sending him backwards against the wall. The remaining coffee splashed all over him. Instead of getting angry, he began to laugh again infuriating James even more. He rubbed his jaw and said, "Well, we might make a man of you yet."

James stared daggers at his brother. He tried to regain his composure, but he lost the battle. Furiously he pointed his finger at him and shouted, "I wish to God you were dead." He stormed out of the office, slamming the door behind him. Before the day was through, James had gotten his wish.

The memory had shaken him to the core. In the distance, he thought he heard his brother's cynical laughter. He looked to his left and there he was laughing hysterically. "What did you think you were doing, buddy boy? Were you trying to free yourself of my ghost when you beat your wife? You could never do anything right. Just like the night our parents were killed. You had to go home and do school work; schooling was soooo important to you. If I hadn't walked you back home, I would have been there to defend them. Their blood is on your head, buddy boy—just like mine."

James took a step forward and the ghost of his brother disappeared. He cried out in anguish and beat his fist against his head. He could still hear his brother's laughter as he fell to his knees. *"Oh God in heaven help me. Please forgive me—for every evil thing I've done."*

His brother's laughter faded in the distance and a stillness swept over the forest. Even the rain had subsided. A strange sensation overtook him like someone calling his name. It wasn't audible, yet he heard it. He sat, resting on his knees perfectly still, waiting to see if he heard it again, but this time, all he heard was the rolling of thunder. It must have been his imagination. He started to get up when he sensed it again.

"James, how do you expect Me help you when you won't accept My love for you."

Again it was not audible, but more like a thought inside his head that wasn't really his thought. James thought at first that he must really be losing his mind and yet he gave into it. *"God, I don't deserve Your love. I've let too many people down…too many people have been hurt because of me…my parents…my brother…and now Mary."* He thought about Mary and began to weep again. His shoulders heaved with each sob. In anguish he cried out, *"God why did you send her to me. You knew she was too much like Nola. You knew how I had failed her."*

"It was to redeem you, to give you another chance."

"I don't understand."

"I gave her to you to show you the beauty of forgiveness. I gave her to you to see that if I could forgive someone whom you deem unforgiveable, I could forgive you as well."

"I don't deserve it God."

"Nobody does; it's My gift. I give it because I love you."

"After all I have done?"

"It's not dependent on what you have done, but on what I have done for you. I sent My Son to die in your place, James. It's time for you to embrace that. After all the times that you sat in My house of worship, hearing sermon after sermon and still you refused to accept this gift of love. It's time James. It's time for you to decide."

James wept. He had never felt worthy of God's love. He had never felt like he had ever measured up his whole life. Even though he had not audibly spoken his thought, James had received an answer.

"I've told you James; no one measures up to my standard. No man is holy enough to stand before me. Only Jesus' atonement makes you worthy. Believe in Me, James. Accept My gift of grace and forgiveness."

"God, I do want to believe. Help my unbelief; please forgive me." He bowed his head and continued to weep. At that moment the rain dropped off to nothing more than a mist. James peered up at the sky just in time to see a ray of light burst through the clouds. The ray spread out into streams of lights. With it, James felt a huge burden lift off of him. He laid down on his back and stared up at the beauty of it. The splendor amazed him at first and then it brought sadness. Softly he spoke as tears slid down his face. *"God, I can't do this; I can't go back and live with what I have done. I don't want to live any longer. I can't take this pain anymore. Take me home. I want to be with You. Please, take me home."*

Amazingly the rays of light seemed to converge until they were overtop of him. They felt warm and inviting. A peace came over him like he had never experienced in his life. If he had finally lost his mind, then he more than welcomed it. A smile broke across his face as he stared up at the brilliant light in the sky. He whispered, *"Thank You God."*

Mary's eyes fluttered, but they were swollen too much to open all the way. She was mouthing words, but they were so soft neither the pastor nor Ida Rose could understand. Reverend Matthews leaned forward to hear better. He listened intently and then a smile curled up on his lips.

"What's she saying?" Ida Rose asked.

He sat up and said, "She's singing."

"Singing?" She leaned down this time and heard it for herself.

"Amazing love…How can it be? That Thou me God shouldst die for me…" She finished and then asked just above a whisper, "Ida Rose? Is that you?"

"Yes, it is dear."

"Where am I?"

"You're in your bed. Reverend Matthews is here with you."

"Reverend," she addressed and then asked, "Where's James?"

"We don't know. We have people out looking for him now."

A lone tear fell out of the corner of her eye and landed on her pillow. "Don't let them hurt him, Parson. Somethin' isn't right with him. He's not thinkin' straight."

Reverend Matthew took her hand in his. He was amazed by her forgiveness and compassion. "We'll do our best."

As night fell, the men slowly trickled in from their search. They were wet and hungry. Ida Rose left Mary in the hands of the preacher as she scrounged up enough food to feed the lot of them. Dejected by the turn of events, no one said much as they ate. A few spoke about how good James had been to them as they had moved into the valley. It was all past tense. One by one, they turned and left to go home, vowing to return tomorrow to continue the search.

Evan had gone into Mary's room and spoken with her. He wanted to stay the night but she urged him to go home. "School starts tomorrow; ya need yar rest."

"We'll cancel school," he said softly, his once proud demeanor had been defeated.

"Ya'll do no such thin'; the children are countin' on ya. Go and get a good night's rest." Her voice may have been weak, but she was still quite spirited. "I have Ida Rose here and Reverend Matthews as well. They'll take care o' me."

He bent down and kissed her hand. He hesitated, wanting to say more, but not in front of her neighbors. He quietly left her room. He passed the men in the sitting room and felt their accusatory stares. He quietly left the house and started back to town.

As darkness filled the night, only Roy and Luke remained. At Mary's insistence she had Ida Rose get them some of James' clothes so they would be warm and dry. They sat by the fireplace and spoke softly, trying not to disturb Mary. Everyone was worried about whether they would find James alive or not. It was a solemn night.

Ida Rose tucked the children in bed and settled in Mary's bedroom on the floor. The preacher joined the other two and slept by the fireplace in the next room. The discussion continued until finally both Roy and Luke drifted off. Only Reverend Matthews was still awake. He spent this time deep in prayer for both Mary and James. He prayed that tomorrow would bring good news.

26

Grief

Some time before sunrise, Luke Myers awakened with a start. He said out loud, "How stupid can I be?" In the silence of the hour, his voice sounded louder than normal. Both Reverend Matthews and Roy Beecham were awakened by it.

Roy mumbled, "What's going on? Luke is that you?"

Luke threw back his blanket and was putting on his boots. He ignored him and mumbled on. "I don't know why I didn't think of this sooner."

The pastor rose up on one elbow and rubbed the sleep from his eyes. "Luke, tell us what's going on."

"I can't believe I didn't think about it sooner," he repeated.

Exasperated, Roy and the reverend said at the same, "What?"

"I think I might know where James is." He didn't immediately elaborate and the two grew impatient. They each asked where only this time they were out of sync. "He's either at one of two places. He's either back at the mill or I'm guessing, he's where this all started— the Breckenridge farm."

Matthews furrowed his brow and asked, "Why the farm?"

"That's where his brother was killed," he said grabbing his coat and putting it on.

"Now hold on Luke," Roy began. "It's still dark; give it another half hour or so and it will lighten up."

He started to object, but both Roy and the reverend agreed. Matthews thought it best for the two to grab a bite to eat first and then head out. "It might end up being a long day for all of us." He got up, went into the kitchen and set some kindling afire in the stove. He pumped some water into the coffee pot. Ida Rose, who wasn't sleeping too sound herself, heard the commotion and came out of the bedroom. She immediately took over the kitchen duties.

The fire had burned down quite a bit, so Roy stirred up the dying embers just enough to bring them back to life. He stuck a few small chunks of wood on them and soon they ignited. It wasn't extremely cold, but the dampness from the leftover rain gave a chill to the air. Roy continued to poke at the fire and think. He wondered how James had faired during the night. If Luke was right, he would have been at the mercy of the elements. Being early summer meant the nights weren't that chilly, but with a man soaked to the bone, it would have been mighty uncomfortable.

Ida Rose set flapjacks on the table for the men. Roy and Luke gobbled down their food and gulped down some coffee. When the two had finished, they put their jackets on and headed for the barn. They saddled James' horses once again and rode off.

Reverend Matthews watched from the window. He said a silent prayer on their behalf as well as for James. He turned to see Ida Rose standing by the fireplace deep in thought. It was strange how still everything seemed this early in the morning. It had an ominous feel to it. He came up beside her and put his hand on her shoulder causing her to jump.

"I'm sorry. I didn't mean to startle you," he apologized.

"I'm just a little jumpy this morning; didn't sleep too well."

"How's she doing?" he asked, referring to Mary.

"As well as can be expected. She stirred once and called out for James, but I got her to go back to sleep." She paused to stare at the fire once again. Then she asked, "What do you think will happen to James when they bring him back?"

"I don't know; I just don't know," he answered, but in his gut he wondered if James would make it back alive.

A layer of fog had risen along the top of the ground. The sun shone weakly through the thick cloud coverage. The men dismounted from their horses at the edge of the woods. They made their way through the underbrush. Luke paused to get his bearings. He looked back and forth searching for any distinguishable marks. "Over there," he said pointing to the left. He recognized the outcropping sticking up from the ground. "It's just beyond there."

Roy obediently went with his companion, but he carried with him some serious doubts. Why would James want to come here? What possible connection could Mary's beating have to do with his brother's death? The two events were years apart. But Roy decided to humor him anyway. He tilted his cowboy hat slightly upward as he scratched his forehead. He watched Luke pick his way through the thistles and then followed him.

As they neared the place, Luke stopped again and searched for any sign that might point to whether James had been here. His eyes scanned again and suddenly lit on something sticking out of the leafy undergrowth. Luke's heart sunk as he realized it was a boot. "There," he said to Roy."

Roy squinted his eyes and made a quick survey. He started to say, "I don't see any…"He stopped when he saw what Luke was pointing to. A sick feeling crept into his belly. Luke swallowed hard and slowly approached; Roy was on his heels. As they came closer, they realized it was what they had feared. Looking down at the man, they saw that it was James.

Mary had insisted that Joshua go to school. Ida Rose came and sat down on the chair beside her bed and gently tried to dissuade her. "Mary, the boy's tired and confused; he's hurting. I know how important schooling is to you, but he needs to be here with his family."

"It'll take his mind off o' everythin'," she countered.

Ida Rose shook her head slowly. "Trust me Mary, it won't. He needs to see you."

Mary started to shake her head in protest, but it hurt too much. "I don't want him seein' me this way." Instinctively she touched her lips and face and felt how swollen they were. She could only imagine how she must look. "It'll only frighten him more."

Reverend Matthews heard the conversation and entered the room. "In some ways," he began. "It'll frighten him, but in another I think it will ease his mind. Right now he is imagining all sorts of things, including that you might die. If he were able to talk to you, it just might give him assurance that you're going to be alright."

"I don't want him seein' what his father did to me." Her voice was choked with emotion. Fresh tears slipped out of the corners of her eyes.

Ida Rose got up from the chair and Reverend Matthews took her place. He gently took her hand and said, "He's going to have to face the truth. The sooner he does, the better off he will be. We can help him sort some things out in his mind. Otherwise, it'll stay there and fester. It might even cause him to be filled with the same rage."

The thought stabbed Mary in the heart. "I don't want that."

He stroked her hand and replied, "I know you don't Mrs. Whitaker. But trust me, it's for the best."

"Ya're probably right, Parson."

"Let me go and get him."

He returned with Joshua a few moments later. The young boy gasped when he saw his mother. Reverend Matthews rested his hands on either side of his shoulders trying to strengthen him. Joshua's eyes flooded with tears and spilled over. He called, "Mama, Mama," and bolted from the pastor. He embraced her with such force that pain shot through her body. It nearly took her breath away. She pursed her lips together and discovered that was the wrong thing to do. Her mouth began to throb again.

"Easy son," Matthews spoke for Mary. He gently pulled him away and then guided him into a chair.

Tearfully Joshua asked, "Are you going to die?"

"Not if I can help it," she answered. She turned her head as far as she could and looked at him through slits. She smiled weakly, even though it hurt.

Joshua tried to return it, but he was preoccupied with so many things. "Why did Dad do it?"

"I don't know, Josh. Yar dad…there's somethin' wrong with him."

"Why was Mr. Sullivan here? And why was Dad so angry about him being here?"

Thoughts raced through her mind trying to come up with an answer that he might be able to understand. She closed her eyes briefly and when she opened them again she said tenderly, "Tis a complicated matter, which I do not have the strength to explain right now." Joshua looked pleadingly at her. "But I will try to later."

The boy seemed to be satisfied for the moment. There was a long silent pause and then Joshua asked, "Where is Dad? When is he coming home?"

"We don't know, lad. We need to pray for him."

Joshua's jaw tightened as he spewed, "I don't think I can; I hate him."

His confession wounded Mary far worse than her abuse. "Don't ya be sayin' anythin' that ya might regret later. Tis not good to harbor ill feelin's, especially to yar own kin." She swallowed hard, remembering all the times she had cried bitter tears for what her father had done. It had taken her a long time to let go of the resentment.

"I hate what he did to you, Mama."

Gingerly, she reached her hand to his cheek and caressed it. "Josh, tis alright to hate the sin, but tis not right to hate the sinner. What yar dad did was wrong, but we have to pray for him. Only God can save him now."

Luke looked at Roy, but neither said anything. He squatted down and leaned over James, placing his ear just above James' mouth. He detected no sign of breathing. With his gloved hand, he reached out and closed his eyes. Whatever had happened to him would remain a mystery.

Roy went back to his horse. He retrieved a rolled up blanket that he had had the foresight to bring this morning. He handed Luke one end and the two spread the blanket out on the ground. Then Luke took the heavy end while Roy grabbed his feet. They slowly lifted the body and placed it on the blanket. Carefully and respectfully they wrapped the blanket around him. Then Roy got some rope and they secured it.

They stood and paused briefly before lifting the body. Roy took his hat off, followed by Luke. Each was lost in his own thoughts trying to come to grips with the loss of their dear friend. Given proper respect, they put their hats back on and hoisted him up, folding his body over Roy's horse. Then Luke mounted his and Roy climbed up behind him, riding double. Luke grabbed the reins of the other horse and they started back.

Overcome by grief, neither man had said anything. Finally, Luke spoke up, "Who's going to tell Mary?"

Roy thought for a moment and then answered, "The preacher."

Mary was asleep when Roy and Luke returned. They quickly lodged the horses in the barn in hopes that no one would see what they had brought back. Luke stayed with the body, while Roy went inside to break the news. Ida Rose immediately met him at the front door. Her face was etched with worry. He just looked at her and shook his head. She fell into his arms and cried softly. He held her momentarily, but he had business to take care of. He motioned for the reverend to come out to the barn. The men disappeared briefly inside. When they came out, they were joined by Luke.

Joshua had come out of the bedroom and saw the concerned looks on everyone's faces. He looked at Reverend Matthews and asked, "Is Dad...?"

He knelt down in front of the boy and answered, "I'm afraid he is."

Immediately tears filled his eyes and he embraced Reverend Matthews fiercely. "It's all my fault. It's all my fault."

Tenderly the preacher asked, "Now why would you think that this is all your fault?"

The boy heaved, not able to say anything for awhile. When he did speak it came out in short bursts. "Because...I...hated him...I wanted him...dead."

"No, son. I don't think you hated your father. You were just so upset with him for what he had done. Those are normal feelings."

"But I prayed…that God would…kill him…and now he's dead. I killed him."

"Then you must be pretty powerful to cause somebody's death," he said, trying to reason with him. "You know Joshua, God doesn't work like that. God is not a vindictive God. Does He discipline? Yes. Does He punish the wicked? Yes. But He does not destroy people out of spite. He is a just God. I trust that He saw the suffering that your father was going through and what he done to your mother…I believe that He was being merciful to him and just simply called him home."

The words of Reverend Matthews brought comfort to Joshua. His body relaxed and he stopped crying. He pulled back and looked at the preacher and asked, "Do you really think he's in heaven with God?"

"I can't say with certainty, but I'd like to think that he is."

Joshua seemed to take comfort in that. He started to go back to his room when suddenly he turned and asked, "What's going to happen to us now? Who will take care of us?"

"God will, Joshua. God will provide."

When Mary awoke, Reverend Matthews was by her bedside. He dreaded giving her the news. It was the one thing he disliked about his calling. Even so, he found that in those times, God provided a certain strength and somehow the right words came.

Mary's eyes fluttered. She turned her head slightly and saw the pastor. "Do ya ever rest, Parson? It seems every time I look over I see ya sittin' beside me."

"Just watching over one of my flock," he said softly. His mouth had gone dry in anticipation of what he was about to do. He reached over and took her hand. "Mrs. Whitaker, we have news about James."

"Tis not good, is it?" she interrupted.

"No, I'm afraid not. Roy and Luke found him this morning. He was dead."

Mary's lip quivered and tears gently fell out the corner of her eyes. She tried to control her emotions. She had a hard enough time breathing without her sinuses becoming congested. She scooted herself up in bed, but her body protest loudly against it. "Do they know if he suffered any?"

"They found him on his back looking up at the sky. Roy said that he had an almost peaceful look on his face."

"Where did they find him?"

"He had gone to the Breckenridge place where his brother had been killed, almost at the very spot."

Mary puzzled over the irony of it all. "I guess that be fittin' that he should die there; he so admired his brother." Reverend Matthews just nodded in agreement, even though in light of what Luke had said yesterday, he thought otherwise. "I want to see him," she said pushing herself up in a sitting position. She swung her legs over the edge of the bed before he could stop her.

"You shouldn't get out of bed," he protested.

Mary found herself agreeing with him. She was in too much pain and had to return to a prone position. "I want an Irish wake for him. I know he wasn't Irish, but I want people to come and pay their respects. That's the least I can do for him now."

"Tell me what I need to do and I'll see that it's done."

"Thank ya, Parson. Ya're a good man."

As instructed by Mary, everyone did their part. Since she was in no condition, Ida Rose and the reverend got the body ready. They were to wash it and then cover it in linen. Roy brought their kitchen table from home to lay his body on; he set it up in Mary's sitting room. Mr. Thompson was nice enough to donate the linen from his store. He also loaned his wife's prized padded rocker for Mary to have something comfortable to sit on during the visitation. She had insisted that she was to be there.

As word spread throughout the community, neighbors brought in food along with their condolences. Mary made sure that the reverend didn't forget to supply whiskey, a pipe for smoking and plenty of tobacco. "James has one somewhere," she said. "It be fittin' for the men to use it." Reverend Matthews was puzzled and she explained. "Accordin' to custom, each man that enters the home must take a puff off the pipe. The smoke was to ward off evil spirits." He gave her a doubting look. She shook her head and said, "I know. I don't hold much cotton to it. God gives and takes life, no evil spirit has any say in the matter—but it be tradition."

Each night around sundown, the candles that encircled James' body were lit and a procession of neighbors would begin arriving. Many were startled at the condition Mary was in. They tried to be polite and well meaning, but the looks on their faces told Mary what they were thinking. The men of course, indulged themselves in some whiskey and stood around telling stories about James—kind things he had done. Some quietly whispered about how he had changed after his brother's death and then the *marriage*. Some insinuated that it was the latter that had caused it.

Hearing these stories warmed Mary's heart, but it also intensified her mourning. Even though their marriage wasn't what she had hoped for, she still felt a sense of loss. She wished she had known this man that people had come to admire. She could have easily fallen in love with him.

She had remained faithful each of the three nights of viewing, greeting each guest courteously. Most of them she had never really gotten to know. Mrs. Cavanaugh and her weasel-faced husband made an appearance. It was hard, but Mary did her best to be cordial to even them. For years, she had fought off biting remarks and accusations. Tonight was no different. Mrs. Cavanaugh couldn't resist one parting shot. As she and her husband proceeded through the line, Mary heard her say, "Poor James, to have to put up with the likes of this woman."

Mary just about came unhinged. *This* woman! This woman was the one that was abused both verbally and physically. If Mary hadn't been so battered she would have come up out of her chair and told her a thing or two. Probably a few years ago, beaten or not, she would have. But fortunately age had given her more wisdom and restraint.

Evan Sullivan had come the first night, apologizing. In a low tone she said to him, "Tis not the time nor place to be talkin' about this. There's already enough rumors goin' 'round about us."

"You're right, but at some point we need to talk." She nodded and he quickly moved on.

On the last night, she raised herself up out of the rocker and made her way to the table where James' body lay. With tears in her eyes she began to sing her favorite lullaby. *"Sleep me child and peace attend thee. All through the night. Guardian angels God will send thee. All through the night."* All the women that were left in the house began to weep with her, especially when she sang the last verse. *"Love, to thee me thoughts are turnin'. All through the night. All for thee me heart is yearnin'. All through the night. Though sad fate our lives may sever. Partin' will not last forever. There's a hope that leaves me never. All through the night.*

Mary kissed James tenderly on the forehead and quietly turned away. Without saying a word she hobbled to her bedroom and closed the door behind her. The wake was over.

The morning of the funeral, Luke brought the coffin he had built. It was a fine piece of workmanship. He had taken the best pieces of oak planking he could find at the mill. The coffin was six sided and narrowed at the feet. He had sanded it smooth and then coated it with an oil varnish to seal it. He placed brass handles on the side and hinges on the lid. It was almost too beautiful to put in the ground.

They placed the body inside it. Reverend Matthews, Roy and Luke struggled to carry it, but they got it to James' wagon and loaded it on it. Roy was to drive the wagon to town with Joshua sitting beside him. Reverend Matthews helped Mary into his carriage with Katherine sitting between them. Ida Rose took care of Michael as she and Roy followed behind. Luke and his wife brought up the rear.

His body was taken into the church. The reverend stayed back with Mary, helping her up the steps and into the church. He seated her on the front pew; Joshua and Katherine sat next to her. Once more the procession of people came through paying their last respects. Many were townsfolk that Mary recognized, but a few must have been business acquaintances. After awhile they all became a blur—all except for two people.

The woman looked to be about Mary's age or possibly a little older. Her light blonde hair was pulled back into a tight bun underneath a black velvet hat. There was a veil that slightly obscured her face. She wore a dark charcoal grey dress that was tailored to her body. But it wasn't so much the woman that caught her eye as the boy that was with her. He looked like he could have been James' son. He had the same dark tousled hair as Joshua, but appeared to be a few years older than him. The two looked like they could have been brothers.

Mary's eyes stayed focused on the boy. A myriad of questions rushed through her mind. Was this a relative? Could the woman have been a wife of Jethro's that she didn't know about? If she was, then why didn't she come over and introduce herself? Or was this the woman from Willard's Crossing? If it was, then that must have meant that he had been seeing her long before Mary came to America. Why didn't he marry her instead? Or had he had an affair with a married woman? Her thoughts ran in circles and got her nowhere. If she hadn't been so disabled, she would have gotten up from her pew and introduced herself to them.

Before she got the fool notion to try that very thing, Reverend Matthews started the service. The congregation sang a couple of favorite hymns and then the pastor gave the eulogy. He said some very kind things about James, including stories that neighbors had shared about his generosity and willingness to give his neighbor a hand.

Mary felt so cheated. She wished that she could have known this man. As she paid her final respects, she leaned over his coffin and muttered under her breath, "James, what happened to ya? What made ya change? Was it me?" She hung her head and wept. Reverend Matthews came beside and supported her. He then led her outside as they closed the lid to the coffin.

They carried the body out to the cemetery that was behind the church building. Some of the men had already dug the six foot deep hole. They set the coffin by the plot; he would be buried next to his brother.

The reverend read from the Bible: "*I am the resurrection, and the life: he that believeth in me, though he were dead, yet shall he live: And whosoever liveth and believeth in me shall never die.* We now commit our brother James to the Lord. May God have mercy on his soul and may we one day be reunited with him."

They slowly lowered the coffin into the earth. Joshua and Katherine clung tightly to Mary and the three wept together. The service concluded and many turned away. The men that dug the hole began refilling it. And so was the end of the life of James Whitaker.

Reverend Matthews again came to Mary's side for support. A few stragglers came to offer their condolences one last time. Mary barely heard what they said. Her attention was focused beyond the throng of people as the woman and boy turned from the cemetery, mounted their carriage and then drove away. They took with them answers to so many questions.

27

Dismissal

After examining the ledger Mary closed it, fully satisfied. "Very good, Mr. Myers," she said softly. She had to admit now that she was glad Mr. Sullivan had taken the time to teach her the basics of mathematics. Otherwise she wouldn't have had the vaguest idea what Luke was talking about.

"Yeah," Luke replied. "James kept meticulous records that's for sure."

She handed the ledger back to him and then got up from James' desk. "I hope that ya're willin' to stay on as manager."

"Yes, ma'am."

She started for the door and then paused. "Ya know I don't know anythin' about this business. Joshua is much too young to come and work here, even though he thinks he can." Luke nodded his head and chuckled softly in agreement. "So I've been contemplatin' on what I should do. I'm seriously considerin' sellin' it. Would ya be willin' to buy it?"

Luke was stunned. It was beyond any of his wildest dream. For a split second his hopes soared as he pictured himself behind James' desk as owner and proprietor. But then reality brought him back to earth. "Mrs. Whitaker, I greatly appreciate the offer, but I don't have that kind of money."

"I've thought o' that. Tis not so much the money that I need, but to be released from the responsibility. So I be wonderin' if maybe we could come up with some kind o' agreement where ya could pay me a little at a time. Maybe ya could even do some odd jobs for me on the farm to help pay off the debt. I'm sure some thin's will come up that I won't be able to do."

Luke rubbed his chin as he considered it. It sounded good on paper, but he wasn't sure about helping her out around the farm. There were already rumors going around about her and he didn't think his wife would be too happy about him spending time alone with her. "Do you have to have an answer today?"

"I understand that ya need to think about it."

"Well, I'd like to talk it over with my wife."

"Take yar time; I'm in no hurry. But eventually, I will have to sell it."

He nodded and opened the door for her. As she left, he said, "Thanks again for thinking about me."

"I can't think o' anyone else that James would want it to go to."

Joshua came home from school and immediately started on his chores. He was the man of the house now and he needed to do his fair share, only he thought he should do more. His mother had been carrying the load for far too long. Mary came out to the barn to check on him. He was cleaning out one of the stalls when she came in. "Joshua did ya not bring yar school books home?" she asked.

"Don't have any," he said, raking up the soiled hay.

"What do ya mean, ya don't have any?"

"They took them away," he replied. "They said there won't be any more school until they can find a new teacher."

His piecemeal of information was frustrating Mary. "Who are *they* and what do ya mean *find* a new teacher? What about Mr. Sullivan?"

Joshua shrugged and said, "I don't know. They just said he wouldn't be teaching anymore."

"And who are *they*?" she repeated.

"Mr. Thompson, Mr. and Mrs. Cavanaugh…"

"Cavanaugh! It figures. She wields a lot o' power 'round here. Did they say anythin' about what was goin' to become o' Mr. Sullivan?"

Joshua shrugged and then continued cleaning the barn.

Mary wrestled with the sheets during the night, worrying about Mr. Sullivan's situation. Her indignation was inflamed by the audacity of Mrs. Cavanaugh. She was tired of her running roughshod over her and who knew how many countless people in town. So when morning came, she decided to take action. To Joshua's surprise, she left him in charge of Katherine and Michael. "I'll be back shortly," she said tying her bonnet. "Make sure ya keep an eye on little Michael; keep him out o' mischief." She turned to Katherine and said, "Don't ya be givin' him any grief."

"Okay Aunt Mary," she said softly.

Mary climbed up into the wagon and started into town. She needed some answers and would start first with Mr. Sullivan. She pulled the wagon up to the diminutive house of the teacher. It sat on the edge of town and was built by the townsfolk ironically with lumber donated by James. It was to house the current teacher which Mr. Sullivan no longer qualified. Mary knocked impatiently on his door. Before he could answer she knocked again. "I'm coming, I'm coming. Keep your pants on." He jerked the door open and was surprised to see Mary standing at his threshold.

She brushed passed him and came into the room. "What's goin' on Mr. Sullivan?" she asked. She looked around and saw he was boxing his things up in crates.

"Well, good morning to you too, Mary," he said sarcastically.

"I heard ya have been dismissed," she said with concern.

"I would have come out to tell you myself, but you basically ordered me to keep my distance, remember? So what brings you here? Aren't you afraid that I'll *soil* your reputation?"

"It appears that we have soiled each other's. Is this what it be all about?" He quietly nodded and then began putting some books in a crate. "Mrs. Cavanaugh's behind this, isn't she?"

He sighed. "Yeah, she did most of the talking."

"What did she say?"

"Oh, she called me an immoral, decadent reprobate."

"Did ya try to explain what we were doin'; that there was nothin' goin' on between us."

He turned and leaned against the table. With an impish grin he said, "Yes, but I don't think she believed me."

Mary furrowed her brow. "What are ya goin' to do, Mr. Sullivan? Where will ya go?"

"Don't really know. They've given me a whole week to vacate the premise. Maybe someone would be kind enough to let me stay with them until I figure this out." His grin broadened. "I could always stay in your barn; they already think that there's something between us. So what's the harm?"

He came towards her and she deftly avoided his embrace. She distanced herself on the other side of the tiny room. "What's the harm? I'm startin' to believe they may be right about ya, Mr. Sullivan. Ya seem to have the morals o' an alley cat."

He laughed and retorted, "And you my dear, think that you're an Irish Catholic nun."

"What's wrong with that? There's nothin' wrong with that kind o' devotion to God. Ya could use a little o' that in yar own life." He waved her off and turned his attention back to packing. "So what are ya goin' to do? Don't ya have some kind o' plan?"

He turned back to her and said exasperated, "I don't know. I've never been in the situation before."

"I'm sorry. Tis all me fault," she said quietly.

"It's not your fault. I'm the one that made advances to you."

"But if I had never asked ya to teach me…none o' this would have happened… and James would still be alive."

"You don't know that. But be honest, is that what you want? For James to be back, abusing you?" he said raising his voice in anger.

"I didn't want him to die," she answered. An awkward silence fell between them. Evan turned back and began to pack again; it was something to do. Suddenly Mary was inspired. "Do ya have some paper and a pen I could borrow?"

"Yeah, somewhere in this mess. Why?"

"I think I have a place for ya to go—at least for the time bein'." Puzzled he handed her some paper and then drew out a pen and bottle of ink from his desk drawer. "I'll write an introduction letter. There's no time to wait for a response. Ya'll have to take it and deliver it to him in person."

Slowly she began composing the letter. Evan inquired what she was doing, but she only raised her hand to silence him. She had not mastered writing as well as reading so she had to concentrate. As she focused on each stroke, she found her thoughts came quicker than she could write them. When she finished it, she blew lightly on the paper to dry the ink. She folded it, placed it in an envelope and wrote something on the outside. She then handed it to him.

"Give this to him and there shouldn't be a problem with ya stayin' with him. It'll at least give ya a place until ya figure thin's out."

He reopened the letter and read it. Then quietly, he folded it and placed it in the inside pocket of his jacket. "Thank you, Mary. I greatly appreciate this."

"I'm glad I could help; tis the least I can do."

Evan came by the Whitaker farm to say goodbye. He pulled his loaded carriage up to the front door. He was met by Joshua who was standing on the front porch along with his shadow, Katherine.

"Is your mother around?" he asked.

"I think she's out back doing laundry," the boy replied. Turning he said, "I'll get her."

Katherine said in with her quiet sweet voice, "I can get her." She ran back into the house.

Joshua hollered back, "You're not supposed to run in the house." A few seconds later they heard a screen door bang shut. "Or slam the door," he added with disgust.

Evan just shook his head in response.

Joshua was a little wary of Mr. Sullivan; he didn't know what to make of the man anymore. He had greatly admired him in the beginning, even thinking that he might become a teacher one day. But after all that had happened, it left him confused. He still didn't fully understand what went on between him and his mother even though she had tried to explain it to him. The confusion came from the murmurings he heard in the schoolyard.

Evan approached the porch, but kept his distance. There was an uncomfortable silence between them. He nervously cleared his throat as he waited for Mary, trying to think of something casual to talk about. All he could think about was how he had let everyone down. "Hey look, I'm sorry," he said trying to apologize. He didn't know why he felt compelled to do it, but it just seemed the right thing to do. "I've done plenty of things in my life that I'm ashamed of, but spending time with your mother, teaching her to read…well that's not one of them."

Joshua listened, but he wasn't ready to respond.

Evan started to say more, but the words escaped him. He was saved by Mary as she came through the door; Katherine was right behind her. When she saw him, she felt a tug at her heart, knowing he was about to leave. "Mr. Sullivan." Her emotions began to betray her, but she was determined not to give into them. "Children ya need to be sayin' goodbye to Mr. Sullivan; he's goin' away."

Joshua reluctantly went and shook his hand. Katherine came and gave him a hug. Embarrassed, she quickly turned and ran off around the corner of the house. Mary told Joshua to run after her to keep an eye on her. They both knew it was a ruse so that Mary could be alone with Mr. Sullivan. He obediently went, but he glared at Evan as he left.

Mary apologized, "He's confused." Evan nodded. Neither could think of anything to say. When they finally did speak, both of them spoke at the same time. They nervously laughed.

Evan said, "You go first."

"I was just goin' to say, that we will be missin' ya."

"We or *you*, Mary?"

"*We*, Mr. Sullivan," she reiterated.

He laughed. There was still a twinkle of glee in his eye even though there was also a heaviness in his heart. "It's only temporary. As soon as I get settled into a new job, I'll send for you and the children."

"Don't be makin' promises ya cannot keep."

He stepped up onto the porch and drew closer to her. Reaching up, he brushed aside a strand of hair that had fallen down. "*I* am going to miss *you*," he said, moving closer, drawing her in his arms. Mary felt something stirring inside her, but it only heightened her bewilderment. Evan tilted his head to kiss her. At the last moment she fought him and pulled away.

Distressed she said to him, "I cannot do this. I just lost me husband three months ago."

He nodded slightly. He dutifully respected her wishes. "But I *will* send for you. I love you, Mary."

"But I don't know if I love ya." Her words stung more than she intended them to. To soften them she said, "I'm just confused right now. So much has happened that I cannot think straight. I do care about ya, Evan…I just don't know if it be in the same way."

He took note that she called him by his given name. That was two times. He surmised that he was making progress. "They say that absence makes the heart grow fonder."

Mary raised an eyebrow and questioned him, "They do?"

He laughed heartily and said, "Yeah, *they* do. And to prove my point…" he pointed his finger at her. "I'm going to leave and while I'm gone, you're going to miss me."

His impish grin made her smile. She shrugged and only said, "We'll see."

He laughed and as he approached her again, she took a step back. "Can I at least kiss you on the cheek?" She gave in and tilted her cheek towards him. He leaned in and gave her a little peck. But while her guard was down, he took hold of her, kissed her passionately and let her go before she knew what hit her. She just stood with her mouth gaped open, speechless. She would have yelled at him, but she had to admit it was a pretty good kiss.

Evan mischievously laughed as he climbed into his carriage. "You'll miss me...you'll see." Tugging on the reins, he turned the carriage around. He waved to her and with his final words he promised he would be back for her. All the while Mary stood weakly waving goodbye.

It took a couple of days for Evan to reach his destination. Thankfully he had found safe accommodations to stay overnight. He didn't get much sleep worrying if anyone might try to pilfer his possessions. He didn't have much in material wealth, but he prided himself in his collection of books. He had scraped together enough money to purchase some of the classics, but the primers had been through a donation. He doubted if he'd ever be that fortunate again.

He rode his carriage along the dusty road looking for his destination. He reached into his inside pocket and pulled out Mary's letter, making sure he had the name right. She had clearly printed on the outside of the envelope: Pederson's General Store. He glanced from side to side, saw a couple of mercantile type stores, but didn't see what he was looking for. Then, just down the street, he caught sight of it. Evan had to take the buggy down the road a ways to find a place to pull off. As he got out, he looked around to make sure there weren't any vagrants around that might steal anything. Thinking it would be safe, he walked down towards the store, hoping that this trip was not a wasted effort.

His footsteps sounded hollow as he walked along the wooden boardwalk that led to the store. He tilted his hat as two lovely maidens passed him. He couldn't keep from turning his torso around to watch them walk away and then continued on. As he reached for the handle of the door, it suddenly opened inward. A burly miner loaded down with a couple of picks and shovels pushed past him. He reeked to high heaven for he probably hadn't had a bath in a month of Sundays. Mr. Sullivan concluded that Jacksonville was going to be an interesting town.

He entered the place and saw a tall, bespectacled man, with thinning light blonde hair. He seemed frazzled with the flurry of activity that surrounded him. Evan surmised that this must have been the proprietor. He surveyed the store as he waited patiently for his turn. He was impressed with how neat and organized everything was.

With the last customer out the door, the owner had a short reprieve. He addressed the lone shopper. Evan stuck out his hand and introduced himself. "I'm a friend of Mary Whitaker."

"Mary!" Henrik exclaimed as his eyes lit up. "How is she? How is Mary Kate and little Michael? Are they doing alright? Are they growing?" His questions came in such a rush, Evan had to raise his hand to slow him down.

"They're all fine; I just saw them two days ago," Evan said.

"Oh, my children; how I miss them so." His eyes filled with tears. Embarrassed he turned his back to Evan and busied himself so that Evan would not see him so emotional. "Mama is so very ill. I've had to hire a girl to help care for her and help me around the store. I didn't vant to send them avay, but vhat else could I do?"

"Mary's taking good care of them; she loves them like her own," Evan replied.

Henrik took his glasses off and wiped his eyes with a handkerchief. He turned and faced Evan. "I vasn't so sure that they vould be after meeting her husband. Terrible brute."

Evan nodded his head and started to tell him that he didn't have to worry about that now, but something stopped him. Maybe it was the fear that Henrik might think it was too hard for Mary to care for them all alone. But it would have been much harder at this point to take those little ones away from her than for her to care for them by herself.

Henrik came back to the here and now. He addressed Evan. "Vhat can I do for you, Mr. Sullivan?"

"I think this letter might explain everything," he replied, handing it to him.

Henrik slid his glasses farther up his nose and quickly perused the letter. The corners of his mouth turned up slightly as he read. When he was finished, he gently folded it and handed it back to Evan. "Sir, I must say that you are a godsend. I could really use some extra help around here and I think you'll do just fine." He started leading him towards the back of the store that he used for storage. "Ve can clear out a spot in the back, move a few boxes here and some over there. I think ve can fit a cot in there for you. I can't pay you much, but vho knows, maybe in a few months, ve can have you teaching again. How's that sound, Mr. Sullivan."

He smiled broadly and said, "It sounds great—and please call me Evan."

28

A Righteous Anger

Mary took the last of James' clothes from the closet. She neatly folded them and placed them in a cedar chest. She had put off this job as long as she could because it made James' death so final. She couldn't decide on what to do with the everyday work clothes that were in the dresser. They weren't really worth saving, but she couldn't bring herself to discard them. After all, she really didn't need the extra space. She stared at the open drawer and then finally decided to keep them for the time being. Maybe she could use them to make clothes for the boys. The Sunday meeting clothes that hung in the closet were a different story. He only had two suits, a few dress shirts and a couple of ties, but that was more than most men in town. She put these in the cedar chest to try to keep them where moths couldn't get to them. In the not too distant future, Joshua would grow into them.

As she put the last of his shirts in the chest, she held it close to her face and drew in the scent of it. After these months, it still smelled like him. It wasn't a bad odor, mostly of lye soap, but it also had the musk scent of a man that was clearly identified as James. Sadly, she placed it in the trunk and slid it off to the side, out of her way. Joshua would have to help her carry it to the barn for safe keeping. One of the things she missed around the house was a man to help with the heavy stuff. James had not always been helpful, but he did assist her with the heavy lifting and toting that she was physically unable to do.

She started to close the closet door, when suddenly she remembered something she wanted to check out. For years, James had hidden a small wooden box on the top shelf. She had discovered it early in their marriage, but out of respect for his privacy, she had left it alone. Besides, it had a lock on it and she couldn't open it.

She brought a chair from the kitchen and stood on it so she could reach it. She gingerly fingered it, sliding it forward enough that she could grab a hold of it and bring it down. Setting it on the bed, she reached into the pocket of her skirt and retrieved a key ring. James only had two keys in his possessions; one was for the sawmill and the other was for this lockbox. Obviously, it was important to him. She felt a little guilty opening it, but James was gone and with it went his privacy.

As she opened the lid to her amazement, she found bundles of letters. She picked them up and sat on the bed beside the box. The letters had a familiarity about them; they were all the letters that Ellingson had written for her. A small spark of anger flamed up at the thought of his betrayal. But it was all water under the bridge now that her husband was gone. She untied the twine that had secured them and then began sifting through them, one at a time.

The anger reignited when she saw the appalling lies Ellingson had written. It was no wonder that James was confused in the beginning and later infuriated with her. Tears of shame and regret flooded her eyes. She felt as guilty as if she had written them herself. After reading several, she couldn't take any more and retied the bundle. But as she replaced them in the box, she saw that her letters were not the only ones he had kept. With shaking hands, she withdrew the other bundle. Her heart began to sink. Was this from the woman that he had had the affair with? Hesitating, not knowing if she wanted to read them, she decided that she had to know the truth. She untied the string, picked up the top letter and began to read.

Mary read each one and cried silently. Her heart ached not only for James, but the woman that he had been in love with long before Mary had any contact with him. She folded the last letter and muttered, "James, ya were a fool; ya should have married her. Hang the world for what they would have thought."

She had finally put the puzzle pieces together, even though she was only getting one side of the conversation. The girl he was in love with was named Finola. She didn't know her last name, because she only signed the letters as *your dearest Finola*. Mary discovered that Finola was in the same predicament that she had been in. She bore a son she claimed to have belonged to James. At first he did not believe her or want to have anything to do with her. But after years of her begging him to come and see for himself, he had given in. One look must have convinced him. Ever since then, he had gone to spend time with the boy. There had never been an affair as far as she could tell. She shook her head and chuckled unbelievingly. James had remained faithful to her all these years.

Quietly she returned all the letters to the box and put them back to the hidden spot on the shelf. One day, when Joshua was old enough, she would bring them back out and together they would read them. He would learn that his father was an honorable man.

The next time she went to town, she had some business to take care of. It had been such a beautiful day she decided that she and the children would walk the distance to town. When they got there, she sent Joshua and Katherine over to the school yard that was off to the side of the church. She carried Michael with her for he was still much too small to be left with them. She could see Joshua getting distracted and Michael wandering off into the street.

She walked over to the sawmill to talk to Luke. Someone told her that they thought he had just stepped into the office. She shifted Michael to the other hip and then proceeded up a small set of stairs that led to the office. She could see him through the glass in the door and knocked. Luke got to his feet and let her in. "Mrs. Whitaker, what a surprise. Please come in and have a seat." He motioned for her to sit behind the desk, but she opted for the wooden chair across from it. She sat Michael on her lap. "What can I do for you?" he asked.

She hesitated and then said, "I'm a little embarrassed to come and talk to ya. It be about me offer o' sellin' the mill."

Luke flushed with his own embarrassment. He had his own reluctance. He interrupted. "Yeah, I've been wanting to talk to you about it. You know, I'm very honored that you made the offer, but I can't see how I could buy it, even given time to pay it off."

Mary smiled softly. It made what she was about to say easier. "Well, tis for the best. Ya see the mill is not mine to sell." Luke gave her a strange look as she continued. "I know about James' other son." The change in Luke's expression spoke volumes. "He is entitled to his share, as well as Joshua."

Michael got fidgety and started fussing. Mary put him against her shoulder and patted him softly; it settled him down for a short time. "I've looked over the bank books and discovered a small sum o' money that was always extracted at the same time o' the month. I believe that it was for the care o' the child. I'd like that to continue."

Luke blinked. He couldn't believe that she would be willing to do such a thing after what James had put her through. "I don't know what to say. But what does this have to do with me?"

"I believe that ya know who she is." He nodded slightly. "I don't need to know. I respect her privacy; she's had her own problems to deal with. I would like for ya to be the courier between us. I have also written a letter outlinin' me intentions, Mr. Myers. I want ya to continue runnin' this mill like it was yar very own. When the boy… I believe his name is James, after his father… when he becomes sixteen, if he be willin', he is to come and work for ya. Ya're to apprentice him and when he is twenty-one and deemed responsible by the two o' us, the mill will be turned over to him. By that time, Joshua will have made his decision on whether to come and work here. They will be co-owners as James and his brother were. O' course, I expect that they keep ya here as manager as long as ya want to work for the family."

Luke was overcome with emotion and a little embarrassed for it. "I don't know what to say, Mrs. Whitaker. That's a generous offer all around. Thank you."

"So ya'll carry out me wishes?"

"Absolutely."

"Good. Here's the letter and a bank draft for the amount for her." She handed it to him and stood to leave. "Thank ya, Mr. Myers. Ya've been a good friend to James and I count ya as one o' me few friends that *I* have." As she walked out the door, Luke realized that he had a new respect for this woman. He wasn't sure if all the stories about her were true or not, but it really didn't matter to him. In his book, she exemplified the love of Christ.

Mary felt a huge burden lift off her shoulders. She walked back to the schoolyard to retrieve her children. She found them taking turns on a swing that hung from one of the large oak trees. She suggested that maybe they could fashion one together at home, although she wasn't entirely sure she could hang it from a tree. Her tree climbing days had long since past.

As they started towards the edge of town, Mary caught Mrs. Cavanaugh out of the corner of her eye. She saw the biddy twitch her nose up in the air and say something to the lady she was conversing with. Mary felt the temperature rise on her anger. There was a little matter she had been intending to take care of. She had been praying about it and now she knew the course of action she was to take. She had a peace with it.

Mary's determination stayed strong until Sunday morning. She argued with herself as God mediated between the two sides, although He was a little prejudiced. His will was for her to stop fighting and be obedient. But she wasn't sure she had the courage to see it through. After today, there would be no going back. She would without a doubt be labeled a pariah.

She left the wagon up the street a short distance. The last thing she wanted was to take someone's parking place. The only thing worse would be to sit in somebody's pew—which was another worry. She ushered the children up the steps and they went in. Hanging back, she strategized where would be the best place to sit when she spotted Ida Rose. She saw Mary and with a surprised look on her face, motioned them to sit with her family. Mary smiled faintly thinking that if she was surprised now, she should just wait.

"Mary," she exclaimed. "It's so wonderful to see you. It's about time you start coming to church."

"Well…" Mary began, trying to come up with something other than the true reason she was here this morning. She ended up shrugging and said, "I thought I'd give it a try."

The pew was a tight fit, but they made it work. It wasn't long until the service began with some singing. That was followed by the passing of the offering plate. Mary hesitated, not because she didn't have it to give, but because of the reason she had come this morning. She felt like a hypocrite, but on second thought, she gave because she liked Reverend Matthews. He had been a comfort to her in her hour of need.

After the offering, the reverend stood behind the pulpit. He cleared his throat and began with a word of prayer. Then he got right into the message. He read from the gospel of John, chapter fifteen where Jesus commanded his disciples to love each other. Mary shook her head softly and laughed inwardly. God really had some sense of humor. The reverend's sermon fit perfectly with what God had called her to do.

She took every word Reverend Matthews spoke to heart. She rather enjoyed being back in a pew learning from God's word. It was a shame that this was going to be her first and last sermon she would hear him preach in this church. Her heart pounded loudly in her chest, knowing that at any moment the service was going to end and she would have to do what she came for. She tried taking in deep breaths to relieve her anxiety and prayed for courage. For a moment it helped until the invitation was given. It was time. Her heart was beating fast and the knot in her stomach had grown three times the size it had been only a moment ago.

As the last verse was sung and still no one had come to the altar, Mary slipped Michael over onto Joshua's lap and stood. She squeezed out of the pew and came forward. A puzzled look came across Reverend Matthews' face. He was certain they had settled the question about her salvation months ago. He surmised that she was coming forward to pray about another matter. He was even more confused when she stood at the altar and did not kneel. One thing about Catholics, they had no aversion to kneeling.

The reverend leaned forward and spoke softly to her. "Is there something I can pray with you about?"

"Oh, I'm sure that there is, but that is not why I'm here. I need to speak to yar congregation. There are some misconceptions that need to be cleared up."

Reverend Matthews hesitated as he contemplated whether this was a good idea or not. He looked into her green eyes, searching her intentions and then he nodded. He wasn't sure what she was going to say, but after everything that had happened, he believed she had that right. He stepped aside to let her pass.

Mary shook as she got behind the pulpit. In her hand, she had the Bible that the pastor had given her. She quietly opened it to the passage she was looking for and began to read. *"Jesus went unto the Mount o' Olives. And early in the mornin' He came again into the temple, and all the people came unto Him; and He sat down, and taught them. And the scribes and Pharisees brought unto Him a woman taken in adultery; and when they had set her in the midst, they say unto Him, Master, this woman was taken in adultery, in the very act. Now Moses in the law commanded us, that such should be stoned: but what sayest Thou? This they said, temptin' Him that they might have to accuse Him.*

But Jesus stooped down, and with His finger wrote on the ground, as though He heard them not. So when they continued askin' Him, He lifted up Himself, and said unto them, he that is without sin among you, let him first cast a stone at her. And again He stooped down, and wrote on the ground.

And they which heard it, bein' convicted by their own conscience, went out one by one, beginnin' at the eldest, even unto the last: and Jesus was left alone, and the woman standin' in the midst. When Jesus had lifted up Himself, and saw none but the woman, He said unto her, Woman, where are those thine accusers? Hath no man condemned thee?

She said, No man, Lord. And Jesus said unto her, neither do I condemn thee: go, and sin no more."

Mary breathed deeply to calm her nerves. She had rehearsed in her mind over and over what she was going to say, but at this moment she had gone blank. She prayed for words of wisdom. "A couple o' weeks ago, some in this congregation took it upon themselves to slander a good man's name without any evidence. The accusations they had against him were the ones they had manufactured in their minds." She paused and looked hard at Mrs. Cavanaugh, who immediately rolled her eyes. She probably would have gotten up and left, but she and her weasel-faced husband were sandwiched in the middle of a row of people.

Mary went on, "this man was accused and convicted without any evidence o' wrongdoin'. He was dismissed from his job. In Deuteronomy, chapter nineteen, verse fifteen, it says that one witness is not enough to convict a man, but that it must be established by two or three. Yet this man had no witnesses to link him with any wrongdoin'." Again she paused and looked directly at the accuser. Mrs. Cavanaugh's eyes narrowed with contempt.

"The crime that Mr. Sullivan committed was to come to me house, every Sunday mornin' to teach me to read. Without his help, I would not have been able to read this passage. As for me, many have accused me o' adultery. I was never unfaithful to me husband James. But that's neither here nor there."

Reverend Matthews stood off to the side and listened intently. It took great courage for Mary to step forward and face those who were slandering her name. In that moment, he had tremendous admiration for her.

Mary continued, "In this passage I just read, a woman caught in adultery has been brought before the Lord to try to trip him up. If Jesus doesn't have her stoned to death, He will have broken God's law and proved that He was not the Christ. But if He puts her to death, then the people will turn on Him. He's in a quandary. What should He do? And so He begins writin' in the dirt. Now it doesn't say what He wrote, but it must have been somethin' mighty powerful to have those men, drop their stones and walk away. He also had said to them that he who was without sin let him cast the first stone. Obviously, none o' these men qualified." She glanced down at the passage of Scripture trying to focus her thoughts. The congregation sat riveted, taking in every word.

"When the Lord looked up, the men were all gone. He turned to the woman that was waitin' to be put to death and asked her where they were. And when she replied that they had left and that there was no one to condemn her, He told her that neither did He condemn her. He said to her, *go and sin no more.*"

"In this story, Jesus makes a bold statement that the one that was without sin should cast that first stone. As I said, the men were disqualified, but lest we forget, there *was* one person there that was without sin. He had every right to put her to death for breakin' God's law. But instead, He forgave her because He knew that in a short period o' time, He would stretch out His arms and take the punishment that she deserved and die in her place. That's the kind o' God I serve—the One who is full o' mercy that did the same thing for me."

Reverend Matthews stood entranced by this woman's understanding of the Bible. He had studied this passage numerous times, heard others preach on it, but had never picked up on what she was teaching today. He recognized that indeed God was working in this woman's life. No one had that great of insight without being led by the Holy Spirit.

"Now some o' ya must find yarselves holier than God, because ya're still standin' there with yar rock in yar hands. Ya're chompin' at the bit to be the arm o' justice for God. But if I remember right, His Word says that *we have all sinned and fall short o' His glory…and that it is through grace that we have been saved.* None o' us have the right to be self-righteous or to have a holier-than-Thou attitude. We have no right to judge anyone accordin' to our own standards, which some o' ya have." She surveyed the crowd and saw who was really listening and who was biding their time until they could get out of the church building and cluck their disapproval.

"I have done some things in me own life that I am ashamed o'. Some o' which could be said to be far worse. But me Lord has granted full amnesty to me, though I do not deserve it. And outa me gratitude I will serve Him until me dyin' breath. Now, ya may say what ya want about me, but I said me peace and I will leave ya. And ya can rest assure that I will not be back to disrupt any more services." She heard something disparaging come from the direction of Mrs. Cavanaugh, but she wasn't sure what was said. Unfazed she said, "I thank ya for listenin' to me side o' the story."

She closed her Bible, tucked it under her arm and marched down the aisle to the pew she had been sitting in. She took Michael back from Joshua and then the tiny family made their way to the back of the church and exited. No one else left their seat. Their eyes shifted from the doorway to Reverend Matthews. Everyone was waiting for what his reaction would be.

He slipped behind the pulpit and gripped the sides of the lectern. Quietly he said, "Mrs. Whitaker said in much less time than I, a greater sermon than I think I have ever heard. I believe we all should return to our homes and contemplate what we heard today. See if you can see any correlation between what Mrs. Whitaker spoke from her heart and what I spoke about today: *"This is my commandment, that ye love one another, as I have loved you."* He prayed and then said. "May God's Spirit come upon you and give you insight into His Word."

He dismissed the crowd. Some quickly got up and left, namely the Cavanaughs, while others hung around to hear what other people's opinions were. Reverend Matthews stayed behind his pulpit deep in thought about Mary and how God was working in her. He wondered what else God would do through her in time. It might be one amazing story to hear someday.

29

Do Unto the Least of My Brothers

It had been another hot and dry summer in the Umpqua River valley. Autumn wasn't appearing to look any better. All through the long months, Mary tried desperately to keep the garden going. She and Joshua loaded up the wagon with as many water barrels they could find. Then they set about the enormous task of filling them, bucketfuls at a time. When they were filled, she drove the team out to the field and they began spreading trails of water up and down each row. It kept the garden going, but just barely. The fruit that was bore at harvest time was piddling compared to all the other years. Yet she was thankful that they would have a harvest this year.

The irony of the whole thing was that after most of the pickings were in, the rains came down in torrents and Mary had a new problem. She discovered they had a leaking roof. The water barrels were now converted into rain barrels, collecting streams of water that poured through the ceiling.

It was on one of those days that Reverend Matthews came calling. He had both a hat and an umbrella, but neither did him much good. He pulled his buggy up to her front door and carefully slid down to the ground, hoping that he didn't continue all the way to the mud. By the time he reached the shelter of the porch, Mary had come outside to greet him.

"Parson, what in the world are ya doin' out in this kind o' weather?" she asked.

"Getting soaked mostly," he quipped.

"I must say, ya're doing a mighty fine job o' it."

They both laughed softly. "I guess I have to agree with you there."

"Why don't ya come in and sit a spell," she said, motioning with her head. "Maybe I can find ya some dry clothes and a pipin' hot cup o' coffee."

As she went into the house, Reverend Matthews started to protest. "Oh, I'm afraid that I'm too wet; I wouldn't want to drip water into your house." Mary chuckled and looked towards her ceiling. The preacher followed her eyes and saw the water dribbling from the ceiling. His jaw dropped and he asked, "What happened here?"

"The roof's leakin'," she stated the obvious. "Can't understand it; we've never had any problems before."

"Well, maybe with the hot, dry summer, your shingles dried up. It could have caused cracks allowing water to run through them."

Mary nodded and then led him into her bedroom. She went to the dresser and pulled out a pair of pants and a work shirt from out of the middle drawer. She handed him the clothes and then suddenly remembered something. From the top drawer she withdrew a pair of socks and a set of long underwear. "Ya might be needin' these as well," she said slightly embarrassed. If he had been anybody but a man of the cloth she wouldn't have. She looked down at his feet and then added, "I doubt if James has any shoes that will fit ya. We'll have to set those by the fire to dry them."

"Thank you for your hospitality," he said smiling faintly.

"Tis the least I can do. It wouldn't be good to have the only preacher in town to come down with sickness." As she turned to leave the room, she added, "I'll put a pot o' coffee on the stove for ya."

The reverend thanked her again and then changed his clothes. Afterwards he joined her in the kitchen. "I don't know what you want me to do with these," he said, holding his wet clothes.

"Put them over there for now. I'll hang them by the fireplace directly." She wrapped a towel around the hot handle of the coffee pot, carried it to the table and poured them each a cup. She returned the pot to the stove and joined the reverend at the table. "Now tell me, what are ya doin' out in weather like this?"

"Well, when I left, it wasn't raining. I figured after all these rainy days we've had, we had seen the last of them, especially, when the sun poked its head out this morning. I thought it would be a good idea to take advantage of it." He took a tentative sip of coffee and then said, "I was not prepared for the deluge I encountered. I did have the forethought to take an umbrella with me, but when the wind started gusting, it didn't do much good."

She nodded and took a sip of her coffee. Momentary lost in thought, she wondered if she should broach this subject. Being one that rarely held her peace, she plunged ahead. "Don't ya worry what people might say about ya comin' here? I'm not exactly a social butterfly these days."

He grinned and teased, "I just tell them that I'm trying to get you saved."

She laughed with him, but there was a sadness in her eyes. "You know, I thought I was doin' the right thing. I felt God leadin' me to do it. Somehow I thought that I could change people's attitudes. I was so foolish."

He reached across the table and took her hand. "No, you were not foolish, a little naïve perhaps, but not foolish. Mrs. Cavanaugh is set in her ways and she'll never change. She has this community wrapped around her finger because of her wealth. The only one that could have challenged her for power is gone. But James never seemed interested in the politics of church."

Mary nodded in agreement. She said quietly, "James never talked about what went on at the church."

"I've been meaning to have this conversation with you. What you said on that day was truth and we should never be ashamed to tell the truth, even if it's rejected by others. God has given you a great gift, Mary. He has given you insight into His Word. The things that you shared…well, I had never heard it from that perspective before, not from my professors at seminary or for that matter any other preacher. Maybe you saw that Scripture differently than all us, because you've been in a similar place. But I do think that God has some kind of ministry planned for you."

Mary shook her head. "What would God be doin' choosin' me. Ya know me past. How could God use someone like me?"

"That's exactly who He chooses. He chooses those the world would reject, so that no one may boast that it was all about them and not God. Mary, God can use your past to minister to others. Be faithful to Him and He will show you what you are supposed to do."

The young woman lifted the two tin cans up to Evan as he stood on a small ladder that leaned against the shelf he was stocking. He put the cans on the top shelf beside the ones he previously had placed. She handed him two more. He then turned to receive more, but there were none. "That's it. That was the last one," she announced.

"Good," he said descending the ladder. "I was starting to get tired of standing on this ladder. You know, I can't understand why he wants them all the way up there. It makes it hard for the customers to see them and for us to get it for them."

"Mmmm, I agree, but he is the boss, so…."

"We just do what he tells us," he said, finishing her thought.

She waggled her finger at him and replied, "That's right. We just follow orders." She walked around the front counter and waited for the first customer just as always punctual Henrik, exited his living quarters, marched across the store and unlocked the front door. Surprised that no one was waiting to come in, he checked his watch again. He held it up to his ear, making sure it was working properly and then placed it back in his pocket. Evan watched with amusement as this was Henrik's morning routine.

"I cannot understand vhy people are not coming in this morning. I hope they have not chosen to go to the store down the street. Their prices may be slightly better, but they do not have the quality that ve have."

"I'm sure that people are just a little busy right now," Evan assured him like every morning. The man worried about everything like an old man who had lost his entire fortune. The truth was Henrik Pederson was probably one of the wealthiest storeowners in town. He had earned a lot of the gold that the miners had worked out of the ground. Evan reminded the man, "We've had some pretty nasty weather of late. People are probably assessing the damage. I bet they'll be pouring in here soon wanting to buy tools and supplies."

"Oh, good heavens! I hope that I have everything they need," he said, rushing to the back of the store and through the door that led to the storeroom.

Evan shook his head and laughed softly at the man's reaction. Then he turned his attention to the attractive brunette behind the counter. He found her intriguing. Her engaging personality, warm smile and contagious laugh made it easy for him to converse with her. It was one of the reasons he saw promise in this backwoods town—that and the possibility of teaching again. Henrik had gone to the newly formed town council and proposed the building of a small one room school house. He had suggested that each business owner give a small percentage of their income proportioned to their size to help construct it. They were mulling it over.

"Has anyone ever told you how lovely you are?" he asked her.

The young woman flushed and said shyly, "You keep this up and Mr. Pederson might just fire you—and me along with you."

"Not in your life. We've become too valuable to him; he couldn't survive without us."

"Don't be too sure about that, Mr. Sullivan."

"Oh, don't worry about that and call me Evan."

"So what makes you so sure—*Evan?*" she asked lowering her voice for fear that Henrik would find them talking about him.

"He's so lost that he couldn't even keep his children. He had to send them away."

"I know. I feel so bad for him. I thought maybe after I started caring of his mother, he might send for them."

Evan shook his head. "Trust me; they're better off where they are." The girl cocked her head in curiosity and Evan elaborated. "I know her—Henrik's sister-in-law. She's taking good care of them. She loves them as her own." He felt a twinge of guilt talking about Mary. The memory of his promise to return to her came to the forefront of his mind.

"Well, if she truly loves them, then maybe they are better off."

He nodded and said, "There's no one better to care for them."

The first real sunshiny day, a carriage topped the crest of Mary's driveway and then started down. Mary and Joshua were laboriously unloading burlap bags of potatoes they had recently dug up. She shielded her eyes as she peered up the road. She recognized the reverend as he came closer. Self consciously, she took inventory of herself. Her hair was coming loose from her bun, her dress covered with mud, her shoes caked with the stuff and sweat pouring from her face. She took out her handkerchief and wiped her brow.

"Good mornin', Parson," she greeted him. She almost didn't recognize him at first, because he was wearing work clothes. "What brings ya out here?"

"I'm on an act of mercy," he said, hopping out of his carriage. He retrieved a bundle from behind his seat. Mary furrowed her brow, not fully understanding until she saw that it was a bundle of new, wooden shingles. "You need a new roof, so I thought I would provide one."

"Praise be!" she said, trying not to be overcome with emotion. "But ya shouldn't have. Ya're the preacher."

"What difference does that make? Jesus was a carpenter by trade and we're supposed to emulate Him, aren't we?" he said grinning broadly. Mary had no argument to come back for him. Then he turned his attention to their bulging burlap bags. "Hey, what are you two trying to do?"

"We're hauling our potatoes to the root cellar," Joshua interjected.

"That's too much for either one of you; let me do it." Before she could protest, he had lifted a bag to his shoulder. "Point me in the right direction."

Mary was astonished that someone in his profession could be so strong. "Over here," she said softly and then walked him to the open doors that led down to the cellar. He trotted down the steps and placed it with the other bags that were already down there.

When the reverend finished, he had worked up a sweat. "Boy, you sure have a mess of potatoes. Are you going to be able to use all of them?"

"Trust me; we will," she assured him. "They were our best crop. The summer heat took a toll on everythin' else." Still in amazement that he had come to help them, she couldn't keep from staring at him. A warm wave swept over her as she felt God's love and provision for them. She finally snapped out of her daze and she said, "Let me go and fetch ya a cup o' water. Ya must be parched after all that liftin'."

"Yeah, I'm a little dry." Mary went inside as the preacher began unloading the rest of the bundles. "You want to give me a hand with these, Joshua?" he asked the boy, knowing that it would make him feel good to be included in the project.

"Yes sir!" he exclaimed and grabbed a bundle. He struggled carrying it to where the reverend was stacking them. Still they were lighter than the potatoes.

By the time they finished, Mary had a tin cup of cool well water waiting for him. "Thank you," he said and quickly downed it.

"Let me get ya another one," she said and went back inside the house.

As he waited her return, Reverend Matthews turned to Joshua and asked him, "Are you going to be my *gopher*?"

Joshua looked confused. "Huh?"

The corners of the preacher's mouth turned upwards in amusement. "A gopher is a person that helps out by going for things: go-for this and go-for that—gopher."

He grinned and answered proudly, "I can do that."

"Good. You can start by getting me some of your dad's tools."

"Okay," he replied and then sprinted to the barn.

Mary returned with not only the cup of water but a pitcher as well. She watched her son dash off to the barn. "What's he in a hurry for."

"He's going to help," he said taking the cup and quickly drinking it. "He's getting me some tools."

"I don't want him up on the roof," she warned.

"Don't worry. He's just going to fetch anything I need. He won't get any closer than the top of the ladder."

She was relieved and poured him another cup. This one he savored longer. Soon Joshua came toting a long wooden box by the handle. It was just about all he could do to carry it.

"I wasn't sure what all you needed," he said, setting it down rather hard on the ground.

Reverend Matthews handed Mary his cup and then said, "I need a ladder. Where might I find one?"

"Out in the barn," she answered.

"I'll get it," Joshua chimed in and immediately ran back to the barn.

"Wait for me; we can both carry it." He started to follow and then suddenly remembered what he had in his back pocket. He turned and handed her two letters. "Oh, I hope you don't mind, but while I was at Thompson's picking up some nails for the shingles, I also got your mail. I thought it might save you a trip to town."

"Thank you," she said sifting back and forth between them. "Two letters? I don't think I have ever received two in one day before."

"Your popularity must be growing," he teased.

"I seriously doubt that. I'm sure they must be from me brother-in-law, askin' about his children. Be careful on the roof. It wouldn't do for me to have the preacher fall off me roof and get hurt."

"It wouldn't do me much good either," he said laughing.

He trotted to the barn as Mary went back inside the house to the kitchen. She sat down at the table and tore open the first letter, which she recognized as Evan's handwriting. Even though she only felt friendship towards him, she still looked forward to his letters. He had written her practically every day until recently. It had been more than a week since his last one and she wondered when he would write again.

She took it from its envelope and quickly read it. It didn't take long; it was only a page. It was so businesslike that she checked the signature at the bottom to make sure it really was from him. Basically all he spoke about was how well things were going at the store and that he may possibly have a teaching job. And that was it. No flowery talk about how he would be sending for her—just business.

She frowned, wondering what was really happening. The second letter was from Henrik. He wrote to her every so often to let her know how he and his mother were getting along. They were always filled with hope that she would one day regain her strength. She felt sorry for him. He too had gone through so much, losing his wife, dealing with his mother's illness and now having to send his children away. Life wasn't fair, but she was quickly reminded that God never said it would be. In fact, He had said the opposite: *in this world you will have troubles.*

Henrik closed his letter as usual asking about the children. He had sent a small bank note to help defer the cost of their care. Mary had never wanted it. She just deposited it in a special account for the two. One day, when they reached adulthood, there would be a nice nest egg for them. Then he closed the letter, but added a post script. He simple wrote: *"It looks like your dear friend Mr. Sullivan is becoming quite smitten with my nursemaid, Emma."*

Mary sat dumbfounded, clearly not sure how she felt about it. Part of her was hurt, but another part was a bit relieved. Her feelings had never been deep for him. It would have been unfair to him if they had ever married. Of all people, she understood what it was like to marry someone that never truly loved you like you should be.

She folded the letter and returned it to its envelope. She glanced up and smiled at the ceiling as she heard Reverend Matthews crawling around on her roof. He was such a good man. She wondered why he had never married, but just supposed that he had chosen to be married to his work instead. She got up from the table and put the pan of beans on the stove that had been soaking overnight. She was thankful that she had made plenty, since she'd have another person for dinner. She took some kindling and started a fire in the stove and then went about peeling potatoes.

When the meal was just about ready, she called the *men* in to wash up. She got Michael settled into the high chair and then took the cornbread out of the oven. She had Katherine set the table; it was her newest chore. She could hear Reverend Matthews and Joshua joking as they came into the house. It warmed her heart to hear Joshua laugh again.

"I wasn't expecting you to feed me," Reverend Matthews said.

"Tis the least I can do after all ya're doin' for us." She invited him to sit down and then set the food on the table. As they gathered around the table, she asked the reverend to say grace and he agreed. He took hold of her hand and then Joshua's, as they formed a circle. The custom was new to her, but she rather liked it. They bowed their heads and he blessed the meal.

As they ate, the reverend and Joshua talked about the day's events, with Joshua doing most of the talking. When he finally took a breath, Reverend Matthews took the opportunity to compliment Mary's culinary skills. "You're a marvelous cook, Mary—I mean, Mrs. Whitaker. Your talents cease to amaze me."

"Thank ya, Parson. And ya can call me Mary…makes no difference."She felt color rise to her cheeks. She hadn't been complimented much her entire life. She found it a little embarrassing.

"And you can return the favor by calling me by *my* first name. You know, everyone calls me either reverend or preacher or *you* call me parson.

It's been a long time since I've heard my name." It suddenly occurred to him that she might not remember it. "It's Seth, by the way."

"I know. It just seems disrespectful."

"When people call you by your given name, do you feel they're being disrespectful to you?"

"Well, it depends on who it is. But I don't mind ya callin' me Mary, Parson."

"It's Seth," he repeated. "We're friends, right? Friends call each other by their first names."

Mary hesitated and then relented. "Seth."

He smiled and said, "Now that wasn't too hard was it?"

"No, I guess not." She felt embarrassed again. It *was* hard for her.

He took a bite of food, chewed on it and then swallowed. There was something else he was chewing on. It was something important he needed to say to her, but wasn't sure how. "Mary, I need you to pray about something for me."

It took her aback. People were all the time asking him to pray for them, she had never thought about a preacher needing someone to pray for him. "Sure, what is it?"

"I've been feeling really restless the last couple of months. I've been feeling like God is calling me somewhere else. I'm getting the impression that I'm supposed to go to San Francisco. I've contacted my bishop about it. I want to make sure that this is really what God wants."

Mary's heart sunk. She was just getting comfortable around him, considering him a friend. For heaven's sake she just called him by his name and now he was leaving. Everyone she came to care about left her. He was just following suit. Maybe she was meant to be alone. The only one that seemed to not desert her was God, but sometimes she wasn't too sure about that.

Quietly she said to him. "I'll pray for ya…Seth. I'll pray that God's will, will be done."

"Thank you, because I really need it. I have a lot of major decisions coming up and I need God's wisdom."

"Well, I have faith that He'll give ya guidance in all yar decisions." And with that Mary made up her mind to withdraw her emotions from their relationship.

30

Proposals

"You did what?" Evan asked. His face had suddenly gone ashen.

"I just vrote and told your dear friend that it looked like you vere getting close to Emma," Henrik replied. "Did I do something vrong?"

Evan caught his breath along with his temper. He placed his hand on the man's shoulder. "No. It's just that I wanted to tell her about it."

Henrik nodded. "I'm sorry. I thought I vas maybe doing a good thing."

Evan shook his head in resignation. "It's alright." He went back to the storage room where he kept a cot and plopped down on it. He unfolded the letter and reread it. It was short and to the point.

"My dear Mr. Sullivan,

I was pleased to hear that you are getting along so well with Henrik. He is a good man and can be a good friend for you. I was also glad to hear that you may be teaching again very soon. You are such an excellent teacher that it would be a shame if you were not afforded the opportunity again. You taught me well and I will ever be in your gratitude for that. I also have heard that there is a new love interest in your life. Tis good to know that you are moving on with your life.

Sincerely,

Mary O'Shea Whitaker

Evan had difficulty breathing, like all the oxygen had been sucked from the room. There was a heaviness surrounding his heart. Sure he'd admit that he had an infatuation with the girl, but Mary was a woman—a very strong willed woman. He missed the combative play they had in their relationship; the spark of fury in her eyes when he teased her until she struck back, often with venom in her words. She was fiery and passionate, a rare find. He smiled sweetly as he thought of her, but it quickly faded. He may have just lost her for good.

He sat on his bed feeling defeated. His mind whirled with thoughts on how he could fix all this. The only solution he could find was to return to Windsor and talk to her. He would use his charm to win her devotion back. At least he hoped he could.

Mary was deep in thought as she took a handful of ground corn from the large bowl she had cradled in her left arm. She sprayed it on the ground and the chickens gathered, clucking with excitement and quickly pecked at the ground. She took another handful and tossed it. Then she stood watching them eat, but not really seeing them. Her thoughts had turned to the reverend and his imminent departure. Even though he had still not fully committed to it, in her heart she knew he was going. She would miss him dearly. He was like a comfortable pair of shoes. She felt like all her life, she had worn ill-fitting shoes that had belonged to someone else. They pinched her feet and caused undue pain. But when Reverend Matthews had come into her life, she had a strange sense of ease around him, like a perfectly fitted shoe.

She started to turn to go back to the house, when she suddenly saw a man walking towards her. He appeared ghostlike, emerging from the thick fog that enveloped the countryside on this late autumn morning. Mary nearly dropped the bowl she was carrying and let out a short cry of surprise. When she realized that it was the reverend, she hung her head feeling rather foolish for her reaction. She looked up at him, wondering if he was just a mirage she'd conjured in her mind, since she'd just been thinking of him.

"I'm sorry; didn't mean to startle you," he said to her. He was neither a ghost nor a mirage.

"I just didn't know ya were here. I didn't hear yar carriage. What brings ya here this early in the mornin', Parson?" He gave her a disapproving look and she corrected it. "Seth."

He smiled broadly and said, "I received news and I just had to share it with someone. Yesterday afternoon I got a letter from my bishop. It seems that things may be working out for me."

"Oh?" she said walking back towards the house. She felt a grip tighten around her heart. She set the bowl on a stump just outside the door and then invited him in. He followed her into the house, excitedly talking about what the bishop had written. She quickly shushed him. "The children are still asleep," she whispered.

He apologized and they went into the kitchen. Mary started a fire in the stove in preparations for breakfast. "Have ya eaten yet?" she asked him.

"No, I've been too excited. I was busting to tell someone and you're the only one I *can* tell."

She nodded as she pumped water into the pot to make some coffee. She turned and tried to mirror his excitement. She feigned a smile and asked, "So how soon do ya have to leave?"

"Well, I haven't committed to it just yet," he answered, his eyes darting around. "There are still some decisions I have to make; plans to finalize." She looked at him curiously, but he didn't elaborate. "The leaders of the church are still making plans. Someone will go, whether it's me or not…well, I want to make sure this is what God wants."

She saw his enthusiasm and said simply, "God gives us the desires o' our hearts."

"Yes, but I think that as we grow in our faith, it becomes more about our desires coming into line with His desires. I want this to be about His desire and not simply mine."

"Parson—Seth, God has given ya a passion for this; it be His will." She had to turn away and busy herself before her emotions betrayed her. For some strange reason she was feeling very alone. "Ya know, Jesus taught that if a son asks for bread, would a father give him a stone instead? If he asks for a fish, would he be given a serpent? If a father who is evil knows to give good gifts to his children, how much more will God our Father give good gifts to those who ask Him? He has put this desire there for a reason; He won't disappoint ya."

Seth smiled faintly. How many times had he given advice to his parishioners with similar Scriptures? Now he was the one being instructed. "Mary, you really have a gift. You need to pursue this. You can teach others about God's Word."

She scoffed at his remarks. "Who would I teach? No one in this county would listen to me."

"Who says you have to stay here?"

His words slowly sunk in. She turned and looked intently at him. "I have responsibilities here. I have this farm to look after, then there's the mill and I have to provide for me children."

"Luke's taking care of the mill quite nicely—at least that's what I've heard. The children can be provided for wherever you go. It's the farm that's holding you back. Is this farm that important?"

She looked towards the ceiling, thinking. "The farm has never been important to me; tis just a place to lay me head at night. I have never truly felt like this was me home. I don't know if I will ever feel that way about any place."

"Then answer the question: What's holding you back, Mary?" She didn't answer him. Instead she turned her attention to peeling potatoes. Seth came up from behind and put his hand on her shoulder. "Sorry, I didn't mean to push so hard. Hey, can I give you a hand?" She peered over her shoulder at him in disbelief but said nothing. "What? I'm a decent cook. You know, I've had to learn a lot about cooking over the years or starve."

She handed him a knife and asked, "How are ya at peelin' potatoes?"

"Haven't lost a finger yet," he quipped.

"Ya work on them and I'll mix up a batch o' biscuits," she replied. Even though her heart was heavy, she still managed a real smile for him this time.

As they worked together preparing the meal, Seth filled her in on the rest of the letter. "Well, it seems they've put a bid in for a piece of property that would be great for starting a mission church. As a matter of fact, the building started out as a Franciscan monastery. It was later abandoned, changed hands a few times and then became a brothel before being abandoned again."

Mary felt a twinge of shame. She had seen the streets lined with bordellos when she passed through nearly ten years ago. She had seen the vacant eyes hidden behind false smiles and had felt for each woman. The memory of her own incarceration made her shudder.

Seth continued to ramble. "You know, it's kind of fitting in a way…this brothel being turned back into a mission. Did you know that San Francisco was named after Saint Francis of Assisi; it's Spanish for Saint Francis. Anyway, he had lived a life filled with debauchery before giving himself to Christ. So in a way, this building is kind of a metaphor for him…from a den of iniquity to a place of sanctuary. Maybe we should call the church Saint Francis. What do you think Mary?"

"I think that would be a fine name."

Evan pushed the horses too hard. He hadn't driven this reckless since all hell had broken loose on that day at the Whitakers' farm. He slowed them to a reasonable trot to allow them to catch their breath. Anxiety filled his gut. He just wanted to fix everything, but the more he tried the worse things had gotten.

At this point, he had no idea what he was going to do. He told Henrik last week that he needed to check on something he had left behind in Windsor. He asked for a few days off to return. But Emma, the country girl turned nurse, had sensed what this was about. The days leading up to his departure, she had been cold and distant. This was supposed to have been an innocent flirtation. It wasn't supposed to hurt anyone. But yesterday morning, as he prepared to leave, he saw the pained look in Emma's eyes and it cut deep into his heart. He hadn't expected that.

So now what was he supposed to do? He had made his promise to Mary. After all that she had done for him and what he had put her through, he owed it to her. He needed to get back and straighten everything out. Why else had he driven his team at breakneck speed, trying to get to Windsor as fast as he could? But the closer he got, the bigger the knot in his stomach grew. He questioned himself that maybe all the feelings he had for her were merely flirtations as well. Maybe he was totally incapable of loving anyone. It was a big question mark for him, one he hoped he could answer before the day was through.

There was a chill in the air as heavy clouds descended over the countryside. Mary and Joshua set about their farm work, as Katherine, taking more responsibility, watched after Michael. He was becoming a handful but she rallied to the task, keeping him occupied while Mary fed the animals. A sharp gust of wind buffeted her as she reached the barn, nearly tearing the faded rust colored shawl off her shoulders. She cinched it tightly around her and went inside. Joshua was sitting on a stool milking their cow.

"Brrrr," she announced as she closed the door behind her. "It be gettin' nippy out there. The clouds look like snows comin'."

"Not cold enough yet," he said absently. Finishing the milking, he patted the cow on the rump, stood up and then carried the full pail over to his mother. She took notice that the boy had grown several inches since his father had passed away. She peered down and saw that his britches were far above his ankles. She was going to have to sew some new clothes for him.

"It may not be cold enough *yet*, but it doesn't change the fact that it feels like it could. It won't be too much longer."

He toted the pail over by the door and then returned to help her feed the horses. He had already given Beulah their cow some hay in her trough; she was now munching on it. He would have to clean out the stalls later in the day. It was an endless chore that Joshua was beginning to dislike. "Why can't cows and horses clean up after themselves? Why do we have to do it all the time?"

"They take care o' it in the wild," she said, cutting the twine off a small bundle of hay. She then began refilling the trough as Joshua toted a bucket of water for the horses. "Tis man that domesticated them and put them in barns. It be our responsibility to care for them."

He found her answer unsatisfying, but continued about his chores. When they finished, Joshua picked up the pail of milk and started carrying it to the house. As Mary turned from closing the barn door, she heard a carriage approaching. She expected it to be the reverend, since he was becoming a frequent visitor. As she squinted her eyes against the glare, her jaw dropped. "Now what in blue blazes is he doin' here?"

The carriage suddenly pulled up beside the barn. Evan Sullivan hopped out of it and was at Mary's side almost immediately. Joshua had turned back so quick that he spilled some of the milk. For a split second, he thought about pouring it all over his former teacher, and then thought better of it. It would be a waste of good milk.

"Josh, why don't ya put the milk in the kitchen for me? I think Mr. Sullivan wants to speak to me about a matter." The boy narrowed his eyes in mistrust, but did what she told him. In rebellion, he closed the door behind him a little louder than usual. She turned her attention to her visitor. "So what brings ya all the way from Jacksonville, Mr. Sullivan? I imagined that ya would be too busy plannin' yar weddin'."

"Who said I was getting married," he declared, perturbed.

Coolly she said, "No one, but Henrik implied that there might be forth comin' nuptials."

"Well, he's mistaken."

"Really? Not even if it be our own weddin'," she teased, not really meaning it.

"Now, that's different."

Mary shook her head and then said, "Mr. Sullivan, marry the girl."

"I came to set things right. I promised to marry *you* and take care of *you*."

She looked at him tenderly and said, "I don't need to be taken care o'. God has provided. Besides ya don't owe me anythin', includin' an explanation. Marry the girl; she'll make ya a good wife."

"How do you know? You've never even met her."

She chuckled and said, "Because ya have impeccable taste in women." Mary reiterated, "Marry the girl; have a good life."

He shook his head in amazement. He had travelled this far, only to be turned down. "What about you, Mary?"

"I'll survive. I always have."

"Can I at least kiss you goodbye?" His mischievous smile spread across his face.

Remembering what happened the last time, she was not going to fall for it again. She lifted her hand to him and teased, "Ya may kiss me hand." He obliged and then peering up at her, tried to think of something clever to say, but it escaped him. He felt an emptiness in his heart, but also some relief. "Goodbye, Evan." It was the third time she had ever called him by his first name.

"Goodbye, Mary. I will never forget you. You have forever imprinted yourself on my heart."

She cocked her head sideways and said, "Ya have to get over me; ya have a new woman in yar life. Don't mess it up."

He nodded and climbed up into his carriage, but before he could leave, another carriage started down the drive. Evan turned and saw that it was Reverend Matthews. He quickly spun his head around and quipped, "Preacher's here; you sure you don't want to go ahead and marry me."

She put her hands on her hips and said, "Ya're incorrigible."

"Thought I'd just take one last shot at it," he said, laughing softly.

They watched the carriage come down and pull beside Evan's. Evan tipped his hat slightly and greeted him, "Reverend."

Seth furrowed his brow and answered, "Mr. Sullivan?"

The expression on the pastor's face told Evan the story. He laughed to himself and then shaking his head, muttered, "At least I lost to a better man."

"Excuse me?" Seth asked, still not clear what was going on.

"Don't worry, preacher. I just came to say my goodbyes to Mary and her family. You see, I'm about to get married. I just wanted to tell Mary in person." The reverend nodded slightly, but was still in a fog. Evan turned back to Mary and said, "Goodbye, Mary. *You* have a good life; you deserve it." He turned the carriage around and then climbed her driveway for the last time.

Seth hopped from his carriage and came to her. He still had a worried look on his face. "Is everything alright?"

Mary smiled faintly and replied, "Everythin' is goin' to be fine."

"I don't understand why he felt he had to come and tell you he was getting married." A feeling of dread was creeping into his gut and he didn't like it. Had the rumors had some truth to them?

"Ya want me to be honest?" she asked. Seth nodded and braced himself. "He had some fool notion that we would marry someday. I never returned those feelin's; they were all in his imagination. The only thin' I felt for him was gratitude for teachin' me to read—nothin' more." She didn't know why she needed to explain herself, but he seemed relieved. "So what brings ya here today, Parson—Seth?"

He took a deep breath and said, "I've got great news. I received a letter from my bishop. The owners have accepted our bid for the property. It looks like we're about to set up a mission in San Francisco."

Mary slowly turned and walked towards the house; Seth followed her. "So I reckon ya'll be leavin' soon."

"Well, I haven't accepted the position just yet." She stopped and looked questioning at him. "There are still some things that I need to take care of." He hesitated and then said, "It's all contingent on whether or not I can find someone to help me in this ministry."

It was Mary's turn to furrow her brow. "Someone to help ya?" she asked a little confused.

"You see, I want to reach the men of the city—those who have become disillusioned by the pursuit of material wealth…to show them there's something better. But what I'd really like to see is women who are going through what you have gone through, come to know Jesus. I want to rescue women from the degradation of prostitution. From what I've been told, there are rooms on the second and third floors that can be converted into bedrooms. They can be used as a sanctuary for these women. We can teach them skills that will help them transition into a better way of life. But I can't do *that*; it wouldn't be proper for a man to do it."

Mary felt a stirring in her heart, an uneasiness that he was going to ask her something big. She wasn't sure if she wanted him to say more. He grabbed her by the shoulders and said, "Mary, I believe that God is calling you to be that person. You know what they're going through. You can give them hope and show them that there is a way out of that kind of life. God has given you a gift and *you* can teach them His Word as well as things to prepare them from life."

She fought hard not to let her feelings betray her, but lost the battle. Yet Seth was not through with his proposal. "Mary, I don't believe in love at first sight, but when I met you, I sensed there was something special about you—that you were different. I felt God telling me, that here was the genuine article…someone truly sincere in their faith; someone that had gone through so much for His name sake. He told me that I was to take care of His lamb. I wasn't sure what He meant at that time, but now I do. Mary, I have fallen in love with you. I don't know exactly when it happened. Maybe I realized it the day you defended yourself in church. But all I know is, I can't do this without your help and I sure don't want to live the rest of my life without you in it. I don't know how you feel about me, but I'm asking you to marry me. So how is it…will you marry me?"

Mary tried to catch her breath. The world seemed to be spinning faster than she could keep up with. She pinched her face and through her tears said, "Ya know me past; ya know the countless men I've been with."

"Mary, God has forgiven you of all those things. He has casted them into the sea of forgetfulness. If he has wiped them away, then I have too. The only time you need to remember them is when you're ministering to others in the same predicament. Not to continue to condemn yourself, but to have great empathy for them. Remember what the Scriptures says, *there is now no condemnation to them which are in Christ Jesus, who walk not after the flesh, but after the Spirit.* God doesn't condemn you, neither do I. I want you to be my wife." He smiled and added, "I want you to bear my children."

She looked at him with astonishment and flushed at the thought. Then she asked, "What about yar denomination? What would they think o' ya marryin' a Catholic?"

"I told you, some of them went on to be good Methodists; remember my mother is one. She still makes the sign of the cross after she prays. She says it reminds her each time what Jesus has done for her. And here's a little secret: sometimes in my quiet times, I do too."

With her heart full of emotions somehow she managed to faintly say, "Kiss me Seth." He looked at her puzzled. "Kiss me and then I'll give ya an answer."

He looked searchingly in her eyes and caressed her cheek. Tilting his head slightly, his lips gently caressed hers and then he kissed her passionately. Mary felt herself laughing inwardly with joy. It was like comfortable shoes. After all these years, these fit perfectly; it was as though she had waited for them all her life. Seth pulled back and waited for her answer.

She looked intently at him. "If ya are willin' to have me, I would be honored to be yar wife. I too have fallen in love with ya—only I was afraid to admit it."

His smile broadened and then he kissed her again, sealing the deal. They turned and began to walk towards the house, hand in hand. She peered up at him and asked, "So when do we have to leave?"

"Probably not until the first of spring. There are still some things that need to be finalized and some work done on the property to make it livable. But I'd like to go ahead and get married."

She stopped in her tracks, turned and looked at him incredulously. "What would yar congregation be thinkin' o' ya marryin' the likes o' me?"

"Oh, I don't know. Some may not like it, but I think some will be pleased. I was just thinking that the first person I'd like to tell is Mrs. Cavanaugh. I can't wait to see the expression on her face."

Mary shook her head and replied, "Ya're askin' for trouble."

"I think we can handle it. After all we have God on *our* side."

She smiled sweetly and then this time she was the one that kissed him. "I love ya, Seth. I dearly love ya."

He pulled her into his arms and held her. "And I dearly love you."

Note from the Author

God can do crazy things in your life if you will let Him. He can literally turn your life upside down. You see, from an early age I was told, "Oh, so you're going to be an artist when you grow up." I thought that was my calling, so I pursued it and had some minor success. It seemed like I was on my way, when suddenly doors of opportunity began to close. It was as if God was asking, *"Do you want this? Do you really want to be an artist? Because if you do, I can give it to you. But I don't think you do."*

The truth was I didn't want it. As an artist, I felt unfulfilled and empty. What glory was I really giving to God? So I began praying, *"God if these are not your dreams for my life, then give me new dreams—give me Your dreams.*

Then something wonderful and bizarre happened. In January 2014, as I was reading a book, I suddenly had a crazy thought. *"I can do this. I can write a book. It's not that hard."* Who in their right might thinks such a thing. It was either God or a moment of insanity. But after a week of it nagging me I said, "Well, if you think you can do it then you better start putting pen to paper." So I did.

I have to admit that at first it was a little difficult. I was trying too hard to sound like a writer. But once I relaxed the words seemed to flow, so much that I couldn't type or even handwrite it fast enough.

Sounds like a great dream doesn't it? So why did I fight it? Fear. I was afraid to fail. I also had so many doubts that God would do this for me. Who was I that God would choose to bless in this way? I made myself miserable and drove everyone crazy who were trying to encourage me, crazy. I fought and wrestled with God that this was too crazy and that nothing would come of it. At one point I announced to God, *"But I'm just a hillbilly from West Virginia."* He immediately answered back, *"And they were just fishermen from Galilee."* He reminded me, *"for nothing is impossible with God." (Luke 1:37)*

So what's the lesson to my story? That if you'll totally surrender to God's will for your life, willing to do anything, He just might have a wild adventure waiting for you. You just need to trust Him and let your faith be bigger than your fears. (I'm still trying to learn that one!) Then you need to get out of the boat. You might sink a few times, but remember Jesus is right there to catch you; He'll never let you drown. He'll reach down and pull you back up and maybe—just maybe, you might end up walking on water.

Loretta Y. Stewart